A Novel of the Clay Shamus
by Michael Panush

AIRSHIP 27 PRODUCTIONS

The Dagger Men
© 2016 Michael Panush

Published by Airship 27 Productions
www.airship27.com
www.airship27hangar.com

Interior and cover illustrations © 2016 Zachary Brunner

Editor: Ron Fortier
Associate Editor: Fred Adams Jr.
Marketing and Promotions Manager: Michael Vance
Production and design by Rob Davis.

ISBN-13: 978-0692678954 (Airship 27)
ISBN-10: 0692678956

Printed in the United States of America

10 9 8 7 6 5 4 3 2 1

CLAY SHAMUS
Volume One

Chapter One
GARDEN OF EDEN

Crisp grass crunched under Emmet Clay's boots. He stared ahead, past the rolling meadow that served as the heart of Arcadia Park, and to the swath of ornamental trees and statues that formed the closest thing to a forest to be found in the city he had made his home. Something about the closeness of the trees, and the way the statues of forgotten Greek Gods, monsters, and heroes seemed hidden by the tangled branches and consumed by vines made the forest seem sinister instead of quaint. Beyond the trees, the skyscrapers of Sickle City reached up into a pale sky. Distant and unreachable, the rows of great buildings reminded Clay of the background for an altar in some strange temple. The occasional picnicking family or couple strolling arm in arm through Arcadia Park didn't notice the darkness of the forest, but they still stayed away from it. Clay wasn't afraid, though. He had a job to do.

He stepped onto the stone path and approached the entrance to the woods, his hands in his pockets. Clay got a few odd looks—just like he got everywhere. He appeared to be a particularly bulky man—a mountain in a trench coat—with broad shoulders, a dome of a head, a slab for a nose, and uncombed, straight, mud-colored hair. He wore a brown suit and vest under his trench coat, the tie loosely knotted. His fedora shaded his face.

Clay wasn't on the job alone. Zipporah Sarfati, his fellow detective, stood next to Clay. She pointed at a stout figure standing on the stone road leading into the forest. "There's our man, Clay." Zipporah, like Clay, was a Jew—but she came from a wealthy Sephardic Family which had settled in the Levant. Her father had given her topnotch fencing lessons when she was young, and she had put them to bloody use in the Great War. Now two scimitars rested on her back, each in its own scabbard. She sported a worn, thin sweater and a long dress over stolen Turkish officer's boots. Her dark hair, long and curly, framed her coffee-colored face.

"He mentioned that there's some kind of trouble in the forest." Clay's youngest friend, Harvey Holtz, stood on his tiptoes to peer into the woods. "What do you think it is, Mr. Clay?" Harvey was not yet a Bar Mitzvah—a boy no older than twelve. An argyle vest and scarlet tie under a checkered coat covered his thin frame. His bright blue eyes peered out at the world through round spectacles, and he had very dark hair, straight and neatly parted. Scrawny and slight, Harvey contrasted greatly with the bulk of Clay. Still, the books contained in the satchel slung on Harvey's shoulder, made him quite valuable in Clay's business.

"I suppose we'll find out," Clay's voice came in a deep rumble. "Detective Flynn seems eager for us to get to work."

He walked ahead of his friends and neared their employer, a detective in the Sickle City Police Department. Like most cops, Detective Ollie Flynn was as rotten as a blackened banana. He worked for Harvey's father, just like Clay and Zipporah did. He had a growing belly poking against his dark blue suit, and kept his derby tilted back over his pudgy face. A fringe of red hair covered his scalp, and a cheap, noxious cigar smoldered in his mouth as Clay, Zipporah, and Harvey arrived. Detective Flynn looked like he always did—consumed by a mix of impatience and fatigue.

He removed his cigar and regarded Clay and his friends. "Mr. Clay. Good to see you. How go things in Little Jerusalem?" He used the common nickname for Haven Street—a home for the city's Jews.

"You should know, detective." Zipporah could never resist a snide jab. "It's your bailiwick."

"And I'm always happy to assist the good citizens of Haven Street," Detective Flynn glanced at Harvey. "Particularly your father, lad. My compliments to the rabbi, by the way." He was always polite when he mentioned Rabbi Herman Holtz, Harvey's father—and the man who really controlled Haven Street.

Harvey removed his newsboy cap and crumpled it in his hands. "Thank you, sir. I'll be sure to let him know." Rabbi Holtz had raised his only son to be polite. It was one of the many reasons Clay liked Harvey. "So, what exactly can we help you with, detective?" He peered around Detective Flynn, gazing into the forest. "Is there something inside the woods causing trouble? Maybe Mr. Clay, Miss Sarfati, and I can get rid of it?"

Detective Flynn turned and looked back at the cluttered swath of greenery. "I hope you can. You see, for a couple weeks now, there's been reports of strange figures watching folks as they perambulate through the park. The watchers hang back amidst the branches and boughs, just sort of staring at the good folk of our fine city as they wander past. Then, one of these phantoms emerged and fell upon a visiting councilman taking an evening stroll with a lady. It apparently stole her favorite cloche hat before absconding back into the cover of the woods. The councilman didn't want word about this little ambush to get out."

"Why not?" Clay asked.

"His fellow stroller? Not his wife. Anyhow, he gave me a ring and asked if I could solve the problem. I knew immediately that this sort of situation can best be handled by some of Rabbi Holtz's fine employees." He pointed to Clay. "You're the shamus to call, Clay. You can find out whoever's lurking in those woods, and—if you have to—eliminate them."

Zipporah snorted. "We ain't torpedoes, Flynn."

"Those big blades on your back argue otherwise, my dear," Flynn replied.

"Well, perhaps we won't need a violent solution." Harvey smiled hopefully. "Did this councilman describe his attacker?"

"He mentioned that the fellow was green," Detective Flynn explained.

Clay cocked his head. "Green?"

"It's what he said—perhaps the assailant had a green pea coat on, or a rather emerald complexion. Or perhaps he had green skin." He pointed to the woods. "That's a mystery you'll have to solve."

Harvey withdrew one of the volumes from his satchel. He flipped through the pages. "I'm not sure about green people. This is an accounting of various mystical animals from the Talmud. Perhaps a green fellow is included in here. Or it might be one of the magical beasts in King Solomon's famed menagerie, which has somehow made it to Sickle City." He pushed up his spectacles as he made his way through the dusty pages.

"We'll find out soon enough." Clay patted Harvey's shoulder. "Come on. Let's go for a walk in the woods."

They started down the trail and entered the forest. Detective Flynn stepped aside, his hands on his hips. Harvey gave him a wave as the stone pathway curved around, blocking the detective from view behind a row of intertwining trunks and branches. Green men running about in Arcadia Park? It certainly seemed strange. But Clay knew that strange things existed in this city, and everywhere in the world. He was one of them. While most people saw Clay as simply a large lump of mobile muscle, he had a different nature that he kept hidden from the world. Rabbi Holtz knew, and so did Harvey and Zipporah—but not Detective Flynn, though he probably suspected. Clay had to keep the secret, or every scientist and scholar in the world would want to examine him. Like most supernatural things, he kept to the shadows. He liked it better that way.

The pale sun seemed to fade as Clay and the others walked further into the woods. Harvey stayed between Zipporah and Clay, his nose still in his book. He stumbled on the cobblestone pathway and Clay caught him and steadied him with a heavy hand. "Oh, thank you, Mr. Clay." Harvey looked up from the book. "I don't really see anything about green people in here. That does sound sort of swell, though. I wouldn't mind seeing a green person." He closed the volume and returned it to his satchel. "Detective Flynn seemed a little angry."

"Probably worried about the Officer's Union business," Zipporah muttered. "And the strike."

"A strike?" Harvey asked.

Clay nodded. "The Sickle City cops are trying to unionize—and the city bigwigs don't like it." Those city bigwigs took the form of the Wigwam Club, a political machine that reliably kept votes going to candidates used to looking the other way. Edwin Eames, the Grand Sagamore of the Wigwam Club, had a particular hatred for unions. "They're all worried about Bolsheviks, anarchists, or Marxists." Clay shook his head. "As if they had a chance of taking over this city." He had plenty of experience with Bolsheviks. "I read about the situation in the papers."

"Oh. I hadn't heard about those kinds of things. I mostly just stick to the Katzenjammer Kids." Harvey stared ahead, peering through the woods. "It's sort of d-dark in here, isn't it?" His voice faltered a little as they neared a clearing, where a gazebo rested amongst several shattered columns meant to resemble the pieces of an ancient temple.

Zipporah moved closer to Harvey. "Don't worry, child. You are safe with us."

Harvey smiled shyly at Zipporah. "Thank you, Miss Sarfati."

Something moved in the underbrush behind them. Clay spun around, his fists swinging at his sides. Unlike Zipporah, Clay didn't bring any weapons. His fists would be enough. He took a step off the path, his boots settling in dirt, and stared at the mass of branches and vines. They rustled and the leaves waved on the branches—but that could only be the wind. Clay drew closer. He pushed aside a branch and looked through the shadows near the boles of the trees. Only dust and leaves greeted his gaze. Clay released a slight creak and stepped back to the trail.

He faced his friends. "Nothing."

"That noise..." Zipporah had withdrawn a scimitar. "I can sense an ambush, Clay. Battling the Turks in the deserts and mountains of the Levant gave me those sorts of instincts, and ample opportunity to sharpen them. I swear we're being watched."

"But by what?" Harvey squinted at the canopy. "Oh." He released a small squeak of surprise.

Leaves fell from the branches and floated down to the path. They came in a riot of rich brown, reds, and orange, so it seemed that fire was dancing its way down from the sky. The leaves fell on their coats and the cobblestone trail. Something else fell as well—a slim, human figure that landed neatly on its feet. Clay stared at the newcomer. At first, he thought that it was some costumed figure, one that belonged in a masquerade ball or an avant-garde theatre production. But then he noted that wrinkled, knotted bark formed the skin of the creature, marked with projecting leaves and branches, and twisted lengths of wood formed the feet and hands. A thick nest of leaves and twigs served as the creature's hair, with two hollows acting as eyes. That seemed to pass for the botanical figure's face. A few autumnal leaves graced the plant creature, but most of its vegetation remained bright green. It stood slowly, emitting a rushing whisper like wind through a forest.

Harvey stared at the creature and this pale face split with a grin of recognition. "It's an Adnei Hasadeh—a Man of the Fields!" He pointed to the Tree Man as it moved closer to them, two vines dragging from its arms and snaking across the pathway. "'Field' just means vegetation in this instance. They're mentioned in the Talmud as being mixtures of plants and men. I don't think they're Kosher, by the way."

"He doesn't look Kosher." Zipporah moved in front of Harvey. "Are they friendly?"

"I don't think the Holy Books say much about that. Maybe some of the sages mention it." Harvey reached to his satchel. "I could look it up, if you'd like."

"I think we're about to find out." Clay stared at the Man of the Field and raised both his fists—a warning that even a plant would understand. Then more wooden legs clicked on the pathway. Two more Tree Men had slipped out of the underbrush and now approached them. One Tree Man had a round chest, like an oaken barrel. The other had grown thorns all over his long, thin, branching fingers. It made him look like he carried a double set of brass knuckles, edged with spikes and ready to do damage. This Tree Man wore a cloche hat. It didn't exactly fit on the branches, and sort of hung to the side and dangled beside the Tree Man's face.

Zipporah faced the Tree Man in front of them. "They're just big trees," she muttered. "Why don't we cut them down?" She moved closer, and reached for her second scimitar. A rare shaft of sunlight caught the blade, and it gleamed like gold. The Tree Men's hollow, empty eyes moved to the sword. They emitted the same rustling sound—full of fear and anger— and then attacked in the same moment.

The Tree Men moved far faster than plants. The creature with the thorny knuckles raced toward Clay, swinging up one of its hands in a rapid uppercut. Clay didn't have time to avoid the blow. The knuckles smashed into his chest and knocked him back. The Tree Man seemed heartened by its success. It lashed at Clay again—this time aiming for the face. Its knuckles reached Clay's cheek, the thorns gouging down. But that was where its success ended. The knuckles broke against Clay's cheek. The thorns refused to sink in. Clay felt the thorns gouge him and the wood snap and shatter. He slugged the Tree Man next. His blow rammed into the trunk, smashing aside bark. The Tree Man fell hard to the ground. Clay kicked it, and sent it rolling away from the stone path. He faced the next foe, squaring his shoulders and ready for the melee.

He was made of something stronger than wood. Clay was a golem, composed of hardened earth. Like some golems, he could project an illusion to hide his true nature—which the Tree Men had just discovered. Clay let his illusion drop, giving the Tree Men a quick glimpse of his true form. Compact, light brown earth formed his body, with two round river stones serving as eyes. Now that the Tree Men had seen exactly who he was, it was time for the battle to end.

The portly Tree Man hastened in front of its fallen companion, and advanced on Clay. This Tree Man seemed slightly older, with a thick beard of moss covering the top half of its round chest. Clay swatted at the Tree Man, hoping to upset it with a quick jab. His fist crashed against the wooden skin of the Tree Man, but the plant stayed upright. Then the Tree Man rammed both of its branches into Clay's chest. The edges of the branches unfurled and wrapped around him, the wood digging into his side and holding on. The Tree Man's arms flexed and it pushed Clay hard. He tumbled from the trail and crashed into a decorative stone pillar. The stone broke under his weight, and fragments of ornate marble rattled to the ground next to him.

"Mr. Clay!" Harvey scrambled to his side. "Are you all right?" He moved in front of the Tree Man, who closed in on Clay with its branches held high. The Tree Man with the thorny fingers came to its feet as well. They both seemed intent on attacking Clay while he was down. Clay hastily came to his feet and stepped protectively in front of Harvey.

Zipporah had problems of her own. The first Tree Man advanced on her, its vines cracking through the air like whips. Zipporah ducked under the swinging vines, and then her blades slashed down together. Her service to the British Army in the Mesopotamian Campaign had earned Zipporah a feared nickname, after a battle where she had taken on a handful of Turkish officers and won: they called her the Maid of Megiddo. Clay saw why she had been given the moniker. She parried the vines, her scimitars weaving in rapid tandem, and then attacked the Tree Man with a flurry of rapid strikes. One sword sheared off a length of fingers. Another plunged deep into the Tree Man's chest. Sap dripped down from the wound and hit the ground.

Clay tore his gaze away and met his attackers. Thorny fingers struck him first—the fist landing a spiked uppercut on his chin. Clay ignored it and let the Tree Man get closer. He took more punches to his chest and shoulders, letting the thorns rip his suit jacket and damage his skin. Then the vegetable attacker got close enough. Clay grabbed the circle of wood that passed for the Tree Man's neck and held tightly. His fingers broke bark. He spun the Tree Man around and rammed its head into the jagged top of the broken stone pillar. Wood cracked and the Tree Man sank to the ground.

A vine whipped through the air and reached Clay's face. It encircled him, speeding around twice before knotting, tightening, and tugging him back to the cobblestone trail. Clay only caught glimpses of the world around him, as the vines enclosed his vision. He tried to grip at the vines and tear them off, but the bearded Tree Man held them tightly. Thorns jabbed out of the vine, stabbing into Clay's skin. Clay creaked in panic and his hands flailed in the air.

On his forehead, his creator had written down the Hebrew word for 'Truth'. Those simple letters—which sounded like 'Emmet' when spoken aloud—kept him alive. If the characters were obscured or changed, it would resemble the Hebrew word for 'Death'. Then Clay would become nothing more than a pile of dirt. What passed for life would leave him, and he would be gone forever. Now, the Tree Man had him in a death grasp, and the thorns from the vine would rip away the letters.

Harvey knew the danger as well. "No!" He ran to the Tree Man. "Please, don't hurt him.."

A blow from a branch struck Harvey. He spun back, stumbling and falling to his knees. Clay caught a glimpse of the boy as he stood up. Pure fear appeared in his eyes. Clay finally got his hands around the vines. He tugged at them, making the vegetation snap. He might be able to rip the vines away in time.

Zipporah charged toward him. Her scimitars hummed through the air. They hacked through the vines, causing sap and juices to spray into the air. The vines went limp. Clay ripped them free from his head and tossed them aside. Now, he was free. He glowered at the Tree Man. The leaves of the Tree Man shook, as if in a heavy wind. Clay had the feeling that the plant was afraid. He charged toward the Tree Man, blocked a blow from its branch, and then drove his hand into the bark of his foe's chest. His fingers dug in and held. Clay held the Tree Man aloft. Its legs, like gnarled roots, waved crazily. Clay pulled back his fist, preparing to smash the wooden creature to kindling.

"Wait!" Harvey cried out the word and stepped close to Clay. "Please— just hold on a moment. Okay? Just for a moment." He pointed to the three Tree Men. Zipporah's opponent lay further back, one of its arms hacked off by her sabers. "We've beaten them. We don't need to destroy them."

"They attacked us, Harvey," Clay glared at the Tree Man, his rage building as he remembered the vines around his face. "They attacked that councilman."

Zipporah nodded. "Nobody will miss a trio of trees."

"Maybe they didn't know what they were doing when they attacked the councilman," Harvey explained. "And maybe they only attacked us because they thought we could be a threat. The sunlight shone on Miss Sarfati's blades. It made the steel get really bright, and they probably assumed we wanted to chop them down. So they attacked, to protect themselves. It's what anyone would do." He moved closer to Clay. "Please, Mr. Clay. You don't have to do this."

Was that true? Clay had been created for one purpose—to destroy. He had been forged from the earth as a weapon, capable of dealing enormous amounts of damage while most weapons broke on his hide. That's what he had first been tasked to do, after he had been given life in the Old Country of war-torn Eastern Europe during the Russian Revolution. But America was different. Clay stared at the Tree Man, looking into the hollows of its eyes and the surrounding mass of moss. The Tree Man seemed as breakable as dry wood now.

Clay set him down. He pulled back his fist and bowed his head, in a quick nod. The Tree Man didn't attack. Instead, it waved its hands to the other Tree Men. They picked themselves up and came to stand next to the barrel-chested Tree Man. The Tree Man with thorny fingers pushed torn bark away from its face. They stared at Clay, Zipporah, and Harvey. Neither side attacked.

"We can figure something out," Harvey said. "We can all live together. This is America, after all—and lots of different people live together." He bowed to the Tree Men. "I don't know if you can hear me, or understand English. I'm not sure how you came to Sickle City either. Maybe some seeds were accidentally brought along from a hidden grove somewhere, and you took root here. Maybe every forest spawns its own Men of the Field. But you're here now, and you can live happily."

"We should just chop them down, child," Zipporah said. "It might be easier."

"No, Miss Sarfati." Harvey pushed up his spectacles. "Please—do you understand me?" He pleaded with the Tree Men.

The elder Tree Man rocked its body back and forth—a sort of vegetable nod.

"You see? We can figure something out—a peace treaty, perhaps." He did his best to straighten his vest and tie. "Okay, how about this: you guys can live here in Arcadia Park, but you can't pop out and scare people. Sickle City can be frightening enough without plant people creeping around in the park. You also can't steal anybody's hat." He pointed to the cloche hat. "In fact, I think we're gonna need that back. Please?"

The Tree Man with the thorny knuckles removed the cloche hat and tossed it to Harvey. The boy caught it.

"Thank you." Harvey pointed back to the woods. "You can still stay here, if you want. I'll talk to my father and Detective Flynn. Maybe he can bring by some fertilizer for you guys? Or water you?" The Tree Men rustled indignantly. "Okay. We don't need to water you." He held out his hand. "We'll make sure nobody bothers these trees, or you, for as long as you want to stay in Arcadia Park. How's that sound? Are those terms acceptable?"

For a few seconds, the Tree Men just stared at him. Then the fat Tree Man extended its branch-like hand—not to Harvey, but to Clay. Evidently, they respected Clay now that he had beaten them. Or maybe they recognized something of themselves in Clay—a kinship. They were made of wood, after all, and Clay was made of earth. He accepted the Tree Man's hand. They clasped for a while, and then the round Tree Man moved back. It waved to the others. They stepped back into the woods, slipping in amongst the branches and leaves, and fading into the underbrush. If not for the sap on Zipporah's blades and the broken bark, twigs, and leaves on the ground, they might have never appeared.

Zipporah stared at her swords. "I'll need to clean them. This damn sticky sap." Then she smiled at Harvey. "You were right to avoid a battle. I hope they stick to the terms you set for them, and we don't have to pick a fight with plants again."

"They'll uphold the terms," Clay said. "I trust them."

"Well, at least that problem is solved." Zipporah returned her scimitars to her scabbards. "This city has enough troubles, after all."

"Like the possible police strike?" Harvey asked.

"Exactly." She motioned to the forest path. "Let's go back to Haven Street. Detective Flynn will be happy to know that we solved his problem. Now he can go back to collecting bribes in peace, and we can receive a nice chunk of dough from your father." She started down the forest trail, alongside Harvey. "Come along, Clay. We're due back at Haven Street."

Clay stayed in the clearing for just a few moments. He liked Harvey's solution. Even though he was used to killing, he didn't enjoy it—and he hadn't really taken any lives since he came to America. But Zipporah was right as well. His new home was full of troubles. He wondered how many of them could be resolved without bloodshed. Clay let out a creaking sigh, slid back into the comfortable skin of his illusion, and followed Harvey and Zipporah out of the forest.

When Clay had first arrived in America, he had gone to Haven Street. The seaside neighborhood was the first stop for many immigrants, and Clay had been just another new arrival to America, straight from the chaos of war-ravaged Eastern Europe. Haven Street had once belonged to the Irish, but Jewish immigrants from Eastern Europe had populated its tenements and cluttered streets since the turn of the century, and their ranks had only swelled after the Great War. Because he was a golem, he never quite fit in. Still, Haven Street—Little Jerusalem—was the closest thing he had to a home.

He looked at the busy street from the window of his Studebaker automobile with Zipporah in the passenger seat and Harvey in the back. Peddlers packed the sidewalks, advertising their wares even as the sun began to dip in the distance. Chasidic Jews, with their long coats and ear locks, clumped together as they strolled along the street, while playing children, workmen, sailors from the nearby waterfront, pushcarts, wagons, and automobiles did their best to share the street. Laundry dangling from clotheslines hung from tenement windows, overlooking everything. This was Neptune Row, the first home of most immigrants and the poorest section of Haven Street. Clay sped past it on his way to their destination.

Soon after his arrival, Clay had visited Rabbi Herman Holtz—the younger brother of the man who created him. Rabbi Herman Holtz had listened carefully to Clay's story. At first, Rabbi Holtz didn't believe that Clay was a golem. Rabbi Holtz's older brother, Chaim Holtz, had excelled at Yeshiva School before immigrating to the New World with his two younger brothers. He had eventually grown distasteful of America and returned to the Old Country. Rabbi Holtz knew his brother studied Kabala and had mastered the Ten Stages of the Sephirot, but had he really created a golem? Soon, Rabbi Holtz had realized the truth, and decided that his older brother's golem would now work for him.

He had given Clay a special home, in a place where even an oddity would fit in. Clay approached it now, the rickety dock of amusements known as Palisade Park, which jutted out into the cold Atlantic on a large pier. He halted the Studebaker on the sidewalk, and he and his friends walked out and entered Palisade Park. They headed down the dock, under the shadow of the twirling Ferris wheel and the rattling roller coaster that always seemed on the verge of collapse. Tents and booths offered fortune telling, midway games, roasted peanuts and popcorn, and other treats and diversions for the residents of Haven Street to buy with their nickels and pennies. Everything in Palisade Park had been painted in gaudy, carnival colors. Zipporah worked there, doing swordsmanship exhibitions when she wasn't helping Clay serve Rabbi Holtz. Like everything on Haven Street, Rabbi Holtz owned a piece of the amusement park.

Near the street, the Elephantine Hotel beckoned. The strange structure resembled an elephant, towering up from the dock and facing the horizon with its painted, pale blue eyes. Gray planks formed the elephant's trunk and its back, while a blue and scarlet howdah held up a viewing balcony, where visitors could look out at the city and the mist-shrouded sea. The oversized wooden elephant seemed to sag on its foundations, as if it wanted to lower its carved head and sleep. Clay, Zipporah, and Harvey walked up the small stairwell to the porch, and headed through the double doors to the lobby.

The owner of Palisade Park, Professor Wallace Wellington West, waited for them inside. His red suit, red bowtie, and red top hat blended in with the scarlet velvet carpet of the lobby. Pictures of elephants loomed down, flanking him as he beamed at his tenants. "Mr. Clay. Miss Sarfati. It is a grand thing to see you." He had upturned mustachios, giving him something close to a permanent grin. Professor West—every word in his name was a lie—was a Polish Jew and showman who ran Palisade Park for Rabbi Holtz. He always did his best to serve as a gracious host, though he did have an unfortunate flare for the dramatic. "Another valiant battle against the forces of supernatural darkness?" he asked.

"Something like that," Clay agreed.

"We fought Men of the Field, Professor West," Harvey explained. "They're, ah, tree people."

Professor West smoothed his mustachios, tracing them with forefinger and thumb. "Marvelous. A shame you didn't recruit them to the Park. Perhaps we could stick them in pots near the entrance and have them offer fruit from their bodies to passersby?" He pointed down a side passage. "I'm afraid you have some guests. Your father, my dear boy, is present, along with his bodyguard."

"Rabbi Holtz is here?" Zipporah asked.

"And very keen to see you." Professor West waved his hand down the passage. "I'll bring you to him, and provide some tea and cakes." He strolled to the hallway, humming some circus tune to himself as his loafers sank into the carpet.

They followed him to the parlor, a sumptuous chamber with a number of Morris chairs and a Chesterfield couch set around a glass coffee table. Four brass elephant sculptures held up the coffee table, matching the elephant paintings on the wall, and the elephant head mounted above the mantelpiece. Sure enough, Rabbi Herman Holtz reclined in the Morris chair at the head of the room. He came to his feet when Harvey entered, and the boy hurried to his side. They quickly embraced. Rabbi Holtz wore a somber, respectable black suit and fedora. A neat beard crusted his chin and upper lip, and he wore round spectacles that matched his son's. Everything about him looked scholarly—but that was far from the truth. Herman Holtz had been a criminal since his first arrival in Haven Street as a young man. He had been just another up-and-coming hoodlum until the Eighteenth Amendment was passed, the sale and transport of alcohol was banned, and the Prohibition Era began.

The Federal government offered a number of exemptions to Prohibition— one of which was alcohol for religious purposes. Rabbis could brew and sell wine, and Holtz was quick to take advantage of it. He managed to turn a few years of Yeshiva in his home village into a career as a rabbi, purchased a failing synagogue, and became the bootlegger and gangster king of Haven Street. Now, with Harvey standing happily at his side, he resembled nothing more than a good Jewish father.

"Papa, we encountered these Men of the Field in Arcadia, while we were working for Detective Flynn," Harvey said, excitedly recounting the afternoon's adventure. "They were sort of like plant people? And Mr. Clay and Miss Sarafti battled them after they attacked, but we eventually arranged a kind of peace treaty."

"I'm glad to hear it, *boychick*. Flynn's a *goy*, but he's a good person nonetheless." The Rabbi faced Clay and Zipporah. "These Men of the Field, these plant people—they gave you no trouble?"

"Nothing to write home about, sir," Zipporah said.

"Good." Rabbi Holtz patted Harvey's shoulder. "Still, I think that's enough excitement for the day. Monk will take you back to Atlas Avenue, and to home. Then, you can finish your homework for school and get some rest."

"Papa..." Harvey worshipped his father—but still seemed annoyed. "I can stay here and offer more help to the greatest detectives on Haven Street. What if you give them a case that requires some of Uncle Chaim's books, or some esoteric knowledge and—"

"Come on, son." Monk Moss, Rabbi Holtz's bodyguard, reclined on the couch, with his boots on the coffee table. "You give your father a break. He's got business to discuss with Mr. Clay and Miss Sarfati, and it ain't the sort that concerns you." Monk wore a rumpled, checkered turquoise suit with an oversized bowtie and a straw boater's hat. Like Zipporah, he had served in the Great War—but for him, that conflict had been just a break between endless battles and brawls in the Sickle City underworld. He and Rabbi Holtz had come up together, and he still proudly served in his role as muscle.

Harvey looked at Clay and Zipporah. They both nodded. "We'll see you tomorrow, Harvey," Clay said. He liked the boy—and knew that Harvey had few other friends. It might be strange for Harvey to want spend his days with a golem and a swordswoman, but Clay didn't want to deny their friendship. "You go and get your homework finished."

"Okay," Harvey agreed. "Goodbye, then." He clasped his father's hand. "Goodbye, papa."

"Goodbye, *boychick*." Rabbi Holtz nodded to Monk. "You check his homework, okay? Make sure it's correct."

"Ah, boss, I ain't that skilled in arithmetic," Monk muttered.

"Do your best."

Monk and Harvey left the parlor. The boy gave his friends a quick wave, which Clay returned, and then followed Monk outside. The door closed behind them, and Rabbi Holtz, Zipporah, and Clay remained in the quiet parlor, alone except for the countless elephants.

Rabbi Holtz adjusted his spectacles. "I appreciate you looking after the boy. He has few playmates. The other kids around Haven Street—I think their parents tell them to avoid me and my family. They think we're *goniffs*, even if they go to my services every week." He snorted. "Let them think what they want. I still protect them. And the children at his private school, the sons of our city's elite—well, to them he is just the child of a Jewish criminal. He has you as friends, and I'm glad of it."

"He's useful to have around," Zipporah said. "It's no trouble."

"What do you need from us now?" Clay asked.

"It's not me. But Sid Sapphire." Rabbi Holtz said the name softly, like he was invoking the name of a powerful god. Sid 'the Shark' Sapphire was perhaps the largest Jewish gangster in the city. Rabbi Holtz might run Haven Street, but he passed up his tribute to Sid Sapphire. The Shark ran a criminal network that spanned multiple continents, with a specialty in smuggling valuable artifacts from Europe, Asia, and the Middle East, and selling them on the black market. He had used Zipporah and Clay a few times, but only for the most serious cases.

Clay listened carefully. "What does he want?"

"We'll find out tonight. He wants to meet at the Garden of Eden." That was Rabbi Holtz's speakeasy, located below a Kosher butcher's shop on Marigold Lane. The Garden of Eden catered to locals eager for alcoholic libation, as well as Uptown types who wanted a thrilling place to drink at a cheap price. Clay couldn't drink—he couldn't eat either—but he had visited the Garden of Eden a few times anyway.

Zipporah nodded. "Any clues as to his purpose? What sort of mood is he in?"

Rabbi Holtz shrugged. "You might as well try to predict the weather as fathom the mind of someone like Mr. Sapphire. But whatever else he is, he is a *macher*—and if he wants your services, you'll need to give it to him." He stood up, and reached for his overcoat. "I'll see you tonight at eight in the Garden of Eden. Come early. Mr. Sapphire values promptness." He walked to the door of the parlor, paused and glanced back. "And thanks again for looking after my son." He departed, with his eyes downcast—a strangely forlorn figure.

After he left, Zipporah stood up, one of her swords in its scabbards in each hand. "I better go and do a quick exhibition—show the swells and the locals a little excitement of flashing blades and unparalleled speed and skill as I cut up watermelons. Earn myself a few coins from passing the hat around after I show off." She watched as Clay settled into the Morris chair in the corner. "You gonna be jake, Clay?"

"Yeah." Clay folded his massive hands.

Zipporah looked at her swords. "If my fencing master knew what I was doing with the skills he had taught me, I think he'd skewer me on general principal. If some of my old friends from the Great War knew— well, they'd understand."

"What about T.E. Lawrence?" Clay asked. Zipporah always liked telling stories about the famous general she had served with.

"He'd understand as well. He was always a practical fellow." Zipporah headed to the door. "We'll leave in an hour, Clay. That should be all the time I need to make a few bucks." She stepped outside, leaving Clay alone in the parlor. It made the room seem bigger.

Clay went to the radio in the corner and fiddled with the dials. They usually listened to radio shows with Harvey here, but Clay preferred music. He found a station with some warbling, slow jazz, and listened to the strumming instruments and lilting voice of the singer. Clay returned to his seat, and looked at his thick hands. He flexed his knuckles. He could have smashed the Tree Men to pieces, breaking and tearing and crushing until they were nothing but twigs. They presented a challenge, but Clay had been built for such acts of destruction.

He smelled smoke. Clay stared at the doorway. A thin line of smoke curled around the doorway, leading into the hall like a trail. The dark smoke hung in the air, flickering before fading out—as if some torch had been waved in the room and then dragged away. Clay came to his feet. He hurried through the door, and stumbled into the hallway. The line of smoke remained, a dark thread weaving across the hall and past the rooms of the guests. Clay hurried after it. He reached a back door, and pushed it open. Clay stepped into the chill evening air, under the Elephantine Hotel. The line of smoke led down a ladder poised at the edge of the pier. Clay needed to see what was causing the strange emanation.

The ladder brought Clay to the gravely beach. At high tide, this place would be underwater. Now, the dark soggy rocks rested under the towering forms of the pillars holding up the pier. Clay weaved around the pillars, until he followed the smoke to a patch of dirt right below Palisade Park. The roller coaster rumbled overhead, and piping calliope music sounded faint against the rumble of the ocean.

The smoke welled up in a cloud right under the pier. It blended in with the shadow, and Clay had to struggle to see it. The smoke coiled up and straightened, becoming a column—and then features appeared in the blackness. A woman's face emerged, with glowing letters on her forehead.

Clay smiled. "Lilith Shadowborn." He crossed the gravel and neared one of the few other golems who called Sickle City home. "How have you been?" He offered his hand. Lilith took it with a clawed shadow. It felt solid and slick in his hand, like was shaking hands with an icicle.

"Well enough, Mr. Clay." Lilith Shadowborn had been forged by a group of educated alchemists in the Enlightenment Age. Clay had been built to destroy, but Lilith had been made to satisfy curiosity. After her creators had proved that they could make life, they hadn't known what to do with her and had cast her out. Lilith had wandered the world ever since. Sometimes, Clay envied her freedom. Other times, he pitied her. "And you?"

"Well enough," Clay repeated. "You ever tangled with Men of the Field?"

"Plant people?" Lilith nodded. "They are a kindly race, as welcoming as the forests they protect—but don't cross them." She floated closer. "You have come into conflict with such creatures? That's odd. They are normally peaceful. Something has agitated them." Her eyes glowed coal red, framing a feminine, shadowy face.

"What do you mean?"

"It's why I came to you. You, Mr. Clay, are a man of many flaws—"

"Thanks."

Lilith flashed a smile—lost in shadow. Only her eyes glowed. "But you are a good man nonetheless, and have a keen sense of duty. That's why I came to you. Unlike most golems, I can enter the world of the spirits. I float alongside the Dybbuks and the Ibburs, the malevolent and benevolent shades, and listen to their stories. Lately, those voices have been raised in a chorus of fear and desperation."

"Of what?"

Lilith shook her head, making the smoke undulate. "I do not know. But something is coming to our city, Mr. Clay. Something of great power, and of deep evil. I suggest you prepare yourself for this incoming force."

"I'm prepared."

"No. You only think you are." Lilith rested a smoky hand on Clay's shoulder. He couldn't feel the weight. "Goodbye. I need to gather more information, and see what exact threat is heading our way. I'd tell you to keep your eyes open—but you are a golem, and you can never truly close your eyes." She turned away from him, floating into the darkening air above the sea. Clay followed her a few steps, his boots crunching on the sand. Lilith faded into nothing. Clay raised his hand to wave after her, but she had already vanished. What sort of danger had she been talking about? Clay didn't know. At the moment, he had to prepare himself for the Garden of Eden.

That evening, Clay and Zipporah arrived at the entrance of the Garden of Eden. Monk waited for them on the sidewalk, scratching one of the curling knife scars on his broad face. He gave Clay and Zipporah a nod as they arrived, and motioned to the Kosher butcher shop behind him. "You fellows hungry? I hear they got good pastrami and can mix a fine egg cream."

Clay grumbled. He didn't like being reminded about food he couldn't eat. "How's the company?"

"Not so good." Monk opened the door. "But what are you gonna do? Come on in."

They walked past the sliding doors and into the butcher shop. A single bored clerk sat the counter, rearranging the complimentary pickles in their bowl of brine. He nodded to Monk as they walked behind the counter, and to another door. That brought them to the store room, where several hunks of meat dangled from hooks. Monk moved past the sides of beef, selected one and pulled it aside to reveal a closed metal door. It looked inconspicuous, the kind of door that would lead to a simple storeroom. That was just what Rabbi Holtz and all the gangsters who worked for him wanted. Local cops could be paid off, but Prohibition Agents were another matter. It was best to hide the speakeasy, just in case the investigating Prohibition Agents happened to be honest.

Monk hauled open the door, revealing a cement stairwell. "Here we are." He removed his straw boater's hat and started down the stairs. "Welcome to the Garden of Eden." Monk stepped into shadow. Clay and Zipporah followed him. The stairwell brought them to a barren lobby, where two gorillas in matching tuxedoes watched the door. They nodded when Monk approached and opened up. Beyond that door, the Garden of Eden waited.

The speakeasy occupied several rooms—interconnected cellars and basements, strewn with colored lights and separated with diaphanous green curtains. Rich green carpets, like the top of a billiard table, covered the ground, and paintings of pastoral scenes covered the walls. The Garden of Eden offered a full bar, with every kind of illegal liquor available behind a large counter with a traditional brass rail. More adventurous drinkers could move to the round tables at the center of the Garden of Eden, facing a small stage where a Negro band, up from Hogshead Street, crooned their way through a rapid jazz number. At the center of the speakeasy, a giant tree stretched out and apparently held up the ceiling with its branches. Colored lanterns dangled down from the boughs of the false tree, adding a shine to every table and cup. Couples wheeled before the stage, fringed dresses flying as polished shoes tapped to the beat.

The usual mix of thirsty locals, dedicated boozehounds, and adventurous scofflaws packed the place. A couple of them glanced at Clay. One Uptown boy, a towheaded youngster sporting his father's monocle and with a young flapper on his arm, opened his mouth to make some doubtlessly witty comment. Clay glared at him and the kid's mouth slammed shut. He turned meekly back to his drink as Clay and the others strolled past.

Zipporah stopped by the bar. "Gimlet, please."

The bartender, a stolid lump of a fellow in a dark vest and shirtsleeves, prepared the drink with practiced speed. "Sure, Miss Sarfati. On the house, as always."

"Perks of the job." Zipporah grabbed the cocktail and followed Clay and Monk as they crossed the room. Monk brought them to a damask partition. "So, Monk, you got any idea what Mr. Sapphire wants with folks like me and Clay?"

"I suppose you'll have to sit down and see." Monk pulled aside the curtain. "Hello, boss. I brought them down, just like you asked." He held the curtain while Clay and Zipporah ducked into the booth, and then let it drop. Monk took up his position outside, his hands folded. He was muscle, and Sapphire obviously didn't want any extra ears hearing what he had to say.

They entered the secluded booth. A round table rested in the booth, where two sets of drinks stood untouched on the dark polished surface. Rabbi Holtz sat at the table, his arms folded. Across from him, Sid 'the Shark' Sapphire savored a cigarette in an ivory holder. Sapphire seemed more like a mannequin in a store than a man. Every fold of his dark tuxedo, and the black overcoat hanging limply over his shoulders like a cape, looked neat and pressed. His hair had been composed and straightened with copious pomade into a rigid dark, graying mass. His bloodless lips curled around the end of the cigarette and emitted a puff of smoke. It drifted up before half-closed gray eyes, which settled on Clay and Zipporah as they sat down. The only color on his dark tuxedo belonged to the brilliant blue flower, serving as his boutonniere. He smiled without showing his teeth.

Next to him, his main enforcer tucked a toothpick between his lips. Isaac 'Kid Twist' Deutsch committed murders for Sid Sapphire and was quite good at his job. His fedora covered his bald head, a pair of smoked glasses hid his eyes, and thick black gloves covered his hands. His arms, big and meaty, didn't look like they belonged on his slightly tubby body. Clay had seen him in action with a pistol, a piano wire garrote, and an ice pick on a few occasions. Kid Twist seemed sedentary now, but Clay knew that could change in an instant.

Zipporah settled down next to Clay. She stared at Sapphire. "Good evening, Mr. Sapphire. What's the rumpus?" She was never one for formalities, despite her privileged upbringing. "We hear you got a job for us."

Sapphire turned to Rabbi Holtz. "Is she this rude to you, Rabbi?"

Rabbi Holtz lowered his eyes. "She's simply eager to get to work, Mr. Sapphire."

"Heh." Kid Twist removed his toothpick. "Ain't we all?"

"How can we help you?" Clay wanted to change the subject, before Sapphire had a chance to grow angry. "Rabbi Holtz said it was big."

"And so it is." Sapphire waved his cigarette holder in the air, letting strands of dark smoke drift in a loose spiral in the dim air. "As with all important matters, it concerns money—namely mine. A very profitable revenue stream, Mr. Clay, is jeopardized. I want you to assure that it's safeguarded for the foreseeable future."

"What revenue stream would that be?" Clay asked.

"There's so many to choose from." Zipporah counted on her fingers. "Bootlegging. All the speaks like this one. Your rackets, including the work you do for the big shots and swells Uptown, gambling, smuggling, and—"

"That last one," Sapphire said. "That's where the trouble is."

"Mr. Sapphire runs a very profitable business in ancient artifacts," Rabbi Holtz explained. "He ships them in from Asia, the Middle East, and Africa, and sells them to wealthy men from around the country. These days, when there's so much chaos and upheaval in the world, it's easy to get your hands on some valuable objects. Naturally, it's a rather cutthroat trade. Mr. Sapphire's managed it well, with some help from me and our friends. But it seems that somebody doesn't know that this is Mr. Sapphire's business and is trying to get a piece for themselves."

"Did an artifact get pinched?" Zipporah asked.

"Not just one." Sapphire's lips swept downward, forming the hint of a frown. "An entire shipment. You see, I bring the shipments in through the sewers. The kinds of artifacts we're talking about—the kind the silver spoon *Goyim* have a taste for—are too valuable to be handled by even my most trusted men in the ports. Instead, I have the goods offloaded from foreign cargo ships at sea, and brought into the sewers on rowboats. The little boats paddle their way to a sewer station, right under my Uptown offices. Last night, that rowboat was attacked. Every artifact inside was stolen." He drummed his fingers on the table, as if he was already impatient for results. "One of my men was killed. The other escaped and spun some *fakakta* story to me about what happened."

Clay listened carefully. "Who was it? Who did the hijacking? A crew from Hogshead? Or maybe the Black Hand or a Chinatown Tong?"

"It could've been a rival crew," Zipporah suggested. "Turk Brownstein and the Tidewater Rats hang around on the docks north of Haven Street. The Rats are a desperate bunch, and like hijacking shipments of contraband booze, because they know the bootleggers can't go to the cops. Maybe they're responsible?"

"No." Sapphire dismissed their suggestions with a cursory shake of his head. "The Italian Families and the Tongs respect me. They need my smuggling routes and financing. As for Hogshead? Those *schwartzes* could never have found out about the shipments. And Brownstein's a *landsman*. His Rats are animals, but they know what would happen if they crossed me." He pulled aside his cigarette and stubbed it on the table, crushing it against the polished wood. "This is somebody new."

"An out-of-town crew?" Rabbi Holtz asked.

"Sure," Kid Twist said. "And we want to give them the proper Sickle City welcome."

Sapphire leaned closer. "Tomorrow evening, another shipment's going through the sewers. I'm gonna have every one of my men, from the croupiers at my casino to the torpedoes doing shakedowns, talk about it, so that any listening ears in the city will catch on. But there won't be any artifacts on the rowboat. Instead, it's gonna be you. You'll float in, encounter whatever attacked my men, and find out where they're laying low. Then you will return my artifacts."

"You leave the rest to us," Kid Twist said. That meant that all Clay and Zipporah had to do was identify the thieves. Kid Twist and his compatriots would hunt down the robbers and dispatch them in the proper style. The unfortunate thieves would probably be floating in the bay or end up in some alley, shot, stabbed, bludgeoned, or simply strangled.

Zipporah sipped her gimlet. "I got a question—why do you need me and Clay for this? You got plenty of palookas who can handle this sort of heat. Why us?"

"Two reasons," Sapphire explained. "First off, there's the artifacts that were pinched. This batch came from British Palestine."

"The Holy Land," Rabbi Holtz said.

"Exactly." Sapphire leaned back in his seat, listing the contents of the shipment. "Ancient stone ritual objects, for the most part. A sacred Babylonian prayer dish or two. But the key to the whole collection was a figurine from King Herod's time—allegedly for demonic worship. Supposedly, the stone depicted Asmodeus."

"The King of Demons." Rabbi Holtz spoke without looking up.

"Second reason is because of the report delivered by the incident's survivor." Sapphire rolled his eyes. "He kept yapping about swords. Shivs of some kind." He turned to Kid Twist. "What was the exact word he used?"

"Daggers," Kid Twist said.

"Nobody in this city uses daggers," Sapphire said. "It's weird business. That means it's your specialty, so you take care of it. All you need to do is identify the thieves and get back what's rightfully mine. I'll see that you're properly rewarded." He glanced at Rabbi Holtz. "Something else. I want your son to go along. He knows this magic business extremely well. He probably knows all about Asmodeus and King Herod, and whatever ghoul, ghost, or goblin is wielding daggers."

Rabbi Holtz's expression saddened. "Harvey's only twelve, Mr. Sapphire."

"Rabbi." Sapphire put his hand on Rabbi Holtz's arm—in almost a parody of a friendly gesture. "How old were you when you went to work for me and torched your first newsstand? Younger than your son, by a good year or so, I'd wager. Besides, I insist." Rabbi Holtz had no choice but to follow Sapphire's orders.

Clay stood up and adjusted his coat. "We'll protect Harvey, sir. Don't worry."

"You see?" Sapphire asked. "Nothing to worry about. So you agree, then? Harvey can accompany Mr. Clay and Miss Sarfati?"

"Yes." Rabbi Holtz didn't sound happy about it.

"I'm giving you and the boy a compliment, Rabbi," Sapphire said. "Your son's a genius. I'd say he's even smarter than your older brother. What was his name? Chaim?" Rabbi Holtz flinched a little at the name, and so did Clay. Chaim Holtz had built Clay and given him life. "What's the matter? You don't want him to follow in your brother's footsteps?"

"Flee America and return to the Old Country?" Rabbi Holtz shook his head. "Abandoning me and his baby brother and sinking into his studies of Talmudic nonsense and Kabala junk? I'd give my left eye to ensure that didn't happen."

Sapphire grinned, finally revealing his teeth. His smile had a predatory edge, as if he wanted to lean over and start eating whatever he grinned at. Clay knew why people called him The Shark. "Would you rather he ended up like you, then?" Sapphire asked.

Rabbi Holtz stared at him. "I'd give my right eye to ensure that didn't happen."

"Hmmm." Sapphire released a muffled, quiet laugh. He was still laughing as Clay and Zipporah walked away from the table, leaving Rabbi Holtz to his guests. They had been given their assignment, and Clay didn't feel like sticking around.

Was Rabbi Holtz ashamed about what he did—acting as the pillar of Haven Street's religious community when everyone knew that he was a kingpin who ran every racket in the neighborhood? He certainly didn't advertise his career to Harvey, who simply believed that his father protected Haven Street from outside threats. Clay supposed that he couldn't blame the rabbi for hiding the truth.

He and Zipporah walked back to Palisade Park, just as it closed up for the evening. The last guests of the night walked past them, ushered along by the park workers. A drunk snoozed against the base of the Ferris wheel, and one of the park's clowns blasted him with a spray of seltzer to wake him up and get him moving. Professor West stood on the porch of the Elephantine Hotel, overseeing his kingdom. The rickety roller coaster looked almost ghostly in the fading light, like the rib cage and spine of some shadowy animal. Shadows made everything in the Palisade Park look a little odd. Maybe it was best to close it up this late.

Zipporah stifled a yawn as they walked past the tents and booths and approached the Elephantine Hotel. "I think I'm gonna head to sleep, Clay. Get a little shuteye while I can." She paused at the porch of their hotel. "You'll be all right?"

"Sure. Sleep was another thing that a golem couldn't do.

"Okay." She held out her hand. "Huh. It's raining." Sure enough, a few drops pattered down from the sky. More joined in, pouring down over the pier and splashing into the sea. The rain pounded against the brim of Clay's fedora. "You want to come inside?"

"No. I don't mind the rain."

He didn't let Zipporah ask him any more questions. Instead, he turned around and walked into the amusement park. The lanterns and electric lights of Palisade Park flickered off, covering everything in darkness and shadow. Clay wanted to be alone, and Zipporah understood that. The battle with the Tree Men, Harvey's hasty peace treaty, the meeting with Lilith, and the new job from Sapphire—all of them reminded Clay of what he was and what he had been built to do. He needed to think about that, and so he strolled around the garish decorations, now turned into fantastic silhouettes by the moonlight and shadow.

The storm worsened. Clay walked to the railing, past a rigged ball toss game, and looked out over the sea. Lightning crashed in the distance. The waves rolled and crested, tipped with points of white, before they fell down into the ocean. Clay knew storms very well. Years ago, right after his creation, he had experienced a blizzard.

He had wandered out of the little cabin and into the plains of Eastern Russia, while the wind tore into the hillsides and threw up endless volumes of snow and sleet. The wind had blasted his body and knocked him down, but he always managed to come to his feet. The tempest almost pulled him off the plains and dragged him into the air, and the snow nearly buried him, but Clay held fast. When the storm ended, Rabbi Chaim Holtz had emerged from the cabin and gazed at him.

Chaim, with his tangled white beard, skullcap, and dark robe, looked like a figure out of the ancient past, as opposed to his contemporary brothers. He had the pleasant round face that Harvey and Herman Holtz shared, at least. Chaim looked at his creation, and nodded slowly. He held out his hands, and he and Clay linked fingers. "My creation—you can stand against anything but the power of the Almighty," Chaim had said. "You are ready."

He had given Clay instructions. The next day, an army of marauding Cossacks neared the small shtetl where Chaim had made his home. In the wild days of the Russian Revolution, Cossacks pledged themselves to the White Army fighting for the Tsar, the Red Army fighting for Lenin, Trotsky, and the communists, or the various warlords and independent armies carving their way through the countryside.

Some Cossacks spurned any flag. They attacked everyone, looting and killing for their own gain instead of a cause—though every army looted and pillaged in that chaotic, mad conflict. Cossacks had long hated Jews, seeing them as weak targets and objects of revulsion, and now they turned against them in endless bloody pogroms. Chaim Holtz decided that the Jews needed a protector, just as they did in Medieval Prague when Rabbi Judah Loew had made the first golem. He crafted a golem, gave it no name, and sent it to battle against the Cossacks.

As he had been ordered to, Clay met the Cossacks. They charged across the open plains in a great horde, snow flying from the hooves of their horses. Their sabers reached high, shimmering in the moonlight. Laughter left their bearded faces when they saw a single Jew standing against them. They had charged him, ready to cut him down. Clay met them. Their sabers shattered against Clay's sides. Their carbines and revolvers thundered into his belly, but barely made him pause. Then Clay had attacked. He tore Cossacks from the saddle and ripped them to pieces. His punches shattered bones. He ripped off limbs and broke skulls. Horses and men died under Clay's blows. A wagon with a mounted machine gun—a Tachanka—rode against Clay. It didn't stand a chance. Clay killed the crew and the gunners and then grabbed the machine gun from the wagon. He turned that gun on the survivors and mowed them down as they tried to attack.

When the battle had ended, not a single Cossack remained alive. Clay returned to Rabbi Chaim Holtz, his arms and legs covered in blood. Sabers had been stabbed in his chest and shoulders and remained wedged in his skin. He stood before Rabbi Holtz, a giant in his enemy's gore. Rabbi Chaim Holtz had shuddered.

He had cursed his creation. "Abomination!" He roared the word, realizing what he had done. "Monster! You are a killer in the eyes of the God—and in my eyes! Be gone from here!" Chaim had pointed away from the shtetl, and so Clay had left and wandered through Russia—a hulking, forlorn figure with no discernible purpose.

Eventually, he wandered north and encountered a strange scene. Soldiers in olive green uniforms and tin bowler helmets had been outnumbered by a large force of Bolsheviks. Clay waded into the battle, intervening on the side of the soldiers—who happened to be Americans. They had been sent to Russia alongside the Allied Intervention, England, France, Japan, and many other countries fought the Bolsheviks. These soldiers belonged to the Polar Bear Expedition, and they welcomed Clay back to their camp, even if they didn't know exactly what he was.

The doughboys gave Clay his name by asking him some simple questions. "Where'd you come from?" The answer was Clay. "What does that scribbling on your head mean?" The answer was Emmet. After that, everyone called him Emmet Clay. He fought alongside the Polar Bear Expedition, engaging in numerous risky missions for them until the Revolution ended and the communist victory was clear. The grateful American colonel brought Clay back to America and looked up Rabbi Chaim Holtz's brothers on Haven Street. Clay had been working for the younger Rabbi Holtz ever since.

Now, he turned away from the ocean and stared over the dark amusement park. Statues of Indians, clowns, imps, and animals grinned at him, strange and frightening in the darkness. Another face appeared in their ranks for half a second—a hairless face, with pale skin surrounded by dark tattoos. The mouth opened, uttering a single word—"Golem"— and then the strange face vanished. Clay stared at the shadows. He must have imagined it.

Still, his imagination was correct. Clay was nothing more than a golem. He emitted a low sigh and trudged back to the Elephantine Hotel for the night.

Chapter Two
UNDERGROUND

The day after the battle with the Tree Men in Arcadia Park, Clay and Zipporah prepared for their next job. They sat together in the parlor of the Elephantine Hotel, readying themselves for the case to come. This assignment had come from Sapphire himself, and they knew they couldn't foul it up. Clay flexed his fingers, making fists and preparing for a scrape. He tried a few blows, rapid jabs in the air followed by powerful right hooks. He pantomimed punching the elephant statue in the corner, aiming his blows at the round head and tusks. Just because Clay hit like an avalanche didn't mean that he could afford to avoid practice. He watched and imitated some of the best pugilists in Steele City, to make every blow hit harder. Because he didn't care for guns or blades, finding them unwieldy and imprecise, he had to be sure he could rely on his knuckles. They hadn't failed him yet.

On the other hand, Zipporah had plenty of weapons. She sharpened her scimitars and placed them in their scabbards, then set the sheaths over her shoulders. The Maid of Megiddo had taken them from the bodies of

The mouth opened, uttering a single word – "Golem."

dead Turkish officers, and cared for them ever since. She had set a valise on the glass coffee table and carefully undid the straps. The valise fell open, revealing a variety of British army pistols, a bayonet, and a few black and white pictures. One showed T.E. Lawrence himself, standing tall with a younger Zipporah at his side in a wide, pale white desert. Clay stopped shadowboxing and looked at the picture.

"A friend?" he asked.

Zipporah shrugged. "He was my commander, Clay. But yes, I suppose he was a friend. Just like Rabbi Holtz is now." Her hand moved to a trio of grenades—Mills Bombs, that looked like ridged, olive green metal fruit. "Think I ought to bring a grenade? A pineapple might come in handy."

If their previous missions were any indication, there would be certainly be a need for firepower. "Bring the grenade," Clay said. Zipporah tucked the Mills Bomb in her pocket, and came to her feet as the door opened.

Professor West poked his head in. He had been applying pomade to his dark hair, and it glistened in the afternoon sunlight. "Young Harvey is at the door. I believe he wishes to invite you to some sort of event. He seems most insistent."

They gathered up their supplies and headed to the porch. Sure enough, Harvey waited for them on the wooden planks, staring out at the gaudily painted structures of the boardwalk. He turned around when Clay and Zipporah emerged, a smile splitting his pale, freckled face. "Mr. Clay, Miss Sarfati—I would like to invite you to see a political speaker at the Sylvan Cafe." He sounded like he had carefully practiced this invitation in his mind. "My Uncle Herbert invited me by telephone after Mr. Moss drove me home from school, and told me that I should bring my friends. I can think of no one else I would rather go with." He pointed down the street. "It's in North Haven Street. Would you guys like to attend?" Enthusiasm leaked from his words.

Clay considered it. "Uncle Herbert?" That was Harvey's young uncle—and Rabbi Holtz's baby brother. "And the Sylvan Cafe?"

"This is Bolshevik business, ain't it, child?" Zipporah asked. Herbert attended university and had fallen in with several radical organizations. The Sylvan Cafe catered to Bohemian types, and would be a fitting place for a radical speaker.

Harvey examined his Buster Browns. "I suppose it might—but Uncle Herbert promised that it was enlightening and important. He's very smart, and he knows all about this sort of thing. Would you like to go with me?"

"I've had enough of Bolsheviks in Russia," Clay muttered.

"Come on, Clay." Zipporah patted his thick shoulder. "Humor the kid.

Besides, I like Herbert. He's a good pup, and he cares for his nephew. I say we go. You never know—you might learn something."

Clay released a rumbling groan as he stared at Harvey. He couldn't deny the boy's request. "Fine. We'll take the Studebaker."

"Swell!" Harvey's smile almost made it worthwhile.

They headed to the waiting Studebaker and left Palisade Park. Haven Street had been glutted with the usual afternoon traffic, and it took them an annoyingly long time to arrive at the Sylvan Cafe. Clay parked a block away, and they headed toward the large crowd gathered before the wide glass windows and conglomeration of leafy plants surrounding the outdoor section of the coffee house. A crowd had already gathered, made up of scruffy North Haven Street types, mixed in with a few Little Jerusalem natives who seemed eager to hear the speaker. Young men and women with red armbands moved around, handing out flyers with insistent eagerness. Clay and the others reached the back of the crowd and sidled in, trying to get a view of the speaker. Harvey stood on his tiptoes and craned his neck, searching for his uncle.

Herbert Holtz spotted him first and hurried over. "Harvey!" Herbert embraced the boy, and then offered his hand to Clay and Zipporah. "I'm delighted that you could make it." Herbert had the same pleasant round face of his older brother and nephew, though he sported a few strands of boyish stubble. He wore a rumpled gray suit, with mustard stains on the vest, and the knot of his tie looked like it couldn't quite handle the task that had caused its creation. Like Harvey, he wore a newsboy cap and round spectacles. He pointed to the speaker. "This is Enrico Neri, with the Socialist Worker's Alliance. We disagree on a few key points, but he's still a wonderful man and a fine speaker."

Enrico Neri stood on a chair from the Sylvan Cafe, which gave his small frame some much needed height. He had graying wafts of hair and pince-nez perched on his Roman nose. His hand cut the air mechanically as he spoke. "And for what purpose was this Great War, in which so many young men lost their lives? Did it improve the lots of their families? Did it make the world better, this great conflict which is burned into the memories of so many? No. The blood of workers was once again shed to enrich the wealthy. So it has always been, and so it is now." He had a thick Italian accent, but somehow his words managed to be audible. "A change is needed, comrades. A change to Sickle City, to America, and to the world! A change in which the worker fights not for the gold of the rich, but to make himself free of oppression and tyranny!" Cheers followed his words.

Herbert jabbed his fist proudly into the air, adding his voice to the roars.

When the shouts finished, Herbert turned back to Clay, Zipporah, and Harvey. "I would like to introduce you fellows to someone else as well." He glanced into the crowd, and motioned for someone to join him. "This is Comrade Bethany Hark, of Shanghai."

Bethany Hark moved awkwardly to stand next to Herbert, her long legs carefully directing her between the members of the crowd. The Chinese girl seemed around Herbert's age, but wore a Westernized woman's shirt and a golden, striped tie under a long overcoat. She even had a bowler hat, framing close-cropped hair. "I am pleased to meet you." She spoke English extremely well, with a trace of a British accent. Clay accepted her handshake, and she gave him a curtsey that looked practiced. She turned to Harvey. "You are Herbert's nephew, young man?"

"Yes, ma'am." Harvey smiled shyly. "Are you really from Shanghai? In China? What's it like over there?" He leaned closer, lowering his voice. "I've read numerous pulp magazines about the secret mysteries of the Orient, so I have a decent idea."

"You do?" Hark seemed amused.

"Yes, ma'am. It's full of ancient Tongs and Triads, and evil assassins, and opium dens, people dying the Death of a Thousand Cuts." He glanced at Clay and Zipporah, who shrugged. "Or at least, it is in the stories."

Hark shook her head. "It's dangerous enough without things like that."

"Bethany was raised in a Christian orphanage, before finding her place with the growing communist party in Shanghai's International Settlement," Herbert explained. "She worked diligently for her comrades before incurring the wrath of some local capitalist and his petty gangster cronies. That necessitated a rapid flight to America's golden shore, where we became acquainted." He smiled weakly, looking between him and Hark. "We belong to a few of the same organizations."

Zipporah nodded politely. "Pleased to meet you, Miss Hark. I'm Zipporah Sarfati."

"And I'm Emmet Clay. We work for Herbert's brother, Rabbi Holtz." Bethany bristled a little at that. Herbert must have told her some details about Rabbi Holtz's business. After all, that was what paid for Herbert to attend University.

"It's good to meet you, Mr. Clay." Hark retained her pleasant expression. "Rabbi Holtz is a good man. There are many like him, in Shanghai."

"Rabbis?" Harvey asked.

"Not exactly," Herbert added.

Clay pointed to the speaker. "What do you make of that fellow, and the Bolshevik stuff he's spewing?"

They turned and looked at Neri, as he reached another portion of his speech. "Sickle City, like all cities in America and in the industrialized world, now stand at a crossroads. One path leads to the same grinding capitalist existence that has always polluted the world. You can see the results everywhere around you. The poor pack into crowded tenements. They struggle in factories. They are spat on by the rich, and called dirty and stupid. Some advance, some do not—and the failure of those who remain mired in poverty is blamed only on their character and not on a system which is inherently unequal." He jabbed his finger into the air, as if he was trying to puncture a hole in something. "But there is another path, my friends. Our comrades in Russia follow it as we speak. Are there struggles and problems? Of course there are. But at its core, they struggle for something better. It is a struggle we should all join."

Hark listened carefully. "You don't agree with that, Mr. Clay?"

"I don't like Bolsheviks," Clay replied.

"But don't you think that things are unfair? That the rich have so much and the poor so little?" Hark arched an eyebrow. "This is called the Land of the Free, where immigrants from around the world can arrive and succeed. In Shanghai, they dream about this country, tell stories about it. I'm sure they did the same in the land where you were born, Herbert. But then we immigrants come here and what do we find? The same cruelty from police, the same rich men with their mansions out of town, and their corrupt politics. The same ineffective charities, which ease the consciences of do-gooders and kindly dowagers, without addressing the real problem. It may be better than your home, but is it *much* better, Mr. Clay?"

"My home was full of war and death," Clay said.

"So was mine. Capitalism is cruel in America—but it is crueler in Shanghai. Do you not agree?"

Clay let out an annoyed creak. "Perhaps. But is a revolution necessary to change things?"

"A lot of people say it is, Mr. Clay," Harvey chimed in. "Or at least, a great insistence on unions. I was looking up articles about the policeman's union that you said had Detective Flynn worried, and some of the labor organizers made a lot of good points. Policemen work really hard in this city, and their pay is so low. I think they should strike, if that's what they n-need to do to get their point across, I mean." He seemed a little nervous, not used to speaking out on these sorts of issues.

"And leave this town without police?" Zipporah asked. "Are you certain, child?"

Herbert snorted. "What would it matter? The cops are servants of the rich anyway."

A harsh shout came from the street leading to the Sylvan Cafe, amplified by a speaking trumpet. It blared over Neri's speech, and he faltered. Clay and the rest of the audience turned. A column of mounted police approached—uniformed cops on the back of powerful, black chargers. They carried billy clubs and sported Sam Browne belts and peaked caps, with goggles protecting their eyes. Other officers followed on foot, toting bulky shotguns and clubs. They formed a line of black across the street, and didn't appear to be eager to listen to Neri's speech. Clay formed his hands into fists as his stony skin creaked in panic. He needed to get his friends to safety.

"Case in point..." Herbert muttered.

The cop with the speaking trumpet pointed a gloved finger at the crowd. "This is an unlawful assemblage!" The trumpet gave his voice a loud, tinny urgency. "You are discussing illegal, subversive topics. Disperse to your homes immediately or face the consequences." Nobody moved. The crowd glared at the cops, daring them to try something. Neri folded his hands and carefully removed his pince-nez. Clay's panic grew. The cop sighed. He sounded weary. "Come on, you goddamn yids. Leave or we'll make you leave."

"You will not insult my audience!" Neri cried. "Or threaten them. We have the right to freely assemble, and to speak freely as well." He scowled at the cop. "Besides, I am not a 'yid', as you charmingly put it. I'm from Campania."

"Goddamn greaser, then." The cop nodded to his friends. "Clear them out."

That was all it took. The cops spurred their horses, who broke into a gallop. They charged for the crowd, their hooves pounding on the pavement in a rapid, terrible drumbeat. It reminded Clay of the Cossack charges he had battled in the Old Country—though the snow always muffled their hooves. The policemen brandished their batons, which shone in the gray sunlight, and reached the audience before they had a chance to flee. The billy clubs rained down, the momentum of the charge adding more power to the blows. Clubs bashed aside Haven Street residents and locals, sending them reeling and tumbling to the street. Blood and teeth struck the sidewalk and the gutter as the audience dropped. Some of the mounted police smashed their way into the outdoor cafe, and their hooves shattered tables and chairs. Screams and shouts of pain joined the whinnying of horses as the batons rose and fell. The other police moved in, cuffing and arresting everyone.

Harvey panicked. Clay knew the boy had experienced danger before while helping Zipporah and Clay—usually in the form of some Talmudic demon or antediluvian monster with a complicated name and too many teeth—but never anything like this. He drew closer to his friends, motioning for Herbert and Hark to join him. "Why are they doing this?" he asked. He turned to Clay, as if the golem knew the answer. "Why are they just attacking, Mr. Clay? Mr. Neri wasn't hurting anyone. Why are they doing this?" Clay didn't have time to answer. They needed to leave.

A cop on horseback spotted Herbert and charged him. He galloped through the crowd, smacking the back of a young woman's head with his baton and dropping her, then turning his club on Herbert. The baton hummed through the air, ready to connect to Herbert's chin—but Hark grabbed the boy's arm and tugged him out of the way. Her eyes flashed. Perhaps in Shanghai, she had dealt with this kind of thing before—or maybe worse—and knew how to conduct herself.

Clay moved in. He faced the horse and glanced at the cop. The officer had a drooping nose, which seemed almost too low on his face. His eyes widened behind his goggles when he gazed at Clay's size, but he raised his baton anyway. Clay struck first, delivering a rapid right hook to the horse's head. Hair pressed against his knuckles. The horse let out a single whinny and its legs slipped on the ground. Its hooves slid on pavement and then it dropped. The cop tumbled from the saddle and crashed to the ground. He rose growling, going for the pistol on his belt.

Zipporah grabbed his head and drove it into her knee. He groaned a final time and dropped; the revolver still in his hand. Zipporah glanced at the others. "We need to get out of here—now. If I get pinched, they'll find the Mills Bomb in my pocket and we'll probably be deported. Or shot."

"Mills Bomb?" Herbert asked.

Clay grabbed Harvey's hand and started forcing his way through the crowd. "Follow me. Stick together." They moved toward the end of the melee, pushing their way around officers swinging away with their batons and wheeling, whinnying horses, as well as the terrified audience. Clay shouldered an officer walloping a towheaded kid with the butt of his shotgun, knocking the cop into the gutter and clearing a path. He pointed to the mouth of an alley, just across from the Sylvan Cafe. The others got the message.

They scrambled out of the brawl in progress and hurried across the street. Clay and Zipporah ran together flanking Harvey—who still seemed consumed with a mixture of fear and confusion. Herbert and Hark followed, holding hands as they moved together over the road. The mounted cops didn't notice them. They had plenty of other people to beat, after all.

The alley offered long shadows and a relief from the scuffle. Clay slowed his pace. Harvey slipped on a piece of trash come from a set of overflowing bins on the concrete, and Clay reached over to steady him before he fell. He winced and thanked Clay with a nervous nod. Hark and Herbert joined them, and paused for breath. They stood together, saying nothing and breathing heavily after their close escape. Clay was just glad that Harvey hadn't been hurt.

A loafer clicked on the alley floor. Clay raised his fists and Zipporah reached for her swords. "Easy there, Mr. Clay. No need to gut me, Miss Sarfati." Detective Ollie Flynn emerged, his hands raised. He had his gabardine coat hanging open, revealing the stubby revolver in his shoulder-holster. "I'll not run you in. You don't need to worry about that."

Herbert knew Detective Flynn—and didn't like him. "What are you doing here?"

"I seem to remember Haven Street being my bailiwick. Came to watch the festivities. Make sure things didn't get out of hand." Detective Flynn waved his hand at the alley. "This seems like a luxury box, you know."

"You just watch, Detective Flynn?" Herbert asked. "You can't s-stop this?"

"Ah, the mounted boys won't kill anyone. They're just knocking around a few Reds, is all." Detective Flynn shrugged. "They need this little dust-up, too. Let's them work out their frustrations after having the union proposal rejected by the mayor and his Wigwam Club backers again. And besides, who gives a damn about a bunch of Bolsheviks? Pardon my language, of course." He grinned at Clay. "You fought those Reds in their homeland, didn't you? You know what I mean."

Nothing excused the sheer violence going on just outside. "These people don't deserve this."

"They're agitating for the destruction of the country which has given us all so much. They deserve every blow we give them." Detective Flynn pointed to Herbert. "And shame on you, lad, for exposing Harvey to this sort of claptrap and the accompanying violence. I'm taking the pair of you back to Rabbi Holtz's house. Mr. Clay and Miss Sarfati, you're welcome to come along. I hear he's got a job for you, and he can send you off properly."

"If you think I'll walk away from my comrades—" Herbert started.

"Herbert." Hark patted his arm. "You need to stick with your family. I don't have that luxury. Don't throw it away."

"There's some wisdom." Detective Flynn pointed to Hark. "Now, why don't you find your own way back to your heathen enclave, with the rest of your Yellow brethren." He grinned at Herbert. "I can't wait to see what the rabbi's gonna say when I tell him your best girl is slant-eyed—"

"Don't talk about her!" Herbert looked like he was going to slug Detective Flynn.

Hark kept her grip on his arm. "Goodbye, Herbert. We'll see each other tomorrow, at the meeting." She gave him a quick kiss on the cheek. "And it was very good to meet all of you. Particularly you, Harvey Holtz. You are a perfect little gentleman, just as your uncle said." She patted him on the head, causing his face to redden. Even when he was terrified, Harvey could still be embarrassed. "As the detective said, I can find my own way back."

She turned down the alley, ducked around the dumpster, and hurried away. "Goodbye!" Harvey called, waving after her. "It was nice to meet you, Miss Hark!" He gave her a parting wave as she left, and turned back to Herbert. "You really think papa will be mad?"

"We'll have to see, child," Zipporah said. "Now let's get moving. We have work to do."

They headed down the alley, following Detective Flynn. He brought them back to his car and drove around the block to Clay's Studebaker. They both headed back to Atlas Avenue, where Rabbi Holtz kept his house. Behind them, the melee had mostly ended. The cops handcuffed the audience and dragged them aboard waiting paddy wagons. The Black Marias would speed them to the downtown Station House, where they'd be tossed in the drunk tank, perhaps worked over a few more times, and shoved back on the street without being charged. It wasn't right, but it was America—Clay's adopted country. It was better than the chaos of Russia, of course, but Clay kept thinking about Hark's words. Could there be an alternative? Maybe not the utopia promised by Herbert's socialist friends, but something else? It was a question that Clay just couldn't answer.

ᛉᛉᛉ

As expected, Rabbi Holtz was not happy. He and Herbert lived in a small manor, next door to the King Solomon Synagogue, which Rabbi Holtz had purchased when it was near bankruptcy and turned into the largest place of worship on Haven Street. A maid and cook kept the house running, and always gave Harvey a home that he was happy to return to. Now, that didn't seem to be the case. The cook served them a quick dinner of cold chicken and cucumber salad in the large dining room. Clay sat next to Zipporah on one end of the table, with Harvey and Rabbi Holtz at the other end. Herbert took the middle, but didn't seem too keen on sitting down. The dining room could have belonged in the home of any palatial residence, with the tasteful refinement of the upper class. Only the touches of Judaism—silver Shabbat candlesticks in the center of the table, framed images from holy books, and a gilded mezuzah on the wall— marked it as unique.

They ate silently for a little, crunching on the cucumbers and slicing the chicken. The cook hadn't provided Clay with a plate of food he couldn't eat. That spared him some embarrassment, at least. Rabbi Holtz carefully skewered a chunk of cucumber, dripping in sauce, and crunched on it loudly. He pointed the fork at Herbert. "Do you remember the meals you used to eat, Herbert?" He asked the question calmly, like any friendly bit of conversation.

"Frankfurters from the stand on the corner," Herbert said. "And chicken soup. Chaim always had a way with chicken soup. I remember that you'd bring back a hot dog when you returned from some job in the evening, wake me up, and let me eat. We would share the same bed, and you never complained about the crumbs."

"I would steal those meals. Oftentimes." Rabbi Holtz raised another cucumber. "You don't remember at all what we ate in the Old Country. I do—as much as I want to forget the taste and the growling of my belly. America has given us so much, and now you insult our adopted land by spending time with these communists, these Marxists. This anarchist filth!" He let his fork fall and it clattered on the plate. "And you bring my son to these people, straight into danger? It is a *shanda*!"

Herbert flinched. The word *shanda* meant shame—but the mention of Harvey, and the vehemence of Rabbi Holtz's words, must have truly burned. "I did not mean for the police to attack. You know I would never cause harm to my dear nephew. You know how much I care for Harvey."

"Papa..." Harvey stared between his uncle and his father. "You don't need to—"

"If you care for your nephew, why would you drag him to meet your subversive friends?" Rabbi Holtz asked. "Why do you hate this country, which has been so good to us? America has given Harvey a safe place to grow up, and you a good education at the university. We are American, Herbert, and we must respect the land that has given us so much."

"So I turn a blind eye to the oppression of the poor? The exploitation of the people on this very street?" Herbert slammed down his fork and pushed back his chair. "You talk about how much you love America, but you know something? If you didn't break the law on a regular basis, if you weren't a bootlegger and some, some gangster king of Little Jerusalem, then—"

Harvey turned to his uncle. "Please, Uncle Herbert, don't call him—"

"You say that I'm a *shanda*?" Herbert continued, his rage growing. "What about you? You lie, sin, swindle, and sell bootleg liquor thanks to your phony rabbi's license. You're a *shanda*, brother. A common criminal who thinks that he's some protector of his people, a modern day Maccabee, when he's nothing more than a common *goniff*."

Clay rested his thick fingers on the table. "Rabbi, we could leave if you wish."

Zipporah nodded. "Perhaps we could go to the study, or—"

"Stay right where you are." Rabbi Holtz kept his tone level. He stared at Herbert. "Call me whatever names you like. Your older brother certainly did. I suppose I shamed Chaim, just as I shame you. I'll tell you what I told him. I will do whatever it takes it takes to protect my family. That includes Harvey, and that includes you—whether you like it or not. Even if I disagree with your politics, I'll watch over you." He leaned closer. "Now what's this I hear from Detective Flynn about you falling for some Oriental twist?"

"Papa." Harvey stammered as he tried to befriend his uncle. "Miss H-Hark is really nice. She was very kind to me, and she's from Shanghai, and had all kinds of adventures there. She protected Uncle Herbert from the attacking police, and—"

Herbert pushed back his chair. "I'm leaving, Herman. I won't let you insult her."

"I'm merely describing her. She's an Oriental. Lower than a *shikse*, even." Rabbi Holtz shook his head. "A *goyish* woman, maybe I could understand. At least she'd be white. But someone from Chinatown? What can you possibly see in her?"

"I don't believe I could ever convey my feelings." Herbert reached for his hat. He paused to squeeze Harvey's shoulder. "I'll see you later, Harvey.

Thank you for coming today. I'll let Miss Hark know that you stood up for her." He headed for the door and then paused and looked at Zipporah and Clay. "The same to you. Goodbye, Mr. Clay—and goodbye, Miss Sarfati." He stepped through the door and closed it behind him. It fell with a resounding bang, and silence once again returned to the dining room.

Rabbi Holtz sighed. "I'm sorry you had to hear that."

"Why are you so mean to him, papa?" Harvey asked. "Uncle Herbert's a swell fellow, and he really likes Miss Hark. You didn't need to call her those names."

"I know." Rabbi Holtz rested his hands in the lap. "Perhaps I didn't mean what I said. I just got angry. I provide for Herbert, just as I did when we were boys. I put money in his pockets, food in his mouth, and he insults me. It causes anger that should not be in the heart of a holy man." He smirked suddenly. "Not that I am a holy man." He leaned over and patted his son's head. "You like the chicken, *boychick*?"

"It's pretty good," Harvey said. "Can we have pastrami some time?"

"Perhaps tomorrow. I'll have it delivered from the butcher shop above the—" He caught himself before mentioning the name of his speakeasy to his son. "Delivered from the butcher shop, I mean." He glanced at Clay and Zipporah. "You're ready for tonight's work, I take it?"

"Always ready, sir." Zipporah had finished her meal. Surviving in the desert had taught her not to waste. She glanced out the window.

Clay glanced out the window, which overlooked Atlas Avenue—the richest section of Haven Street. "It's sundown," Clay said. "We should be leaving soon." The sun had set, bathing the street in shadow. It turned the numerous ancient oaks into large, outstretched outlines over the sidewalk, and made the King Solomon synagogue look like a giant tombstone.

"Sapphire will send a car around. He'll have everything ready." Rabbi Holtz leaned closer to Clay. "I'll send Monk and Cohen to another sewer entrance. They'll meet you inside, in case you need any help. It should be fine. Perfectly safe." He was trying to reassure himself.

The dining room door inched open. Monk Moss poked his head in. He held his straw boater's hat in his hand. "Boss." He jabbed a finger into the hall. "There's a Rolls Royce outside—one of Sapphire's cars. It'll take Clay, Zipporah, and your boy to the coast. They'll be taken out to a tramp steamer, put in a rowboat, and sent into the sewers from there."

Zipporah pushed back her chair. "We'd better get moving." She smiled at Harvey. "Come along, child. No time to waste."

"Okay." Harvey turned back to his father. "Goodbye, papa. I'll be back later. I'll be careful—I promise." They embraced, and he and Zipporah joined Monk in the hallway. Clay moved to join them, but Rabbi Holtz left his seat. He gripped Clay's arm.

"Clay." He lowered his voice. "Do you think I'm a good father?"

"I'm not sure how to answer that." Clay paused. He paused for a few moments. "You're a better father."

"Better than who?"

"Than your older brother."

"Ah." Rabbi Holtz released Clay's arm. "You know what's crazy? I often wish Chaim was here. When he was in America, he hated it and I hated having him here. He wanted to study his holy books and debate on obscure passages of the Talmud, without caring at all for making a living and putting food on the table. That was my concern, and yet he never approved of my decisions. Maybe I want him here so I could tell him 'I told you so.' Prove that he was wrong and I was right. Or maybe I just miss him."

"I miss him," Clay said. "Despite everything."

"You take care of yourself, Mr. Clay. And you watch over my boy."

"I will, Rabbi." Clay walked through the open doors, and followed his friends. They headed outside, into the shadows, to solve the night's mystery.

An hour later, they floated through a sewer entrance on a small motorboat. They had followed Sapphire's exact route for smuggling his artifacts—joining a tramp steamer as it approached Sickle City, and boarding a petite, maneuverable motorboat, which was loaded into water bright with reflected stars. From there, they had zoomed to the dark coast. Above the land, the skyscrapers reared up and sparkled like pillars of light. Zipporah managed the motorboat, and used a flashlight and a small map to navigate. They found a sewer entrance, a round tube leading to a canal, and buzzed the motorboat inside. Then they floated down the canal, zooming along above a trail of bubbles. Clay settled in the back, closer to Zipporah, while Harvey sat in the prow. They all carried flashlights, which gleamed through the tunnel.

The light revealed Sickle City's mammoth sewer system—an ancient collection of tunnels dating back to before the Victorian Age. They stretched for miles under the surface, crisscrossing and forming hubs like subterranean cathedrals, lubricated by an endless river of sewage and water. This canal seemed small, but they floated past numerous branching forks and hallways, all lost in shadows. Rats appeared to be the only residents. They clumped together on the sheer, cement banks of the canal, and scurried away when the flashlight beams passed them. The smell wasn't too bad, and Zipporah and Harvey used scented handkerchiefs to help them cope. Clay simply ignored the stench.

Harvey pulled his coat closer. He looked back at Clay and Zipporah. "Who do you think is right?" His voice echoed through the hallway. Clay and Zipporah stared at the boy. "My uncle, I mean, or my father?"

"Right about what?" Zipporah asked.

"About America." Harvey pushed up his spectacles. "I've read a lot of books, but I'm still not sure what to do in this situation, or what I should believe. There's injustice and inequality, but America has been really good to my father, as well. It's given us a great house, and two servants who are really nice, as well as people like Mr. Moss and Mrs. Cohen—and you Miss Sarfati, and Mr. Clay too. I can go to a good school, and Herbert can go to university. It's given us all kinds of great things."

Clay didn't know what to say. Should he tell Harvey that Rabbi Holtz had only acquired all those great things by breaking the law? Somehow, he didn't think that would help matters. "It can be a hard country nonetheless," he said.

"Yes," Harvey agreed. "I suppose it can. That's why I think Herbert is right, as well. Maybe they're both right, in their own way." He stared at his Buster Browns. "I know my father shouldn't have said those things about Miss Hark. I've b-been called similar names, by some of my classmates. Not exactly the same, of course, but still insults. About my Hebraic heritage."

"Bunch of heels," Zipporah said. "Don't listen to them. I remember when one of the Tommies in our unit was giving me lip because of my ancestry. I broke his nose and he never raised his voice again."

"So I should break their noses?" Harvey asked.

"Don't do that," Clay said. "But you're right—you shouldn't insult other people, just because they're different. After all, if you can't get along with other human beings, you have no hope at all of getting along with me."

Harvey grinned. "That's a nice way of putting it, Mr. Clay. Do you think—"

"Wait." Zipporah raised her hand and Harvey fell silent. "Does anyone notice the air getting colder in the canal?"

She was right. The air had suddenly grown chilly. Clay could sense the temperature, and the cold crawled its way up his arms, across his shoulders, and down into his gut. It didn't particularly bother him—he had been forged from nearly frozen Russian ground, after all—but he certainly noticed. Zipporah and Harvey both shivered. Harvey buttoned up his checkered coat and stared in amazement as mist left his mouth. Zipporah's breath did the same. The coldness came from the air itself, as if the entire tunnel had been turned into an icebox.

Frost appeared on the walls of the tunnel, forming curling, white spirals against the cement. The ice shone in the beams of the flashlights, so that the sewer canal seemed to be running through pale blue light. Ice appeared in the canal, smaller chunks bumping against the hull of the motorboat. The motor blades cut against ice, spraying some in the air in a white slush. The water continued to solidify, cracking and groaning as the motorboat moved against it. Then their vessel lurched to the side as the surface of the canal solidified completely. It could go no further. The ice surrounded the motorboat completely, trapping them in place. Clay stood up in the boat. It rocked a little, but stayed steady, fixed in place by the ice.

He didn't know exactly what had happened, but he knew the cause. "Magic."

"This is a powerful spell, Mr. Clay." Harvey reached into his book with shivering hands. "Cripes. I wish I had some gloves." He flipped through the pages. "It comes from someone who has mastered the various regions of the Sephirot—the Ten Emanations of God—and also, the—"

"The Qlippoth." The voice came from further down the dark hall. Clay turned his flashlight down the tunnel. A figure approached, big as a bear and nearly as hairy. He strode into the light, his hands folded in the thick sleeves of his dark robe. Every inch of this newcomer seemed covered in dark, bristly hair. He had a thick beard, long hair—partly set in ringlets— and bushy eyebrows. His beard and hair matched the dark fur of his long, flowing kaftan and the round fur cap on top of his head, so it all seemed composed of the same substance. "They must master the Qlippoth, the evil and impure husks that come from distancing oneself from the divine. I have mastered both."

Zipporah pointed at the stranger. "You certainly ain't mastered a razor and scissors. You ever been to a barbershop?"

His dark eyes fixed on her. "I am a disciple of Isaac Luria, and will let no razor ever reach my beard." He pointed to Zipporah. "You speak out of turn. You do not know a woman's place. It is very typical of American women. They disgust me, with their short skirts, and the free and disrespectful behavior. And have you seen the way that these 'flappers', as they are called, style their hair? Disgraceful. Still, you will learn. You and your people will all learn." His eyes moved to Clay. "You seem to be in charge. Did Sapphire send you?"

"Who are you?" Clay asked.

"Yossel Geist." He rested a hand on his robe. "Rabbi. Of the Dagger Men."

"Dagger Men?" Harvey asked. "Aren't those the rebels in Ancient Judea? Didn't the Romans wipe them out?"

"The Roman Empire is dust," Geist continued. "The Dagger Men remain." He walked closer, his tone changing and becoming almost pleasant. "Now, let's get to business. What artifacts are you protecting? They must be strange indeed, if Sapphire gave them such odd guards. Some sort of shrew in the guise of a woman, a clumsily made golem, and a little boy—very odd guards indeed."

"I want to slug him, Clay," Zipporah said. "Then hack off his beard."

Rabbi Geist ignored the threat. "Give me whatever you have in the motorboat and you may pass."

"We ain't got nothing." Zipporah reached for her blades. "Sapphire sent us, all right—to find out who robbed him. You Dagger Men or whatever you call yourselves might've survived the fall of Rome, but you won't be around much longer after pissing off Sid the Shark."

"You need to learn the proper way to behave." A smile split his bearded face. "The Dagger Men will be fine teachers."

He clapped his hands, and then the icy surface of the canal shattered in a dozen places. Flakes of ice flew through the air, the powder white and faint in the low beams of the flashlights. Skeletal bodies emerged, smashing their way to the surface. They broke the ice and pulled themselves up, frost dripping from their bones and their armor. Clay stared at the soldiers that Rabbi Geist had summoned. He recognized them from one of Harvey's books on Ancient History, where he had seen them arrayed in colorful crimson rows before armies of charging, half-naked barbarians. Like the soldiers in the history books, the Roman legionaries wore round metal helmets and jointed armor, with rectangular shields and small, lethal swords. But these legionaries had only bone behind the visors of their helmets. Skeletal hands gripped their swords and shields, which had been splotched with rust and frayed. They looked like they had just been unearthed from some ancient tomb.

Harvey recognized them as well. "Roman legionaries—these are the guys who battled the Dagger Men, thousands of years ago in Ancient Judea! They put down the Judean Rebellion, but the fighting was very fierce and lots of people on both sides died."

"Looks like Rabbi Geist wants us to end up like these Romans," Zipporah muttered.

"We won't," Clay replied.

A legionary clambered into the side of the motorboat, moving over the rim in a single step and approaching Clay. He pulled back his sword, but Clay slugged him first. A rapid blow to the Roman's chest shattered metal and bone alike. The legionary fell back, fragments of bone and broken steel flying from the shattered skeleton. It fell on the ice, which cracked under its weight. Clay turned to the next legionary, who swiped his sword in a rapid slash. Zipporah's scimitar parried the blow. She pushed back the sword while Clay punched the legionary in the skull. The helmet and skull left the skeleton's neck and hurtled through the air. Clay could hear it bounce against the stone wall and fall to the frozen surface of the canal.

The skeletons swarmed the motorboat. Even as Clay and Zipporah dispatched a pair of the legionaries, more scrambled aboard and went to work with their swords. The skeletons slashed the short blades at Harvey, apparently thinking nothing of killing a child. Clay doubted they had much intelligence. Magic alone animated their ancient bones, and it knew no mercy. He stepped in front of Harvey, the boat rocking, and took three swords in his back. The blades, splotched with rust but still sharp, jabbed into his shoulders and tore his trench coat. One wedged deeply into his back and stuck there. Clay spun around, dealing a wide, sweeping blow that smashed apart the three legionaries and tossed them from the boat. He reached behind his back, grabbed the sword, and wrenched it out. Another legionary neared him and he stabbed the point straight into the skeleton's skull.

But even as Clay and Zipporah fought, the legionaries continued their advance. It seemed that an entire Roman Legion had somehow been hidden in the sewer canal, and now rose up with a mad eagerness to deal damage once again. Clay and Zipporah fought together, his fists and her sabers hacking and bashing aside the skeletons, but the legionaries still closed in. Zipporah received a cruel cut to her chin, and she flinched back at the sudden blood. Harvey stood between them, trying to stay upright as the motorboat twisted in the ice. Clay glanced down the tunnel. Rabbi Geist had vanished further down the frozen canal. He had apparently decided to let his undead minions finish the job.

Harvey pointed off the back of the boat. "Pilums! Or pila, to use the plural. Mr. Clay, Miss Sarfati—duck!"

As he spoke, a trio of legionaries moved behind the boat, armed with oversized spears—each ending in a lethal point. The skeletal arms twisted and threw, sending the spears hurtling through the air. Zipporah grabbed Harvey and pushed him down, then dropped as well. Two spears flew past their heads. The next thudded into Clay's upper chest. If it had reached his forehead, it could have turned him back into a lump of earth. The legionaries reached for more spears—pila , as Harvey had called them—and prepared to throw again.

Then the motorboat creaked, the edge screeched painfully against the ice and began to descend. Sword points smashed through the bottom of the vessel, jabbing into the air. The blades punctured the wood, dripping with ice water as they reared into the low light. Clay grabbed Harvey by his collar and hauled him up—just before a spear could pierce the boy's foot. Another sword point nearly missed bisecting his foot. The legionaries had gotten under the rowboat, and had stabbed holes in the hull. Water poured in the through the holes. They would be sinking soon.

Clay glanced at Zipporah. They both knew their only option. "Ready for a walk on the ice?" Zipporah asked.

"Why not?" Clay set Harvey gently down on the other side of the ice, and hopped over himself. His boots slammed down. The ice cracked and trickles of cold water pressed over his boots—but it didn't shatter completely. It could hold their weight. Zipporah dealt with another skeleton, driving her sword into its rib cage and smashing several of its bones, and then leaping nimbly to join them. They hurried away from the boat, down the canal.

Their shoes clicked and slipped on the ice. The carpet of slick, frozen sewage stretched ahead of them. Rabbi Geist must have frozen a decent part of the underground river, to give his Roman legionaries plenty of means to maneuver. The skeletons used that now. They surged around the trapped, sinking motorboat, and charged after Clay and his friends. More pila hummed through the air. They smashed down into the ice, the points driving into the ice and the poles reverberating as they wedged in place. The legionaries brandished their square shields, using them like the Romans of old.

They couldn't battle that many legionaries. Clay turned back to face the legionaries, walking backwards. He smashed a fist into a Roman shield, his knuckles cracking against wood and steel. He knocked the legionary back, but another took its place. They would chase them, surround them, and use their lethal short swords to hack down Clay and the others.

"Zipporah." Clay's voice groaned as he warded off another sword's blow. "You know what to do."

"True enough," Zipporah agreed. "Looks like I was right to come prepared." She pulled the Mills Bomb from her pocket, then glanced at Harvey as she removed the pin. "I'll throw it and we run." She balanced the grenade in her hands, judged the distance, and then tossed it through the air. The grenade bounced off a legionary's shield and then rolled to the frozen surface of the canal. It bounced on the ice. Clay grabbed Harvey's hand and tugged him along, breaking into a run and sprinting down the tunnel. Zipporah hurried after them.

The Mills Bomb roared to life and did its job. The blast swept through the tunnel, ripping into the skeletal legionaries and shattering them. Red fire and smoke pulsed against their slim bodies. Chunks of bone, ancient armor, ruined shields, and ice from the frozen canal flew through the air and ricocheted off the stone walls. They pattered down on the ground, clattering and scratching against the ice or plopping into the liquid canal. Harvey covered his ears and winced, and Clay's head rang against the concentrated noise of the blast. Still, they stumbled on.

The explosion faded and light dimmed. Clay caught a glimpse of a furry figure and switched on his flashlight. The beam of illumination showed the back of Rabbi Geist's fur coat as he scooted down a side canal, slipped into a shadowy alcove, and vanished. He must had seen them deal with his skeletal soldiers and now sought to escape.

"There he goes," Clay said.

"We'll find him. And have a nice long talk about ripping off Sapphire's goods." Zipporah turned to Harvey. "He mentioned he's with the Dagger Men. They're old, right? From Classical Times? I guess that's why he's commanding a bunch of skeletons."

"The Dagger Men led the Judean Rebellion," Harvey explained. "And they killed numerous Romans—and moderate Jews as well—and then they fought the legions to the end, and—"

"We can talk about this later," Clay said. "For now, we've got to get Rabbi Geist."

They hurried around the corner. A small stone staircase lay in front of them, leading off the canal and into another area. A metal door stood at the end of the stairwell, but Clay wrenched it open. He shoved his way through and his friends scrambled after him. Clay slammed the door and spun around, surveying the hidden room.

It had apparently been some sort of maintenance area, where sewer workers could stash needed tools during repairs—but the Dagger Men had taken it over. A few bookshelves, assembled from abandoned furniture, rested against the walls. Symbols from the Kabala had been etched on those walls in pale chalk, showing the multi-branching Sephirot of divine emanations. A mattress appeared to be the only furniture. Clay turned back to the door. There would probably be a mezuzah. The whole room spread under out a stone ridge, which ran the length of the chamber. Ladders led down to the floor, which had been covered in pages filled with Hebrew scrawl. Rabbi Geist had kept busy.

"Where's Geist?" Clay asked.

"Looks like he skedaddled." Zipporah slid her scimitars back into their scabbards. "Left us his room."

They moved through the room, searching for any clue to the missing artifacts. "Rabbi Geist was just living here?" Harvey picked up a ragged newspaper and examined it. "Just waiting for Mr. Sapphire's shipments? What kind of man would do something like that?"

Zipporah reached the mattress. "A fanatic. I know the type." She moved to a strangely neat pile of papers next to the mattress—bedroom reading for Rabbi Geist, perhaps?—and started leafing through it. "When I served with T.E. Lawrence, some of the Arabs had similar ideas. They were convinced that they were on a holy war, a Jihad, and that God himself was backing our cause. Made them fight like demons in battle, and never dream of giving up. They would even work with infidels like me and T.E., for a chance at victory."

"Anything for their faith," Clay added.

"And I guess the Dagger Men must be the same way." Harvey glanced at the bookshelves, his eyes drifting over the spines of the dusty volumes. "Cripes—these are some very rare and impressive mystical texts. I think he's got an original Zohar over here. That's like the main book of Kabala." He walked over to Zipporah and peered at the collection of papers. "What's that one?"

"Doesn't look like Kabala." Zipporah produced a gilded, square piece of paper." She handed it to Harvey. "What do you make of that, child?"

Harvey looked it over. "It's a ticket—for the Sickle City Museum of Venerable Antiquities."

"Do you know it?" Clay asked. Though he had been in the city for a year or so, he didn't mark himself as an expert.

"Yes, sir," Harvey agreed. "Papa—my father's taken me there a few times. It's an amazing place." Pure enthusiasm filled his voice as he talked. "They've got sections on most of the ancient civilizations, with a place for Greek statues and urns, some Egyptian artifacts and mummies—including an entire chunk of a temple, taken from Egypt itself—and Aztec stuff from Mexico as well. It's quite an impressive collection." He stared at the ticket. "They have a bunch of objects from the Middle East as well, and several artifacts from Palestine."

"So these Dagger Men steal some of Sapphire's artifacts?" Clay said. "And now they want what's in the museum?"

"I suppose so." Harvey's smile faded. "Maybe they're gonna rob it?"

"But why?" Zipporah asked. "Something tells me that all these ancient gewgaws ain't gonna be gathering dust on their mantelpiece."

Footsteps clicked on the stone ledge above the maintenance chamber. Clay glanced up—and his stone body creaked in panic. Rabbi Geist stood there, his hands folded over his thick fur coat. His eyes smoldered in the midst of his beard. Behind Rabbi Geist, a quartet of Roman legionaries wielded more of those long, heavy spears. They didn't come alone. Apparently, the Dagger Men had access to a whole armory of Roman weapons.

Two more skeletal legionaries manned something like an Ancient Roman artillery piece. The wooden device moved about on a pair of wheels, and looked like a giant crossbow. The legionaries had loaded up an oversized bolt, as long as Clay's forearm, and pulled back the great string that would send it flying. Their skeletal hands perched over the controls, ready to fire. Clay doubted that even he could survive having his body struck with that weapon.

"A ballista," Harvey explained quietly. "It's a Roman siege weapon. They might've used it at Masada."

Rabbi Geist raised his voice. "Perhaps they did!" he called. "And what did it matter, for all the arms of the Romans are nothing compared to the will of God. So it was with Joshua, when he destroyed the Canaanites. The shofar horns were blown, and then Israel became the land of the Jews."

"The Romans won, buddy!" Zipporah called. "In case you forgot."

"Rest assured, harpy—I did not. The Dagger Men never forget." He leaned closer, peering down from the ledge. "But that was merely the first battle. Sickle City shall be the sight of another—and the beginning of a final victory for the Dagger Men."

"You picked the wrong town to conquer," Zipporah replied. "Come on down from that ledge and I'll prove it to you."

"I have a better idea." Rabbi Geist nodded to the Roman Legionaries. "Wipe them out."

The ballista twanged—its string making a loud, rumbling twang. It echoed through the chamber and the large arrow shot down like a comet. Zipporah grabbed Harvey's hand and tugged him out of the way as Clay darted to the side. The ballista's bolt still hummed across his arm, its point digging out a trench in his earthen skin. He winced and stumbled as the arrow flew on. It slammed into the bookshelf, smashing through the worn wood and damaging several books. Pages of ancient paper came from the tattered books, floating down slowly and showing Hebrew script and rich illustrations of Stars of David, griffons, and crowns in bright primary colors. Rabbi Geist stared in horror at the destruction of his books. Clay got the idea that the Dagger Man rarely considered the consequences of his actions.

He pointed at them with a shaking finger. "Bring me their heads!"

The legionaries leapt down, a phalanx of the Roman skeletons leaping from the ridge to attack. They raised their shields, forming a neat wall, and jabbed out with their swords. Zipporah pulled her blades, and Clay readied his fists. Still, they couldn't last long against this many skeletons. They needed to flee—even it meant going back into the sewers.

Zipporah nodded to the door at the far end of the room. "Get moving. Watch their swords."

"I think the Roman sword is called a gladius, Miss Sarfati." Harvey adjusted his spectacles. "I, ah, read a lot about Ancient Civilizations. My father buys me a lot of books on that subject."

"Just make sure you don't get stuck with one." Clay patted his shoulder. "Stay close."

They ran for the door, just as the legionaries charged. Clay barreled ahead and rammed his shoulder into the door to force it open. He hurried up the steps, followed by Harvey, and then Zipporah. The Romans charged at the same moment, their bones rustling as they pursued.

The stairwell led back into the sewer tunnel, but Rabbi Geist's spell had faded. The ice had melted, and the sewer canals returned to flowing, filthy water running between two rectangular cement banks. Clay overstepped the bank, momentum carrying him along. He pulled back his boot, before it could fall in the sewer water, and steadied himself on the cement ridge. The legionaries emerged from the stairwell behind them. Clay chose a direction—the one that led further into the sewers—and hurried down the tunnel, still holding Harvey's hand.

Pila whistled through the air, hurled by skeletal hands. Zipporah increased her speed and ran next to Clay and Harvey. The spears crashed down, their stone heads bouncing off the concrete. The legionaries still followed them, their shields groaning against the stone wall as they raised their short swords. The clicks of their boots filled the tunnel. Clay focused on running. The tunnel twisted up ahead, and they ran along the curve.

"Zipporah." Clay couldn't get tired—but his friends didn't have that advantage. Harvey stumbled, breathing heavily, and Zipporah did her best to help him along. She hadn't gotten winded yet—she was used to crossing the desert under Turkish fire, after all—but she couldn't run forever. "You wouldn't happen to have brought another Mills Bomb, would you?"

"Afraid not, Clay." Zipporah grinned weakly. "One's usually enough to do the job."

"So what do we do?" Harvey asked.

The tunnel made another turn. They ran with it, racing past the curved stone tunnel. It straightened out—revealing the end of the river of sewage. Steel grates covered the sewer, providing a long bridge between the two banks. A large cement wall covered most of the entrance, with only a small gap—covered by steel—for the water to flow. Clay stopped as well. They had reached a dead end. Shadows filled the room, but Clay couldn't see an exit. A ladder led up to the ceiling, and perhaps a manhole cover, but Clay didn't think they would reach it in time. Roman legionaries followed them and spread out, forming another phalanx and readying their swords.

Gunfire blasted through the shadows. A rifle roared, and the lead Roman dropped, his skull shattered by an accurate bullet. A woman stepped out of the shadow, carefully working the bolt on her rifle. She wore a leather jacket, a set of bandoliers crossed over her chest, and carried a machete on her belt. Gunfire cast shadows over her weathered, brown face and sleek, dark hair. Clay recognized her as Carmen Cohen—Rabbi Holtz's top enforcer. She had come to help them, just as Rabbi Holtz had promised. She had arrived just in time.

Monk Moss joined her, armed with his trench gun. "Clay! Get Zipporah and the kid out of the way. Leave these skeleton fellows to me and Cohen."

Clay took Harvey's hand and they hastened out of the firing line. Monk fired his trench gun, then racked the pump and fired again. Cohen kept her rifle cracking away. She had ridden with Pancho Villa as a soldadera, and married a Jewish mercenary who served her warlord master. Cohen believed that her family had once been Marranos, and practiced Jewish ritual while pretending to be good Catholics. Now, she had embraced her religion—but hadn't given up her violent ways. She went to work with the rifle while Monk's shotgun roared.

Their bullets cut into the legionaries and destroyed them. Lead ripped through Roman shields and broke bones. The skeletons collapsed, their bones rattling against the metal grate as the weapons did their work. The gunshots echoed through the sewer, and Harvey covered his ears.

Despite the barrage, the legionaries advanced. They charged straight into gunfire, stepping over the bodies of the fallen as they approached. Some legionaries made it through, and closed in on Monk and Cohen. Luckily, Rabbi Holtz's two most trusted torpedoes were ready. Monk swung the butt of his trench gun around, ramming it into the skull of the attacking legionary. Cohen went for her machete. She hacked into the helmet of an attacking legionary, the blade smashing bone and cutting the skull in half.

Cohen returned the machete to her scabbard as the legionary collapsed. "*Cabrone!*" She pointed back down the tunnel. "More of them, charging in. We'd better get out of here, Monk. I don't think they'll follow us into the street."

"Sounds like a fine proposition." Monk nodded to Clay. "Get to the ladder. Up we go."

Clay hurried to the ladder. He scrambled up first, followed by Harvey. His hands gripped the rungs, and the ladder squealed slightly in protest. It held his weight, and he reached the top. A punch knocked the manhole cover out of its mooring. It fell aside, revealing a circle of night sky. Clay grabbed the edges and hauled himself up into a vacant street. He offered his hand to Harvey, and pulled the boy out. More gunfire echoed below them. Zipporah came up next, and then Monk. Cohen hurried up next, firing her rifle as she went. They helped her out of the ladder and slammed the manhole cover. No skeletons followed.

"*Dios...*" Cohen wiped her forehead on her sleeve. "You seem to have a habit of fighting the dead, Clay."

"And we always win," Zipporah said.

"So far." Cohen turned to Harvey. "We've got the Cunningham Touring Car around the block. Let's get you home."

"Okay," Harvey agreed.

That seemed fine with everybody. They hurried down the street, leaving the ancient skeletal legionaries under the street.

᙭᙭᙭

Later that night, they met in Rabbi Holtz's study and listened to Harvey tell the story of the Dagger Men. The boy seemed quite fatigued as he stood before Clay, his Buster Browns planted on the earth-colored carpet. "Okay," he said. "The Dagger Men—the Latin term for them is *Sicarii*—were part of the Zealots, who were the most intense of all Jewish rebels. They got their name because they'd carry these special daggers under their coats, close on some Roman, or someone they thought was a Roman sympathizer, and then pull their blades out and, ah, assassinate them."

Rabbi Holtz frowned. "So we're dealing an order of ancient hitmen?"

"Something like that," Harvey said. "They were the most extreme of all the Jewish rebels—even the other Zealots didn't like them. They killed Jews as well as Romans. Anyone they thought was betraying the Torah. I thought most of them died at Masada, but I guess some survived..."

"And now they're here." Clay folded his hands. "You remember the ticket to the Sickle City Museum of Venerable Antiquities?"

"Yeah?" Zipporah asked.

"That's where they're going next," Clay said. "And we'll be there to meet them."

"Dagger Men." Rabbi Holtz shook his head. "Mr. Sapphire's not going to like this. And neither do I."

Clay nodded grimly. He felt the same way.

Chapter Three
GIANTS

The Sickle City Museum of Venerable Antiquities, like so much in Sickle City, attempted to ape the glory and refinement of Ancient Greece—and only partly succeeded. It occupied an entire block in Damocles Street, just across from Arcadia Park, and featured an arched roof supported by a row of towering, marble pillars and a large stairwell bordered with Classical statues. A polished golden dome topped the entire monstrosity, resembling a small bowler hat on the head of a fat man. Clay parked his Studebaker across the street from the Museum of Venerable Antiquities, and led Zipporah and Harvey up the steps. They paid their admission and headed inside. They had arrived in the midmorning, a quiet and peaceful time even for Sickle City, and sunlight filtering down through numerous windows illuminated the vast lobby and the various exhibits.

After buying their tickets, Clay and his friends approached a large map indicating the exhibitions and their place inside the museum. It looked like a list of every ancient civilization in the world, set in neat squares between twisting hallways on the three floors of the structure. The Aztecs and Mayans, along with other Indian tribes, occupied the first floor. The second belonged to Asia, with a large section for China and Japan. The third—the place of honor—went to the ancients regarded as the forerunners of Western Civilization. Egypt, Greece, Rome, and more had their place here, each in its own chamber.

Harvey's eyes widened as he looked over the various civilizations. "This is swell," he mused. "Papa—I mean, my father has brought me here many times, and so has Uncle Herbert. I always enjoy it. They've got artifacts from everywhere!"

"You like all this ancient civilization business, don't you, child?" Zipporah asked.

"Yes, ma'am. There's just something incredible about all these foreign lands, with all that sort of history." Harvey pointed to a chamber on the third floor. "And look—we Jews have a place amongst them, right between Greece and Rome. I think we can get to the Judean artifacts by going through the Egyptian room, and then we'll be in the exhibition. It says they've got some new artifacts as well, recently uncovered in British Palestine."

Clay followed the boy's finger. "Could be what Rabbi Geist and the Dagger Men are after. We should head there now, and give it a look."

"You don't want to see the stuff on the first floor? They've got Aztec sacrificial knives, and Mayan glyphs, and—" Harvey started.

"Maybe when we're finished with Ancient Judea," Clay said. "Come on."

They headed to the elevator, which whisked them up to the third floor. With its cream-colored walls and golden control panel and brass rails, the elevator resembled a gilded pearl—which matched the rest of the museum. The doors clicked open on the third floor and Clay and his friends wandered out into Ancient Egypt. It looked like someone had picked up Egypt, given it a good shake, collected all the detritus which fell out, and stuffed them in glass display cases or on brass pedestals. Everything seemed quiet and hushed in the expansive chamber; as if a single sound would disturb the artifacts.

Harvey darted to the first display case, where an Egyptian chariot of carved gold stood before statues of animal-headed gods. "They must've found this in a tomb in the Valley of Kings," Harvey explained. He pointed to the gods. "There's Anubis, the falcon-headed god of Judgment. Next to him is Osiris. He's the god of the dead." He moved to the next display, which showed a stretch of hieroglyphics taken from a tomb. "Here's Horus—he's Osiris's son, with the bird head. There's a bunch more gods over there. Oh, and I think there's some mummies." He scrambled to a large glass case in the center of the room, where mummies rested on stiff frames so that their spindly arms formed strange gestures. Harvey moved close to the glass, staring at the mummies in amazement.

Zipporah rolled her eyes at Clay. "Sounds like too many Gods. One's enough for me, I think—and I have my doubts about him." She pointed to the mummies. "Those yeggs look like they're right out of Old King Tut's Tomb. You ever think about that, Clay? Getting yourself preserved for posterity?"

"No need." Clay pointed to a large statue of some pharaoh, a crook and flail crossed over his chest. "I'm more like that fellow—made of something stronger than flesh."

"You won't rot, then?" Zipporah shook her head. "Stupid question. I don't think you'll even age. Or die. Must give you some relief."

"Yeah." Clay turned away. He knew that he wouldn't age or die as normal people did—and that brought him very little succor. He walked over to join Harvey by the mummies. They examined the long-dead Egyptians, their limbs withered by age and shrunk by constraining bandages. The mummies all seemed to have expressions of terror on their faces, as if death had brought them only pain. Clay was considering moving to the next room, the special exhibition hall where the Ancient Judean artifacts waited, when another group of visitors came down the aisle.

They strolled out from behind an obelisk, which had been sliced in half so that its tip didn't scrape the roof, and stopped when they saw Harvey. The family consisted of two parents and a son around Harvey's age, and the boy's eyes fixed on Harvey. "Harvey?" he asked. "Harvey Holtz?" They appeared to be Damocles Street royalty, dolled up in expensive garments. The boy, a tow-headed child, wore a pale blue suit and bowtie under his coat, and had an expression of growing embarrassment on his face when he spotted Harvey.

Hesitantly, Harvey faced the boy. "Darby. H-hello." He turned to Clay and Zipporah. "This is Darby De Vere. He's in my class at the Academy for Prestigious Young Gentlemen." He stared at his Buster Browns, obviously unsure what to do. Clay shared his uncertainty. After all, the De Veres were one of the oldest and most powerful families in Sickle City. They had made fortunes in the shipping and manufacturing industries, and, unlike

…an Egyptian chariot…stood before statures of animal-headed gods.

the Jews of Haven Street, there was no question of their role in civic society.

"You can introduce us," Zipporah suggested.

"Darby, this is Mr. Clay and Miss Sarfati. They're my, ah, my friends. My caretakers." Harvey corrected himself quickly.

Darby's father regarded Harvey as he would a fly on a piece of food. "You're the Holtz boy, aren't you?" He had bushy black sideburns, dusted with gray, and a monocle that seemed wedged in his eye. His pearl gray suit and frock coat belonged to an earlier era, and he held a top hat under his arm. He glanced at Clay. "Danforth De Vere, sir. I'm certain you've heard of me."

"Yes, sir," Harvey said. "I'm the H-Holtz boy."

Darby turned to his father. "He's the one who's—"

"I know, my darling. I am fully aware of the Holtz boy's ancestry." He pronounced 'Holtz' very loudly, and the word echoed over the chamber, around the oversized sphinx's head in the corner and the display cases. He turned to his wife. "It's a shame, I think, that they allow Jews at the Young Gentlemen's Academy. Such a thing would never be allowed in the old days. It's a rather distressing situation for all concerned." He glared at Harvey. "You understand, don't you? The conniving, obsequious character of the Jew is more suited to an education closer to the street. Attempting to teach one of the Hebraic persuasion of the proper ways to behave is an inherently flawed endeavor."

"I, ah..." Harvey stammered. "I don't really think so, sir. I—" His face flashed red.

Zipporah glared at De Vere. "You silver spoon heel. I ought to throw you through that display case for—"

But De Vere had already turned away. "Of course, I'm afraid that goes with the falling standards all across the country. Criminals like the Holtz boy's father amassing fortunes because of Prohibition, boatloads of new immigrants arriving every day with their own debased languages and cultures, and now they even allow their sort in museums—former bastions of learning and taste. Come along, Minnie. There's much else to see."

The De Veres wandered away, giving Harvey and his friends a wide berth. Darby looked over his shoulder and glanced at Harvey. He offered Harvey a quick wave as his parents directed him to the adjacent door, leading to the Greek exhibits. Harvey waved back, but they had already slipped into the next chamber. Then he turned away and closed his eyes. He let out a single shudder, as if he was trying to stifle a sob. Clay had the idea that Harvey had been called similar names at school and faced the same, dismissive prejudice.

He walked over to Harvey and put his hand on the boy's shoulder. "It's not your fault. You haven't done anything wrong. It's just..." He paused, trying to think of the right word. "It's just the way that things are."

"I know." He wiped his eyes quickly on his sleeve. "It's okay. They're heels anyway, like Miss Sarfati said. Darby's nice to me sometimes, but he still keeps his distance. Most of the other boys at school do that." He glanced at Zipporah. "We should get to the exhibition on Ancient Judea." He moved away, stumbled on the polished floor, and then headed to the arched doorway past the obelisk and the sphinx.

Clay and Zipporah trailed after him. "Does Rabbi Holtz know?" Zipporah asked. "Maybe he could arrange a better school for Harvey? Something closer in the neighborhood?"

"He wouldn't fit in there, either," Clay explained. "Not when everyone knows what Rabbi Holtz is and treats him with a mixture of fear and respect." His body creaked a little as he watched Harvey forlornly put his hands in his pockets. "He doesn't exactly fit in anywhere."

"Reminds me of some other people," Zipporah suggested.

"Yeah." Clay fell silent and moved ahead, joining Harvey in the next chamber. He tried to shake those feelings away. They had a job to do, after all.

The Judean artifacts rested in a round chamber, inside the dome that topped the Museum of Venerable Antiquities. They occupied brass pedestals and marble plinths, or rested in glass display cases and shelves. The shards of ancient pottery with Hebrew etched on the sides, rusted swords, clubs, axes, and occasional dusty ram's horn didn't have the grandeur of Ancient Egypt, but the collection did boast quite a few unique items. The most impressive rested in a display case set in the center of the room. A set of giant bones—femurs, ribs, and a single skull—lay on metal frames. Clay and his friends approached the case and stared inside. The skull looked as big as Harvey's chest, while some of the leg and arms bones doubled the size of Clay's limbs.

Zipporah folded her arms as she gazed at the bones."What are these? Goliath's bones, after David and his slingshot got done with him?"

"Not quite, Miss Sarfati." Harvey examined the descriptive plaque. "These were uncovered in a subterranean temple, below Jerusalem. It's supposed to be part of one of the Nephilim." He adjusted his spectacles as he spoke. A professorial lecture helped him forget his earlier feelings, for which Clay was grateful. "These were giants—descendants of angels who were cast out of heaven and mortal women. Most of them were bad guys, and enemies of the Israelites. Supposedly, Goliath was descended from them."

Clay rested his fingers on the glass, near the bones of the giant. "Why would the Judeans keep the bones of their enemies?"

"Well, some Judeans worshipped the gods and forces that others considered evil—just like we have occultists and devil-worshippers today." Harvey walked past the giant bones, and faced another artifact set under a large skylight. "I guess some of them even worshipped Asmodeus."

They joined Harvey in front of the next display—a great stone altar, about as big as a cauldron, set on a marble stand. The stone altar had been covered in Hebrew carvings and occult symbols, all of which surrounded a small depression. Perhaps that was where the blood went during sacrificial rituals. A set of three carved stone heads topped the altar, all connected by stout necks to a coiling dragon. One head belonged to a ram, another to a bird with a thin beak, and the one in the center looked almost human, apart from pointed ears. Golden light cascaded on the altar from the window above, making the whole device gleam. Clay stared at the three faces.

"Asmodeus," he whispered the name to himself. "He's the King of the Demons, isn't he?"

"Yes, sir," Harvey agreed. "He's called Asmodai or Ashmedai as well, depending on who you ask. And he is the King of the Demons, so he's not exactly a nice guy. He's a villain in the Book of Tobit, where he falls in love with a human woman and murders the seven men who try to marry her. But he can also do good stuff as well. King Solomon was able to trick him into building the great Temple in Jerusalem. That story's in the Talmud, where he's more of a trickster."

"But he's not a nice guy," Zipporah said.

"Not at all." Harvey leaned down and looked at the informative plaque. "This belonged to a cult of devil-worshippers in ancient Jerusalem. They must have used it to conduct all kinds of terrible rituals, trying to summon and control Asmodeus."

The altar shone in the sunlight. Clay moved closer to the altar and stretched out his hand. He wanted to feel the arm of the stone on his fingers. It would be comforting. His hand inched out.

His finger brushed the ridged edge of the altar. Suddenly, a deep creaking rang through Clay's body. The museum room shifted; the pale whiteness of the marble obscured by pulsating smoke. Clay stumbled back as the shadows covered him. He turned around, looking for Harvey and

Zipporah. They had vanished. Clay stood alone, lost in a maze of smoke. He could make out features in the distance –canyons and mountains, but all were outlines of smoke. It was a dream of a valley, where nothing was distinct. Clay stared down at the valley floor. Bones lay before him, etched in the same dark shadows. Skulls, rib cages, limbs and more lay in a wild pile. Clay stared at the bones.

A voice whispered in his ear, high-pitched and full of humor. "You've seen this before, man of earth."

"Yes." Clay remembered the plains of Russia. "The bodies of the dead, resting in the snow in the evening. But there was moonlight, then. Not just shadow." He spun around. "Where am I? Who are you, and what do you want?"

"You are in the Valley of Dry Bones, where God took the prophet Ezekiel. But where is God? Nowhere to be found, though his servants are present." Clay kept turning, searching for the voice. "Who am I? You know that, Emmet Clay, just as you know yourself. The King of Demons is calling to you." So Asmodeus had summoned Clay—but why? "And I bring you here, to my shadowy kingdom, for a simple reason. I come to warn you. Evil is coming to your city, man of earth. Evil clothed in the armor of righteousness. Soon, you will see that Man will do far worse things than ever appeared in my shadowy kingdom." Laughter came from all directions. The bones began to shake. "Perhaps that is the greatest joke of all."

"What do you—" Clay started, but then the shadows receded. The bones vanished. Clay stood again in the museum. He gasped and his body creaked. He pulled back his hand from the altar as if the stone burned. Harvey and Zipporah stared at him. Zipporah's hand moved protectively to Harvey's shoulder. "Asmodeus appeared in front of me," Clay said. "He said that—"

Before Clay could explain, the De Veres strolled into the room from an adjacent exhibit. They walked past a collection of Biblical scrolls, and came to an immediate halt. They stared at each other, surrounded by ancient artifacts. Harvey raised his hand in a quiet greeting, which Darby returned, and then Danforth De Vere stepped almost protectively in front of his son.

He nodded to Clay. "A Hebraic goliath. You are one of Rabbi Holtz's thugs, perhaps? Well, you must have some sense. My family and I wish to tour this part of the museum, so why don't you go to a different floor? Perhaps you can return when we are finished. That will spare both of our young charges some embarrassment."

"Danforth..." Minnie De Vere whispered. "We don't need to—"

"Hush, my dear." De Vere waved away her protest with a kid-gloved hand. "This mammoth Jew knows that we are correct."

"I don't think I do," Clay replied.

Zipporah took a step closer, her anger rising. "I think we may leave, Mr. De Vere." She raised a fist. "But I'd like to leave you with something first."

Darby stared at Harvey. "Did your servant just threaten my father?"

"Miss Sarfati," Harvey started, his face going red. "Please, don't cause any—"

The skylight above them shattered. Glass rained down, falling onto the altar. Clay grabbed Harvey and tugged him back as the glass descended. It shattered on the marble floor, forming a shimmering, crystalline blizzard. More windows shattered, breaking one after the other. Glass clinked on the display cases and pedestals. Clay raised his fists as Zipporah reached for her swords. They hadn't expected the Dagger Men to come so soon. Birds fluttered down through the broken windows, and swooped into the exhibition room. The birds had the shimmering, dark feathers of ravens, and the round faces of owls with protruding beaks and bone-white talons. Minnie De Vere screamed. She grabbed Darby and hauled him away, while Danforth watched in terror.

A pair of birds fluttered toward Clay. His fists lashed out, striking together. He punched back both birds, his knuckles ramming through their beaks and cutting through their feathers. Small bones snapped under his blows, and the birds struck the ground as masses of feather and ash. Zipporah worked with her swords, protecting Harvey with a few rapid slashes that cut off the heads of the wheeling birds.

She turned to Harvey. "What are these, child?"

"Broxa," Harvey explained. "They suck goat milk and blood. They're like vampire birds."

The Broxa billowed around the room, soaring around the artifacts on silent wings. A few more sped to Clay and Zipporah, who dealt with them quickly. They moved in front of Harvey, protecting him from the talons. The De Veres huddled near the altar, Danforth and Minnie shielding their son. Clay glanced at them. Despite their bigotry, they did care for their son. Then footsteps clicked on the stone floor. Clay turned around, preparing his fists for another blow.

The servants of the Dagger Men had arrived—a trio of Roman skeletons storming into the exhibition hall with blades drawn. These Romans had frayed plumes topping their rusted helmets, and carried swords with longer blades than the weapons wielded by the other legionaries.

"Centurions," Harvey said."The officers of the legions."

"I'll deal with them." Clay hurried across the room and met the centurions at a charge. He reached the first centurion, which swung its sword as he approached. Clay put the momentum of his charge behind the blow, and rammed his fist into the Roman's chest. Armor shattered. The centurion collapsed, even as its sword slashed his shoulder and ricocheted against his stone skin. The other skeletons moved in, one stabbing a spear into Clay's side, while the next hacked down with his sword. Clay took the spear blow, but the sword aimed for his forehead. A blow from that would damage the carvings and destroy him for good. Clay met the sword with an upper cut, his fist catching the blade and pushing it back. Then he wrenched out the spear and smashed it into the centurion's ribcage. Clay drove a right hook into the remaining centurion, hard enough to rip the skull from its shoulders.

The centurions collapsed, their bones rattling on the ground. Clay kicked them aside and turned back to the hall. Rabbi Geist stood there, flanked by a pair of Roman archers. Their bows twanged and two arrows thudded into Clay's chest. He winced as the shafts burrowed into him, and started toward Geist. The bearded rabbi folded his arms and watched as his archers prepared another set of arrows. The shafts hummed through the air. One grazed Clay's elbow and another arrow wedged into his chest. Then he reached the archers. He grabbed the arm from one, tore the bone from its socket, and smashed the limb against the skull of the other. Both archers collapsed.

Rabbi Geist watched with disinterested eyes. "You certainly know how to destroy, golem. That's no surprise. It's what you were created to do, after all." He made some occult sigil in the air, his fingers dancing as he formed the gesture. "But the Dagger Men were made for a grander purpose. Tasked by God himself with a holy mission. That is why we are here today."

"How about you tell me what it is?" Clay asked. "Before I rip out your beard?"

"Why not ask our leader?" Rabbi Geist pointed to the center of the room. "The *Tzadik* of the Dagger Men stands before you, golem. Quake in his presence." Clay turned around. *Tzadik* was a title given to spiritual masters. Someone of that caliber had to be leading the Dagger Men, if they could pull off summoning armies of dead Romans and flocks of Broxa. Clay had guessed that the true leader of the Dagger Men couldn't be the hirsute Rabbi Geist. He raised his fist as he scanned the exhibition room for any sign of the *Tzadik*.

A swarm of Broxa gathered before the altar, forming a spinning pillar of shimmering feathers. They spun around, their feathers blurring together. Zipporah and Harvey scrambled next to Clay, and watched as the Broxa turned. The vampire birds eventually fluttered away, their wings silent in the still air. A man stood where they had spun, gazing at the altar to Asmodeus. He moved closer to the altar, ignoring the huddled, whimpering forms of the De Veres.

Clay had seen him before—on the pier of Palisade Park, the night before they ventured into the sewers for Sid Sapphire. He had emerged in the rain, marked Clay as a golem, and then vanished into the night. He had no hair at all—not even eyebrows—on his round, pale face. His clothes seemed strangely normal compared to the robes of Rabbi Geist, with only a rumpled black suit and vest over a tattered shirt. With his medium stature and placid eyes, he could have been an average fellow walking down a Sickle City Street, on the way to a job in a factory or the docks—if it wasn't for the endless occult tattoos of Hebrew lettering and strange symbols on his pale skin. They curled around his nose and cheeks, rested on his forehead, and appeared along the back of his head and even his eyelids. More tattoos appeared on his hands. Tattoos were forbidden by Jewish Law, so why would a *Tzadik* cover himself in such images? Clay didn't want to ask.

Danforth De Vere stared at the newcomer. His voice shook. "Who the devil are you?" His voice shook. He might have regarded Harvey as vermin and Clay as an amusement, but this tattooed figure clearly terrified him.

The *Tzadik* folded his hands. "I am Rabbi Issachar Eisendrath. I am the Judgment of God."

Shadows burst from his sleeves and fluttered into the air. Fire followed the shadow, with sparks coiling down and hissing as they hit the marble floor. Wings appeared in the shadow, each outline of a feather trailing fire. De Vere ducked closer to his family, trying to protect them from the strange apparitions. Rabbi Eisendrath guided the flame-winged ravens without moving his hands. They orbited him about him, opening their shadowy beaks and spitting flame. Each bird looked big enough to pick up Harvey in its molten talons.

"The A'arab Zaraq!" Harvey whispered. "Creatures of the Qliphoth— the Fiery Ravens of Dispersion." He turned to Zipporah and Clay. "To control those creatures, to even summon them, must require immense power. They're extremely dangerous—"

"See to the De Veres," Clay ordered. "I'll deal with Eisendrath." He didn't give the others a chance to argue, but hurried past the exhibits and approached this new rabbi.

Rabbi Eisendrath faced him, leaving the De Veres to the ravens. Zipporah and Harvey reached them and guided them away. A raven swooped toward them and Zipporah warded it off with a few slashes from her scimitars. Rabbi Eisendrath didn't seem to care. He hadn't arrived at the Museum of Venerable Antiquities to frighten some *goyim*. Instead, he stared at Clay, watching quietly as more of his ravens swooped around the rooms. Their sparks fell on the Judean artifacts in glittering, flame-colored waterfalls. He pointed at Clay.

"Golem." He said the word slowly, savoring the sound. "Creature of earth. Abomination."

Clay faced him. Behind him, the display case holding the Nephilim bones shattered. A raven swooped inside, its talons wrapping around the ancient bones. More followed. They were robbing the place. "What do you think you're doing?" Clay asked. "You're trying to attack Sickle City? Why? What's the point?"

"The same reason God brought about the deluge," Rabbi Eisendrath explained. "Look at our people, golem—who you were created to defend. They are mocked, insulted, hated, and poor. Truly, we are the wretched amongst the nations." He extended his hands, indicating the artifacts. "Look at these relics of ancient kingdoms, now nothing but forgotten dust. But we can be a mighty empire again, and this city will be our capital."

"You want to conquer Sickle City?" Clay asked.

"And claim it from unbelievers and *Apikorsim*." He casually used the Hebrew term for heretic. "Or the criminals who pretend to be holy men." For the first time, a trace of emotion appeared on Rabbi Eisendrath's face. Anger distorted his features, and he scowled at Clay. "Such as your employer and all his spawn." He leaned closer. "They are bad men, Clay. Why else would they befriend an abomination like you?"

That was all Clay could take. He felt the same cold, driving need to crush bone and spill blood that he felt when he had battled the Cossacks on the plains of Russia. He charged across the room, his boots pounding on the marble floor as his hands outstretched. He wanted to grab Rabbi Eisendrath, shatter his jaw, cave in his chest, and tear him apart. But that was just what Rabbi Eisendrath had been waiting for. He blinked once, and a flaming raven swooped down.

It reached Clay and attacked, stabbing at him with its talons. The claws dug into Clay's chest and lifted him up. The raven's wings beat and carried

Clay into the air. The raven dragged him to the nearest window. Clay struggled against the bird, ramming a fist against fiery wings. Sparks flew as his knuckles carved grooves in the wings, but the raven kept flying. It sped up to the window, and rushed through. Clay had a single look back at the exhibition hall. Zipporah defended Harvey and the De Veres from ravens, while more picked up the altar of Asmodeus. That was what the Dagger Men had wanted—and Clay had let them steal what they desired.

Rabbi Eisendrath's raven reached the window and flew through. Clay struggled against it as cold morning air mixed with the heat from the raven's fire. They soared outside, over the golden dome. The raven stared at him, its beak glowing red hot, and then its claws opened. Clay fell. He hurtled down, bashed against the top of the dome, and kept falling. The arched roof caught him, and he continued his rapid descent. Another final drop sent him plummeting off the roof.

He cracked the sidewalk when he fell. Clay lay on the ground, staring at the gray sky. He groaned. It was all he could do.

An hour after the chaos at the museum, Clay and his friends got some rest in the Elephantine Hotel, back at Palisade Park. Zipporah didn't say much and Harvey stayed quiet as he paged through all of his books on Asmodeus. According to Zipporah, the Dagger Men had stolen the altar and the giant bones, using legionary skeletons to cover their escape as they moved back into the Greek exhibit and then vanished before the security guards could reach them. The De Veres had left as well, in a mixture of panic and embarrassment. Darby had thanked Zipporah for protecting them before they hastened away. Now, Clay and his friends simply sat and waited—knowing full well that they had failed. The Dagger Men had stolen what they wanted, and their mad plan to conquer Sickle City—whatever that was—perhaps neared completion.

Professor West sauntered inside, bringing a tray with cups of tea and pastries. "There, there." He offered his biggest grin. "No need to be glum." He set the tray down on the coffee table. "After all, tomorrow is a brand new day." He jabbed his finger into the air as he made the pronouncement.

"What does that even mean?" Zipporah asked.

"A mere aphorism, my dear." Professor West turned to Clay. "Oh, and there's a phone call waiting for you." He paused slightly, his optimistic facade cracking. "From our mutual employer. You can take it in the lobby."

"From my father?" Harvey asked.

Clay stood. "I'll let him know what happened." He followed Professor West out of the parlor and into the lobby, where the phone waited at the desk. Clay picked up the speaker and receiver and brought them to his mouth and ears. "Rabbi?"

"Hello, Mr. Clay." Rabbi Holtz's voice came over the phone, tinny and faint. "I heard there was a bit of a dust-up at the museum this morning. Some *goyish* bigwig made a stir, but it's nothing a little money can't smooth over. But I guess our Dagger Men friends remain at large?" He sounded busy, as if something else concerned him.

"Yeah."

"Pity. Well, Mr. Clay, I've got another assignment for you. I'm going to a meeting with a whole pack of *goyish* bigwigs, and I need you along as my bodyguard. Edwin Eames, the Grand Sagamore of the Wigwam Club, has called the meeting, and quite a few city authorities will be in attendance— including Mr. Sapphire. I'd ask Monk to come along and watch my back, but his manners aren't the best. You can look imposing and you're smart enough to avoid causing a ruckus. Besides, maybe you can tell them about this Dagger Men nonsense. Perhaps we'll get some help."

"You think so?"

"We have to try. I'll bring the car around to the front of the pier to pick you up." Rabbi Holtz paused. "Oh, and say hello to Harvey, please." The phone clicked empty. Clay hung up as well. He looked at his trench coat, battered and torn from his recent battles. It wouldn't be suitable to wear for this kind of excursion, but he didn't have anything else.

He moved back into the parlor and reached for his fedora. "I'm going to a meeting." He rested the hat on his head. "Your father invited me, Harvey. I'll return when it's through."

Harvey glanced up from his books. "Oh—you better warn them about the Dagger Men."

Zipporah had started a game of solitaire, playing with the same tattered deck that she had used during the Mesopotamian Campaign. "Warn them about the policemen's strike as well." She glanced at her next card and tossed it aside. "And don't let those swells boss you around." She nodded to Clay as he left and Harvey waved. He set his fedora on his head, straightened his tie, and went to meet the rabbi.

He waited for only a few minutes before Rabbi Holtz arrived, driving his sleek Cunningham Touring Car. Clay took the passenger seat and they set off, zooming down Haven Street and heading toward the Uptown

portion of the city. Rabbi Holtz didn't talk much. He had dressed in a
crisp suit for the meeting, and left his yarmulke back at his house. He kept
his hands on the wheel as they arrived on Damocles and drove straight
to Tier Tower—the largest building in Sickle City. Tier Tower sprouted
above the other skyscrapers, a shining pillar of silver and glass with sleek
ridges along the edge and a jagged needle at its pinnacle, piercing the gray
clouds. Rabbi Holtz parked the Cunningham and motioned for Clay to
head inside.

Clay stared at Tier Tower. "We're meeting inside?"

"Not quite," Rabbi Holtz explained. "Grand Sagamore Eames likes to
be a little higher."

They went through the lobby, talked to the clerk, and went to an
elevator in the corner. That carried them up through the entirety of Tier
Tower, rushing past endless floors of offices, and then brought them to the
very top. A single step through a short corridor brought them to a viewing
platform, with all the city sprawled out below them behind brass railings.
Wind whistled through the skyscrapers. Rabbi Holtz shivered a little as he
walked onto the cement floor. A pair of policemen guarded a gangplank
at the edge of the platform, which led to the undercarriage of a hulking
zeppelin. The airship had a sleek, golden deck and a blue gasbag, its engine
humming as it stayed in place.

Rabbi Holtz turned back to Clay. "Watch your step, Mr. Clay. We're in
Eames' world now." He walked onto the gangplank. Clay followed him.
They headed up onto the deck of the airship. Clay felt strange, being so far
from earth. Perhaps it was part of a golem's nature—he didn't like being
kept away from what had given him birth. Still, he followed Rabbi Holtz
onto the deck.

An airship crewman, dressed smartly in a blue coat with brass buttons
and a peaked cap, met them on the deck. "This way, please—and welcome
to the *Heavenly Chariot.*" He stepped through a gilded door, and into a
stately dining room surrounded by high windows overlooking the clouds.
A meal had been set on the white tablecloth, with a maid carefully filling
tall crystal glasses with illegal wine, while a cook spooned some steaming
meat in a creamy sauce on each plate. The other guests had already sat
down, and they glanced up as Rabbi Holtz and Clay entered the dining
room.

Edwin Eames, Grand Sagamore of the Wigwam Club and perhaps
the most powerful political boss in Sickle City, took the head of the table
like some proud patriarch overseeing a family meal. "Rabbi Holtz! It's

wonderful to see you—and it seems you've brought a companion." He waved his hand to the meal. "You're both welcome to the meal." Eames had the fat, contented look of a prize-winning farm animal. He had short, wavy gray hair over a plump face, and wore a white seersucker suit with thin pinstripes. A stiff collar and tie and a diamond stickpin added to his wealthy look. "We have much to discuss." He pointed to the other people at the table as Clay and Rabbi Holtz sat down. "I trust you know Mr. Sapphire."

Sapphire stared at his food and wine, without touching it. He said nothing.

"And I'm sure you know Chief Rufus McNally, commander of our valiant officers of the law." Eames pointed to Chief McNally, who had swaddled his girth in his dark blue uniform. His peaked cap rested on the table, revealing a few strands of white hair, which matched his red face. He sipped illegal wine with a smile and waved to Rabbi Holtz. "There's Danforth De Vere as well, a leading member of Sickle City's business community." Eames nodded to De Vere who sat next to the police chief. De Vere's eyes settled on Clay, but he said nothing. He evidently wished to avoid embarrassment.

Rabbi Holtz nodded. "It's good to see you all. This is my bodyguard, Mr. Clay." He looked at the food and then back at Clay. "He's not hungry." That was a relief. Clay stood back, and didn't have to move food around and pretend to eat.

Eames waved his empty glass at the maid, who hurried over with the bottle. "Now that we're all here, I believe we may address the matter at hand—namely, the nascent threat of unions in the police department, and the specter of an encroaching strike. I know we all watched what happened in Russia with feverish terror, and we may fear similar radicals arriving here."

"Agreed." De Vere sipped wine loudly. "I, for one, would like to know what my elected and dutifully funded civic officials are doing about it."

Chief McNally jabbed his fork into the air, in De Vere's direction. "Calm yourself, Fauntleroy. My boys won't strike. You'll find no Bolsheviks wearing police blue, and that's a fact. No need for a union, either. A pay raise—or at least, the promise of a pay raise—should placate them and take the wind out of the rabble-rousers' sails."

"No union, then?" Rabbi Holtz asked.

"Of course not." Eames snorted. "Do you know how I would look if I even listened to their demands? Why, they'd be painting me the deepest shade of Red in every newspaper from here to Kalamazoo. Besides, their requests are ridiculous. Do you think the city has the money to pay for new uniforms or to keep their living quarters sanitary?" He sipped his wine and leaned back, smiling as the sun crept in through the window. The *Heavenly Chariot* had doubtlessly been purchased with cleverly embezzled city funds. "No. We merely need to wait them out."

"What if they do strike?" Sapphire asked the question without looking at anyone. He still hadn't touched his food. Everyone stared at him. "What if you're wrong, Mr. Eames, and the officers call your bluff? What is our course of action, then?"

"No matter." Eames adjusted his collar. "I already have made preparations to hire a number of private detectives—the Sinclair-Koots Detective Agency." Clay stiffened a little. The name 'Sinclair' was familiar. "They're Great War veterans—good men, doing security work and combat unions as well." He glanced at Clay. "Are you a veteran as well, sir?"

"Yes." Clay didn't elaborate.

"Splendid! Always glad to meet a boy who made the world safe for democracy." Eames raised his glass of illegal wine. "Here's to you." He drank his toast and then turned back to Sapphire. "The Sinclair-Koots boys will maintain order. And even if they can't, I trust you to keep the criminal element in line. You have pull with the Yellow Chinese and the clannish Italians, do you not?"

"That may change." Sapphire stared ahead. "With the circumstances."

"Well, Mr. Sapphire, please do your best to make sure that does not change. Under any circumstances." Eames glanced back over the table. "I just wanted to put your minds at ease—which I have done. Are there any other concerns?"

Rabbi Holtz sighed. "Actually, Mr. Eames, there are." He nodded to Clay. "Tell them about the Dagger Men. You know it better than I."

All eyes moved to Clay. He shifted a little and looked away. He would have to tell them. "Yesterday, my friends and I were sent after some robbers who hit one of Mr. Sapphire's shipments. We discovered that the robbery was carried out by an ancient sect called the Dagger Men. They're Jewish radicals, thousands of years old. Today, they attacked the Museum of Venerable Antiquities. I tried to stop them, and could not." He pointed to De Vere. "You were there, Mr. De Vere. Anyway, I believe that the Dagger Men are preparing to launch an attack on Sickle City. They may very well use the chaos of the police strike to enact their plan."

Chief McNally laughed. "Jewish radicals? What do you they intend to do? Swindle us? Steal our money?"

"They are mystics," Clay explained. "Master sorcerers."

"Sorcery?" Eames offered a skeptical raise of an eyebrow. "I've attended quite a few séances. My wife loves spiritualism, you see—but it seems to be a lot of bell-ringing and table-rapping and nothing more. I'm certain we have nothing to fear from such charlatans."

Sapphire folded his arms. "There are stranger things out there, Mr. Eames. Mr. Clay's helped me banish them, many times. We should listen to him."

"Naturally, I'll take your warning to heart." Eames calmly made his politician's promise. "But I really don't think there's much call for—" He stopped suddenly and sprang to his feet. He hurried around the table and grabbed the maid's arm, tugging her closer to him. His benevolent grandfather act vanished and he suddenly became the political boss who had held power in Sickle City for generations. "What are you doing here? You goddamn shrew, who let you onto this vessel?" He tugged her close, as the police officers in the corner reached for their guns.

The maid shrugged. "A new career, Grand Sagamore. Nothing more." The maid had auburn hair, cut in a classic flapper bob. Her eyes gleamed. "Didn't you say you wanted that for me, after you read my latest column? By the way, I can conjure up quite a few paragraphs about the way you're accosting me now. Unless you want to hurl me over the side of your floating pleasure barge, of course." She winked.

"Ava Silver." Eames released her. "I apologize. This newspaperwoman and her gossip rag, the *Weekly Sophisticate*, have been a thorn in the side of Sickle City for years. My men should have paid more attention to whoever snuck aboard." He glared at Silver. "I'm afraid there's no room for newshounds aboard the *Heavenly Chariot*. You'll have to leave." He glanced back at Clay. "Mr. Clay, why don't you escort her off?"

Silver beamed at Clay. "My. He's a big one." She put her hands on her hips. "How about showing mercy on a poor girl reporter?" She sighed as Clay took a step toward her. "Ah, applesauce. All right, big guy. Let's go." She walked past Clay, heading past the table. Silver paused to grab some wine and took a long sip. "A little top shelf giggle juice for the road." She set the cup down and licked her lips.

Clay crossed the table. "Come on," he ordered. "We're leaving."

"You're no fun, Mr. Clay." Silver trailed after Clay. They moved out of the dining room, leaving Sickle City's powerful to make their plots in peace. Silver gave them a parting wave. "You've given me plenty of information for the next issue of the *Weekly Sophisticate*. Be sure to snag a copy to see your name in headlines."

Eames bellowed out his rage. "Get her out of here!"

They reached the deck and then the gangplank. Eames' pet police officers followed them a little, but Silver didn't make a dash back to the deck of the *Heavenly Chariot*. She waltzed down the gangplank, crossed the observation deck, and stepped into the elevator. Clay hurried over to join her as the elevator doors hummed shut. Evidently, Silver had gotten what she came for. The doors closed and the elevator descended. Silver produced a pad and a pencil. She tapped the tip against the paper as they rushed down through Tier Tower.

"So, Mr. Clay, is it?" she posed the question calmly. "How about an exclusive? What's it like to be the top enforcer of the Big Cheese Heeb on Haven Street?" Clay said nothing. "Oh, tight-lipped, ain't you? Well, how about those Dagger Men? Now that sounds like a scoop worth learning about."

"You believe it?" Clay asked.

Silver nodded. "Uh-huh. I've covered the pagan rites of upper class snobs at their secret society gentleman's clubs and Voodoo in Hogshead Street. I've seen plenty of strange things, so Jewish mysticism would fit right in." She paused as she looked at Clay. "You don't look Jewish, you know. Matter of fact, you don't look like much of anything—except for a guy who spends his free time carrying around automobiles and eating raw eggs. I've heard about most of the people who work for the good rabbi of B'nai Bootlegging on Haven Street, but I don't think I've run into you before, Mr. Clay. What's your story?"

He couldn't tell her that he was a golem. That would have to be kept secret, apart from his few friends. "No story," he said. "I'm just a guy who works for the rabbi."

"Just a simple mug, eh?" Silver asked. "No such thing, in my lofty experience." The elevator doors hummed open. "Look, I'm not being a snob or a bigot. I'm a Jew myself—well, a half-Jew, on my mother's side. Daddy was an upper crust rich boy who didn't stick around, and I keep my mother's name to avoid embarrassment. In return for plenty of dough from my father's family, of course." They stepped into the lobby. "Let me introduce you to my daughter, Mr. Clay."

"Your daughter?" Clay hurried after her as she crossed the lobby, heading to a collection of round couches and Chesterfields set before the clerk's desk. He had been tasked with escorting Silver away from the airship, but—somehow—Silver's brisk manner had turned the tables. She simply acted like she was the boss and everyone seemed to think that she was.

"Sure." Silver pointed to a small girl sitting on the couch, next to what appeared to be a runty, black-and-white dog with a scrunched face. "Sophie, dear heart, come and meet Mr. Clay. He's your mom's latest confidential source."

"That's not—" Clay stammered. "I never said—"

But Sophie Silver had already dog-marked her book, hopped off the couch, and hurried over. Sophie seemed about Harvey's age, with a pleasant face framed by elfin ears. She had her mother's auburn hair, cut to a similar length without imitating Ava's straight, flapper bob. A white pea coat covered a thin sweater and a smart, checkered skirt. She smiled politely at Clay and curtsied. "Good afternoon, sir. I'm delighted that you're helping my mother. She's one of the best reporters in the city and her writing at the *Weekly Sophisticate* is always witty and illuminating." She patted the small dog sitting on its haunches next to her. "You'll find that she'll give you a fair shake."

"That's not—I'm not—" Clay stared at the dog—and found it wasn't a dog at all. "What is that?"

"Lucky?" Sophie asked. "Oh, yes—he's not a dog. He's a panda cub, actually."

"Got him from China on one of my jaunts." Silver picked up the suitcase next to Sophie. She produced a pack of cigarettes and a lighter, and busied herself preparing one. "Had to head into some dangerous, mist-shrouded country to discover him, and decided to bring the little fellow back. He's a cute little devil, isn't he? I suppose when he's bigger, we'll send him to a zoo, but until then, he makes a fine pet for Sophie."

Lucky moved closer to Clay and gave him a quick sniff. Clay stepped back.

"Tell me, Mr. Clay, do you have a ride home?" Silver asked.

They had taken Rabbi Holtz's Cunningham—and Clay didn't have the keys. "No."

"Excellent. I'll give you a ride back to Haven Street and it will give us more time to chat. Nothing like a ride in a luxurious automobile to truly loosen the tongue." She patted Clay's head. "Stay here with Sophie, big fellow. I'll slip into the proper glad rags and off we'll go a-motoring. Ta-ta!" She gave Sophie a kiss on the cheek and hastened away, leaving Clay with her daughter. They stood there awkwardly for a few moments. Lucky tried to sniff Clay again. This time, Clay lowered his hand. Lucky gave his finger a quick lick. Clay pulled away as the rough tongue brushed his fingers and Sophie stifled a laugh.

A few minutes later, Silver returned—completely transformed. She appeared to be every inch the flapper, with a fringed bottle-green dress under a shimmering fox fur coat and a cloche hat. She even had a pair of motorist's goggles, dangling around her neck. She motioned outside and Clay and Sophie fell in step behind her. Lucky followed on his leash, his stubby legs struggling to keep up. They headed out and reached the sidewalk, where the valet brought around Silver's car. She offered him a substantial tip and he tipped his pillbox hat as he shuffled away. Clay stared at Silver's car, a sleek Duesenberg roadster that resembled a steel torpedo and matched the emerald color of her dress. It put Clay's Studebaker to shame.

Silver got behind the wheel and patted the white leather seat next to her. "Have a seat, darling. Sophie, you may take the back. Make sure Lucky's properly secured. I don't want him running into traffic if he mistakes a street pole for bamboo." She turned to Clay as he sat next to her. "Wondering where I got the boiler, Mr. Clay?"

"The question crossed my mind."

"Well, do you recall when I said that my father's family pays me a great deal of money to avoid using their name when I write my columns? It's rather a lot of money. Pays for trips around the globe, fancy vehicles, and young Sophie's education, as well as imported food for Lucky." She started the engine. "Where to, darling?"

"Palisade Park," Clay explained. "Haven Street." Once again, Silver simply hadn't given him time to protest.

"The amusement park?" Sophie asked. "That's a swell home, Mr. Clay."

"Sounds rather dreary to me." Silver hit the gas. "But off we go." The Duesenberg roared into the street. Silver fought for space like a lion at the kill, claiming her pathway through the crowded thoroughfare and zooming off to Haven Street. Clay slumped in the seat, the wind roaring in his face. Silver and Sophie both put on goggles, but he could handle the wind. The meeting with Eames and the others hadn't gone well, and Clay felt a lot better in Silver's company. Though he couldn't tell her the truth, he had a feeling that he could trust her—and that was more than he could say for Eames, Sapphire, and the rest. One thing was for certain: they weren't prepared for the Dagger Men. Clay began to wonder if he couldn't say the same thing about himself.

In the late afternoon, when mist rolled in from the ocean and spilled over Haven Street and the waves growled as they smashed in nautical rage against the supports of the dock, the Duesenberg came to a halt by the entrance to Palisade Park. Silver hadn't bothered with questions as they motored along to the park, but now she killed the engine and glanced at Clay. "Why are you so keen to keep this Dagger Men story hushed up, Mr. Clay?" she asked. "If there truly is some group of religious radicals intending to turn Sickle City in Sodom and Gomorrah, surely the public should know about it? And yet, you seem to desire the whole problem to quietly be dealt with."

Clay stared ahead, following the Ferris wheel with his carved eyes. "That's what I want." He had always kept things secret as a matter of course, and now he needed to come up with a reason why. He fell upon it instantly. "The *goyim* hate us enough already. We don't need to give them any more reasons."

"Well, I wouldn't say that," Silver replied. "In fact, apart from the occasional snobbery, I'd say we Hebrews are as welcome in America as any other collection of immigrants. We're not treated like the Blacks or the Chinese, for instance. My word, the horrors that are perpetrated on those poor souls..." She sighed as she opened the door. "But I do take your meaning. We have found something of a sanctuary in Haven Street, and you don't want to see it jeopardized. I just hope these Dagger Men fanatics don't take that decision out of your hand."

Sophie leaned out of the door, Lucky tucked under her arm. "Can we go in?"

"A superb notion, dear heart." Silver opened the door. "Lead on, Mr. Clay."

He couldn't seem to get rid of them. Clay sighed and led them under the colorful archway and onto the dock. They passed under the roller coaster as it made another circuit, the rumble of the carriage against the wood and the merry screams of the passengers echoing over the crashing of the waves. The sky grew darker, with dark clouds mingling with the gray. Rainfall seemed inevitable. Clay led the Silvers over to the Elephantine Hotel. Harvey waited for him on the porch, seated in a cushioned deck chair before a thick volume on demonology. Zipporah stood a little way apart, struggling through her swordsmanship exhibition. She tried to hack up bananas and pineapples, but the audience didn't seem interested in standing still. The old Australian slouch hat she used to collect donations from spectators only had a few coins and dollars against the weathered fabric. She sheathed her blades when Clay approached.

"Harvey." Clay had to call the boy's name to make him look up. "I'm back."

"Oh." Harvey perked up and carefully closed the book, then bounded down the stairs. "Hello, Mr. Clay. How was the meeting?" His eyes moved to Ava Silver and then darted to Lucky, who rolled over on the planks and whined at the sky. "Is that a panda?" He stared curiously at the panda, the book under his arm.

"Yes." Clay supposed he should introduce the Silvers. "Its name is Lucky. This is Ava Silver, and her daughter, Sophie. Miss Silver works for the *Weekly Sophisticate*. She was trying to spy on the meeting with Grand Sagamore Eames, and now she wants to interview me about the Dagger Men." Clay stared at her. He could state his intention clearly now. "And I do not want to be interviewed."

Zipporah walked over and offered her hand. "Zipporah Sarfati. Pleased to meet you." She nodded to Harvey. "The squirt is Harvey Holtz, Rabbi Holtz's boy. He's a good kid." She pointed to Lucky. "He bite?"

"Not at all. Lucky is very well behaved," Silver explained. "Can't say the same about me, of course."

Sophie glanced at Harvey, who hesitantly held his hand above the panda. "You can pet him, if you wish."

"O-okay." Harvey knelt down and petted Lucky. The panda whined and pushed its head against his palm. Harvey looked back at Sophie, and his face flushed red. He recoiled from the panda, as if petting anything was the furthest from what he desired. He stumbled back, nearly dropped the book, and managed to steady himself. "Good afternoon, Miss S-Silver. I am very pleased to make your acquaintance." He managed a clumsy bow. "I welcome you to Haven Street and I would be honored to provide some information—within reason, of course—to you. Your mother, I mean. Not that I wouldn't want you to interview me, of c-course."

She smiled at his awkwardness. "Thank you, Harvey. Do you live in an amusement park?"

"Not exactly. I h-have my own house, on Atlas Avenue," Harvey explained. "Would y-you like to see it? Perhaps you could see my room, and my collection of pulp magazines and occult texts? I have quite a few sacred books, you know, and I'd be happy to—" He paused suddenly. "Oh. It started raining." Sure enough, the first drops of rain poured down from the sky and fell over Palisade Park in gray curtains. The rain dripped off the roller coaster and the colorful painted booths in the midway, dulling every color. The few guests ambled away, the rain ruining their fun.

Clay and the others stepped under the awning of the Elephantine Hotel, sheltering under the pachyderm's bulk.

Clay watched as Harvey and Sophie continued their conversation. He emitted a slight creak—a chirp of happiness. The boy might have trouble fitting in, but now he seemed to have found a friend. Maybe Ava Silver wasn't so bad after all. Her daughter had given Harvey a bit of childhood normalcy and Clay appreciated it.

But the normalcy didn't last. As they stepped under the awning, Zipporah tapped Clay's shoulder. "Clay." She pointed to the archway. "You remember the giant—the Nephilim bones from the museum?" Clay nodded. "I was wondering why the Dagger Men bothered to pinch a bunch of dusty bones. Now I know why."

"What do you mean?" Clay stared at the archway.

"The rain," Zipporah explained. "It ain't falling like it should."

She was right. The rain came down in dripping lines all over Palisade Park, but it fell at curved angles near the archway. Something invisible blocked the rain, and the drops spilled and fell on this unseen object. Whatever it was moved closer. The archway shuddered and snapped. Wood fell to the ground as the shape moved closer, and then, in a sudden instant, Clay and everyone else realized what had just entered Palisade Park.

The ghost of a giant—of a Nephilim—stood before the porch of the Elephantine Hotel. The giant had shimmering silver skin, as if it had been built of gossamer stretched over a massive frame. Clay barely came up to the giant's chest, which bulged with muscle. Assorted animal skins from a dozen different beasts, including lions, camels, oxen, and perhaps the tanned hide of a man, formed a crude cloak around the giant. It carried a heavy club, which looked like it had been made from a tree trunk and carved into a siege weapon. The giant's face seemed to be mostly beard and teeth, with glowing, pale blue eyes. It headed straight toward them, already raising its club.

Zipporah realized what was happening. "Down!" she cried. She pulled Harvey from his chair. He squeaked in panic as the club hurtled toward the porch. It could have crushed at least three of them. Silver grabbed her daughter and pulled her close, as Lucky released a series of whimpers. Clay couldn't let any of them come to harm. He charged toward the ghostly giant, running down from the porch with his fists swinging at his sides.

The club caught him, striking his side and knocking him hard onto the ground. Clay skidded on the pier, the slick planks carrying him along. He crashed into a wooden devil, and it shattered under his weight. Splinters jabbed at him. Clay grabbed the devil's head and hurled it at the giant. The cherry red wood shattered against phantom muscle and splinters pattered to the planks. Clay came to his feet as the giant trundled toward him, raising its club for another strike.

"I'll distract him! Lead him into the midway." Clay waved to Zipporah and Harvey. "Protect Miss Silver and Sophie!" He moved back, facing the giant. Sure enough, the hulking apparition followed. It may have been big, but it certainly wasn't smart.

"I've got a spell that might get rid of ghosts, Mr. Clay!" Harvey dug into his satchel. "They work on human ghosts—but I don't know if they'll work on a giant ghost." He fiddled through the pages, rain soaking his spectacles and pattering against his face. Clay gave them a quick wave and then turned away. He hurried into the midway, running into the collection of booths offering games of chance and skill. The giant followed him, its club already speeding down like a comet.

Clay ducked as the club took out half of the nearest booth. Striped fabric ripped, the booth's contents—a milk jug toss—flew through the air. A milk jug slammed into Clay's midsection and knocked him down. Baseballs poured out of the milk jug's mouth, bumping into Clay's face in an endless stream. He ignored the pain, spat a baseball out of his mouth, and rolled over. The giant towered above him, its club held high in the rainy air. Clay didn't have time to get out of the way. He braced himself for the club's descent. It would probably smash him in too, or just knock him through the pier and straight into the ocean.

But Zipporah's twin scimitars struck first. She charged at the giant, her blades outstretched. Clay could see her through the spectral giant's body, as if he was watching some distorted picture of Zipporah in a malfunctioning moving picture. She raced in and rammed the blades into the giant's back.

The swords pierced its body. The giant threw back its head and emitted a cry—one more animal than human. It spun around, moving ponderously as it raised its club again. Zipporah leapt to the side, leading into the shelter of a booth offering a shooting game. The club crashed down on the roof, smashing it apart. Zipporah stayed slow, the booth crumbling around her. The giant bellowed and raised the club again. Clay needed to help, but he had the feeling that his fists alone wouldn't be enough. It would be like trying to punch out a mountain.

His eyes moved to the next game—a strength tester aimed at manly visitors trying to impress their best girls. The game consisted of a bell topping a long pole, which could be triggered by striking a weighted spring with a massive sledgehammer. That hammer, lying on its side and slick in the rain, seemed promising. Clay ran for it. He needed to get the giant's attention first so he scooped up a baseball, palmed it, and tossed it back with all his strength. The ball bounced off the giant's back and made it turn. It roared again and started toward Clay.

By then, Clay had crossed the soggy planks. He reached down, grabbed the sledgehammer and spun around. Zipporah emerged from the ruined booth. They stood together, brandishing their weapons. The giant seemed surprised as it prepared to swing up its club. But before the club could land, Clay and Zipporah struck. The scimitars and the sledgehammer smashed the giant's chest together. The sledgehammer hummed through something viscous and thick, like some kind of heavy broth. Clay pulled the hammer back and smashed it down again. Zipporah hacked and stabbed with her swords. The giant howled, unable to swing its club.

Harvey reached them next. He held a small book, a cloth-bound volume small enough to be carried in a single hand. He snapped it open and began to read, his voice high and cracking over the downpour. He raised his hand, forming strange outlines with his fingers, as he hurried through a complex prayer. As soon as he began to read, the giant released another groan and sank to its knees. The club fell away. Harvey continued reading, and Clay and Zipporah stepped back.

The giant released another moan, outstretched its great arms, and then glowed brightly and vanished. It simply faded away, drifting like sparks in a wind, and then it had gone completely. The rain continued, and the boardwalk stood empty.

Clay hurried to Harvey. "Good job." He patted the boy's shoulder. "Now let's get out of the rain."

They returned to the Elephantine Hotel, where Ava and Sophie Silver had watched everything. Sophie looked delighted. She ran to Harvey. "You defeated that entire ghostly creature all on your lonesome? That's remarkable!" She peered at the book. "What did you do use to get rid of that ghost? Are you a sorcerer, perhaps? Or a wizard?"

"I'm not a w-wizard, Miss Silver," Harvey said, the redness returning to his cheeks. "I just used one of King Solomon's spells."

Zipporah nodded to Silver. "First time being attacked by the supernatural?"

"I'm afraid so—and it's not an experience I'm keen to repeat." Silver picked up her pet panda cub and tucked it under her arm. "Come along,

Sophie. We'd better return to our apartment. You have work from your tutors and I have an article to complete." Sophie hurried to her mother's side and followed her down the pier. "Farewell, Mr. Clay. It was grand meeting you." She wiggled her fingers and Sophie smiled.

"Goodbye!" Harvey waved back as they left the dock. He turned to Clay and Zipporah. "They're swell, aren't they?" Clay shrugged. "Well, what do you think we should do now?"

"We were attacked by a ghost, dispatched by the Dagger Men," Zipporah said. "And we know just who to see to deal with ghosts and find out where those Dagger devils are hiding."

"Shlomo Ben Shlomo," Clay muttered. He pointed to the Elephantine Hotel doors. "Come on. Let's get this over with." He didn't want to contact Shlomo Ben Shlomo, but he had little choice. They needed more information on the Dagger Men, and they couldn't leave anything overlooked. For the moment, Clay was just glad to get out of the rain.

Chapter Four
THE FULCRUM OF THE WORLD

With the rain still pouring over Palisade Park, Clay and his friends returned to the Elephantine Hotel and headed to the attic. They took a spiral staircase, which wound to the elephant's upper chest, and walked down a hall leading to the pachyderm's head. A trapdoor in the ceiling came down at the pull of a cord, and then they went upstairs. The rain pattered on the round windows, and all of the gaudily painted amusements in the Park seemed like strange coral in some bizarre reef. Clay gave Harvey a boost up the steps leading to the attic, and followed him. The folding stairs creaked under his weight. Zipporah joined them, and she switched on the lamp in the corner and added some illumination to the round chamber that occupied the space where the elephant's brain would have been. They walked into the attic.

Professor West kept a variety of old show business detritus in the attic, loaded into crates or stacked against the walls in unruly piles. Cut-out posters for sideshow acts, revealing freaks and performers in lurid reds and greens, leaned against the round walls. Old midway games, discarded furniture, broken machinery from the rides, and a stuffed tiger occupied the rest of the attic. Clay didn't care about any of that stuff. His eyes moved to the round fishbowl resting on a card table before a number of newspapers, at the very center of the room.

They approached the fishbowl. A single salmon floated awkwardly in the green water, its body curled so that it fit against the glass. The fish faced them, and reared its body up. Water splashed on the newspapers. The fish's eyes, glassy and dead, settled on Clay. "Well, if it isn't my favorite golem?" He spoke with a raspy voice, an Eastern European accent thick as borscht. "Hello, Clay. May you marry the Angel of death! May you grow like an onion—with your head in the ground!" He bellied up to the edge of the fishbowl, swaying back and forth as he muttered the curses.

Clay stared back, not giving Shlomo Ben Shlomo a reaction. "Hello, Shlomo."

"We got a job for you." Zipporah walked over to the table and stared at the fish. "And we'd appreciate it if you closed your head."

"May you turn into a blintz and be eaten by a cat, you harridan!" Shlomo Ben Shlomo replied. "I'll insult you as much as I want." He bit his lower lip—a funny gesture for a fish. "It's all I can do, in my current, scaly prison."

Shlomo Ben Shlomo was a dybbuk—a malevolent spirit, which possessed others to cause evil and mischief. Clay and his friends had encountered him during a previous case. Thanks to one of Harvey's spells, they had trapped him inside a fish's body. Now, they used Shlomo as an informer for the spirit world. Shlomo wasn't entirely pleased about the arrangement. If he had his way, he'd possess bus drivers and cause traffic accidents, make husbands insult their wives, or use a child's innocent hands to start fires. Clay didn't have much sympathy for the dybbuk.

Harvey gingerly approached Shlomo. "I'm sorry, Mr. Shlomo—but it's very important. We really do need your help."

"And why should I help you, you little rat? Especially after you trapped me here, in this cursed fish?" Shlomo Ben Shlomo demanded.

Clay had little patience left. He towered over the fishbowl and raised a heavy fist. "You oughtn't to be talking to him like that."

"Oh yeah? What are you gonna do, clay man? Kill me?" Shlomo Ben Shlomo grinned, another expression that didn't belong on a fish's face. Somehow, even without lips, Shlomo managed it. "May you swallow an umbrella, so its opens in your belly. May there be salt in your eyes and pepper in your nose. May your head fall off, may you—"

Zipporah withdrew one of her swords. She spun the blade around it, letting it catch the lamplight that filled the dim attic. "You don't like being a fish, Shlomo? What if we cut you in half? How'd you like being half a fish?"

Shlomo paused. "You make a good point."

"We could give you something to make your stay easier here, as well," Harvey suggested. The boy had a good heart. He walked over to the newspapers resting on the table. They gave them to Shlomo to read, so he'd have something to occupy himself while he sat in his fishbowl prison. "I've got a big pile of comics pages at home. You like the Funnies, Mr. Shlomo? I've got the *Katzenjammer Kids*, *Little Nemo*, plenty of good ones. I can bring them, if you'll help us."

"I do like the *Katzenjammers*," Shlomo mused. He turned to Clay, splashing water on the card table. "Okay. What do you want?"

"There's a ghost in Sickle City," Clay explained.

"There's about a million of them, clay man."

"This ghost belongs to a giant." Zipporah pointed to Shlomo. "He's somewhere in town, summoned by a group of mystics called the Dagger Men. They're holed up in the city, staying out of sight while they summoned their ghost. You need to fly out there, track down the giant—his essence might still be in the air—and tell us where they're staying. That sound agreeable, Shlomo?" She raised her sword again. "Or should I take off your tail?"

"It will take some time," Shlomo said. "An hour perhaps."

"We'll wait," Clay said.

"Then I'll do it." Shlomo fixed his shiny eyes on Harvey. "And you'd better bring me those Funnies, boy."

"I will," Harvey said. "Don't try and escape or anything, or I'll know about it and you'll be dragged right back into the fish."

"Which I'll cut in half," Zipporah added.

"I sure am glad I ran into you folks, to set me on the proper path," Shlomo mused. He floated to the center of the fishbowl, gave a little shake, and opened his mouth. A pale shape, misty and faint, burst out of the fish's mouth like it had started to breathe smoke. The cloud briefly formed a figure, which swelled as it emerged into the still air of the basement. A hint of Shlomo Ben Shlomo's human form—with a stiff, wiry beard, dangling side-locks, and permanently squinting eyes—appeared in the air. Harvey hurried to the window in the corner to let the dybbuk out.

He swung it wide, and Shlomo Ben Shlomo zoomed into the rain. He left with another whispered Yiddish curse. "May you grow a wooden tongue!" echoed over the still attic, and then he zoomed away into the sky.

He vanished in a few seconds, released on his mission. The fish lay in the water, floating on its side on the surface of the fishbowl. Now, there was nothing to do but wait.

Clay pulled over a threadbare armchair for Harvey, who slumped on the cushions and yawned. This day had been full of chaos, but Harvey seemed determined to stay awake. He reached for one of the newspaper pages on Shlomo's table and read the Funnies as his eyes drooped. Zipporah settled on a stool and rested her hands on her knees. Clay simply stood. He didn't have muscles or bones to feel weary, but he knew that his friends did. They needed a break, and this was their best chance to get one.

Zipporah returned her sword to the scabbard over her back. She glanced at Harvey and Clay. "What if they're right?" she suddenly asked.

"Who?" Clay asked.

"The Dagger Men, Clay." She stared past him, at an oversized decoration resembling a grinning devil's head, complete with horns and goatee. "I've been thinking about them, while you were at the meeting with Rabbi Holtz and the other swells. They fought the Romans, because the Romans conquered Judea and tried to transform it into a miniature Rome. And look at what happened in Russia, during the Revolution—the pogroms only got worse, and they were bad to begin with. You saw how those upper crust De Vere heels treated Harvey. Maybe Rabbi Geist and Rabbi Eisendrath have themselves a point."

"You think they deserve to rule Sickle City?"

"Well, look who's running it now—the Wigwam Club and Grand Sagamore Edwin Eames." She spat on the ground. "They don't give a damn about anything besides getting out the vote, lining their own pockets, and putting their no-good relatives on the dole. No wonder the police force is ready to strike. They're treated like garbage and they want a change."

Harvey stared at Zipporah. "You really think that, Miss Sarfati?"

"I don't know. I'm just making conversation." She smoothed back her auburn hair. "What do you think, child? You must have a bird's eye view of how things are, as Rabbi Holtz's son. Do the Dagger Men make any sense to you?"

"Not at all, ma'am," Harvey said. "Not one bit." Even though he was tired, he still spoke clearly. "They hurt people. They're cruel. The historical Dagger Men, the Sicarii, were the same way. They didn't just kill Romans— they killed anyone they thought wasn't Jewish enough. Innocent people died at their hands, and these Dagger Men seem to want to do the same thing. If they capture Sickle City, things will definitely get a lot worse."

"And you'd better bring me those funnies, boy."

He stared at his Buster Browns. "The kind of violence they bring, the dark magic they use to fuel their Roman armies, is evil and cruel. It hurts people, and there's no excuse for that. Even if things are hard for the Jews, we can't become prejudiced or mean to those who aren't Jewish. That's always going to be wrong, no matter what." He settled back on the armchair, nervous after his outburst. "I'm sorry, but that's what I think."

"You're a good boy, Harvey," Zipporah replied. "A kind boy." She sighed as she came to her feet. "Besides, the Dagger Men are a pack of rascals. They'd have me trapped in a kitchen, keeping my hair covered."

"We can't have that," Clay said.

"They use violence to get what they want," Harvey added. "And that's never acceptable."

Clay stared at Harvey, remembering what he had done just a few years ago, on the plains of Russia. He had slaughtered his enemies, just like the Dagger Men wanted to do to in Sickle City. What Clay had done was wrong, but that knowledge alone wouldn't scour the blood from his hands. He turned away from Harvey, unable to look the boy in the face. Harvey knew some of what Clay had done, but not the whole story. If he did, he might follow his uncle in calling Clay an abomination. Perhaps Clay couldn't blame him if he did.

The window flapped open, stirred by a passing wind. The dead fish in the bowl shook and wiggled, scattering a few more droplets. Clay hurried to the table, while Harvey sprang from his chair. Zipporah watched as well. They stared at Shlomo Ben Shlomo, who swiveled about to face them. Somehow, his scaly face fused into a glowering frown.

His head jabbed out of the surface, and he stared at Harvey. "I want three Sunday editions," he said. "All the Funnies, stacked up and ready to read."

"O-okay," Harvey agreed. "I can get them for you." He leaned closer. "What did you discover?"

"I found that giant's ghost. One of the *Nephilim*, in God's name." He slid into the water, as if he wanted to escape and swim away. "It nearly clobbered me. I had to fall back, sneak away, and then follow his trail. I did, though. I'm a very good dybbuk. I possessed a pigeon, you see, and—"

"We don't want a story," Zipporah said. "What'd you discover?"

"I was getting to that." Shlomo glared at her. "I tracked him into Sickle Bay, over the water. You know what that was like? I detest water. Reminds me of my current lodgings, in which I am unjustly imprisoned. But I did it, out of loyalty to you." He spun his body around, facing Clay. "Anyway, the ghost led me to Bone Island. You know it?"

"Yeah." Bone Island lay at the center of Sickle Bay, like a nose in a face. Shaped somewhat like a comma, the island contained a center of dark woods with a tail of jagged rocks leading into the ocean. Some of Sickle City's founders, the Puritan Barebone family, had settled there and created a small village called Barebone's Town. Its ruins rested in the center of the woods, rotting away in the sunlight and ocean spray. Recently, Bone Island served as the home for an entirely different group of visitors—bootleggers used the dense woods and rocky coasts to store their wares, before taking them into the city for sale. Law never went that far out into the bay.

Shlomo Ben Shlomo rested his fish head on the edge of the bowl, and watched Clay and his friends. "Well, that's where they are. They're in the ruined village, right in the middle of the island, in this clearing in the woods."

"Barebone's Town," Harvey explained. "Founded by Bathsheba Barebone, the sister of Sinner Barebone, who created Sickle City." He turned to Clay. "We should go there tomorrow, in the morning, and see what we can discover."

"Don't you have school tomorrow, Harvey?" Clay asked. "Your father won't—"

"I'll have to skip it," Harvey said. "This is about the fate of the whole city. I'm pretty sure that's more important than another day at the Young Gentleman's Academy. Papa will understand. He'd want me to go with you. It might be safer than being alone during the day, actually, especially with the Dagger Men after us..."

"I'm inclined to agree," Zipporah added.

"Well, I'm delighted you've made a fine set of plans for tomorrow," Shlomo said. "Do you need anything else from your noble dybbuk servant?" He swiveled to face Harvey, forming another hopeful grin with his lipless, toothless mouth. "And how about those newspapers?"

"We'll bring you the Funnies later." Clay turned to his friends. "Come on."

They walked out of the attic, heading for the trapdoor leading back to the hall. Shlomo called after them, his rasping words echoing over the antique decorations and abandoned carnival games. "Hang yourself with a sugar rope, and you'll die a sweet death! May all your teeth fall out, except one, so that you will suffer! May you—" Clay let Harvey and Zipporah take the folding stairs first, before he descended through the trap door. He slammed it shut, cutting off the last of Shlomo Ben Shlomo's insults. Hopefully, they wouldn't need to rely on the dybbuk again.

Clay nodded to Harvey as they walked down the hall. "I'm going to call your house. Monk Moss can come and pick you up. You should return home."

"I can't stay here?" Harvey asked. "Professor West probably has a guest room—"

"Stay with your father," Clay said. "You have a big day tomorrow."

"Okay, Mr. Clay," Harvey agreed. "But I think I can stay up a little longer. Maybe I can do some more reading about Asmodeus, or—"

"Harvey." Zipporah patted his head. "Here's something I learned in Mesopotamia. You never know when artillery or mortar shells are going to come screaming out of the sky for hours on end and make sleep impossible. Take your shuteye when you can get it. Use every opportunity you can to rest your eyes."

Harvey nodded. "Well, all right, Miss Sarfati. I guess that makes sense. And you guys should get some rest as well."

"We will," Clay assured him. "We've got a big day tomorrow too."

He didn't mention the fact that he needed no rest, and could only slip into a sort of half-sleep if he sat on his bed and concentrated for hours on end. That's what he would do tonight, after Harvey had left and Zipporah had gone to her own quarters. He would sit down and try to clear his mind of Russian snows turning red and the terrible mixture of alarm, sadness, and rage in Rabbi Chaim Holtz's face when he banished Clay into the wilderness. Somehow, Clay knew that he wouldn't entirely succeed, even as he resolved to try.

The next morning, they sped across the cold Atlantic in a motorboat borrowed from Rabbi Holtz. It might have been used for covert deliveries of contraband, but now it carried them over the waves and toward the dark form of Bone Island.

Once again, Zipporah manned the motor and directed them over the sea. Sickle City loomed behind them, the towers lost in a gray fog rising up from the sea, and shimmering with distant, electric light. Clay sat in the bow of the motorboat, across from Harvey. The boy shivered a little under his coat at the rising surf. Maybe he would prefer to be in a warm schoolhouse instead of zooming straight to danger on a motorboat which bucked over the waves, but he had appeared before the Elephantine Hotel in the early dawn anyway, with his satchel of books ready to go. Clay folded his thick hands over his legs and waited.

After perhaps an hour of speeding over the waves, they reached the eastern coast of Bone Island. A set of rickety docks rested before a few cabins serving as flophouses and makeshift taverns for visiting smugglers. Lanterns dangled outside, waving in the rain. Beyond the length of crisscrossing docks, a thick forest of clustered trees covered the island like a curtain. Clay scanned the docks with a set of binoculars. Nobody stood on the quay, even though the lanterns were lit. They would have to be careful. He nodded to Zipporah and she directed the motorboat toward the piers.

They sped to a halt by the biggest dock. Zipporah killed the engine and Clay lashed the vessel to a waiting post. He hopped out first, then Harvey scrambled out of the motorboat and Zipporah followed. They walked down the pier, approaching the tan earth and the waiting trees. Ocean wind made the branches wave, and birdsong mixed with the crash of the waves.

Harvey's face had turned a greenish shade during their voyage over the choppy water, and he sighed as he rested his feet on the earth and wiped droplets of water from his glasses on his sleeve. He grinned as sunlight reached his freckled face. "My father has taken me and Mr. Moss to your cabin in the woods outside the city, but this is very nice as well. I like the ocean being close by." He turned to Clay. "Do you think we'll see any whales? Maybe they could, like, come out of the sea and then swim back inside, waving their flukes in the air?"

"I'll keep my eyes peeled," Clay said.

They neared the dockside tavern—a small cabin with a crumbling roof that listed to the side. A sign hung before the entrance, suspended by a frayed rope that made it lean almost entirely on its side. The saloon's name appeared to be 'the Clamshell', but it danced in the wind and wouldn't stay still enough for Clay to be sure. He turned from the tavern, and then the door slammed open. Clay stopped and faced the doorway.

The muzzle of a Tommy gun protruded from the shadows, aimed straight at Clay and his friends. A well-dressed fellow followed it, stepping into the sunlight with a smile fused to his broad face. He had thin brown hair agleam with pomade, and wore a painfully bright checkered red suit and bowtie, complete with diamond stickpin and a rakishly colored pocket square. A bowler hat tilted back to reveal his grin and twin pearl-handled revolvers rested in crossed shoulder-holsters. A trio of other gunmen walked out from behind the rear entrance of the saloon, dressed in far more sober clothes of dark oilskins, brown leather jackets, and flat caps. They carried pistols. The window opened as well, revealing a double-barreled shotgun. The entire crew made the fellow with the Thompson look even more ridiculous, like a clown at a funeral.

He grinned at Clay. "What's the rumpus, Mr. Clay?"

"Turk Brownstein," Clay muttered. "Step aside."

He and Turk Brownstein had clashed before. Brownstein ran a crew called the Tidewater Rats—a gang of dockside ruffians who made their living with small time smuggling, stick-ups, and hijacking. Sometimes they did work for Sapphire; other times they bothered the bigger gang. Either way, the Tidewater Rats never caused enough real trouble to be dealt with. Still, they were rough men used to violence and Brownstein had a particularly volatile mixture of arrogance, stupidity, and aggression that made him truly dangerous. Clay had hoped that the Rats wouldn't be on Bone Island when he and his friends went after the Dagger Men, but it seemed that wasn't the case.

Brownstein kept the Thompson aimed straight Clay. "Nah. I don't think I will. I'm curious, I suppose." He walked closer, keeping the gun trained on them. "What brings you out here to Bone Island—you going sightseeing with Rabbi Holtz's little boy?"

"That's it exactly," Zipporah said. "Just a little outing. We'll have a picnic later. Watch the birds."

"Sounds peachy." Brownstein withdrew a stubby cigarillo from his coat pocket and stabbed it into the corner of his mouth. "But I'm afraid your little vacation is gonna have to be delayed. I want you and the big man to take your boat back to Sickle City." He pointed to Harvey. "The pipsqueak stays here. Don't worry—I'll take good care of him. Rabbi Holtz can pay me a fat pile of dough to show his gratitude."

Harvey looked from Brownstein to Clay. He didn't quite understand what was going on. "You want to watch me, and my father will pay you? I don't think that's necessary, Mr. Brownstein. Mr. Clay and Miss Sarfati are doing a fine job of looking after me. I don't really need a nursemaid or governess, or anything."

"Jesus Christ, you're a thick one." Brownstein flared a lighter to life. "I'm kidnapping you, you little runt. Get inside the Clamshell and I'll have one of the boys tie you to a chair. Get going or I'll break your nose."

"What?" Harvey asked.

Clay groaned. "You're asking for trouble, Brownstein. Step aside."

"You really want to enrage Rabbi Holtz, Brownstein?" Zipporah asked. "Going after his son is gonna earn you a shallow grave. And don't forget that Sapphire will back the rabbi's play. I don't need to tell you what's going to happen to you then."

"Go climb up your thumb." Brownstein blew a raspberry at Zipporah. "The Shark doesn't even swim in these waters. I don't owe him anything. And Rabbi Holtz? He's old. Doesn't have enough time between writing sermons to manage his business. He's gone soft, play-acting at being a rabbi, and forgotten all about being a gangster. I'll see him at High Holidays and thumb my nose at the bum. He won't do a thing about it." Clay hadn't realized that Brownstein was this dumb. "Now, both of you go back to your boat and dangle. I only need one of you alive to deliver the ransom message to the good Rebbe."

They didn't have time for this—not with the Dagger Men at the center of Bone Island. Clay would have to end this fast. He walked in front of Brownstein, ignoring the Tommy gun aimed straight at his chest. He could take Brownstein, but that left the rest of the Tidewater Rats, and Zipporah and Harvey didn't have his strength. He wasn't sure what to do.

Then, a Tidewater Rat with a stubbly nest of beard and a long-barreled revolver released a fit of coughs. He waved his hand. "Goddamn smoke..." he muttered. Smoke hung in front of his eyes, and then rushed past him like a black cloak flying under its own power through the night. The cloud of smoke undulated and curled in front of the Rat. Two eyes appeared, coal red, and then faint feminine features winked into being. Clay found his limbs tensing. A friend had followed them to Bone Island. Lilith Shadowborn, the smoke golem, flowed in front of the Tidewater Rats, blinding them in a flood of darkness. One fired his pistol, and the shot struck the planks of the wharf and kicked up splinters.

Lilith coiled around them, her coal eyes glancing at Clay and his friends. "Run, Clay!" she cried. "Into the woods. I will meet you there." A tendril of shadow whipped out and lashed across the three Tidewater Rats like a whip. It hurled them back, knocking them onto the patchy dirt and grass. Lilith boiled over them, raining down blows with fists made of shadow.

Brownstein must not have known exactly what was happening, but that didn't stop him from reacting in his usual way. He rammed the muzzle of the Tommy gun into Clay's chest, pressing it against the stone. "Pulling some trick, eh?" he asked. "I'll blow you in half. See what—" Clay didn't give him a chance. He grabbed the sub-gun just as Brownstein pulled the trigger. A burst of bullets ripped into Clay's chest, shredding his trench coat. The bullets didn't stop him. He wrenched the Tommy gun away, and then drove the butt straight in Brownstein's face. Brownstein fell back, sputtering as blood boiled out of his nose. Clay let him fall, and then motioned to the woods.

Zipporah grabbed Harvey's arm, tugging him along. They ran for the cover of the forest, hurrying over the tan earth. The shotgun in the window tracked, the Tidewater Rat inside preparing to fire. Zipporah slashed her sword back, scraping the gunman's knuckles with the edge of the blade. He screamed in pain and pulled back the shotgun, giving Clay, Zipporah, and Harvey a chance to escape. They ran for the woods as a few shots cracked after them. Clay glanced over his shoulder. Lilith's shadowy blows continued to fall, keeping the Tidewater Rats from rising. She could fade away before they knew what had happened.

He reached the woods and ducked around the bough of a stately pine. Zipporah and Harvey followed. They moved together, rushing through the woods on a patchy trail half overgrown with grass and splotches of moss. Harvey stumbled along and finally paused for breath in a clearing. Clay stopped as well, and Zipporah gripped her swords, in case the Tidewater Rats charged after them. Nobody came running through the woods. They had escaped their pursuers.

Harvey turned to Clay. "That was Miss Shadowborn, the smoke golem—right?"

"Yeah," Clay agreed. "She must have tailed us. Perhaps she suspected trouble." He sniffed the air. "She's here."

Smoke slithered out from behind a stout tree. Lilith floated into the clearing. She returned to her human form, even putting a little color in her cheeks. She approached Clay with a skeptical, dismissive shake of her head. "Running straight into trouble, as always. Truly, Clay, you are as heedless as the earth that composes you."

"We came seeking the Dagger Men." Zipporah peered through the trees. "We weren't prepared for Rats."

"You warned me about the Dagger Men, didn't you?" Clay asked. "Before this started, you came to me at Palisade Park and warned me."

"So I did," Lilith agreed. "And I'm warning you again." She seethed out of her physical form, her neck extending so she could look closer at Clay. "The Dagger Men are in the old city, just through these woods. They gather in the old stone church. I did not suspect Rabbi Eisendrath had a sense of humor—no more than he had a sense of mercy, but I can think of no other reason why they've chosen to make that their temporary lodgings."

"You know Rabbi Eisendrath, Miss Shadowborn?" Harvey asked.

"From the old days," Lilith agreed.

"So Rabbi Eisendrath is old as well," Zipporah said. "Immortal, perhaps."

"Dangerous," Lilith corrected. "And he surrounds himself with particularly powerful magic. He and his modern companion, Rabbi Geist, are working on some grand endeavor. I can feel its energy, whistling through the trees like a sour wind." Her coal eyes glowed. "I can't go too close, or they will know of my presence and trap me."

"We have a pet dybbuk who said the same thing," Clay said.

Lilith shrugged. "I am not surprised." She floated back, catching a passing wind and billowing away. "I often find a great deal of similarity between myself and ghosts." Lilith lifted up and floated upwards, curving around the branches of the trees. "Goodbye, Emmet Clay. And please—for the sake of your friends—be careful." Then she was gone, leaving only a few traces of smoke in the gray air. Clay wished that she had stayed.

Zipporah pointed down the trail after a few moments of silence. "You heard her. The Dagger Men are in the church of—what was the town called?"

"Barebone's Town," Harvey explained. "An early settlement, later abandoned for Sickle City, until Bathsheba Barebone returned to it." He stared down the trail, buttoning the clasps of his jacket as he shuffled along. "She was kind of a strange woman—she had all these weird visions, and her own version of Christianity, and a lot of other women joined her in Barebone's Town while the rest of the Puritans stayed in Sickle City. They called her a heretic and she had to hide out here for the rest of her life." He glanced back to Clay. "They say she was a witch."

"It wouldn't surprise me, child," Zipporah said.

They walked on in silence, trudging through the trees. Shadows filled the forest trail, and Clay moved carefully over roots and branches underfoot. Maybe the Puritans had civilized this place once, but Bone Island was all wild now. He stared ahead and spotted the village. It lay on a meadow of thin grass and gravel beside a series of rocky hills, which led down to the coast. Clay moved quietly, as he had in Russia when he went on some raid into Bolshevik territory, and Harvey and Zipporah did their best to follow.

They moved into the deserted main street of Barebone's Town. Not much was left of the colonial city. A few cabins, storehouses and shacks rested on the grass, most crumbling into little more than piles of rubble covered in moss and growing plants. A well appeared in one corner, the stone chipped and broken. Roman soldiers stood at the center of the dismal, abandoned settlement in silent ranks. Clay kept his distance from the skeletal legionaries, who didn't notice them. The Dagger Men had to be here.

At the very end of the overgrown street, the ancient stone church nestled like a predator about to spring. The cross had fallen from the roof, and lay in a stone heap on the grass floor. Light appeared from the bare sills of the church windows.

Clay motioned for the others to follow him. They approached from the side, weaving around the other ruined structures until they neared the gray stone wall of the church. Harvey's shoes kicked up a few pebbles, and they rattled against decayed wood and ancient stones. He winced and Zipporah held up her hand to keep him still. Clay led them to the stone wall, and motioned for them to keep their heads down. He walked to the nearest window and peered over the casement. Shlomo Ben Shlomo hadn't lied. Neither had Lilith. The church housed the Dagger Men.

The pews had vanished from the church, along with the pulpit and everything else. Now, only dead leaves, pine needles, and pebbles covered the floor. A small cot rested in the corner, along with a table holding a lantern, a few ancient scrolls, and other occult tools. The bed was probably for Rabbi Geist. Clay doubted that Rabbi Eisendrath ever slept. His eyes moved to the front of the church. The Dagger Men had created a new altar.

They had taken the stone altar from the Museum of Venerable Antiquities and placed it at the far end of the church. A figurine representing Asmodeus—stolen from Sapphire's shipment—stood on the altar like a miniature dancer on a stage. The figurine had a rooster's beak and crest, lizard's claws, and hooves. Its beak lay open, screaming its rage at nothing in particular. Rabbi Eisendrath stared at the altar as he set a number of strangely colored iron chains in neat rows on the ground. The metal of the chains had a dark blue, shining color. Rabbi Geist stood behind him, examining an ancient book. It may have been stolen from a library. The gold writing on the cover, in English, read 'Diary of Bathsheba Barebone, Puritan Prophetess'.

"It's not here." Rabbi Eisendrath spoke almost to himself as he unfurled the chains. "You know as well as I. We can search all we want. We will not find the stone." He turned suddenly, chain rattling in his hand. "What must we do now, Yossel?"

"Master, the Puritan woman said that the Founding Stone is here." He tapped the pages. "She used it as the key, to access the ley-lines which course through the earth, filled with power. Here, she set her spell, which would grow as the years passed, and ripen like fruit, until it is harvested by the oppressed and used to power some other great spell, and then it will become the very Fulcrum of the World. Perhaps it is hidden here, Rabbi, and we merely must—"

"I do not wish to debate with you." Rabbi Eisendrath turned away. "The Dagger Men do not waste time with debates. We act—just as our predecessors did." He turned back to the altar. "This will be a good place for the binding of the Demon King, at least. It is far from prying eyes. But we must return to the city to find the Founding Stone."

Rabbi Geist bowed his head respectfully. "Of course, master—but we have many enemies in the city. The golem—"

"The golem is a lump of earth." Rabbi Eisendrath snapped out the words. His tattooed face contorted in rage. "He is nothing! I will destroy him, and build a garden from his body." He rattled the chains, striking them against the stone floor of the ancient church. "Our people have outlasted empires. We are the goat—eaten by the cat which is bit by the dog and in turn hit by the stick, which is then burned in fire, doused in water, drunk by an ox, that is slaughtered by a butcher, who withers before the Angel of Death. And still we live."

"Yes, master." Rabbi Geist didn't look up. His hair drooped over his eyes.

Rabbi Eisendrath turned back to the altar. "A golem is nothing compared to the foes I have faced."

Clay's mind raced. The Dagger Men wanted something called the Founding Stone, which would be the key to unlock some ancient spell left by the Puritan founders of Sickle City. But what did they hope to accomplish with that sort of power, which lay buried under the earth? And why did they need Asmodeus, the King of the Demons? Clay listened closely, hoping to find out more. He agreed with Harvey. The Dagger Men's plan would mean nothing good for Sickle City.

"Shall we summon Asmodai, master?" Rabbi Geist gestured to the altar.

"Let it happen at night. It is the domain of Naamah and Lilith, Asmodeus's mother, and he will be at home." He gripped the chain. "These will hold him, no matter his confidence. Now, we merely need to—"

A burst of submachine gunfire ripped through the air, echoing over the forest. A flight of birds left the nearby trees and flapped their way into the gray sky, calling in panic. Clay's stones creaked as he gazed at the source of the gunshots. The Tidewater Rats hadn't learned their lesson. Instead, they had followed Clay and his friends, and now strode into Barebone's Town in a clump, with Turk Brownstein at their head. He fired his Thompson at the ground, kicking up leaves and dust. The Dagger Men noticed as well. Rabbi Geist hissed curses in Yiddish. Rabbi Eisendrath's eyes flashed darkly. He gently set the chains down.

"More criminals," he muttered. "This Babylon overflows with them."

Brownstein walked down the main thoroughfare of Barebone's Town. "Where you hiding, Clay?" He aimed his Tommy gun at the ruined buildings. "That was slick, what you did—grabbing my heater and pasting me like that. Don't matter. I'm gonna put some bullets into you, Clay, and enough times to be sure. Don't matter how big you are. You got that? I'm Turk Brownstein! Ain't no one bigger than me!" He gave the Thompson another burst, blasting into a ruined storehouse. Chunks of wood and stone fell from the shots.

The Roman legionaries noticed their approach and charged down the street, their shields raised. The Tidewater Rats opened fire, their bullets ripping through shields and skeletal bodies. The legionaries dropped, but more emerged from the alleys and raced out to attack. The Tidewater Rats stared in amazement at the legionaries, then leaned on the triggers of their guns. Clay guessed that they had decided to gun everything down first, and figure out why they were being attacked by ancient Romans later. Rabbi Geist walked out of the church to meet them, snapping his fingers and summoning more the legionaries. Bullets and shattered, dusty bones filled the street. They needed to leave.

While the battle raged, Clay turned away from the window and glanced at Zipporah and Harvey. The boy hadn't been able to see inside the church, but he must have heard what was going on. "We need to go." Clay kept his voice low. "Let the Rats and the Romans have each other."

"Amen to that," Zipporah agreed. "We'll slip back to the docks and skedaddle."

They turned away, staying low as they moved down the alley to flee—but Rabbi Eisendrath stood in their way, neatly blocking their path.

It didn't make sense. How could he be in the church one moment, and appear outside the next? Clay groaned. He hated magic. He walked quickly in front of Harvey and Zipporah, his fists swinging at his sides. When they met before, Rabbi Eisendrath had thrown Clay out of a window and down to the street. What would be the outcome now?

Rabbi Eisendrath folded his arms. "The golem. How much did you hear?"

"Enough," Zipporah said. "We'll stop you, Rabbi—whatever you're planning."

"How come you wear tattoos?" Harvey asked the question suddenly. Rabbi Eisendrath stared at him. The boy stepped back, moving closer to Clay. "Y-you're not supposed to have tattoos if you're Jewish, Mr. Eisendrath. If you have tattoos, you can't be b-buried in a Jewish cemetery."

"Well, boy, I find that acceptable." Rabbi Eisendrath ran his finger down his cheek, tracing the outline of an occult symbol. "I will never die. Of course, I cannot say the same for you." His eyes flashed. Fire split the air behind him, and two of the giant ravens swooped down from the air with sparks trailing from their burning wings. They were the A'arab Zaraq, the Fiery Ravens of Dispersion, and they swooped down on Clay and ZIpporah. But this time, they were ready.

Zipporah pulled both her swords and drove them upwards. The tips of the blades plunged into the chest of the raven, spilling sparks and dripping flame on the grass. Clay lunged for his, striking the bird with a rapid fist to the beak. He grabbed the raven's neck and hauled it out of the sky, then slammed his boot down on the bird's head. It was like kicking a dying campfire. Chunks of burning feathers and sparks filled the air. The raven's wings flapped, and Clay pulled back his feet before his trousers caught fire. Then he grabbed Harvey's hand and ran back to the street. Zipporah joined him. More ravens soared past them, shrieking and trailing sparks.

They scrambled across the street, just ahead of the battle between the Tidewater Rats and the legionaries. The Rats had fallen back, and now stood at the edge of Barebone's Town. Brownstein raked the legionaries with automatic fire, but the skeletons continued to attack. Clay ignored them. He dragged Harvey into the cover of the forest and they hurried away from the town. They raced into the shadow, their shoes crunching on fallen leaves and pine needles as they hurried through the tall trunks of the trees and neared the rocky hills.

"Golem!" Rabbi Eisendrath's voice came from the trees. "You know what we are doing." Clay stopped and spun around, his fists raised. He looked at the shadowed trees, but couldn't see Eisendrath. His voice seemed to come from the air itself. "But if you were what your creator intended you to be—a defender of the Jewish people—then you would not stand against the Dagger Men. Instead, you would join us. But you resist and that truly makes you an abomination."

"That's not true!" Harvey shouted into the woods. "It's not true at all!" But they had stopped running for just a moment, and that was what Rabbi Eisendrath wanted. A weighted net hurtled down from the forest and fell on top of Harvey. The folds of the net wrapped around the boy. He hit the ground, wincing as the fabric pulled him down.

More nets hurtled through the air. One wrapped around Zipporah and she sank down next to Harvey. Two hit Clay, and he grabbed the nets and started to rip them free, even as they clung to his arms and slowed him. He stared through the holes in the net, as more Roman skeletons marched out to attack—but these weren't legionaries. Instead, their bones bore the sparse armor and elaborate, round helmets of ancient gladiators.

Rabbi Eisendrath walked out from behind a stout tree, just ahead of them. Once again, he had managed to travel in an instant, thanks to his magic. He walked calmly toward them, his hands in his pockets. Two gladiators flanked him, both armed with steel tridents. They aimed them like spears, preparing to strike the nets. More gladiators slipped out from behind other trees. These bore round helmets that hid their skulls, and carried short, lethal stabbing swords. Clay tore at the net, tugging at the bonds. They ripped slightly, and a gladiator approached him and stabbed him with its trident. The trident aimed for his face, the three points reaching for his forehead. If they scratched the words on his forehead, he was finished. He fell back and landed heavily on the ground. The three points hovered above his face, ready to stab again.

Zipporah pressed her scimitar against the net, slicing it open—until another trident stabbed down and pinned her sword to the dirt. She froze; her hand still on the sword. Harvey lay on his side, whimpering slightly. In the distance, the gunshots had faded. Maybe the Tidewater Rats had made the smart play and escaped. Clay wished that he and his friends could do the same.

"Gladiators." Rabbi Eisendrath moved between the two trident-wielding skeletons. "They used to make them battle in the arena—shedding blood for the entertainment of crowds. Truly, they were a debased and wicked people." He pointed to Clay. "And can you truly say that your Americans are much better?"

"We're not the ones animating skeletons," Zipporah replied. Evidently, she had lost all sympathy for the Dagger Men.

"It is a necessity," Rabbi Eisendrath explained. "Noah regretted the flood. Lot regretted the fate of his wife. And yet, in their hearts, they knew it had to be done. So do I." He crouched in front of Clay, as the gladiators surrounded them with blades drawn. "I detest my long life. I detest what I have had to do. But I think of what Christians and *Apikorsim* and all the other villains of the world have done to me, and I regret nothing at all." He reached out, his hands moving to Clay's head. Clay recoiled and tried to crawl back. His limbs rubbed dirt as he tried to escape Rabbi Eisendrath's hands. "Sometimes, I think it would be better to never have been born, and face a peaceful oblivion. Perhaps it's best that I give that gift to you, golem."

"No!" Harvey managed to come to his feet. He charged to Clay, only for a gladiator to casually spin around and bash him with the handle of his sword. The gladius's handle rammed into Harvey's face and he crumpled. Rabbi Eisendrath's fingers drew closer.

A rock smacked into the rabbi's head, banging against his ear. He hissed and pulled back, his hands flying to his forehead as if that was what needed the most protection. He stumbled back, gritting his teeth and sucking air through his teeth. Clay stared at the woods as Ava Silver, the flapper reporter, raced out from between the trees. She had her purse in her hand and the wind ruffled her dark flapper bob as her boots pounded over the dust.

"Well, speak of the devil." She raced over and withdrew a pearl-handled, snub-nosed revolver from her purse. "What a marvelous coincidence, running into you here." The gladiators surged toward her, raising their weapons. Silver's pistol flashed, punching bullets into their skulls. She fired quickly, the revolver's shots popping and echoing against the trees. Fragments of ancient steel and bone spun to the ground. "A gat does come in handy." Silver returned the pistol her purse. "How you been, Mr. Clay?" She knelt down next to him, and pulled a silver-bladed switchblade from the purse.

"I've been better," Clay said.

"There it is." Silver sawed the cords of the rope with her knife. "A sense of humor."

The net snapped and Clay's strong arms did the rest. He pushed it aside and came to his feet. Silver went to work on Zipporah's net next, while Clay faced the remaining gladiators. A short sword swung at his chest. Clay took the blow and rammed his fist into the gladiator's ridged helmet. Metal broke under the blow and the gladiator collapsed in a rustle of bone and rusted armor.

Zipporah came free. She and Silver both hurried to Harvey. Their blades moved down together, and sliced through the net. Harvey rolled over and came shakily to his feet. He had gained a bloody nose, and held his hand over his face. Blood welled between his fingers and his eyes were pained beneath his spectacles. Zipporah offered him a handkerchief and he accepted it, then quickly cleaned up the spilled blood. Clay saw the wound and shuddered. He had one job—to protect Rabbi Holtz's son— and he hadn't been able to do that.

Behind them, Rabbi Eisendrath groaned. He stood back, moaning. His hand came away from his head, shaking. Why was he so concerned about a thrown rock bashing him? His face had gone pale, making the dark lines of his tattoos stand out even more. He pointed to Silver. "You will pay for this. Whoever you are, I will see you weep because you—"

"Threats? I've heard plenty of those before, from plenty of mugs like you." She fired into the ground next to him, kicking up dust. Rabbi Eisendrath stumbled back, somehow still frightened from the blow to his head. "I covered the Great War in France, buddy. I'm pretty sure there's nothing you can do that'll scare me." She turned to Clay. "I bet I can get what I need from an interview with you. No need for an exclusive with Nosferatu here." She pointed past the trees, to the rocky hills overlooking the ocean. "Come on, Mr. Clay. I'll give you and your pals a ride home."

"Fine by me." Zipporah patted Harvey's shoulder. "Let's go."

They hurried through the trees, running past Rabbi Eisendrath. He glared at Clay as they passed. For a second, their eyes met—and something about the rabbi's face caught Clay's attention. His eyes seemed far too gray and far too round. He pulled away, refusing to look at Clay, and then they had left him behind as they scrambled through the trees. A couple weighted nets flew after them, wrapping around branches and trunks and rustling as they hit the dirt. Zipporah kept Harvey moving, and they avoided the nets. The gladiators didn't give chase. Clay would have to remember to go for the head the next time he and Rabbi Eisendrath battled.

The forest gave way to a few rocky hills. They scaled them easily enough, though Harvey slid down the gravel and had to crawl up on his hands and knees before stumbling to his feet. Clay helped him down the hill, and then they neared a gravel beach when Silver's vessel waited for them. She had a sleek speedboat of cherry-colored wood floating in the water, with Sophie behind the wheel. Lucky, her pet panda, sat on his haunches on the side seat, watching the waves hit the beach uneasily. Sophie waved to them, and Silver waved back.

"A little runabout, darling." Silver pointed to the boat. "Quite expensive— but then again, I can afford it. Would you care to go for a spin?"

Skeletal feet stepped on the rocks behind them. Roman legionaries emerged, followed by a squad of archers with arrows already notched to their bows. The Dagger Men seemed determined not to let Clay and his friends escape alive.

"We'd be delighted, ma'am. Thank you," Harvey replied politely.

They ran down the rocky slope and crossed the beach, as skeletal legionaries fired a salvo of arrows into the air. The arrows fell down, striking the gravel. One settled in Clay's back, but he ignored it and kept running. They reached the surf next. Clay grabbed Harvey, hauled him out of the water, and set him over the railing and inside the speedboat. Zipporah pulled herself over and Sophie helped her mother into the boat. Clay stepped into the speedboat next. The vessel shook under his weight and he settled in the stern. Sophie had already gotten the engine going. She spun the vessel around as legionaries hurried to the beach. Silver gave them the last shots of her revolver, and then the motor purred to life.

The speedboat zoomed away from the beach and flew into the open sea. Lucky lost his footing and slid across his chair, making forlorn yips as he neared the edge. Harvey grabbed a fistful of fur and pulled the panda back from the edge. He gingerly handed Lucky to Sophie, and the cub whimpered as she held him. The motorboat sped away, trailing a white wake.

"Are you okay, Harvey?" Sophie pointed to Harvey's nose.

"Oh, I'll be fine. It's already s-stopped bleeding, Miss Silver." He settled into his seat and looked back at Bone Island as it slid away into the mist. "Rabbi Eisendrath is a terrible person," he said. "He has too much hate. Far too much."

Silver looked up from the controls. "What was with those Roman skeletons of his? I recognized the armor from my time in Italy, covering Blackshirts and Fascists. Mussolini's boys love all that Roman crap. I didn't expect to see ancient armor up and walking around." She stared at the turf. "I came over here because I learned that a recently formed corporation, Dagger Limited, purchased a plot of land on Bone Island, intending to do some excavations. They apparently paid with ancient Roman coins. I figured I'd come over, snoop around, and ask a few questions. I wasn't expecting this."

"They're Dagger Men," Zipporah explained. "Lunatic fanatics with access to powerful magic."

"They want to conquer the city." Clay decided he could tell Silver the truth—she had already seen walking skeletons and God only knew what else during her visit to Bone Island. Lying wouldn't get him anywhere. "They mentioned that they need the Founding Stone, but can't find it on Bone Island." He paused. "I don't know what that is."

"I do." Harvey brightened up. "It's this big stone that was the center of Barebone's Town, back when Sinner Barebone founded it. He carved the Barebone name in this big stone, and it represented the new colony. He left it in Barebone's Town when he founded Sickle City, and Bathsheba Barebone had it. But in the Victorian Age, they moved it from Bone Island and into the city."

"Where, child?" Zipporah asked.

"City Hall," Harvey explained. "We saw it on a field trip." He smiled shyly at Sophie. "Have you ever been to the City Hall?"

"I have tutors. I don't really go to school," Sophie explained. "I have seen the pyramids, though. And the Great Wall of China, and the Tower of London, and some other places."

"Cripes." Harvey whispered. "You're like some kind of globetrotting hero..." His face flushed red.

"We're well-traveled, dear heart," Silver added. She turned to Clay and Zipporah. "But this is one scoop that's a little too big, even for me." She sighed. "I hate to say it, but we need to tell Edwin Eames about what's going on. If these rabid rabbis want the Founding Stone for some kooky spell, the damned rock must be safeguarded." She gave the wheel of the speedboat another twist, sending it zooming over the waves. "We'll go straight to the Wigwam Club and meet with him. Tell him what happened and see what he can do about it."

"Why, Miss Silver," Zipporah said. "You sound almost like a responsible citizen."

"Let's not go that far," Silver said. "There's nothing like putting one's self in the center of a story. The readers of the *Weekly Sophisticate* are well aware of that fact. Now, let's see where this story leads." She directed the speedboat over the sea, returning to Sickle Bay. Sickle City loomed above them, lost in the mist. Clay settled down and listened to Harvey and Sophie talk in quiet tones about all their various travels and adventures. Lucky crawled over to his lap and rooted around in his tattered trench coat. He leaned back and let it happen as they returned to the city.

The Wigwam Club rested on Damocles Street, about a block away from Tier Tower and Arcadia Park. For nearly a century, this political club had hoarded all power in Sickle City, like a dragon hoarding its gold. It resembled a neo-classical junk heap, all gilded pillars and statues of swooping American eagles looming from the ceiling as ornate chandeliers. American flags bedecked the walls, covering everything in limp displays of red, white, and blue. When Clay and his friends arrived, the place was in an uproar. Clerks darted about through the narrow halls, carrying piles of spilling paper. Phones rang continuously, adding to the cacophony of increased conversation. Clay and the others settled into a waiting room, where ward bosses, businessmen, police officers, and even honest citizens crowded together on the tiled floor and tried to get an audience with Edwin Eames. His harried secretary struggled through appointments as the minutes ticked away.

Harvey stared at the chaos of the Wigwam Club as security guards hauled out a squad of reporters. Flash bulbs clicked and glowed as their photographers snapped pictures of the mess. "Is this all because of the police strike?"

"You hit the nail on the head, kid," Silver said. "I think old Edwin spoke a little too soon in his big fancy zeppelin about the strike dying down. The policemen in this city are treated like garbage—it's no wonder so many of them take bribes as a matter of principle—and now they're being treated like upstart Bolsheviks when they try to get something a little better. They're gonna strike, and then this whole city will have no law."

"For how long?" Clay asked.

Zipporah settled into her seat. "Long enough for the Dagger Men to make their play, whatever it is." No one had even asked her to leave her scimitars outside. She probably could have come inside toting a machine gun and nobody would have noticed. She called to the secretary. "We need to see Mr. Eames. It's important."

"He's not taking any visitors at the moment," the secretary said, trying to be polite. "Regrettably, he is busy with important matters of state. If you would continue to wait patiently, then I'm certain—"

"Tell him that Rabbi Holtz's representative is here," Clay suggested. "That might get him interested."

The secretary nodded weakly, his pince-nez glasses slipping down his sweaty nose, and ducked into Eames's office. A moment later, his head reappeared in the door. "Grand Sagamore Eames will see you now," he said. He held open the door as Clay and the others filed inside. Lucky snapped his teeth at the secretary, who sighed and shuffled back to his desk.

Eames' office had the refined, elegant look of a place that was more for display than actual use. A desk the size of a grand piano housed rows of sculptures of majestically flying eagles and Revolutionary War soldiers in attitudes of heroism, and assorted plaques, trophies, and decorative trophies and weapons that he had earned in his service. Vast bookshelves occupied the walls, overlooking the sort of walnut furniture found in smoking rooms in gentleman's clubs. Eames himself sat in shirtsleeves behind the desk. A window looked out on the street behind him, giving him a great view of Arcadia Park—but he wasn't paying any attention. He torched a Cuban with his desk's lighter as Clay and his friends came in. Another man stood in the corner, ramrod straight and staring at the books.

Clay removed his fedora. "Mr. Eames." He nodded. "I'm afraid we've got some bad news."

"And what a shock it will be for me to hear it, after I've had nothing but joyous tidings since the sunrise." Eames put his feet on the desk as he sucked in cigar smoke. "Clay, let me introduce you to a fellow man of action." He waved his cigar at the fellow in the corner. "Orton—get over here."

"I don't think we have time for pleasantries, Eames," Silver said. "We've got a warning for you, and something tells me you better hear it."

"My dear Miss Silver—I'm starting to wish I had thrown you off my airship yesterday." Eames stood up and threw his arm around his other guest. "This is Orton Sinclair, one of the founders of the Sinclair-Koots Detective Agency. His valiant guards will be defending our fine city from all threats, especially after the worthless police force goes on strike."

Sinclair approached Clay. They recognized each other instantly. "Clay?" Sinclair asked. "It's good to see you." He looked just like Clay remembered him, when they served together in the Polar Bear Expedition, with a stiff bearing, reddish handlebar moustache, and hooded, dark eyes. He wore his black suit and bowler hat like a uniform. He and Clay shook hands. "I suppose things haven't changed that much. I'm still hunting Bolsheviks, though now my quarry resides in America."

"Hunting Bolsheviks?" Harvey asked.

"Exactly, young man." Sinclair answered briskly. "You see, the Bureau of Investigation regards the upcoming police strike as an opportunity. The enemies of America, many of them aliens—Polacks, Hungarians, Jews, and that sort, will attempt to rise up and create some sort of Marxist Revolution. But we can snatch them up first and see them swiftly deported. The Bureau's paying me and my detectives a great deal of money to assist them, and we'll be earning additional funds protecting the city for Mr. Eames. This is good work, Clay. Perhaps there's a place for you at our side." He turned to Silver. "But what was your concern, ma'am?"

So Sinclair hadn't left the soldiering game—though now he worked for hire. And if he was going after Bolsheviks, then Herbert Holtz might end up in the crosshairs. He was an immigrant, after all, even if he had come over when he was barely old enough to walk.

Zipporah glanced at Harvey, recognizing his panic. "One thing at a time." She pointed to Eames. "Clay already told you about the Dagger Men. Well, we were just spying on them and we found out a little more. They're going to try and create some sort of spell, which they'll use to conquer Sickle City."

"It depends on the Founding Stone, sir," Sophie said, holding a squirming Lucky in her arms. "You need to protect it."

"The Founding Stone?" Eames asked. "That old museum piece at City Hall? They've got it right in the lobby, you know, so that every visitor can see our noble heritage." He slumped on his desk. "And you believe that these Dagger Men will make an attempt to capture the stone, as an ingredient in some mystical recipe? And they'll use the chaos of the police strike to attempt this theft?"

"Yeah," Clay said.

"Well, it's certainly an interesting story. And I'll try to have some detectives guarding City Hall—but there are so many other potential targets for looting or anarchist sabotage that we must defend." Eames sat at the table and rested his head in his hands. "Here's a moment of honesty, a rarity, I know. When the strike is over, I'm not certain this *city* will remain standing. But I will do my best. I owe Rabbi Holtz that at least." Eames stubbed his cigar out on the desk, ignoring the way that it burned the wood. "Now, do you have any other concerns?"

Before Clay could reply, a chant reached the office. "Policeman's strike is here to stay! Better conditions! Better pay!" The chant came from a crowd marching out of Arcadia Park to stand in the street. "Policeman's strike is here to stay! Better conditions! Better pay!" Some policemen wore their blue uniforms while other dressed in civilian clothes. They wielded their signs and marched straight up to the Wigwam Club, bellowing their slogans.

Eames looked out the window and whimpered. He glanced at Clay. "No more visitors. Get out."

"But the Dagger Men—" Harvey started.

"You heard him." Sinclair spoke with a cold tone. "Get out."

There was nothing else they could do. Clay turned around and Zipporah and Harvey followed him. The Silvers joined them in the hall. They left the Wigwam Club and walked down the marble steps. The protesting policemen stood before them, shouting their slogans as reporters snapped photos. A small crowd had gathered to watch, some of them joining in with the chant.

Silver took her daughter's hand. "Come along, Sophie. We'll catch a cab back to the apartment. I think we'll want to be indoors for what's coming next." She waved goodbye to Clay, Zipporah, and Harvey as they walked down the steps. "You should do the same. Get somewhere safe, Mr. Clay—and it was a thrill working with you!" They moved down the sidewalk, Sophie dragging Lucky on his leash.

Harvey waved to them. "Goodbye!" Then he turned to the crowd. "Oh, Uncle Herbert. Hello!"

Herbert Holtz walked over, Bethany Hark at his side. He shook hands with Clay and Zipporah and patted Harvey's head. "Hello there." A boyish smile filled Herbert's face. "Bethany and I were in a Northside coffeehouse when we heard the news and had to come see it for ourselves."

"And it seems the rumors were true," Hark added.

"Isn't it marvelous?" Herbert extended his hands, as if he wanted to embrace the police.

"What do you mean?" Zipporah asked.

"The strike—workers asserting themselves and agitating for their rights." Herbert squeezed Harvey's shoulder. "This could be it—the beginnings of revolution in America, and an end to capitalist tyranny. Perhaps other workers will soon follow the police, and they will become the vanguard of a revolutionary struggle."

He seemed delighted, but Clay didn't share his enthusiasm. The strike had begun and there would be no law in Sickle City until it ended. The Dagger Men would take full advantage of the chaos. As far as Clay was concerned, only misery lay ahead.

Chapter Five
STRIKE!

They took a cab straight back to Haven Street, only to find Uptown boiling in an uproar over the strike. Newsboys stood on every corner, loudly hawking extras and announcing that the law in Sickle City had vanished. The upper class citizens of Damocles Street acted accordingly. They hastened over the sidewalks, packed into their luxury automobiles and cabs, and struggled to make it home to their families before the lack of law led to chaos. A few accidents slowed traffic even more, as automobiles rammed into each other in their haste to escape. Arcadia Park emptied completely. Even the birds left the thick copses of forests and decorative Greek ruins, escaping into the sky in vast clouds. Clay wondered if the rats and pigeons of Sickle City wanted to leave as well, to get away from what would soon happen. He envied everything with wings.

With traffic a wild crawl of honking horns and packed intersections, it took them nearly an hour to return to Haven Street. As soon as they reached the border of Little Jerusalem and the seaside, poorest neighborhood of Neptune Row, Clay ordered the taxi to swing to the curb and let them out. They would make better time on foot. He paid the cab driver double, and the taxi careened back into traffic with a flurry of honks from its horn. Clay stood next to Harvey and Zipporah, looking over the desolate expanse of Neptune Row. Vending stalls stood empty on the sidewalk, the street had no occupants, and every door and window had been closed. A single draft horse, absurdly large, trotted forlornly down the road and stepped into an alley.

Harvey looked at the street in horror, his face becoming a panicked shade of pale. "W-what happened? Where is everyone?"

"They must have fled—expecting violence," Zipporah explained. "There's one place they would go, child—your father's synagogue." She pointed down the street. "We should be there too. We need to tell Rabbi Holtz what we discovered on Bone Island. If there's trouble, maybe we can help."

"Trouble?" Harvey stared up at Clay. "What do you mean? Do you think we're in danger?"

"Everyone's in danger," Clay replied. "Come on."

A quick walk down the street and turn around the corner brought them to Atlas Avenue, the wealthier section of Haven Street. Rabbi Holtz and Harvey had their house near the end of this wide, tree-lined block. Closer to Neptune Row, the King Solomon Synagogue offered a constant sanctuary. It loomed over the street, a rectangular structure of somber gray stone under the shade of several leafy trees. A large cement sign displayed a Jewish star and the name of the synagogue in Hebrew, English, and Yiddish. Unlike every other business and tenement building on Haven Street, the doors of the King Solomon Synagogue stood open, and ready to offer sanctuary to anyone who needed it.

Clay led his friends past the lawn and to the door. Monk Moss and Carmen Cohen leaned against the stout pillars flanking the entrance, both watching the empty street. Monk had his trench gun leaning on his shoulder, while Carmen had a hand firmly wrapped around her machete.

They nodded politely as Clay, Zipporah, and Harvey approached.

Monk leaned over and patted Harvey's head. "How's it going, little fellow? Solve some mysteries on your day off from school?"

"A few," Harvey said. "What's going on here?"

"We're protecting our people," Cohen explained. "The city's got no law at all, not with every worthless *cabrone* in blue on strike. Soon enough, all the scavengers are gonna come creeping out of their holes, eager to steal as much as they can. Old scores can be settled, and new crimes committed without fear of arrest. Haven Street could be a tempting target." She patted the handle of her machete. "We're here to make sure it ain't so tempting."

"We'll help," Clay explained.

Zipporah nodded. "Amen to that. Say, how's the rabbi?"

"He wants to talk with you." Monk jabbed a thumb into the hall. "He's in his office, getting some things ready." He grinned at Harvey. "You'd better bring the boy with you. The rabbi's been worried sick about him, and seeing that Harvey's all right will put his mind at ease. You go and see him, then come out here and stand guard."

"Could I stand guard too?" Harvey asked. "Maybe I could—"

"We're going to see your father." Clay put his hand on Harvey's shoulder. "Come on."

He steered the boy into the synagogue, with Zipporah trailing behind. They stepped through the barren marble lobby and entered the main synagogue hall. The residents of Haven Street packed the place—perhaps a hundred or so people crowding the pews or sitting in the aisles. Men and women huddled together, clutching quickly chosen bags of their most precious belongings. Children played, stepping around the seated adults, or slept on the wooden pews or floors in makeshift beds of jackets and crumpled hats. Even several Chasids, with their ear-locks and beards, huddled together in their own corner of the synagogue. They had all gathered here, seeking the protection that they knew Rabbi Holtz could offer. Back in the Old Country, they had done the same thing whenever Cossack pogroms threatened to break out. Here in America, the old nightmare had come true, and all they could do was gather together and pray for the best to a God who never seemed to listen.

Harvey looked them over. "My father will protect them." He spoke quietly. "And you'll help too, Mr. Clay—and so will Miss Sarfati. If there's trouble, these people will be safe." He looked up at Clay. "Right?" Hope made his voice quiver.

"Yeah," Clay said. "Come on."

They walked through the synagogue. The citizens of Haven Street pulled back, clearing a path. Parents pulled their children close. Fingers pointed at Clay and his friends, and hushed whispers filled the synagogue. Harvey turned away, focusing on staring ahead at the distant door beside the large, silver cabinet where the Holy Torah scrolls rested. He must have heard the whispers—the same ones leveled at him wherever he went in Haven Street—but he ignored them, and walked ahead to the door. Zipporah held it open, and they passed through a small corridor into the back room, which Rabbi Holtz had turned into his office.

Bookshelves lined the chamber, surrounding a desk currently covered in weapons and ammunition. A pair of rifles, a shotgun, and numerous pistols sat on the dusty wood, beside several holy books. Rabbi Holtz stood behind the desk, carefully sliding bullets into a revolver. Detective Flynn sat in the Morris chair in front of his desk, talking quietly. They both ended their conversation as Clay and the others entered.

"Papa!" Harvey hurried around the desk and ran to his father. They embraced quickly. "I'm sorry I missed school, but we went to Bone Island, and found the Dagger Men, and I think we know their plan. Well, we sort of do." He stammered as everyone looked at him. "They're gonna try to capture the Founding Stone, the first stone laid by the settlers of Sickle City, and cast some kind of spell on it. You see, the Founding Stone is part of an enchantment left by the witches of Bone Island, which has been building for centuries, and we think the Dagger Men want to use it."

"What will they do with this magic, *boychick*?" Rabbi Holtz asked.

Harvey rested his hands in his pockets and looked at his Buster Browns. "I don't know."

"I can promise you that it won't be good," Zipporah explained. "They had some chains in Bone Island—magic chains—and they were talking about summoning Asmodeus himself and hogtying him, though I couldn't tell you why."

"We told Edwin Eames," Clay explained. "The Dagger Men might very well use the chaos caused by this strike to make a move on City Hall. We should be there, to defend it." He wanted to see Rabbi Eisendrath again, and defeat him once and for all. "Maybe we can defeat the Dagger Men for good."

Detective Flynn withdrew himself from his Morris chair—a slow and laborious process. He looked like he hadn't slept or changed his pale blue suit for at least a trio of very busy days. "I think you might have more pressing problems, Mr. Clay." He pointed to the window in the corner of

"Papa! I'm sorry I missed school today."

the office, overlooking Atlas Avenue. "A few policemen are keeping tabs on the city, passing around updates and trying to make sure everything doesn't go completely to Hell. They told me that someone in the Rookery had the great idea of raiding Haven Street, as you Heebs have fortunes squirreled away. They could be coming any second." The Rookery was the poorest section of Sickle City, a slum of outcasts and outlaws with respect for nothing but an intense hunger.

"Fortunes?" Harvey asked.

"Bigoted heels," Zipporah said. "The same as anywhere."

Rabbi Holtz picked up his revolver. "We can't count on the police to protect us. Not that we ever could—not really." He glanced at Detective Flynn. "No offense, detective."

"None taken, Rabbi." Detective Flynn came to his feet. He reached for his bowler hat, which rested on the edge of the desk. "But I wouldn't take it personally. This sort of thing will be happening all over the city. It will end when Eames wises up, swallows his pride, and calls in the National Guard or the Marines or the like. Or when he caves in and gives the striking officers what they want and they go back to work and restore order. Until then, I'm expecting more looting and riots." He sighed. "Another sunny day in Sickle City."

"You're leaving?" Zipporah asked.

"I've got to check in with the other officers, and see what else is transpiring. If there's any pertinent information concerning the Dagger Men or City Hall, I'll give you a ring—as long as the telephones still work, of course." He paused, his hat in hand. "Oh, and Rabbi? It is close enough to the end of the month, if you don't mind."

Rabbi Holtz pulled open the bottom drawer of his desk and grabbed an envelope, thick with cash. He tossed it to Detective Flynn. "Take it and go."

"Grand." Detective Flynn pocketed the bribe. "You're a saint, Rabbi—or you would be, if your people had such things." He walked to the door, then paused and his feigned joviality vanished. He looked straight at Clay. "You look after your friends, Mr. Clay. Stay safe and good luck."

"Thank you." Clay turned back to Rabbi Holtz as Detective Flynn left. "Should we go to City Hall, to protect the Founding Stone?"

"Not yet, my friend. I need you here." Rabbi Holtz removed his spectacles and began cleaning them with his handkerchief. His hands shook as he automatically scraped the fabric across the lenses. "If what Detective Flynn is saying is true, this mob will soon be approaching Haven Street. They'll come here—searching for silver candlesticks and golden Torah covers and breastplates, and all the finery that the greedy Jews hoard. I'll need you and Miss Sarfati to frighten them off." He stared at Harvey. "And I want my son here, where we can protect him."

"But the Founding Stone and the Dagger Men—" Harvey started.

Rabbi Holtz's voice went firm. "You'll stay here, *boychick*. We'll look after our own."

"But the whole city's at stake!" Harvey's voice cracked, squeaking in a mixture of fear, desperation, and anger. "Everybody will suffer if the Dagger Men succeed. Maybe we can frighten off the mob really quickly, and then—"

"*Goyim*, you mean." Rabbi Holtz walked out from behind the desk and towered over his son. "The Dagger Men threaten the *goyim*—the same *goyim* who march against us, just as they did in Russia. They have nothing but disdain for us, and this proves it. We will always be Yids in their eyes, and never fit in. No wonder they make us their targets."

"That's n-not true, sir," Harvey said. "We're Americans—just like the people on Damocles Street, or Hogshead Street, or Chinatown. We're all Americans, and we need to look out for each other. Uncle Herbert's right about that. These differences, race or religion or whatever, just cause problems." He lowered her voice. "We're all Americans, and we need to protect each other and take care of each other. That's the right thing to do." He lowered his head.

"You're a good boy, Harvey." Rabbi Holtz cupped Harvey's chin, making him look into his eyes. "But you're wrong." He withdrew the revolver and slid it into his coat, and then selected a double-barreled shotgun. "Mr. Clay, Miss Sarfati—please follow me outside." He started to the door, and then glanced back at Harvey. "Please stay here, *boychick*. Stay safe."

"We'll be back soon, child," Zipporah added.

"And then we'll go to City Hall," Clay promised. "Don't worry."

Harvey watched as they walked to the door. "Be careful!" He waved goodbye as they stepped into the hall. "Please, be careful." He nearly whispered the final words, and then Rabbi Holtz closed the office door. His son would be safe now. He nodded to Clay and Zipporah, and motioned back to the synagogue hall.

They walked through once again, Clay and Zipporah flanking Rabbi Holtz. Zipporah pulled out her scimitars, and rested them on her shoulders. Rabbi Holtz toted his shotgun. The synagogue residents fell silent and stepped aside. A few muttered prayers or well wishes in Hebrew or English. They bowed their heads as the defenders of Haven Street walked outside.

Monk and Cohen waited in the doorway. Cohen removed her fedora as Rabbi Holtz, Zipporah, and Clay walked outside. "Detective Flynn left a few minutes ago, but we've got some more guests now." She pointed down the street. "I don't think they're here for services."

The mob from the Rookery had arrived. They clustered together, marching in a mass down the center of Atlas Avenue and heading straight for the King Solomon Synagogue. Clay counted at least three score men, along with several women and numerous teenagers and children, who walked with the same vehemence and dark purpose as the other would-be looters. They carried the weapons of the street—axe handles, baseball bats, lead pipes, broken bottles, and knives. Others carried bricks or paving stones, ready for throwing. They didn't bother with the other businesses flanking the street. Rumor had given King Solomon Synagogue riches, and they wanted their share.

Clay and his friends looked over the mob. How could five people, even with guns, stand against such a mob? Clay could wade into their ranks and start killing, but even then he would be overwhelmed. Besides, he had no desire to spill that much blood. Rabbi Holtz and the others seemed to feel the same fears. The mob drew closer, spitting hateful shouts into the cold air. "Goddamn Christ-killers! Let's take back what they stole! They been secretly running the world—I read this book that told me all about it!" The anti-Semitic shouts echoed over the street, as the mob prepared itself for violence.

Zipporah readied her blades. "Sure are a lot of them."

"Nuts." Monk removed his straw boater's hat and scratched his head. "You know something? I ain't even a Jew." Clay stared at him. "I'm serious. I'm German, Dutch, and a little Irish. But me and the rabbi been friends since we was both in short pants. That's why I've been helping him." He racked the pump on his shotgun. "Good a reason as any, I suppose."

"What do you want to do, Rabbi?" Cohen asked Rabbi Holtz. "I can drop the first couple. Make them scatter."

"No." Rabbi Holtz watched the mob over his spectacles. "If we open fire, they'll charge and wipe us out. I don't want us killing any of them, either. This strike will end, one way or the other, and then there'll be countless witnesses to the five murderous Jews who struck down innocent Christians in the street of their own city." He gripped his shotgun. "We need to scare them."

"We'll need bigger guns for that," Clay said.

"I think I have just the ticket." Cohen pointed back to the King Solomon

Synagogue. "It's waiting in your basement, Rabbi Holtz—a little souvenir I brought back with me after serving so long with Pancho Villa. That might make the mob afraid."

"Get it, Mrs. Cohen," Rabbi Holtz said. "And hurry."

Cohen raced back to the synagogue, her boots clicking over the street. While she ran, the mob drew closer. The fellow serving as their appointed leader moved to their head, and pointed at Rabbi Holtz with a baseball bat, studded with nails. "Christ Almighty, I can almost smell the stink of vermin on you." He had his sleeves rolled back, revealing thick forearms covered in tattoos of curling serpents. "I'm tired at looking at your big-nosed faces. Step aside, Christ-killers, and let us take what we want." His face went red with rage under his walrus moustache.

Rabbi Holtz gazed up at the big fellow. "You're not going one step further."

"What are you gonna do about it, Mr. Kike? You think I—"

Without hesitation, Rabbi Holtz swung the barrel of the shotgun into the mob leader's head. The barrel cut the skin of his cheek and knocked his head to the side. He tried to raise his bat, but Rabbi Holtz had already rammed the butt of his shotgun into the thug's knee. Bone splintered and the fellow collapsed. Rabbi Holtz kicked him, driving a loafer between his ribs. He moved back, swinging his shotgun to cover the mob. That gun alone didn't stop them.

A few more brave souls charged out, calling for their friends to help. Brickbats hurtled from the hands of the mob, arcing in the air before clattering down in a painful rain. A brick banged against Clay's shoulder, and he ignored it. Zipporah caught a rock against her chest, and she grunted and sank down. Clay wanted to run to her, but there was no time. The mob's toughest hurried out to meet him and Clay steeled himself for a brawl.

The first to reach Clay looked like he knew what he was doing—he had the stance and muscles of a prizefighter, with a crushed nose and cauliflower ears that proved he lost as many bouts as he won. He swung at Clay, feinting from the right before swinging a rapid left that connected. All the boxer did was bruise his knuckles. He pulled back his hand, wincing as he shook his fingers, and Clay dealt him a haymaker that sent him sprawling to the street. The next member of the mob struck Clay with a pickaxe handle. The wood shattered as it slammed against Clay's shoulder, the force of the blow making Clay stumble. He prepared to hit back, when a flying brick bounced off his eyes. Gravel rattled across his face. Clay stumbled back.

Zipporah moved in on the fellow with the pickaxe handle, an oversized brigand with a protruding gut and a porkpie hat which seemed far too small for his massive head. He swung the remains of the pickaxe handle at Zipporah, and she met it with her swords. The scimitars cut the pickaxe handle apart. The looter had a second to look at his former weapon before Zipporah slapped his cheek with the flat of her blade to upset him, and toppled him with a swift elbow to the chin.

Next to her, Monk Moss and Rabbi Holtz dealt with other, eager members of the mob. Clay could see them from where he stood, dealing damage at every rioter coming their way. Monk had slung his trench gun over his shoulder, and used a trench club from the war with great effect. The club consisted of a hollowed grenade topping an iron bar. Monk broke bones and smashed teeth out of mouths with rapid strikes. He tackled one rioter, knocking the fellow down and then working over his face with a few rapid strikes. Rabbi Holtz simply bashed anyone close with the butt of his shotgun. The two of them had grown up in the slums of Haven Street, and knew just how to win a back-alley brawl. They dealt with every member of the mob who came their way.

Still, Clay knew they couldn't last long. He grabbed an extended arm, ignoring the meat cleaver slashing against his sleeve, and hauled his attacker into the air. The stout, towheaded looter wailed as Clay sent him soaring through the air and back into the mob. He turned to the next target, only for a rain of bottles and bricks to pelt him. He raised his hands, sheltering his head—which only inspired the mob to increase their barrage. A brick banged hard into his face, right below the holy words. Clay moved back, trying to put his back to the mob.

"Clay!" Zipporah noticed. "Don't worry. We can hold them off—get further back up the street, and—" A brick slammed into her back. Zipporah gasped and crumpled, her sword dipping and pointing to the street. Zipporah winced, but returned to a swordsman's stance as more of the mob surged closer. She kicked wildly, keeping the attackers back.

Clay moved closer to her. He punched madly, using wide sweeps of his arms to hold back the attackers. Rabbi Holtz fired one barrel of his shotgun, shooting above the heads of the Mob. They ducked back, the looters hurrying away from the blast—but their courage would come again, and they would charge and Clay and his friends would be overwhelmed. Already, another volley of brickbats flew toward them. Bricks shattered and rattled on the street, and Clay stepped in front of the others, to take as many blows as he could.

Monk realized what was happening as well. "We can't win." He spat, his drool a pale red. "They outnumber us." He returned the trench club to his coat. "We need to start killing them, Rabbi. I know you don't care for it, being a holy man and all, but I think blasting a few skulls wouldn't go amiss."

"No." Rabbi Holtz stumbled as he moved out of Clay's shadow, readying the shotgun butt for another strike. "No deaths. Not on Haven Street."

"Admirable, Rabbi." Zipporah pointed her scimitars at the mob. "But I don't know if we—"

"No one dies on my command." Rabbi Holtz glared at her. "I could not face my son, if that happened." It was true enough. Clay looked at his fists as his body creaked. He could start killing as well, but that would turn him back into the cold, violent machine he had been in Russia. He couldn't go back to that, and he knew that the rabbi felt something similar.

The mob recovered its rage. Their broad-shouldered, tattooed leader picked himself back up. He rubbed blood from his mouth. "Rush them, boys!" he roared, waving for the mob to group around him. "Maybe those damn Hebrews will get a few—but they won't get us all!" He pointed a broken bottle at Rabbi Holtz, the edge glinting in cold sunlight. "But you leave that one to me." He waved the bottle like some general's sword, and the mob advanced.

"You want to reconsider, Rabbi?" Monk withdrew his trench gun and leveled it at the mob. Bricks and broken bottles clattered around his boots. "Maybe I could just kill a few of them, and you wouldn't have to tell little Harvey nothing about it?"

"No." Rabbi Holtz glanced over his shoulder. "There's no need."

Carmen Cohen walked out of the King Solomon Synagogue, holding a large canvas bundle in her hands. She stepped carefully to the sidewalk, reached the street, and let the canvas fall away from what she carried. A heavy machine gun, the kind used to devastating effect on the Western Front, rested in her hands. Cohen prepared it with practiced precision and speed. She snapped open the tripod and rested it on the ground, then fell to a kneeling position. One hand gripped the handle of the gun while the other threaded in the belt of ammunition. She rested her hands on the trigger, her eyes calm as she swiveled the machine gun to face the mob.

Rabbi Holtz pointed to Cohen. "Run to her!"

They dashed up the street, hurrying through a rain of brickbats. All the detritus of the streets tumbled around them. Clay could feel bricks bouncing off his shoulder. Zipporah caught another, somewhere on her back. She fell, and Rabbi Holtz grabbed her arm and tugged her along before she could reach the street. Behind them, the mob charged—emboldened by their sudden retreat. Their feet rang out against the stone, as they raced straight for King Solomon Synagogue. They were blood-mad, full of the same greed and prejudice that had filled the Cossacks in the Old Country. Clay felt the urge to stop running and start killing, but Cohen had other ideas.

She fired the heavy machine gun into the air. Bullets roared in the street, kicking up a spray of sparks and dust. Cohen fired into the air again, sending a burst hurtling over the head of the charging mob. The sudden, terrible roar of the machine gun brought them to a halt. A few blasts from shotguns or revolvers could only stop one or two of them—but a heavy machine gun would wipe out the entire mob in a matter of seconds. Cohen kept firing over their heads. Members of the mob tossed down their weapons. She sent a burst at the leader, a single bullet which shattered the bottle in his hand. He gasped, his fingers bloody from the broken glass.

After the staccato blasts, Cohen let the machine gun fall silent. The mob had stopped its charge, but still stood around in the street—unsure what to do. Rabbi Holtz walked in front of the machine gun and faced the mob. "On a single word from me, you will all be cut down. You understand me?" He roared out the words. His voice echoed over the silent street. Rabbi Holtz pointed down the street. "Go somewhere else. Haven Street is protected." The mob simply stood and watched him. Bravado and fear battled in their brains. Rabbi Holtz turned to Cohen. "Give them another blast. Let them know we're serious."

"Si, Rabbi." Cohen sent another couple shots rattling into the air. The bullets hummed over the heads of the mob, even knocking off a tall fellow's straw boater's hat. They began to break. Members of the mob drifted away, heading to the safety of alleyways or simply walking back down the street. Cohen kept the machine gun trained on the remaining men.

Their leader gripped his bleeding hand. He glanced at his mob and they stared at him—waiting for his order. "Let's go to Chinatown. Those heathen Chinese are the lowest scum in the city. I bet they have all kinds of fine goods, hidden away and ripe for the taking. Or maybe we'll go to Hogshead Street, teach the Negroes a lesson or two. Those darkies deserve it." He turned away and started walking, doing his best to keep his head up. Cohen sent a shot whizzing past him, and he broke into a run, almost tripping in his haste to flee.

That did it for the mob. They dispersed or fled, scrambling away from

Haven Street. Clay watched them leave and lowered his fists. For the moment, Haven Street was safe. He looked at his friends, who had helped protect the street, and noticed the injuries they had taken. They needed rest and safety—but the police strike continued, and so would the lawlessness.

"Back to the synagogue." Rabbi Holtz offered his hand to Zipporah. "Well done."

"It was Cohen's doing, mostly," Zipporah said. "Nothing like a heavy machine gun to make folks decide on a different course of action. I used one of those a time or two in Mesopotamia, out in the desert. Damn useful weapons."

"True enough." Cohen picked up the machine gun, using a rag to hold the burning barrel. "Damn heavy as well. When I was younger, I could carry this across the desert, set up on some hill and wipe out a pack of Federales. No longer, though. Still, I suppose it served its purpose." She started back to the synagogue, and the others followed.

But as they neared the entrance, the double doors slammed open. Harvey hurried out. "Papa, I just got a call about Uncle Herbert!" The words spilled out of him in his panic. He darted in front of his father. "He's in trouble, very big trouble, and we need to help him. Detective Flynn just called, and he said that—" Harvey paused and looked at Monk and Zipporah. "Oh, Miss Sarfati. Mr. Moss. Are you okay?"

"Just a bit of a scrap," Monk explained.

"We'll live, child," Zipporah said. "What about your uncle?"

Harvey turned to his father. "Detective Flynn just called. He heard from some of his fellow officers that these private detectives Eames hired—the Sinclair-Koots Detective Agency—have found out where Herbert is staying. He's at the Bower Green, a greenhouse cafe in Finch Bower. They're gonna capture him and maybe then they'll deport him! Or interrogate him, and torture him." Harvey grabbed his father's hand. "We have to help him."

"We are needed here," Rabbi Holtz explained. "I'll call Eames and some of my friends, explain about Herbert, and see if we can—"

"There's not enough time." Harvey turned to Clay. "Mr. Clay, Miss Sarfati—could you please go with me and rescue Herbert?"

Zipporah stared at Rabbi Holtz. He shook his head. "You need to stay here, Harvey, where it's safe. Your uncle has made some very foolish decisions. Cavorting with communists and radicals, involving himself with a—with a *shikse*. He should have expected something like this."

"I don't care." Harvey let his father's hand fall. "He's my uncle and he's your brother. I love him and I won't let him be deported or hurt." He stepped back. "I'm going to Finch Bower and I'm going to warn him and rescue him. Even if y-you say I shouldn't." Harvey rarely disobeyed his father, but he seemed willing to now. He stepped back, stared at Rabbi Holtz, and then turned and ran—going the wrong way down the empty street.

Rabbi Holtz sighed. "His mother could be just as willful," he mused. He looked at Clay and Zipporah. "Go with him. Other mobs could be around—other looters. I am needed here, with my people. Monk and Mrs. Cohen can help me." He offered his hand to Clay. "But please protect my brother, and my son. Can you do that, Mr. Clay?"

"I will," Clay promised.

He shook Rabbi Holtz's hand. "Harvey! My automobile is this way." Harvey stopped running and reversed direction. He followed Clay and Zipporah as they crossed the street, went another block and reached the Studebaker. Clay drove, while Zipporah took some bandages from the glove compartment and did her best to cover her cuts and bruises. Harvey watched her from the passenger seat, terrified by the sight of his wounded friend. Zipporah offered him a quick smile as they drove along. In the distance, smoke rose from fires started elsewhere in the city. Gunshots rang out from the direction of the Rookery, the cracks loud and clear. The riots would continue, just as Detective Flynn had promised. Clay hoped that some would come to their senses soon, before the Dagger Men made their move, or it might be too late for the entire city.

Finch Bower lay to the north of Haven Street, the center of Bohemian life in the city. Neat houses with colorful gables bordered the wide, tree-lined street, surrounding coffee shops, restaurants, and jazz clubs. Normally, the streets would be full of couples strolling together, artists composing pictures of the scene, and diners enjoying the outdoor cafes. Instead, everything seemed deserted. Looters had smashed up a coffee shop, destroying furniture and spilling milk out into the street. It trickled down a storm drain as the Studebaker drove past.

They sped to the center of Finch Bower, where the Bower Green rested on a wide green lawn. The rioters had overturned a carriage on the street, and its wheels spun in the light wind. The spokes cast long shadows over the pavement. Harvey held his breath as the Studebaker circled the lawn and the Bower Green, an oversized octagonal glasshouse full of greenery. The frosted glass prevented anyone from seeing anything inside beyond muted shades of emerald. Clay drove around, looking for any looters, or sign of the Sinclair-Koots Agency. He didn't see anything. They had either arrived on time, or far too late. He parked the automobile at the back of the lawn, and they emerged into the cold sunlight. Clay's boots settled on the grass.

"He's in there, I think," Harvey said. "We'd better hurry—before the detectives get here." He crossed the grass, with Clay and Zipporah close behind. Harvey glanced back at them. "Do y-you think my father will be angry, Mr. Clay?"

"He'll understand," Clay said. "Herbert is his brother."

"But he and Herbert have been fighting—they had that huge argument at my house, just two days ago." Harvey stopped running. "Maybe—maybe my father sort of wants Herbert to be deported, so he doesn't have to deal with him anymore."

"That's not true." Zipporah stepped closer to Harvey. "They are brothers and they love each other. They both love you as well. There's a bond among you three, and it will never be broken. Your other uncle, Chaim Holtz, has that bond too. They may have had their arguments, but if Chaim Holtz showed up tomorrow, they would welcome him with open arms." She smiled. "My parents are dead and I had no siblings. I have no family at all—but you do, child, and you should never take it for granted."

"Thank you, Miss Sarfati," Harvey agreed. "Now let's save my uncle."

A brick pathway cut across the grass, leading to the entrance of the Bower Green. The door had been shut, but swung open when Clay put some pressure against it. They walked into the Bower Green. It only had a few occupants—about a half-dozen of Herbert's radical friends, who sat at the round tables amongst the endless shrubbery, hanging vines, and long rows of flowers that filled the greenhouse. Warmth filled the air and Herbert and his friends had shed their coats and stood in vests and shirtsleeves. The Bower Green contained a few tropical birds and butterflies, which seemed to feel the agitation that had settled over the city. They fluttered from branch to branch, adding creaking calls that rang off the glass panes in the walls.

Herbert sat at the table near the entrance, next to Bethany Hark. They had both been enjoying mugs of tea. Herbert sprang up when Harvey entered. "Harvey—my God." He ran to the boy. "What are you doing out here? You shouldn't be here, Harvey—not with the city like this." He glared at Clay. "Take him back to Haven Street. My brother will protect him."

"We came to warn you, Uncle Herbert." Harvey pointed to the door. "The Sinclair-Koots Detective Agency was hired by Mr. Eames to police the city, during the strike—but they're just using the chaos as an excuse to arrest everyone they think is a radical, so they can hand them over to the Bureau of Investigation and they'll be deported, or tortured, or killed."

Hark almost calmly sipped her tea. "The same happened in China— and happens still. I should have expected that the purges and crackdowns in Shanghai would soon come to America as well. I'm just surprised it took so long."

"Sinclair-Koots." Herbert slumped in his seat. The other Bohemians gathered around them, listening closely. "I know of them. They're strike-breakers, mostly, serving as security for the bosses and breaking the skulls of working men trying to earn their rights." He stood up and straightened his vest and spectacles, trying his best to look noble. "The capitalist running dogs are coming for me. I am not surprised and I am not frightened. I am prepared to face any consequence for the international revolution and liberation of the—"

"You need to run." Clay didn't have time for Bolshevik bleating. He moved in front of Herbert, cutting off his speech. "I don't know if the Bureau of Investigation wants your friends, but the detectives are coming for you. I know the man who leads them, Orton Sinclair. We fought together in the Polar Bear Expedition. He is a cunning and determined soldier, and he will catch you if you don't run."

"I'm not running, Mr. Clay." Herbert folded his arms. "I will stay here with my comrades and I won't be frightened by some servant of capitalism who went to war against the Russian proletariat when they attempted to—"

Zipporah grabbed his arm. "This isn't the time. Don't be stupid."

"Please, Uncle Herbert," Harvey added. "Come with us."

"I—I can't just run away and leave my comrades." Herbert looked at Hark, as if she would affirm his words. "Right?"

"I think you should, Herbert. You are a very good young man, and a willing member of the class struggle—but you can be a real sap at times." Hark leaned closer. "Go with your nephew. We'll disappear into the city. You don't deserve to be deported for what you believe."

Herbert looked like he was going to agree, when a chorus of motors came from outside. Clay's stony body creaked in panic. It was too late. The Sinclair-Koots Detective Agency had arrived. Clay and everyone inside the Bower Green could watch their approach through the windows of the glasshouse, and the open door. Three armored cars rumbled over the curb and into the grass. They had bulky, square armored plates covering their forms, and swiveling turrets with detectives manning the machine guns in the cupolas. The armored automobiles came to a halt in front of the Bower Green, deposited a number of detectives on the lawn. They assembled before the glasshouse, checking their weapons as they shifted their packs and plated armor.

Clay hurried to the doors. He slammed them shut, then grabbed a table and used that to force the doors closed. Clay crouched down and motioned the others to do the same. He could still see what was happening through the glass windows in the door, and watched as the detectives moved closer. Orton Sinclair led them, a speaking trumpet at his side.

Sinclair raised the trumpet to his mouth. "Herbert Holtz! We know you are inside—a reliable informer has appraised us of your presence. We will give you an opportunity to come out and give yourself up. We'll hurt you; perhaps break one or two of your ribs. But that's a mere matter of principle. If you continue to hide, you dirty Red, then we will come in and get you, and by God, we will truly hurt you when we bring you out." Like all the Sinclair-Koots detectives, Sinclair wore a modified doughboy uniform. They had the tin bowler helmets over olive green uniforms, but they sported armor plates on their chests and on their arms and legs as well, and goggles hid their eyes.

Harvey grabbed his uncle's vest. "Don't go!"

"Talk to him." Zipporah tapped Clay's shoulder. "You fought together. You were soldiers, in Russia. Perhaps you can convince him to change his mind—tell his Bureau masters that he couldn't find Herbert Holtz, and go home without causing any trouble."

Clay doubted it would work—but he had few other options. He raised his voice. "Corporal Sinclair!" he called. "This is Emmet Clay!"

"Is that you, Clay?" Sinclair called back, his voice rendered loud and tinny through the speaking trumpet. "What are you doing there, alongside Bolsheviks and subversives? Have they captured you, perhaps? Taken you hostage, somehow? I can scarcely give that credit."

"I'm protecting Herbert Holtz," Clay called back. He glanced at Herbert. "He is a brother to the man I serve. He's the uncle to a boy who I care for, a great deal. I can't let him come to harm." He walked to the window in the door and stared out, letting Sinclair see his face. "Please, Sinclair. I had my fill of bloodshed in Russia. I know you did as well. You're tired of sitting in freezing trenches, of bloody last stands against charging Bolshevik infantry, and ducking down from bursts of machine gun fire spat from tachanka wagons. Go home. Leave Herbert here."

Sinclair paused. "You want me to stop, Clay. Is that it?"

"That's about right."

"Well, I'm afraid I can't. I am a patriot and I will not have my country destroyed from within by communist agitators."

"Herbert couldn't agitate a dinner party," Clay replied. "He's a harmless kid."

"Mr. Clay..." Herbert started, but Sinclair spoke again.

"I need to capture him, Clay. I need to fight." Sinclair paused. "I am a soldier. I remember the horrors of the Polar Bear Expedition all too well, but there is nothing else for me. What am I to do? Work in an office? Man a store? I am a fighter, and I need to fight. That means working with my detective agency and defeating America's enemies. Even if that means fighting an old friend." His voice became more sure—more of a commanding officer giving orders. "Now, we are going to enter that greenhouse and bring out Herbert Holtz. Will you stand against me, Clay?"

"I will," Clay replied.

"That is a pity—but I'm afraid it can be nothing more." Sinclair waved to the armored cars. "Fire."

The machine guns on the tops of the armored cars roared to life. Clay grabbed Harvey and pushed him down, under the cover of the nearest table as a storm of lead reached the Bower Green. Bullets shattered the countless glass panes. For a second, Clay thought he was in a blizzard in the land of his creation, one of the wild dust-ups of wind and snow that struck the Russian plains like blows from God. The glass fell, glittering and shimmering, and smashed against the tables and shattered. The ringing of breaking glass mixed with the roar of gunfire, creating a strangely delicate cacophony. A spike of glass struck Clay, grazing his arm before shattering on the floor. He could survive that kind of damage, but the others were not so lucky. The Bohemians ducked for cover, hiding under the tables, to avoid the falling glass. Clay hoped they would be safe as the chattering machine guns ended—and then he heard a pained, almost quiet whimper from Harvey.

A chunk of glass, a jagged spire the shape of an icicle, had punctured the boy's arm. The jagged tip stabbed into his skin, and redness seeped into his sleeve. Harvey didn't cry out. His eyes widened and he shook, but he didn't scream. Clay should have known something like this would happen. He was a killing machine, a weapon, a golem—but his friends were not. He felt sick and his body creaked as Harvey's blood dripped slowly to the ground.

The others noticed as well. "Oh no." Herbert looked at his nephew, unable to take his eyes away from the wound. As soon as the gunfire ended, he ran. He broke out from under his table and dashed across the Bower Green, shattered glass smashing under his feet, and heedlessly scrambled to his nephew. "Oh God—I should have departed as soon as you arrived—I should have fled. I should have given up everything, instead of grandstanding..." He looked even more pained than Harvey. He dropped to his knees, already tearing his coat to make a bandage. "Don't worry, Harvey. We'll get you out of here. We'll keep you safe."

"Let me, Herbert." Zipporah reached him next. "There's needle and thread in the auto. We'll bandage the wound as best we can, and then we must flee." She went to work, doing her best to staunch the flow and then gripping the glass. She glanced angrily at Herbert. "I trust there's no more disagreements on that score?"

"No. We'll flee. We've got no choice." Herbert sounded defeated. Clay almost felt sorry for him. He pointed to the rear. "There's a door in the back. We can escape." He raised his voice, calling to the other Bohemians hiding out in the Bower Green. "I think we'd all better flee. We can plot revolution another day—but not now."

Hark started getting their radical friends out from under the tables and toward the door. They stayed low. Hopefully, the remains of the frosted glass meant that the detectives outside couldn't spot them. Clay glanced back at the door, which swung dangerously on busted hinges. It wouldn't last long, and he doubted that Sinclair was a man of patience.

Sinclair's voice boomed through the speaking trumpet. "All right, Clay—we're coming in. We're going to grab Herbert Holtz and anyone with him. If I were you, I would stand respectfully aside. I don't want to label you as an enemy of the state as well."

Clay glanced at Zipporah. She had removed the glass spike from Harvey's arm and now wrapped a bandage around the wound to stanch the bleeding. Harvey closed his eyes and still didn't say anything. He shivered wildly, and Herbert put a hand on his shoulder to steady him. Clay pointed to the door and Zipporah shook her head. She needed more time. Clay decided that he could buy it for them—even if it meant clobbering a few Sinclair-Koots detectives.

He came to his feet and took a step closer to the doorway. "You really want to do this, Sinclair? You don't remember what I was like, in Russia?"

"I remember well enough, Clay—you were big, and strong as an ox. But I've been thinking about how best to defeat you, and I believe I have a solution. I'd rather not utilize it, but I will bring you down if I must." Sinclair sounded serious. "I will extend you the same courtesy that I'm giving to Herbert Holtz. This is your last chance. You surrender immediately or we're gonna come inside and take you. What'll it be, Clay?"

Zipporah glared at the door. "Stop your goddamn blathering!" she roared. "And get it over with!"

That spurred the Sinclair-Koots detectives to action. Their boots tramped on the grass, breaking bits of shattered glass as they crossed the porch and reached the door. A rapid kick forced the door from its hinges. It spun almost slowly, twisting to the side before clattering to the ground, and the detectives charged inside. They seemed inhuman in their bulky armor and goggles, like armored demons rushing up from an uncaring Hell. Clay squared his shoulders as the detectives hurried inside. They carried night sticks and trench clubs, as they wanted to take their prisoners alive. Clay felt a bit better when he saw their armor. He could do some damage and wouldn't have to hold back.

The first detectives came at Clay in a row, their clubs humming down and bashing against him. Clay took the blows, letting the clubs rain against his arms and chest. He let the detectives get closer, and then swung with both fists. One blow struck a detective's chest, the knuckles leaving thick dents in the steel. The detective crumpled, and Clay brought the other down with a rapid kick to the chest. The detective fell heavily into a table and it broke under his armored weight. Clay moved back, as Zipporah finished her work on Harvey's arm and joined him.

More Sinclair-Koots men poured in through the door. A spiked trench club whistled at Clay's face. He caught it, his palm stopping the falling club and his fingers closing around the spike. "Herbert!" Clay wrenched the club out of the detective's hand. An expression of surprise appeared on the detective's goggled face, before Clay rammed the bottom of the club against his helmet and dropped him. "Get Harvey and get out of here! Get through the back! We'll join you shortly!"

Harvey called back, his voice thin. "But Mr. Clay, what about—"

Zipporah parried two clubs with her swords. She rammed a handle into a detective's face, shattering his goggles. "Run, child! Go!" She caught another club on the back of her scimitar, and dispatched her attacker with a swift kick.

Clay grabbed a chair, picking it up by the back and swinging it in rapid circles. The heavy wooden chunk of furniture smashed aside the detectives, knocking them off their feet as it began to break. The legs fell aside, and then the seat and back shattered as well. Clay kept swinging and tossed the ruined chair to the ground. That held the detectives back, or at least knocked them off balance for precious seconds. Clay and Zipporah moved back, heading further into the Bower Green. Glass crunched under their feet. Clay couldn't see what had happened to Harvey, Hark, and Herbert, but he hoped he could join them after exiting through the back.

Then another boot settled on the glass. Sinclair stepped inside, armed with a heavy, long-barreled revolver. "Hello, Clay." He turned the pistol on Clay, gripping it with both hands. "I told you I had a way to defeat you." The revolver roared twice. The noise echoed over the glasshouse, ringing over the shattered panes. Tropical birds and butterflies raced away, terrified by the deafening blast.

The bullets carved into Clay's knees. He sank down with a gasp, feeling gravel and dust slipping away from him. Clay hit the ground, nothing more than an oversized lump of earth. The wound would fade, but Sinclair had targeted his joints specifically to slow him down. The bullets wedged deep into Clay's legs. He would need to pull them out, but he simply didn't have time. Sinclair moved closer, keeping the gun trained at Clay. Zipporah moved in front of him, but Sinclair swung the revolver about and covered her.

"Don't." Sinclair kept the gun ready. All around him, his detectives picked themselves up. They groaned, and several of them leaned against overturned tables or slumped down, too battered to do much else. Sinclair watched Zipporah. "You're a soldier too, aren't you?"

"I am," Zipporah agreed. "The Maid of Megiddo, they called me. And I don't spend my time hunting down innocent college students with a penchant for Karl Marx."

"No." Sinclair moved closer, still keeping his gun trained on Zipporah. "You merely serve some Jew Gangster, like Clay here." His eyes, hidden by his goggles, switched back to Clay. "That's what you do right now, is it not? A sad fate for a soldier. But no sadder than mine, I suppose." He walked closer. "Your forehead is your weakest spot, I think. I saw the way you tried to protect it, in Russia. I am not entirely sure what you are, Clay, and I doubt any soldier in the Polar Bear Expedition truly knew. But I am certain that if I put a round through your forehead, you will die."

Harvey dashed in front of Clay. "No—please—don't do that, sir." His words spilled out as he ran through the back door, and raced to Clay.

Harvey gripped his hastily bandaged arm, and his face had drained of color. Clay could only imagine all the pain and torment the boy had been through today, but he still rushed to protect his friend. Harvey stepped in front of Clay and faced Sinclair. "Don't hurt him." He repeated the words loudly, but his tone remained plaintive. "Please. You were friends together. You don't have to do this. Please don't hurt him."

Sinclair stared at Harvey. "Step aside, son. There's no need for—"

"My father said that we couldn't trust the *goyim*—people who aren't Jewish, I mean. But my uncle doesn't believe that and neither do I. You're not Jewish and Clay is—or he sort of is—and you were friends in Russia." That wasn't entirely the case, but Clay didn't want to contradict Harvey. "So you can lower your gun. You can let us go. You can prove that Jews and gentiles can work together."

"Step aside," Sinclair repeated. "Before I—"

"You would hurt a child, Sinclair?" Zipporah asked. "Some soldier you are."

"That's not—I would never—" Sinclair glared at Zipporah. "You subversive strumpet! You need to—"

Zipporah didn't give him a chance to finish his sentence. She crossed the space between her and Sinclair in a single step, and then grabbed his gun hand and pushed the pistol to the side. Sinclair struggled to swing it back, but Zipporah rapped his helmet with the handle of her sword. She hit the brim of the tin bowler. It tilted down, blocking his vision. Zipporah slugged Sinclair in the throat, and shoved him hard to the side. He tumbled straight into a collection of brush, falling through leaves as vines tangled around. Branches shattered under the weight of his armor, and leaves covered him.

"You should never turn your back on a soldier," Zipporah told him. "Clay, Harvey—let's go."

"I think Mr. Clay might have some trouble walking," Harvey said.

"We'll help." Herbert and Hark appeared in the back door. They ran to Clay, along with Zipporah. Even Harvey helped. They gripped Clay's arms, and pulled him off the ground. Clay forced his legs to work. He could feel the bullets inside of him, grating against his body when he tried to move his knees. He rested his feet on the ground and tried his best to move them. Somehow, Zipporah, Herbert, and Hark helped him along. Clay limped to the distant door.

Hark glanced over her shoulder. "We need to hurry. The detectives are recovering from the drubbing you just delivered. They don't seem ready to let us leave."

"Then let's dangle!" Zipporah cried.

Clay pushed himself to move into a tottering run. He blundered through the back door, smashing it open with a swing of his fist. He ran madly across the lawn, momentum carrying him along. Herbert and Hark hurried after him. Zipporah held Harvey's hand. They hurried across the lawn as the first gunshots cracked after them. Bullets flew through the Bower Green and cut over the lawn. Some struck the dirt, kicking up puffs of grass. Clay spotted his Studebaker, resting across the street. He nearly fell in the gutter, but forced himself up and hurried to the car. He wrenched open the door and got behind the wheel.

The others reached the car next. Zipporah and Herbert took the back, with Harvey seated behind them. The boy's wound had begun to bleed through his bandages. Zipporah pressed the bandages tighter and motioned for Herbert to help her. "Drive, Clay!" she ordered. "Get us out of here!" Behind them, the Sinclair-Koots detectives came out of the Bower Green. They left the glasshouse, raising their side arms. The armored cars rumbled around the structure, aiming their machine guns to destroy the Studebaker. But Clay's feet wouldn't move. He forced his foot over the gas pedal as he turned the key in the ignition, but his leg wouldn't bend. The engine roared, but the car didn't move. Hark thought quickly. She leaned over and stomped on Clay's boot, forcing it to hit the gas. That sent the Studebaker rushing down the street. Machine guns rattled as they fled, spitting lead into the street, but Clay's arms worked fine and he could drive.

He sent them zooming down an alley, then turned another corner and kept speeding along. A few more moments of frenzied driving took them away from Finch Bower and closer to Uptown. Clay rolled along a nondescript street before pulling over. He opened the glove compartment and withdrew a short, thin hammer and chisel for himself and a needle and bundle of thread, along with a roll of clean bandages, for Zipporah and Harvey. He wordlessly handed the medical supplies to Zipporah, and then rolled up his trouser legs and got to work with the chisel.

Silence filled the car as Clay used the chisel to find the bullets and the hammer to wedge them out. He drove the chisel into his leg and let the bullets clatter to the floor of the car. Clay grabbed them and tossed them out the window. A jar of clay waited in the glove compartment as well. Clay used that to fix up the wounds.

"What exactly are you doing, Mr. Clay?" Hark asked. Clay stared at her. She had seen the whole thing.

"Mr. Clay has a sort of skin condition." Herbert talked quickly. "He has a very hard dermal layer, but requires certain poultices and ointments. He just applied some. How are you feeling, Harvey?"

"It still hurts a great deal, Uncle Herbert," Harvey said. "But it will heal, right?"

"Pass me the flask, Clay." Zipporah smiled at Harvey. "It will heal. I'll give you something for the pain."

"Just don't give him too much." Herbert watched nervously as Clay reached for a silver flask in the glove compartment.

Dutifully, Clay handed Zipporah a flask of bootleg whiskey from the glove compartment—some of the rabbi's wares that they kept inside, strictly for medicinal purposes. Zipporah gave Harvey a few quick sips. He sputtered and coughed, and then settled back into his seat. "I'll be okay," he said quietly. He looked at Herbert. "You should go back to Haven Street. Papa—my father will protect you. And it will make him feel better, to have his family around him."

"But you'll go with me, right?" Herbert asked.

"I'm sorry—but there's s-something else we need to do." Harvey stared in the distance, his voice going hollow. "City Hall. The Dagger Men. The Founding Stone."

In the chaos of the strike, the riots, and the Sinclair-Koots Detective Agency's attempt to abduct Herbert, Clay had almost forgotten about the Dagger Men. Rabbi Eisendrath and his goon, Rabbi Geist, were still out there. The Dagger Men could be making their move already, going into City Hall to steal the stone and conduct their final spell. Eames had said he would post guards, but he could easily have been lying—and what good would a few guards do against the Dagger Men? Harvey needed time to rest and heal, but Clay knew that they needed the boy's knowledge. His respite would have to wait, for just a little longer.

Herbert bowed his head. "There must be someone else—someone you can call."

"It's a Jew's business, Herbert," Zipporah explained. "And we need to deal with it ourselves."

Hark opened the passenger door. "I'll get Herbert to Haven Street," she explained. "And then I think I'll go to Chinatown. I have friends there. People from the Party, and some of the Tongs. They can take care of me." She paused. "You're all welcome there, of course. Chinatown doesn't like outsiders any more than Haven Street does, but I'll make sure that there's a place for you."

"In case things get bad?" Clay asked.

"In case things get worse," Hark replied. She offered her hand. "Goodbye, Mr. Clay. And please, Harvey, look after yourself." She waved to Herbert. "Come on, Comrade Holtz. I'll get you back home safely." She gripped his shoulder, and almost hauled him out of the car.

They paused for just a moment. Harvey and his uncle clasped hands, and then Herbert and Hark turned away, hurried down an alley, and vanished into the shadows. Clay watched them go. He couldn't say that he liked Herbert overly much, but he hoped that the young man would make it safely back to King Solomon Synagogue. In the meantime, they had their own tasks. Clay started the engine, massaged his knees to force the extra clay into place, and began the drive to City Hall. The Dagger Men could be waiting for them—along with the doom of the entire city.

City Hall lay at the top of Jupiter Hill, the center of Sickle City's old money. The city fathers must have had Mount Olympus in mind when they created the structure, which had a hulking, classical appearance and gazed down at the rest of the city like God in Heaven. Statues of past mayors, Civil War generals, and the other antique heroes of Sickle City flanked the marble steps in mid-strut, as if they would stroll proudly through the large wooden doors. The effect was rather ruined by the riots in the distance, the smoldering fires casting smoke throughout the city, and the way that the doors had been thrown open to show the shadowy lobby. The place appeared to be deserted.

The Studebaker rumbled to a halt on the curb. Clay and his friends got out. Battered and damaged from their various battles, they still faced up the stairs and looked at the open doors. No guards were in sight. If Eames had dispatched any, they certainly weren't currently guarding the place. Clay moved his legs. They already felt better. Golems healed quickly.

Zipporah pointed to the doors. "What do you think, Clay?"

"The Founding Stone's just inside, Harvey?" Clay asked.

The whiskey had taken effect. Harvey leaned against the car. "Oh? Yes. That's right. We visited it on a field trip. It's just through those doors."

"Then we'd better—" The pounding of hooves on marble cut off Clay's words.

The Dagger Men had indeed arrived, and now their servants came to defend them. Cavalry raced through the lobby, with skeletal riders on skeletal horses. These cavalrymen had once served the Romans, but now they rode for the Dagger Men. Long swords flashed in skeletal hands, rusted and thin, while their skeletal horses' hooves resounded off the marble. The skeletons of large dogs, easily the size of Harvey, ran with them. Their mouths opened, flashing their fangs. They would be baying if they had any flesh between their ribs. Instead, their bones merely clattered. Clay sighed. His friends couldn't defeat that many skeletons—but perhaps he could.

He turned to Zipporah. "Do you have a grenade?"

"I took one from Rabbi Holtz's office." Zipporah withdrew the pineapple grenade from her pocket. "What do you—"

"Keep Harvey back." Clay grabbed the grenade. "Leave the Dagger Men to me."

"Clay, you can't—" Zipporah cried.

"I'm a soldier," Clay muttered. "Just like Sinclair. I need to fight."

He pulled the pin and tossed the grenade at the charging skeletons, then ran after it. The grenade exploded soon after hitting the ground, the blast enveloping the first skeletal horses and riders. Bones flew through the air, along with rusted chunks of armor and broken weapons. Clay reached them next. He hurled himself into the skeletons, lashing out with his fists as swords broke against his body. He decapitated a skeletal horse with a punch, shattered the ribs of a rider, and kicked away an attacking dog. With several rapid punches, he cleared his way up the stairs. His legs still ached, but he forced himself through the open doors and into the lobby.

Light flashed as Clay entered. A large mosaic, resembling a compass surrounded by the different symbols of the zodiac, occupied the floor. The northern point of the compass pointed at the Founding Stone itself—a simple lump of rock around the size of a safe. Words in Latin and English had been carved into the front. They had faded over the years and Clay could barely make them out. Rabbi Geist stood next to the stone, his hand outstretched and reaching for the rock. Clay took a step toward the Stone, and then something else clicked on the tile. He spun around.

Rabbi Eisendrath stood next to him, appearing from nowhere. "Golem. Why do you persist in this folly? Perhaps it is not your fault. Perhaps you were made incorrectly."

"Leave the Founding Stone," Clay ordered. Energy crackled from Rabbi Geist's fingers and shot into the stone. They wrapped around the rock, the coils of lightning rapidly circling the stone. "Leave it!" Clay cried.

"Should we destroy him, master?" Rabbi Geist asked.

"No." Rabbi Eisendrath formed rapid patterns with his fingers. "He can bear witness—and maybe be taught how a golem should behave. The Nehemoth Night Specters, from the Qliphoth , will begin your lesson."

Insects buzzed out from the sleeves of his simple coat. They swarmed over Clay in a dark tide, growing in size as they reached him. Insects the size of monkeys landed on Clay, their bodies covered in asymmetrical spikes. They drove those spikes into Clay's shoulders and knees. He moved toward Eisendrath, swinging blindly. One blow connected. Rabbi Eisendrath fell hard to the ground, then rolled over and returned to his feet. That strike should have broken his ribs, but Rabbi Eisendrath seemed not to notice. Clay didn't have time for surprise. The Nehemoth Night Specters drove into his legs and he collapsed. Rabbi Eisendrath towered above him and waved his hand in another occult pattern, and then Clay saw nothing at all.

Chapter Six
KING SOLOMON'S WORM

After the darkness came, Clay dreamed. He walked along the cold snow, the frost crunching under his boots as he trudged along down a silent, white plain. Clay knew where he was—the wasteland of Eastern Europe, the crossroads of Empire where the Jewish people had settled. He was back in the Pale of Settlement, the land of his creation. Wilderness stretched in every direction. A forest lay along the horizon, distant and dark. Right before Clay, a village lay nestled in a gentle valley, glowing with lantern light like gold in the snow.

The village had snow along the rooftops and porches of the various cottages. A synagogue sat at the far end, a simple, square structure with an arched roof. Clay could make out the designs of curling vines, lions, griffins, and unicorns etched along the sides. It was beautiful. This was a shtetl, a village for the Jews of Eastern Europe. Clay moved toward the shtetl, imagining families in their warm houses, children asleep in their beds, and fires crackling in every hearth. He reached out, as he walked, as if he could grab the shtetl and bring it close. But no matter how much he walked, the shtetl drew no closer. Clay forced himself to continue as snow fell.

Someone appeared at his side, matching his pace. "A fine night, isn't it?"

Clay turned. He stared at a man in a long black coat, with hair glistening with pomade and split fashionably down the middle. He had a pale face, with a calm, easy smile. "Perfect for a stroll." He pointed down to the shtetl. "Look at that charming little village. A place of safety and kindness, ever at the mercy of greater powers. It will not last long in this cruel new century, I think."

Clay stopped walking and faced the stranger. "And what will?"

"Perhaps those that were made to weather any storm. I'm sure I'll be around. Man always has need for the King of Demons." Asmodeus smiled, revealing teeth as white as the surrounding snow. "I'm needed now, as a matter of fact, by the very men who have captured you."

"The Dagger Men."

"Yes." Asmodeus leaned closer. "Normally, I can fathom the minds of men. They are simple things, after all. They have simple desires. But I do not know why King Solomon captured me, when he did, and I do not know why the Dagger Men have done the same. You see, every so often, the ways of men become mysteries. King Solomon is my own father, and I still never understood him. I think that is the case with these Dagger Men as well."

"What about golems?" Clay wondered.

"The ways of golems..." Asmodeus whispered the words as he turned back to the snowy plains. "They are even simpler to understand than men. Golems have only one desire. No matter what else they may think, their single desire will control them completely."

"What is that desire?"

"To do whatever it was that they were created to do." Asmodeus extended his hand, taking in the sweep of snow and the village below. "And you know exactly what you were created to do."

A shudder ran through Clay. He turned away from Asmodeus, and the distant village. Clay tried to run, to dash across the snow and somehow escape the company of the King of Demons. But as he turned, a rush of snow rose from the ground. Phantom winds blew from all directions, lifting up the powder and swirling it around Clay. He clawed at the snow, trying to push his way through. Still, the winds and snow rose. Clay slipped on the snow and sank to his knees. A blizzard wrapped around him, the wind howling as the snow and frost flew into his face. Clay crouched lower and dug his hands into the snow. He wanted to burrow under the cover of snow and reach the dark, peaceful earth. It would embrace him, as it had before he was created, and he would be safe. Darkness surrounded him, warm and calming.

Then it flashed away. Vision returned to Clay's eyes. He stared into the hairless, tattooed face of Rabbi Eisendrath. A scowl covered the face, deepening the dark lines of the tattoos. Rabbi Eisendrath stood up and folded his arms. Clay tried to move, but could not. He had been placed into a coffin, his arms and legs pinned with glittering blue chains. He shook and strained, his limbs tugging at the chains. They did not budge.

"Electrum," Rabbi Eisendrath explained. "Try all you wish. They will not crumble."

He stepped back, letting Clay look around. The Dagger Men had apparently returned to the sewers below Sickle City, where they had another base. They had formed a place for rituals on a round cement island, surrounded by a miniature lake of dark green water. Pipes and tunnels projected from the distant walls, pouring more green-tinged water into the lake. It seethed and stank. Rabbi Geist stood behind Rabbi Eisendrath, preparing candles for the ritual. He held a handkerchief over his mouth for the stench, but Rabbi Eisendrath didn't bother. Skeleton centurions stood at the corner, watching the water with swords drawn. The altar to Asmodeus sat on the island, opposite the Founding Stone. A large lantern rested in the center of the island, bathing everything with amber light.

Rabbi Eisendrath pointed to Clay. "I wanted you to see this, golem. I want you to see the power of God, come to bring low this Babylon." He walked closer to Clay. "I could rub out your name, you know. Turn you back into a useless lump of earth. Who knows? Perhaps you would be happier. But it is better that should observe. You were created to defend the Jewish people, just like your predecessor in Medieval Prague. You should see how we do the very same."

"You're not protecting anybody." Clay stared back, defiant to his captors. "You're hurting innocent people. You've tried to hurt my friends, and you want to hurt countless others—just because they're not Jews."

"*Goyim.*" Rabbi Eisendrath spat on the ground. "All my life, I have been under the boot of *goyim.* Their cruelty and hate falls upon me like rain on a blasted plain." He lowered his head, unable to meet Clay's gaze. "I have suffered, golem. I have been brought low and been forced to bow before false kings. It is the same for my people. The same for you. But now, that is at an end." He looked to the ceiling, his hands outstretched. "This day marks the beginning of the Age of Daggers. Finally, the Hebrew people can lift their heads high."

"You're only going to bring more trouble for the Jews of Sickle City. They'll get blamed for your actions. They'll suffer." Clay strained against his chains, struggling to move his arms. The electrum clung to him like spider webbing, sticking against the sleeves of his trench coat. "All you're going to do is cause more pain."

"Then let there be pain!" Rabbi Eisendrath cried. "Justice is worth pain—and do we not deserve justice?" He spun to the side, facing Rabbi Geist. "My student, are the preparations finished? Can we begin to conjure the King of Demons?"

Rabbi Geist had set a number of fat, black candles on the altar. He placed them in the proper slots, and adjusted each wick so that it stood tall. "We stand ready." Rabbi Geist walked back to the center of the island, where a torch lay on the ground. He held a lighter to the oil-soaked rag wrapped around the torch and let it burn. "Let the veil between our world and Gehenna be shattered. Let the King of Demons come through." He paused as he looked at Rabbi Eisendrath. "And may I just add, Master, how grand it is to work with you. You have the wisdom of the sages. Isaac Luria himself unwrapped the mysteries of Kabala no better."

"Thank you, my son." Rabbi Eisendrath approached the altar. He reached down and grabbed a coil of bluish electrum chains, crackling with energy. "I was right to seek you out, and you were right to follow me. Now, we will do what Luria, the Baal Shem Tov, and all the rest never could. We are going to bring the exile of our people to an end."

Clay shook in his chains. "You'll be stopped." He glared at them. "My friends are still out there. They'll come for me, and then we'll stop you. I'm going to smash my way out of here, and then I'm going to rip you both to pieces."

"Golem." Rabbi Eisendrath glared at Clay. "Silence yourself or I'll rub out your mouth and you'll never speak again." That made Clay shut up. Rabbi Eisendrath nodded to Rabbi Geist. "Now, my son. Light the fire that will burn the world."

With a shaking hand, Rabbi Geist touched his torch to the candles. The wicks caught and flame danced above the altar. The figurine of Asmodeus— chicken-headed and lizard-featured—glowed in the light of the candles. Smoke wrapped around it and seethed up to the ceiling. The smoke had the color of obsidian, dark and shiny, and it billowed up in a vast column. Fire light sent shadows dancing over the altar. Rabbi Geist and Rabbi Eisendrath chanted together, speaking a strange mixture of Aramaic and Hebrew. They waved their hands, forming their fingers into inscrutable patterns. The smoke seethed and roiled. Part of it became solid.

Asmodeus stepped from the smoke. He looked like he had in the dream—with the same fashionable dark hair split down the middle. He wore an Edwardian suit now, with a stiff collar and scarlet waistcoat. A silver watch chain projected from his pocket. Asmodeus rested his white loafers on the floor and looked around, humming to himself. When he turned to look at Rabbi Geist, and slipped into profile, he changed. A rooster's comb appeared above his head. Reptilian, scaly fingers showed on his hands. He replaced the illusion quickly.

The King of Demons pointed to Rabbi Geist. "My," he said. "He's a hairy one."

"Now!" Rabbi Geist cried.

Rabbi Eisendrath swung the chains and let them fly. A lasso slid over Asmodeus's shoulders, slipped down to his arms, and tightened. Rabbi Eisendrath pulled and Asmodeus fell to the cement surface of the island. Both rabbis sprang on Asmodeus, working quickly with their chains. They wrapped his arms and legs, and put another length of chain around his throat. In a matter of seconds, their work had finished. They moved back and looked at Asmodeus, who lay on the ground—covered in chains, and strangely unconcerned.

"Demon." Rabbi Eisendrath pointed to Asmodeus. "In the name of the Most High, we bind you."

"Oh, very well." Asmodeus sounded almost bored. "Consider me bound. And I don't think you're doing this for God. You are no holy servants, seeking to battle demons. That sort of nonsense is the domain of Christians." He sat up, ignoring the chains biting into his chest and tangled around his arms. "No. You brought me here because you have a purpose. Well? I'm right, aren't I? Out with it, then. Tell me what you want so I can appease you and return to Gehenna."

Rabbi Geist withdrew a short sword from his robes—a slim blade in the style of a Roman gladius, but with the same silver and glowing blue color of the chain. "An electrum blade." He pointed the tip at Asmodeus's face. "Still your tongue, demon, or you'll taste it."

"Yossel." Rabbi Eisendrath put his hand on the younger man's shoulder. "Don't let him antagonize you. It's what he wants."

"Quite right. Now what do *you* want?" Asmodeus asked.

"The Shamir." Rabbi Eisendrath spoke the word calmly, while Rabbi Geist still held the sword. "Bring it forth, or we'll start cutting."

Asmodeus paused. "The Shamir—the worm that cuts through solid stone. King Solomon's worm." He sat up on his elbows. "King Solomon summoned me to his presence, just as you did, and asked for the Shamir

"My. He's a hairy one."

so he could build the first great Temple, the holiest of holy places, without needing to cut stones. King Solomon was my father, you know. My own father, and yet he ordered me about as if I was a slave. Now, you wish to do the same." For the moment, his good humor left him. His smile vanished, and a snake's forked tongue flicked in and out of his mouth. "Tell me why. What do you intend to do with the Shamir? The temple is gone. Judea is dust. What use do you have for the worm that tunnels through stone?"

"It's no business of yours, demon," Rabbi Geist explained. "You claim King Solomon fathered you? Impossible. You lie." He walked closer, pushing past Rabbi Eisendrath, and lowered his short sword. "You heard my master. Give us the Shamir or I will take your hands, and your feet, and the nose and ears from your face. We will do with the Shamir what we must."

"It seems I have no choice." Asmodeus's eyes shifted. They settled on Clay. "What did I tell you, man of earth? In the Valley of Bones, I told you that righteous men will do more evil than demons. Now, you will see the truth of my words." He faced Rabbi Eisendrath. "It won't help you, you know. Whatever you do will not change who you are."

"Enough." Redness appeared in Eisendrath's tattooed face. "Bring forth the Shamir."

"Here it comes." Asmodeus opened wide.

His jaws opened like the lid of a case, snapping all the way back and hiding his eyes and chin. Only darkness filled his face. Shadows spilled from the ring of teeth, and crept down his cheeks and chin. Rabbi Eisendrath hastily slipped his hands into a pair of scaly gloves. He withdrew a set of tongs, made of glittering electrum, and approached the maw. Clay strained his head, craning his neck to watch. Rabbi Eisendrath jabbed the prongs into the open mouth. They vanished in shadow for a moment. Then Rabbi Eisendrath pinched them down and caught something. He pulled it back, struggling a little before wrenching the tongs free.

They held the Shamir. King Solomon's worm had been caught between the two iron jaws of the prongs. It wriggled madly, waving its tail and head in all directions. The Shamir resembled the earthworms that Clay had seen crawling through mud during rains and in the gutters of the city. However, this Shamir had opalescent colors on its ridged, dripping flesh. Pale blues and greens rested amongst the ridges, so the worm seemed more like some thin gem stone than a living thing. A mass of spikes covered its head. They pulsed and shook as Rabbi Eisendrath held the Shamir aloft. Asmodeus's jaws returned to normal, and he watched as well.

Rabbi Geist took a step closer to the Shamir. The worm shook and a silver drop fell from its spikes. The drop hit the cement, which hissed and burned. A small strand of stream whistled up. Rabbi Geist bowed his head. "We have it! This creature divided the stones to build the temple, and now it is ours!"

Clay followed the Shamir as Rabbi Eisendrath walked across the cement island. "What are you going to do with it?" he demanded.

Rabbi Eisendrath stopped. He looked back at Clay. "You know," he said. "In what passes for your heart, you already know." Then he crossed the island and reached the Founding Stone. He whispered something to the Shamir, and the worm stilled its wriggling. "Prepare the case." He gave his orders to Rabbi Geist. "This won't take long."

The prongs opened and the Shamir landed on the surface of the Founding Stone, right above the carved stone words bearing the name of Sinner Barebone and the Puritans who had created Sickle City. The Shamir wiggled about and then got to work. It curled around the ancient stone, leaving a trail of shimmering pale blue juice. Steam rose wherever it moved, following the trail. The juices settled in the stones for a few moments, filled with steam, and faded away. Letters remained. Clay watched them silently. He even forgot to struggle. Rabbi Eisendrath was right. He knew exactly what the Shamir was doing and what it was carving in the first stone of Sickle City.

It only took a few moments before the Shamir finished. It slid off the stone and fell to the ground. Rabbi Eisendrath scooped it up with his prongs and dropped it into a lead case stuffed with cotton, supplied by Rabbi Geist. Carefully, they closed the lid of the case and set it down. Steam still seethed from the surface of the stone. Everyone watched and waited for the steam to fade, to see the Shamir's work. Rabbi Geist impatiently waved his hand, clearing it away. Then they stared at the stone and they saw what had been done.

The Hebrew words for 'Truth' had been etched on the ancient stone— just as they were etched on Clay's forehead, and on the forehead of every golem in existence. They stood boldly over the words in English, as if proclaiming that they had more authority. Now Clay knew why the Dagger Men had stolen the Founding Stone. It controlled the energy created by the women of Bone Island, the witches and mystics led by Bathsheba Barebone. That magic had been pulsing under the city, waiting for the right spell to claim it. The Dagger Men had just created the spell to use that magic. The Shamir's power had helped them. Now, the Founding Stone—

the center of Sickle City—had been turned into a golem. The rest of the city would follow.

The walls began to shake. Sewer waters splashed, causing waves to smash against the cement island. Dust rained down from the ceiling. It must be even worse up above, as the city shifted and changed. Rabbi Eisendrath stood before the Founding Stone, breathing in the still air as he stretched his hands out in the direction of the sky. Sickle City was his golem now.

The shaking faded. The waters stilled. Soon, the only noise was Clay rattling his chains, trying to free himself. Everyone ignored him. "The first tremors," Rabbi Eisendrath whispered. "The first sounds of new life coming into the world, and the rebirth of the Jewish people."

Asmodeus let out a surprisingly high-pitched giggle. "You foolish little rabbi. For all your knowledge, you're not very smart at all, are you?" He sat up, his calm, jovial manner returned. "The Shamir will be your undoing, just as it was Solomon's. He built the first Temple with demon's magic. It laid a curse onto the stones, which seeped down and reached King Solomon's people. It cursed them forever, and now that curse will go to you and the Dagger Men. You've lived for centuries, nursing your hate in the shadows of the world. No longer. You and the bearded man are the last of the Dagger Men, and the demons will laugh as you fail."

"Silence!" Rabbi Eisendrath grabbed the electrum blade from Rabbi Geist. He approached Asmodeus, raising the sword high. "This is the hour of my victory. The first day of the Age of Daggers. Nothing you can do will stop me."

"Not I, dear Rabbi Eisendrath," Asmodeus explained. "But the golem will."

Both Dagger Men turned to face Clay. They approached the coffin, their hands swinging at their sides and ready for more rituals. Clay continued shaking the chains. If they were going to destroy him, he would go down fighting. "Get rid of him, master," Rabbi Geist whispered. "Change the word on his forehead from 'truth' to 'death.' Let him rejoin the earth. I know there may be a kinship between you—"

"A kinship?" Rabbi Eisendrath demanded. "How can their possibly be a kinship between us?"

While they argued, Clay looked past them and stared at the sewer water. It still rippled, the green surface stirred by chunks of cement and stone falling from the ceiling. But something rose out of the water, emerging from the spreading ripples and extended into the air. Smoke boiled out of the water, though no heat had been delivered to the sewer. An entire cloud came out of the lake, and sailed toward the round cement island. Clay realized who it was, and felt an immense gratitude. No matter the danger he faced, his friends hadn't abandoned him.

Lilith Shadowborn reached the cement island. She moved soundlessly over the ground, floating along as her sharp features appeared from the smoke. She floated past Asmodeus and neared the coffin, a hand on her lips. Clay understood. They could slip away, and then find and warn the others about the Dagger Men's great spell.

Rabbi Geist and Rabbi Eisendrath still talked. "I am sorry, master. I apologize with all my soul. I did not wish to—"

"You still have much to learn, Yossel. I pray that God gives me the wisdom to tutor you properly." Rabbi Eisendrath sniffed the air. "Hold on." He walked past Rabbi Geist, scanning the little cement island. "We are not alone." Lilith coiled closer to the coffin, trying to float out of view. "I smell magic, old and powerful."

"Excuse me?" Asmodeus pointed to the coffin. "Right behind there."

The Dagger Men spotted Lilith in the same second. Her smoky limbs went solid as surprise and then rage filled with the rabbis' faces. Rabbi Geist called the centurions, shouting an order in Hebrew. They withdrew their long swords and charged.

Lilith met them. Twin plumes of smoke emerged from her hands and then became solid—forming twin swords of shadow. She parried the first centurion's strike, repelling the sword with a rapid blow, and jammed her next blade into its chest. The shadow cut through ancient armor and bone. A slice cut the skeleton in half. Lilith moved to the next, driving a shadow into its skull and piercing its plumed helmet. She turned to Clay. "One moment, Mr. Clay, and then you shall be free. I suggest an immediate retreat. I cannot last against these Dagger Men for long." As she spoke, Rabbi Geist and Rabbi Eisendrath prepared another spell, adjusting their fingers in arcane preparation.

"They've chained me," Clay muttered. "And where am I to go?"

"I'll deal with the chains." Lilith swung a sword back, the point of the blade humming through the air. The sword struck the chains and split the electrum. Shining links shattered and fell to the ground, glowing like stars as they bounced on cement. Clay tumbled from the coffin and fell to the ground. "Into the water, Mr. Clay!" Lilith cried. "Filthy it may be, but we must all do horrid things from time to time." She raised her blades as more skeletal centurions closed in. "I will find you later, and then we will decide how to save this city."

She was right—there was no time to linger. Clay ran to the edge of the island, gathering momentum as he shook off the last pieces of the electrum chains. They clattered to the ground, ringing and bouncing as he ran to the edge. Rabbi Eisendrath called after him, and stretched out his hand. Clay ran faster. He reached the edge and jumped.

The sewer water reached up and dragged him down. Clay sank like a stone. He had never had much luck with swimming before, and soon he reached the bottom. Luckily, this time he had the current on his side. It slammed into him, dragging him along the sewer floor and then hauling him up and carrying him along. Clay didn't need air—he didn't need to breathe—and he let the water rush him into the mouth of a large pipe and down a tunnel.

He banged against the walls, occasionally getting stuck against a portion of the tube or in a grate—but he used his strength to smash aside the obstacles, free himself, and continue floating along. He went through another grate, and deeper into the sewers. The world went green and brown around him, and his trench coat sucked up the sewer water like a sponge. Still, he continued floating along. Around him, tremors still ran through the city. It was a golem now, and the Dagger Men owned it. Clay tried to banish that fear as the current dragged him along.

Finally, he found himself in a passage without much water, below a ladder and a manhole cover. Clay clambered up the ladder and rammed his fist into the manhole cover. After a few moments of pounding, he popped it off. He pulled himself out of the hole, and into a small back alley, opposite Damocles Street. Clay came to his feet and leaned against a wall for a few moments, then stared at the state of his clothes. The trench coat and suit jacket would have to go, and his fedora was already gone. He tore off his coat and suit, and tossed them in the alley, then stumbled to the sidewalk in vest and shirtsleeves. He reached Damocles Street.

The police strike and the riots had taken their toll. Overturned cars rested in the deserted street, and many of the upper crust shops on Damocles Street had lost their windows and much of their merchandise. Clay walked down the empty street, passing a smashed automobile and examining what had once been a jewelry store. Either the owners evacuated their wares or the thieves had been thorough. Nothing inside remained.

Clay continued walking along, shaking off droplets of sewer water and most of the stench. He needed to get back to Haven Street and find Rabbi Holtz, Zipporah, and Harvey—hopefully, they had escaped from the Roman skeletons at City Hall and made it to safety. Clay needed to tell them what had happened and prepare them for what came next. He wasn't sure what that would be, but he had a feeling it would be violent. The Dagger Men had turned Sickle City into a golem, but what exactly would they do? Clay supposed he would have to wait to find out.

He passed the remains of a hot dog stand. Buns lay in the street, spilling out from the inside of the stand and lying in the gutter and across the pavement. Pigeons and rats dined on them, eating as much as they could. They hardly noticed as Clay walked past. He stared down the street and looked into the park. The looting had faded in this part of Damocles Street, but it was doubtlessly happening elsewhere. Evening had already reached Sickle City, and nightfall would probably just make the riots worse. Clay sighed as he wiped sewer water from his face. He had a long way to go.

A hum of motors cut through the eerie silence of the street. Clay turned around, readying his fists as two armored automobiles shot across the open pavement like metal torpedoes. Sinclair-Koots detectives manned the machine guns in the cupola, already fingering the triggers and preparing to fire. They must have been patrolling the city and spotted him—just another bit of bad luck in a day full of it. Clay glanced up the street, wondering if he could run. He doubted that he could, and there were no other options beside standing and fighting.

The armored cars rumbled to a halt, their brakes screeching before they stopped. Their side doors opened and the Sinclair-Koots detectives emerged. This time, they came prepared. The score of detectives had abandoned their armor, and now sported khaki uniforms with Sam Brown belts and peaked caps, like they were all officers in the Great War. Rifles and shotguns aimed at Clay, along with a pair of Thompsons. He stared at them, not afraid of their bullets.

"It's the big one, sir!" A stout detective with a face full of stubble racked the pump on his shotgun. "The big Bolshevik, from Finch Bower. That goddamn Red broke two of Lucas's ribs. Let's put him down now, before he gets a chance to charge."

"Hold your fire." Orton Sinclair walked out from behind the armored cars. He had his long-barreled revolver raised, and trained on Clay's forehead. Clay shifted a little. Sinclair knew his weakness—even if he didn't know what a golem was. A barrage from the other detectives could immobilize Clay, and a bullet from Sinclair would finish the job. Sinclair moved closer. He sniffed. "Christ, Clay. You smell like a sewer. Is that where you've been? Hiding out after you escaped from the greenhouse?"

"Something like that," Clay replied. "Look, I need to get to Haven Street and—"

"Clay, you're not going to Haven Street. Your Jew friends will have to wait." Sinclair leaned closer. "You're coming with me, to the Wigwam Club. Eames is there, along with more of my men. The others are combing the city, searching for other agitators and subversives." He took another step closer to Clay. "You're not on any list. You're not wanted by the Bureau of Information or the State Department. In fact, Clay, I doubt that more than a few other soldiers from the Polar Bear Expedition know that you exist. But I won't have you interrupt my investigation. I understand why you did what you did, but I won't have it happen again. I'm certain that you understand that."

Another detective cocked his Thompson. "Let's waste the kike, sir. We ain't got the time to—"

"You will hold your fire!" Sinclair roared the words. He turned back to Clay. "Well? What's it going to be?"

Once again, Clay had no choice. If he picked a fight with these detectives, he would lose—and then he would never reach Haven Street. If they brought him to the Wigwam Club, maybe he could find a way to get a phone call to Rabbi Holtz and warn him about the Dagger Men. Edwin Eames would be there, and he might be able to help as well. Clay sighed. He held out his hands. "Are you going to handcuff me?"

Sinclair shook his head. "Not an old friend like you. Now get moving."

They walked him back to the armored cars. Sinclair yanked open one door, revealing a small area in the back for the detectives to sit on a pair of short benches. Clay went to the back of the chamber, with half-a-dozen detectives surrounding him, all armed and eager for a fight. Sinclair sat across from him, his revolver in his lap. He rapped his fist on the wall, alerting the drivers. The armored car sped down the empty street, followed by its partner. The movement jostled the detectives a little, but they mostly stayed upright and waited for the ride to end. They were all soldiers and used to long waits. Clay was as well. War had taught them all to be patient.

The armored cars sped around Damocles Street and soon arrived at the Wigwam Club. The center of politics in Sickle City now appeared to be a last bastion of law and order—a fort in the wilderness. Sandbags had been placed before the entrance, and more Sinclair-Koots detectives manned a pair of heavy machine guns facing the street. The armored cars stopped in the street and deposited Clay and a few detectives before speeding away.

More detectives pushed the door open, allowing Clay, Sinclair, and a few guards into the lobby. The place looked much like it had earlier in the day, though every visitor waiting to see the Grand Sagamore had gone home. Overturned chairs lay on the ground, and detectives played cards or loaded their weapons in the corners. The abundance of American flags and eagles overlooked it all.

Eames himself stood behind the receptionist's desk, talking loudly on the phone. "I don't care for your excuses!" He sputtered as he blared his words into the speaker, while the receiver shook in his hands. "If you don't have the fuel, you find it. Steal it from some motorists, perhaps. Say that you are requisitioning the gas on behalf of the civic government. Flash a pistol if a badge doesn't work!" He turned around, noticing Clay for the first time. "I need the *Heavenly Chariot* here on the double. Do you hear me? On the double! I want to be sailing safely away by evening." He slammed the speaker and receiver down and sighed as he slumped against the desk. "How are you, Clay? Come to visit me? Warn me about the Dagger Men?"

"He's a prisoner, sir." Sinclair marched next to Clay. "Caught defending known Bolsheviks. We're keeping him here until further notice."

"He's a Bolshevik, eh? I might have expected such a thing." Eames stared at Clay, his face the color of tallow. "Everything else is going wrong. Do you know there was some sort of earthquake that just struck Sickle City—as if the terror of the riots and looting and the police strike were not enough!" He walked out from behind the desk, glad to have someone on whom he could pour out his troubles. "Thankfully, the tremors did not damage the city itself. Instead, they shattered roads and broke every bridge connecting us with the surrounding countryside."

"How bad is it?" Clay asked.

"As bad as can be," Eames explained. "The roads were rendered impassable. No vehicle can drive over the disrupted asphalt, or cross the broken bridges. If the National Guard was going to enter Sickle City to restore order, they would have to come from the coast and land on the docks—many of which have also collapsed—or fly in via airship. And of course, the preparations for those things take time. I haven't even called them yet."

"Why not?" Clay demanded.

Eames stepped back. "W-well, I kept on wondering how that would look. What would my candidates think of me if I couldn't have order in my city without relying on the Federal government? I would be humiliated, so I naturally dawdled a bit on the fateful decision. Lately, I have been too busy to make the necessary entreaties. I had to arrange for my own private airship to come by, pick me up, and direct me to safety. Once I have left Sickle City, I can begin opening the necessary channels and see about bringing in help."

Clay drew closer, drawing himself up to his full, intimidating height. "Call them now. Tell them to send all the help they can—and many soldiers." He paused for a moment, before deciding to invoke the name of his former commanding officer, who had led him and Sinclair in the Polar Bear Expedition. "Send word to Colonel Menelaus Montgomery Rook and tell him that—"

"Clay." Sinclair spoke calmly. "You are a prisoner. You can't make Mr. Eames do anything."

"Quite right, Mr. Sinclair—though I do appreciate the sentiment, Mr. Clay. I'll make all the calls you'd like, after I leave the city. Why don't you go and wait in the Founders' Hall? It's a big comfortable room, where we talk club business over brandy and cigars." He spun about, undoing his bowtie with one hand and sucking in breath. "I need to go to my office and pack. There're certain documents, numerous records, that should not fall into the wrong hands." He hurried to the back, shoving aside the door and almost diving into his office.

After he left, Clay turned to Eames. "Can I make a call? One phone call. That's all."

"Make it quick," Eames ordered.

Quickly, Clay dialed up the King Solomon Synagogue. He waited as the phone rang, and then Rabbi Holtz's voice came over the phone. "Yes?"

"Rabbi, it's Clay." Clay talked quickly. "I've been captured by the Sinclair-Koots people. I'm at the Wigwam Club, on Damocles Street." He needed to get to the warning quickly, but he had to know something else first. "Harvey, and Zipporah, are they—"

"They're fine, Mr. Clay. Harvey's getting some rest in the next room. Zipporah's helping get some freshly made chicken soup to my other guests." Rabbi Holtz barely paused for breath. "You're a prisoner, Clay? We can help you. Just give me some time and I'll call Sapphire and—"

"No time." Clay cut him off. "The Dagger Men have succeeded. They stole the Founding Stone and used the Shamir to carve holy words in the rock. They've turned all of Sickle City into a golem. It's under their control. I think the spell will take another hour perhaps, to truly work, and then I don't know what will happen. They've already cut off the city from the outside world." Clay tried to jam his words together, so he could tell them all to Rabbi Holtz. "They're going to try to conquer it, I think. To make some kind of second Jerusalem—another temple. Rabbi Eisendrath mentioned the Age of Daggers."

"Clay, don't worry. We'll—" Rabbi Holtz's voice went silent. The line clicked dead. Clay fiddled with the dial a few more moments and then set the speaker and receiver back. He lowered his hands. Somehow, the Dagger Men had stopped the telephones from working.

Sinclair stepped closer to him. "Conversation over?"

"Yeah," Clay muttered.

"What do you talk about, anyway?" Sinclair asked. "You and your Jew pals. Trade stock tips, perhaps?" He shook his head. "It doesn't matter. Come on, we're going to the Founders' Hall like Mr. Eames said. I'm on his dime and I'll do what he asks." He tapped the butt of his revolver when Clay didn't move. "Get moving, soldier."

They left the lobby, crossed through a small corridor, and entered the Founders' Hall. This wide chamber served as a meeting place for the Wigwam Club, when they wanted to talk private business and discuss bribes, patronages, and assure that their candidates would always get the needed votes. Leather armchairs and Chesterfield couches rested around glass coffee tables, and the air stank of aged tobacco and alcohol. Skylights looked up at the night sky, while electric lamps covered everything in a warm glow.

The walls belonged to oversized portraits of the founders and leading citizens of Sickle City. Clay looked them over. It didn't take long for him to find Sinner Barebone, a severe, hawk-nosed Puritan dressed all in black and scowling under a Puritan's black hat. His sister, Bathsheba Barebone, had another portrait across from him. She wore a black robe and cradled a white goat in her arms as her fierce eyes stared at the viewer. She had just been a young woman struggling against the confines of Puritan society by delving into powerful magic—and she might have been the one to set in motion spells and rituals that would bring Sickle City to its knees.

Clay selected an armchair and settled down. Sinclair walked to the liquor cabinet and prepared a drink for himself. Ice cubes clinked in a round glass, followed by golden bourbon. Sinclair swished it idly as he walked back and stood in front of Clay. "Fine quarters, this building," he said. "Particularly compared to the place we garrisoned in Russia."

"I remember. We never truly owned that ruined castle. The snows had conquered it, long before we got there. They never gave it up." Clay rested his hands on his knees. "We had to keep fires burning at all times, and sleep under thick blankets." He hadn't bothered with any of that, being used to the cold—but he could see the discomfort and pain the snow caused for his fellow soldiers. "And then the bodies of the Bolsheviks froze on the ice."

"So many of them. You could slip on frozen blood during the counter-charge that finally forced them back." Sinclair had a tentative sip of bourbon and then set it on the coffee table. "I served in France before Russia, Clay, and I sometimes can't tell which was worse. I still see them, you know, whenever I close my eyes."

"I just did," Clay explained. "In a dream I had, a few hours ago. I walked across the plains of Russia, and listened to the howling of the wind."

"The howling of artillery rounds and mortar fire is what I hear. Rouses me at night whenever I try to sleep. Sometimes I wish the fire really would fall from the sky, if only to stop me from wondering when it would finally come."

Suddenly, Clay perked up. "Do you remember when Sergeant Sanders went off to piss?"

"And ran straight into a patrol of Red Cossacks?" A smile appeared under Sinclair's moustache. "The poor bastard came running back, chased by an army of those bearded devils with their swords in the air, ready to cut him in half, with his—"

"With his trousers fallen around his knees." Clay shook his head at the memories.

"Here's to those far off lands." Sinclair raised his glass in a mocking toast. "And all the good men who died there. Died for nothing, I should think, as the Bolsheviks won and we crawled back to our country after giving all of Russia to the Reds." He drank deeply, and shuddered. "But we made the world safe for democracy, at least. A thousand hurrahs to that noble sentiment."

"It has not been easy for you." Clay looked at his former friend. "To live in peace."

"No, Clay. It hasn't." Sinclair almost snapped at him. "And it's been the same for you, I'd wager." He sighed as he settled into a chair. "It was different for my grandfather, I think. He was in the War Between the States, you know. Marched through Georgia. He came back and he was a hero. I lived in awe of him. Everywhere he went—pats on the back, parades, salutes." His smile vanished. "But not you and me. Forgotten soldiers from a forgotten war. We didn't even have the good sense to win. Now look at us—I command a pack of bloodthirsty killers who threaten striking miners and you serve some bootlegger rabbi."

"Do you think it's possible?" Clay asked. "To have a better life after coming home?"

"Possible?" Sinclair weighed the question. "Probably not. But at least we can hope." He pointed at Clay. "You have friends, at least. The wild woman with the sword. That nice little fellow with the spectacles." He finished the bourbon, upending it and drinking down the rest. "I don't have much of anybody."

Clay didn't know what to say to that. Sinclair had been his friend—but that had been long ago, half a world away, when they battled the Bolsheviks with rifles and bayonets. Now, Sinclair was his captor, and a casual anti-Semite in the bargain. Clay settled into his seat and gazed up at the skylight overlooking the Founders' Hall. The night sky shone down, the stars faint and distant amongst dark clouds. But something else appeared in the window. A shadowy shape moved to the center. Then, a set of long, thin cracks ran through the glass.

Sinclair didn't notice. He had refilled his glass and now walked around the billiards table, spinning the white ball on the green felt. He hummed to himself as he knocked back the bourbon, and then raised his voice in song. "Johnny get your gun, get your gun, get your gun. Take it on the run, on the run, on the run." He jabbed his finger into the air. "Hear them calling you and me! Every son of liberty! Hurry right away, no delay, go today. Make your daddy glad, to have had such a lad. Tell your sweetheart not to pine—to be glad her boy's in line!" He let out a sudden gasp and sunk into his chair. "What's it for, Clay? All the pain. All the suffering? What's the goddamn point?"

Up above, the skylight shattered. Glass rained down in a flurry and struck the billiards table. Sinclair jumped back and reached for his pistol. He had it half out of its holster when Zipporah Sarfati swung down from the ceiling, leaping down with a rope wrapped around her waist. She swung low, a child on a swing, and zoomed straight for Sinclair. Both of her boots struck him square in the chest.

Sinclair tried to stand, his motion slowed by pain and drunkenness. Zipporah didn't give him the chance. She reached him in a pair of steps and cracked her boot heel against his face. The back of Sinclair's head hit the carpet. Zipporah withdrew a scimitar and pointed it at the detective's throat. "Move and I take your life's blood," she ordered. Sinclair gurgled and stayed still. Zipporah gave Clay a thumbs-up. "How's your evening, Clay?"

"Not great." Clay walked next to Zipporah. "You're here to rescue me?"

"And I didn't come alone."

Rustling and the crunch of shattered glass came from the shattered skylight. Harvey Holtz peered down, and he unfurled a rope. He started to shimmy down, wincing as the rope swung back and forth. His hands weakened and he dropped the last few feet. Clay ran under him and caught the boy before he could hit the ground. He gently deposited Harvey on the carpet. Harvey smiled weakly at Clay and massaged his wounded arm. Clay could see the bulge of bandages under his sleeve, and hoped that the boy was healing.

"Hello, Mr. Clay. We're going to save you." Harvey brushed dust from his coat and straightened his tie. "My father told me that you called, and that you were a prisoner, and we knew that we had to help you." He paused, his exuberance fading. "He didn't like it, sir. And Zipporah didn't either, but I insisted. What if there's some magic that I can help you with? Besides, things have calmed down at Haven Street. There's no more mobs, or anything—though the earth did shake a little."

"That's the Dagger Men's doing," Clay explained. "They summoned Asmodeus, stole the Shamir from him, and had it inscribe a charm in the Founding Stone. They turned the whole city into a golem." He could see the fear in Harvey and Zipporah's eyes. "I'm not sure what that means, but the Dagger Men need to be stopped."

"Aces," Zipporah agreed. "First things first—we gotta get you out of here." She kept her sword tip hovering above Sinclair's face. "We can leave the Doughboy here. Mrs. Cohen's across the street in the rabbi's Cunningham. We get to that, and we can drive back to Haven Street."

"Good." Clay patted Zipporah's shoulder. "And thanks for your coming. Both of you."

"Of course, Mr. Clay," Harvey said. "You're our friend. We'll always be there to help you."

From the ground, Sinclair let out a slight moan. Zipporah pulled her sword away and returned it to the scabbard on her back. She headed to the door, followed by Clay and Harvey. A quick kick opened the door, and then they scrambled into the corridor. Other detectives lurked in the Wigwam Club, but Clay figured they could slip past them, maybe duck out of a rear exit and work around to find Cohen and the automobile.

Behind them, Sinclair sat up. Clay looked over his shoulder. Their eyes met. His old friend stared at Clay, a bruise shadowing his cheek, and then raised his voice. "The prisoner is escaping!" he roared out the words, and stumbled to his feet as he went for his pistol. "Block the exit! Capture them alive! Don't let them reach the street!" Sinclair may have been sour about his service in the Polar Bear Expedition, but he still sought to do his duty.

"Nuts!" Zipporah cursed. "We should've cut his throat."

"That's murder, Miss Sarfati," Harvey pointed out. "We can't do that."

They left the corridor and hurried into the lobby, where the Sinclair-Koots detectives had already prepared to meet them. About a score of the detectives assembled in the lobby, overturning chairs and aiming their rifles and Tommy guns into the hall. One Thompson fired early, an undisciplined soldier leaning on his trigger. Bullets stitched the wall. Clay grabbed Harvey and hauled him back, before the boy could run out. He and Zipporah crouched by the wall as the Tommy gun rattled. The bullets sawed through an American flag, and the strips of striped cloth floated down. One bullet hit a large brass eagle, knocking the bird from its perch with a ring. It bounced on the ground before landing at Clay's feet.

Clay glared at Zipporah. "You've got a plan for getting out?"

"I came prepared, Clay." Zipporah reached into the pocket of her coat and withdrew a round steel cylinder, topped with a ring. She pulled the ring and tossed it aside. "We used to use these little fellows in the war. Toss them into a machine gun nest from horseback, and the gunners could see nothing. We'll make a dash for the exit soon—just stay together and keep moving."

A quick underhand throw sent the cylinder flying into the lobby. It struck the marble floor, rolled under a chair, and then began spewing smoke. The smoke grenade expelled great gouts of blue smoke, which billowed around the room, seeped over the furniture, and obscured everything. The detectives stumbled about, waving their guns and shouting in panic. Zipporah chose that moment to run. Clay and Harvey followed her, and they dashed into the mass of smoke together.

The detectives couldn't fire into the smoke cloud for fear of hitting their own. Clay could hear their commands, even if he couldn't see anything in the smoke. "Get to the doors—don't let them out!" He kept running, still holding Harvey's hand, and bumped into someone in a khaki uniform. He caught a glimpse of the detective, a stout fellow with a lazy eye, as the Sinclair-Koots man tried to raise his Thompson. Clay slugged him, driving a heavy fist straight into his gut. Another blow knocked the detective onto his back.

He kept moving, tugging Harvey along and nearing the door. Another detective stumbled out of the smoke and took up a position in front of the door. He had a weasel's grin and packed a carbine rifle– which he aimed straight at Clay and Harvey. "Not another step, you big, Bolshevik bastard," he ordered. "I'll cut you in half if you—"

Zipporah's scimitar slashed down from the smoke. The sword hacked into the wooden stock, splintering the wood and smashing apart the metal. She stepped from the blue fog and grabbed the surprised guard's shoulder. A head butt shattered his nose and sent him reeling, and another punch knocked him into the door. Zipporah stepped over him and pushed open the door.

She pointed down to the street. "Shall we?"

"Why not?" Clay and Harvey hurried out next.

They raced down the steps, approaching the machine gun posts. The detectives inside turned to meet them, trying to swivel their heavy machine guns completely around to face the stairs. Zipporah was ready. Another pair of smoke grenades flew from her hands and landed in the sandbags. Smoke poured out as they ran down. Zipporah leapt into the first nest, her feet landing on the edge of the sandbags. Rapid kicks took care of the gunners, and Zipporah motioned for Clay and Harvey to follow. They hurried past the sandbags and into the abandoned street.

The Cunningham Touring Car waited for them. It sped out from around a corner, the engine and tires screaming, and braked hard right in front of Clay and his friends. Cohen manned the wheel, sporting a pair of driver's goggles. Clay picked Harvey up and set him into the back, and then Cohen scooted over to let Clay take the wheel. She had her rifle leaning against the passenger seat and stood as she readied the gun. Zipporah hopped into the back next to Harvey. Cohen worked the bolt on the rifle, and aimed it straight at the steps of the Wigwam Club.

"Good to see you, Clay," Cohen said. "*Cómo estás*?"

"Eager to leave." Clay turned the key, preparing to leave.

"Clay!" Sinclair's voice came from the steps. "You are not leaving! Kill that engine and come out with your hands up! Do that and I'll let your friends walk out of here alive!" Despite himself, Clay turned to look. Sinclair came down the steps, his revolver at his side. More detectives followed him. Some of the smoke had wafted away, giving the machine guns a clear shot at the Cunningham Touring Car. "If you attempt to flee, we will fire—and you will be destroyed. Don't make me do such a thing, Clay—not to a fellow soldier." Sinclair's voice sounded pained, but he still covered the Cunningham with his revolver.

Perhaps they could still escape, but then the Sinclair-Koots armored cars rattled out from behind the Wigwam Club, speeding into the street. The guns in their cupolas swiveled to face the Cunningham. Clay kept his foot poised above the gas pedal, unsure what to do. Zipporah pushed Harvey's shoulder, keeping the boy's head below the windows of the Cunningham. Sinclair reached the bottom of the steps. A handful of detectives followed him, and they advanced on the car. The armored Sinclair-Koots autos stayed put, watching everything.

Cohen at least knew what to do. She gripped her rifle in one hand and pulled a pineapple grenade from her leather jacket pocket with the other. She stepped onto the runners. "Drive, Mr. Clay," Cohen ordered. "Leave me. I'll hold them off. I can kill a hundred of these fools and slip away before they return fire." She glared back at Clay. "Go!"

"Wait, p-please!" Harvey stammered. "We can think of some peaceful solution! We don't have to fight!"

Sinclair and his detectives drew closer. "Out of the car, Clay!" He aimed his revolver at Cohen. She covered him with her rifle. "Tell your greaser friend to stand down or, by God, I will put her down." He cocked his pistol, ready to fill the street with death. Cohen's thumb neared the pin of the grenade. It looked like nothing could stop the battle.

Then the earth shook. Tremors ran through the street, filling it with long cracks. Glass shattered on the windows of the Damocles Street skyscrapers. The trees in Arcadia Park shook and several collapsed. Pigeons lifted up in a thick cloud and raced into the dark sky. The Cunningham rolled backwards and rumbled to the side. One of the Sinclair-Koots Armored Cars slammed into the other, and they both careened across the street and smashed against a nearby brick wall. A street light fell from its moorings and shattered against the asphalt. The detectives in the street struggled to keep their footing. The whole city shook.

"W-what's happening?" Harvey asked. "Is this an earthquake, perhaps?"

Clay knew the answer. "No. It's the Dagger Men."

Almost as soon as it began, the earthquake stopped. The street ceased shaking. Silence filled the city, apart from distant shouts, and the calls of pigeons, along with a few more crashes as momentum and gravity did further damage. The Sinclair-Koots detectives had lowered their guns, as had Cohen. Throwing lead at each other just seemed pointless now. Everyone stared around the street, wondering what would happen next. They didn't have to wait long.

A deep, melodic noise rang through all of Sickle City. Every window and bit of shattered glass shook at the noise, which resembled the brassy burst of a trumpet. The sound seemed to come from the street itself, as if all of Sickle City was clearing its throat. More rumbles came from the steps of the Wigwam Club. The statues moved. Civil War generals stretched their arms, and politicians in their top hats and frock coats waved their hands. Their stone mouths opened, and the trumpeting noise projected from their throats as if they were part of one stone choir. The whole city appeared to sing. The noise wasn't particularly harsh, but it still seemed eerie and terrible. Harvey spun around in his seat, looking from the singing statues to the surrounding buildings.

Then he pointed to the skyscraper next to the Wigwam Club. "Look! It's Eisendrath!"

Clay folded his hands into fists—but Rabbi Eisendrath himself hadn't arrived. Instead, his tattooed face had been projected onto the side of the skyscraper, like a screen in one of the moving pictures he took Harvey to see. The window sills and cement and brick of the building distorted Rabbi Eisendrath's face, but those tattoos and that scowl were unmistakable. However, unlike the silent movies, sound came from Rabbi Eisendrath's mouth as it moved. The effect was uncanny, and Rabbi Eisendrath's voice projected from the building, the street, and the mouths of every statue in the city. More images of Rabbi Eisendrath appeared, taking up every wall. He appeared on the street as well, and the sidewalk. His image blossomed on the steps of the Wigwam Club, and on the dome roof. Everywhere Clay looked, Rabbi Eisendrath's tattooed face stared back. He must be giving this message to everyone in town. Sickle City spoke with the rabbi's voice.

"People of Sickle City—non-believers, Philistines, and Romans!" Rabbi Eisendrath's hairless face loomed above them, several stories high. His open mouth could have swallowed them all. "I come bearing joyous news. No longer will you labor under the control of corrupt politicians, cruel gangsters, and decadent tycoons. Your city now belongs to the highest authority of all. Sickle City is no more. Now you reside in the Second Jerusalem, the Holiest of Holy Cities, and the center of an Empire of God!" Clay shivered as the voice continued. "Do not be afraid. Rejoice in your newfound freedom, and the glory that will come to you as the beloved of Adonai, Our Lord and Our God."

Silence followed his words. He seemed to be giving them some time to let the proclamations sink in. The Sinclair-Koots detectives stared at each other, unsure what to do. Even Cohen lowered her rifle, her eyes darting between the talking statues and the image of Rabbi Eisendrath. His eyes, big as automobiles, scanned the street.

"In time, you will learn the ways of the Lord." Rabbi Eisendrath continued his speech—or was it a sermon? "Do not be afraid, for I will instruct you as Abraham did to the Israelites. You will learn how to dress, and how to eat, and to behave. The uncertainties of modern life, the struggle to discover one's way, will vanish. The Torah will provide every answer. I will be a patient teacher, like the priests of old, and God himself will aid us. We will give sacrifices to him, as they did in the days of the Temple, and He will make our new kingdom strong."

"He's instituting a theocracy," Harvey said, his voice a whisper. "This is terrible!"

"Is it really that bad?" Zipporah asked. "The Torah does have a lot of wisdom in it..."

"That's very true, Miss Sarfati—but it also has stuff about keeping slaves, and killing people with stones, and all kinds of violent, awful things. The people in Chinatown, and the Christians, and everyone who isn't Jewish will also be in great danger." Harvey pointed to the massive image of Rabbi Eisendrath looming above them. "And he's the one who's interpreting all of it! He's the one who says that God is telling him to do things, and he'll interpret the Torah or the Word of God any way he wants to ensure that he stays in power."

Rabbi Eisendrath continued. "There will be some who disagree with this new course. That is understandable. There are always Greeks, always Romans, who stand against the Chosen People. In every generation, they rise against us. But now, their hour of destruction is at hand." The sound of marching skeletal feet came from further down the street. "Stand against the Second Jerusalem, and you will meet such a destruction. If the United States government attempts to enter my Jerusalem, then they will learn destruction as well. So speaks the voice of God." His frown deepened. "I will be cruel to any who stand in my way."

Cohen aimed her rifle at the wall of the skyscraper, as if she could kill Rabbi Eisendrath by shooting his projected image. "I get the bad feeling he's talking about us," she muttered. "I think we'd better get out of here."

"Every window in Sickle City will be my eye." Rabbi Eisendrath's eyes scanned the street. They seemed to settle on the Cunningham—though that had to be Clay's imagination. "Every paving stone will be my fist. Every bit of energy will be my beating heart. Remain in your homes and do not attempt to flee. More instructions will come soon. Pray to the True God and know that this city belongs to the Dagger Men." His eyes closed and his image vanished. It faded from all the skyscrapers. The moving statues shut their mouths, though they still moved on their pedestals with creaking and rains of dust. His ultimatum had finished.

Clay turned to his friends. "He can see us. He said that every window would be his eye—and the city is an entire golem. He must know where we are, and he's already coming for us." Clay thought quickly. "Harvey, do you have some means of hiding from him?"

"I think so, sir." Harvey reached into his satchel. "Just give me some time..."

Zipporah pointed across the street. "Looks like we ain't the only ones thinking about escape."

Edwin Eames' private zeppelin, the *Heavenly Chariot*, rose up from behind the Wigwam Club. Eames must have arranged for the airship to land in the pavilion behind the Club, so he could hurry aboard. Now, the ornate airship flew into the air. Moonlight glittered on the intricate designs of the undercarriage as it ascended. Clay squinted and he could make out Eames on the deck, gripping the railing and watching everything.

A shriek came from the dark cloud. Hordes of black-winged birds swooped down, their talons glittering as they fell upon the zeppelin. Harvey gasped and turned away. Talons slashed into the canvas. Gas leaked out. The entire airship dropped downward, and then spun to the side. The undercarriage smashed against the top of the Wigwam Club. Metal shrieked and the airship flew past and drooped into the street. The Broxa—the vampire birds who served the Dagger Men—wheeled and darted around the downed zeppelin. Eames' attempt to escape had failed.

"He doesn't want anybody getting out," Harvey said.

"Nobody gets to leave his kingdom." Clay shook his head. "His Second Jerusalem."

"You're right, child," Zipporah said. "This guy is a nut."

Skeletal Roman cavalry appeared around the corner. A full column came riding down the street, their hooves clattering on the asphalt. Roman skeletal soldiers stood in the saddle, pulling back their pila for a salvo. Others carried lances or long swords, held high and ready to attack. They charged straight for the Cunningham, ignoring the Sinclair-Koots guards as they rode along. Sinclair shouted an order and the detectives turned their guns on the Roman skeletons. Guns chattered and bones broke under the barrage—but the cavalry rode closer.

Now, Clay could flee. He slammed on the gas and the Cunningham zoomed down the street. He made the engine roar, pressing down the gas pedal all the way. The cavalry rode closer, their swords flashing. In a few more moments, they reached the car. Skeletal horsemen rode on both sides of the Cunningham, and their swords flashed down and stabbed into the metal. A gladius jammed into Clay's shoulder. Zipporah pulled Harvey back, just as a spear punctured the upholstery where he had been sitting. Swords jammed into the long hood of the Cunningham, denting the metal and reaching the delicate motor inside.

Zipporah stood in her seat and fought back, slashing with her sabers. Cohen fired her rifle, blasting Roman horsemen out of the saddle. She blocked a sword with her rifle, and then swung the gun over her shoulder. "This isn't working." Cohen popped the pin of her grenade. "Time to try something new." She grabbed the collar bone of the nearest Roman rider and jammed the grenade in his face. When her hand pulled away, the grenade remained stuck in the skull's mouth. "Now drive, Clay!" Cohen cried. "*Vamos!*"

He punched the gas again, giving the wheel a twist as well. The Cunningham smashed its way through a pair of skeletal horses and riders. Bones flew through the air, bouncing on the street and crunching under the wheels. Clay drove on. Behind them, the grenade went off. It caught the first ranks of Roman cavalry, and the explosion finally stopped their charge. Skeleton men and horses rode on, their bones full of flame until they collapsed. Clay made it around the corner and kept going.

Harvey caught his breath. He withdrew a book from his satchel. "Here's a spell that should wrap a cloak around us, so that we can't be seen by supernatural means. I hope that will keep Sickle City from looking at us." He flipped through the pages. "It's an easy spell. I can just read it out loud and we should be okay. I just need to—Mr. Clay, there's golems in the road!"

Clay peered through the cracks on the windshield. Sure enough, a dozen golems blocked the road. They were rough creations—little more than conglomerations of bricks fused together by magic into the rough shape of human beings. They had no features and resembled lumps of orange bricks with arms, legs, and small nubs for heads. The city had spat them out and assembled them. They were the fingers of Sickle City, now forming into a fist and running to attack.

There was no time to avoid the golems, who had already charged. Clay hit the brakes. He spun the wheel. It didn't matter. The foremost brick golem reached the Cunningham Touring Car and threw itself into the hood. Metal crunched. The motor smoldered and popped. The weight of the crash sent the Cunningham spinning to the side—over the sidewalk, and into a nearby wall. The automobile would never drive again. Clay took his hands off the wheel as the golems closed in.

Chapter Seven
GOLEM CITY

The brick golems had a strange gait—a sort of shambling limp that dragged their lumpy limbs over the street. Magic, and not gravity, held the bricks together. Some stuck out at odd angles, jutting into the air as the brick golems closed in. But their funny way of walking didn't matter. Their hands had the appearance of clubs, with red bricks jabbing out like spikes on a morning star. They closed in at the same moment, a half-dozen of them with more further up the street. Clay's eyes moved from golem to golem. There was no way out. He hopped out of the smashed Cunningham, his boots landing on the dusty street. Behind him, Cohen, Zipporah, and Harvey scrambled out of the automobile.

"Harvey." Clay kept his tone calm. "Do you have the spell that will hide us?"

"I found it, sir. I s-suppose I better start reciting it." The book shook in Harvey's hands. The boy was terrified. "The spell should make it so that Rabbi Eisendrath won't be able to see us. Not with magic, at least. He won't be able to sense us either. But it w-will take some time, Mr. Clay. I'm sorry." He lowered his head and began to chant in quiet, urgent Hebrew.

Zipporah and Cohen moved next to Clay. "Shall we buy the rabbi's son some time?" Cohen readied her machete.

"Yes." Clay faced the first brick golem. "Remember, these are golems. Aim for the head."

A brick fist swung at Clay's chest. The brick golems had strength, but no intelligence. They were mindless constructs, summoned from raw magic, given an order, and now carrying that command out to the best of their abilities. The brick golem didn't know to attack Clay's forehead, but even a mindless, powerful blow could still do damage. Bricks smashed against Clay's chest, sending cracks rippling through his body. Red dust poured from the golem's fist, and it pulled back its arm to attack again. This time, Clay was ready. He weaved to the side—a boxer's move—and then grabbed the golem's forehead and jabbed down with his thumbs. They pushed through the rough sides of the bricks forming the golem's face. Clay kept the pressure until the brick golem collapsed. It tumbled to pieces, and soon a pile of bricks lay at Clay's feet. He kicked them aside.

The next brick golem tackled Clay, moving from a clumsy run to an awkward jump. Its sheer weight brought Clay down. He struck the street. Pavement bashed into his back as the brick golem's fists rained down heavy blows. One smashed into Clay's chin and another walloped his cheek. A few more blows, and those brick fists would reach his forehead. But Zipporah and Cohen reached him first. Cohen's machete and Zipporah's scimitar slashed down in the same moment, carving into the golem's forehead. They erased the letters, and a torrent of bricks spilled over Clay.

He rolled over, pushing them aside, and stumbled to his feet as another brick golem reached them. This one swatted Cohen, delivering a rapid blow that knocked her back. She fell into the ruined car, landing next to Harvey with an almost quiet grunt. The boy knelt next to her, trying to help her as he stammered through complicated Hebrew words. The brick golem advanced.

Clay reached it first. A powerful, rapid right hook smashed into the brick golem's face. Dust flew, along with red fragments of brick. The golem dropped. Clay had already turned to the next foe as bricks clattered against the street in wild syncopation.

Zipporah had drawn her second sword. She slashed both blades in the air, sawing at the forehead of one brick golem and dropping it with a well-timed slash—but her injuries slowed her. She moved next to Clay. "We can't stop them, Clay." She lunged out, delivering a stab to another brick golem. An arm of bricks caught the blow, and sparks flew as the sword stabbed down. "They are too many and too strong. And we cannot run."

"No options, then," Clay muttered. "You and Harvey should go and—"

The rapid honking of a horn drained out Clay's words. A familiar sleek gray Dusenberg automobile roared down the empty street, the horn blaring endlessly. Its headlights cast two yellow beams into the darkness, almost fantastically bright. Ava Silver gripped the wheel like she was trying to strangle it, her knuckles white as she gave it a twist. The Dusenberg slid to the side, the tires screeching over the pavement as it stopped right in front of the wrecked Cunningham Touring Car. Ava kept the engine running as she pushed up her motorist's goggles. She grinned like she had won a round of cards in a friendly game—but Clay could see fear in her eyes.

Silver gave them a wave. "Hello there, fellows. I think your auto's gone bust-o. Care for a ride?" She pointed to the brick golems. "It seems you're in a bit of a tight spot. I can guarantee a way out and a good place to stay. How about it?"

Harvey turned from the shining Dusenberg to Clay. He still mumbled Hebrew words. Clay knew the answer immediately. "Best offer we're gonna get. Let's go." He faced an attacking brick golem and caught its outstretched arm as it attempted a punch. Clay's fingers ripped around the arms, grabbed one brick, and pulled it free. He smashed the brick into the golem's forehead, destroying the creation in a burst of dust, and kicked aside the results. Then he ran to Cohen to help her to Silver's car. Zipporah got Harvey aboard, while Silver held the door open.

They clustered inside, Cohen groaning a little as Silver sent the Dusenberg zooming away. "How's that spell coming, *niño*?" she asked Harvey, a bit of motherly kindness drifting into her voice. "Almost finished?"

Another complicated set of syllables spilled out of Harvey's mouth. He coughed, cleared his throat, and then nodded. "It's finished, ma'am." Then he glanced over his shoulder. The brick golems ran after them, moving in a clunky jog as they pursued the Dusenberg. The automobile outpaced them, but they kept running—and as long as they ran, Rabbi Eisendrath could see Clay and his friends through golem's eyes. Harvey stared back at his book. "Oh no. I hope I didn't make a mistake, or pronounce something wrong, or—"

"Don't worry, child." Zipporah patted his shoulder. "We can outrun them."

"Let me give something a try." Silver gripped the wheel. "See if that amends the situation." The Dusenberg shifted to the side, and then sped into a side street. Scraps of newspaper and litter flew through the air, stirred by the wind as the automobile rushed by. Silver zoomed into the side street and hit the brakes. The automobile lurched, making everyone rock in their seats. Harvey bumped his head against the back and dropped his spectacles, which Zipporah swiftly returned. After that, they stayed quiet apart from the rumble of the car's engine.

Behind them, the brick golems ran on, into the shadows—as if they were still chasing a car down Damocles Street. The clatter of their feet echoed over the city, and eventually vanished. Clay settled into his seat. They had escaped. He turned to Silver. "You say have a safe place to stay?"

"Sure," Silver agreed. "My apartment." She hit the gas. "I bet Sophie will be pleased as punch to see you, Harvey. She's taken a shine to you, I'm happy to say." She turned the automobile around and began to drive, as

Harvey flushed a deep red. Clay was glad that he had found a friend—even after the whole city had been taken over by insane fanatics.

ฅ ฅ ฅ ฅ

Ava and Sophie Silver resided in a luxury penthouse apartment in the swanky Pepperdine Arms—when they weren't traveling over the world in search of news stories. Currently, the apartment building had turned into a fortress. The haggard, uniformed doorman carried a shotgun under his arm, and he moved aside to let Silver and her guests inside. They had dropped Cohen off as she approached, so she could make her way back to Haven Street and let Rabbi Holtz know that Clay had been rescued. She had taken a pounding in the skirmish with the brick golems, but Clay had a feeling she would be all right. She had survived the Mexican Revolution, after all.

Silver unlocked the door and motioned for her friends to follow. "My humble home." Her shoes clicked on the tiled floor as she stepped into a broad parlor. "And your humble home as well, for as long as you need." Comfortable Morris chairs faced a large radio, while an overstuffed couch rested near a wide window overlooking the entire city. Artifacts from Silver's travels had been mounted on the wall—African masks, rich tapestries, and photographs of numerous world-leaders. Framed newspaper articles joined them, showcasing some of Silver's best work for the *Weekly Sophisticate*. Candles rested on the glass coffee table and in the kitchen, holding back the shadows.

As soon as they entered, Sophie and Lucky hurried from the back room. Sophie embraced her mother. "You're okay, mom? And did you rescue them?" She spotted Harvey and the others and beamed. Lucky scampered to Harvey, who gave the excited panda cub a cautious pet. "You did! I knew you would."

"They're very tired, Sophie. Why don't you stand back and give the boy a little rest?" Silver pointed down the hall. "I got a pair of guest rooms you can use. The power flickers in and out, but the water's still running, if you want a dip in the bathtub."

"Should we?" Harvey asked. "There's so much to do, and—"

"Child, I learned long ago that you never pass up an opportunity to sleep." Zipporah pointed down the hall. "Come on. Let's get some rest. I'll help change your bandages." She put her hand on Harvey's shoulder and steered him toward the bedrooms, then glanced at Clay. "Would you mind standing guard, Clay?"

Clay didn't need to sleep, so the job was perfect for him. He sat down in front of the door. "I'll stand guard," he agreed. Silver gave him a thumbs-up and then led Sophie back to her room as well. Clay settled into the darkness. He watched the candle flames gutter and jump, and then turned his eyes to the door. He had done this before, many times, in the wilderness of Russia when he stood guard for the soldiers of the Polar Bear Expedition. Now, he was fighting another war. He sighed as he waited for night to end.

Morning came quickly, then Clay's friends joined him in the kitchen next to the parlor, where they had breakfast. The icebox remained cold, and they dined on milk and cereal, with sliced apples and even a few Oreo Sandwich Cookies for desert, which Harvey and Sophie enjoyed. Clay stayed near the window and watched as they ate.

The window overlooked a northern portion of Damocles Street, but the view stretched out over most of the city. Clay's eyes scanned the skyscrapers, now still and dark, and the empty road. Smoke trickled into the sky from several locations throughout Sickle City, forming curling black serpents against the gray sky. A thicker plume came from the direction of Arcadia Park. Had the Dagger Men torched the ornamental forests in the park? Clay thought about the Men of the Fields, the plant-people he and Zipporah had battled before this mess with the Dagger Men. That seemed so long ago now. He absurdly hoped that the plant-men would be all right.

Then footsteps came down the street. Clay stared downwards. A procession of Roman skeletons marched down Damocles Street, led by a towering golem composed from a chunk of skyscraper. The strange creation had the general outline of a man, and an automobile would only come to its knees. Glittering glass covered most of the golem's body, with steel supports and girders holding everything in place. Chunks of rebar formed thin, spidery fingers and projected from the golem's thick, cement hands. Roman legionaries marched behind it in silent formation. Behind them came a line of prisoners, tugged along on ropes fixed to iron collars. Clay squinted at the prisoners. Sure enough, it was the Sinclair-Koots Detective Agency. Orton Sinclair and Edwin Eames walked with them, trudging along and occasionally tugged by the ropes in their collars.

He moved back, noticing Zipporah's gaze. "What's the rumpus, Clay?"

"Sinclair's captured. Same with the other detectives, and Eames." Clay went to the round table, where Harvey, Sophie, and Silver enjoyed their meal. Lucky sat on the table, enjoying milk and crushed bamboo in a porcelain bowl. "The Dagger Men must be moving through the city, removing any threats to their control."

…a towering golem composed from chunks of skyscraper.

Harvey set down his spoon. He had dribbled milk on his shirt and chin. "Oh no. We need to get out of here—right now." He hopped down from the stool. "We're endangering Miss Silver and Sophie. The Dagger Men will see them as their enemies, and they'll come for them and—"

"Easy there, little fellow." Silver handed him a napkin. "For starters, Sophie and I are in danger even without you showing up. We tangled with the Dagger Men on Bone Island, remember? We ain't exactly on their Christmas card lists." She patted the counter. "Besides, I know what the Dagger Men want. They'll have me dressing in the proper *Frum* style—wearing a long dress and working in a kitchen until my dying day. I want to help fight them, however I can. And don't worry. Sophie and I are used to danger."

"I want to help too," Sophie agreed. "We'll fight the Dagger Men, however we can." She glanced at her mother. "But how exactly do we do that?"

Clay considered the question. "We need to assess our strength, before we can move against the Dagger Men."

"And that means getting back to Haven Street." Zipporah swiveled in her stool and faced the window. "No easy feat. Even with Harvey's spell shrouding us, there still must be countless guards around Haven Street. The Dagger Men know about Rabbi Holtz. They might have made a move to capture him and they could be waiting for us, already." She patted Harvey's shoulder. "Don't worry. Your father is a tricky fellow. He wouldn't let a bunch of dusty Roman skeletons trap him."

"I know he wouldn't, Miss Sarfati," Harvey agreed. "He has my uncle to look after as well. He would never let Herbert come to harm." He sounded like he was trying to convince himself. "So, if we can't go to Haven Street, what do we do?"

"I may have a solution," Silver explained. "Remember, we're not the only mugs who are gonna be picking fights with our new benevolent biblical masters." She gave Lucky a pat, and the panda cub rolled onto his back and wiggled his feet in the air. "The Dagger Men have little love for anyone who doesn't embrace their particular brand of Biblical Judaism. And quite a few people in Sickle City have no place at all in their perfect Second Jerusalem."

Zipporah folded her arms. "What do you mean, exactly?"

"The Negroes of Hogshead Street," Silver said. "And the Chinese. The Dagger Men have no love for those poor fellows, who have already suffered in the riot. Besides, there's amateur sorcerers and crime bosses in those neighborhoods who pose a threat to the Dagger Men's magical monopoly. I happen to know a fellow in Hogshead Street who will certainly become a target for the Dagger Men. If we can get to him first..."

"He might help us!" Harvey nodded his agreement as he faced Clay and Zipporah. "And there's Miss Hark—Herbert's friend. She resides in Chinatown, and is friendly with some of the Tongs. She might be able to help us as well."

"And the Tongs work with Sid Sapphire," Zipporah said. "They're the Shark's allies in the smuggling business."

"So what do you think?" Silver asked.

Clay rested his thick hands on the counter. "Hogshead Street." He remembered the dismissive way that Rabbi Holtz and Sapphire referred to the residents of Hogshead Street. "Can we really trust the *Schwartzes*?"

"Mr. Clay." Harvey's voice went stern. "T-that kind of bigotry has no place here. My father sometimes uses that word, and I hate when he does. It's insulting and mean. It's a slur, just like the names that my classmates call me." He tried to draw himself to his full height, but the stool swiveled under him, making him look ridiculous. "The Dagger Men are bigots. Their prejudice gives them strength. If we're going to fight them, we'll need the help of everyone in Sickle City—especially the residents of Hogshead Street. Please, don't say any more horrible things l-like, like that word ever again." His courage faded from him. "That's what I think, at least."

Sophie patted his shoulder. "Well said, Harvey."

"Thank you, Miss Silver." A smile crossed Harvey's red face.

Silver nodded. "Don't you worry, Mr. Clay. I know at least one Negro who can hold his own in any mumbo-jumbo scrape, and you can bet your bottom dollar that he'll help us out of this jam." She picked up her purse, pausing to withdraw her snub-nosed pistol and check the ammunition. "Besides, I know Hogshead Street. I visit all the time."

"You do?" Zipporah asked.

"Sure. Best jazz in town." She nodded to Sophie. "You're coming with me, darling—but Lucky's gotta stay here. I'm not dragging a panda cub across the city today."

"Mom..." Sophie sounded annoyed as she swept Lucky into her arms.

"No discussion on that matter." She grinned at Clay and his friends. "And I'd be honored if you went with me as well."

"You should go, Clay," Zipporah said. "And take Harvey. I think I'll go to Chinatown." Her scimitars had been resting on the kitchen table, next to the milk and the package of Oreo Sandwich Cookies. She grabbed the scabbards and strapped them over her shoulders. "I'll see if I can find Miss Hark, and Sapphire. He does business with the Ghost Brothers Tong, and they operate out of a joint called the Benevolent Merchantman's Association."

Clay watched as she readied her blades. "How do you know?"

"I worked security for the illegal casino in the Benevolent Merchantman's Association's basement," Zipporah explained. "Those Chinamen have quite an operation." She moved to the door, and paused. "It'd be better if we split up. Confuse the Dagger Men. I'll meet you there." She offered her hand to Harvey. "Be careful, Harvey."

Harvey took her hand and clasped it. "You too, Miss Sarfati."

Then she opened the door and stepped into the hall. Clay, Silver, and the children got ready next. Harvey and Sophie put on their coats, Silver loaded her revolver, and then they followed Zipporah's path to the hall and to the elevator, after leaving a good amount of bamboo for Lucky. The Dusenberg waited around the block. Clay flexed his fists as the elevator brought them down to the lobby. He wondered what exactly was waiting for them in Hogshead Street. Harvey was right about there being no place for bigotry now. Compared to the Dagger Men, almost anyone was their friend.

※ ※ ※

Hogshead Street had been hit hard by the riots following the police strike. While only one mob had hit Haven Street, several had fallen on the Negro neighborhood. Fueled by hatred, they had torched tenements, destroyed businesses, and looted everything. Now, the street lay quiet and empty. The overturned, burned-out husks of destroyed cars lay in the street. Silver weaved the Dusenberg around them, and stuck to the back alleys and side streets. Smashed furniture and broken shelves joined the ruined cars. They had been tossed out in the looting. The residents stayed in their shabby apartments or rundown stores, peering out and carefully watching the Dusenberg—doubtlessly wondering if Clay and his friends presented a threat. Clay didn't blame them.

Silver took another turn, and then drove her automobile down a straight cement road elevated along a fetid, green canal known as the Cut. A sluggish, manmade river, the Cut wound through the eastern half of Sickle City and emptied into the bay. Several docks jutted out into the still waters of the Cut, where rows of boats floated. The Cut was used for smuggling, as well as transport. Great volumes of bootleg booze must have flowed through the manmade river.

After driving a few more blocks, Silver parked the car on the bank of the Cut. A rundown gambling joint overlooked the river, the sort of establishment where questions were never asked and bets could vary from pennies to fortunes. The square structure had the general shape of a tomb, with a pair of dull neon dice above the entrance. Clay and the others left the car and examined the shabby casino.

"The Snake Eyes Social Club." Harvey read the joint's name. "Your friend's in here, Miss Silver?"

"That he is, darling," Silver agreed. "Don't let appearances deceive you. It's a truly charming little place. Now, follow me, and try not to touch anything." She led them to the door, gave it a pull, and then a loud knock. After a few more moments of waiting, the door creaked open just enough for the muzzle of a double-barreled shotgun to emerge and aim at Silver. She put her hands on her hips. "Easy there. We're just here to see the doctor."

The shotgun wavered and then retracted. The doors opened. The fellow with the shotgun returned to his place behind the bar, his gun resting on his shoulder. He had a fringe of white hair, a perpetual frown, and sported suspenders over a frayed shirt with a band collar. He took up position behind the bar, rested his gun on the counter, and stared at Clay and the others. The Snake Eyes Social Club looked much like the bartender— tired, aging, but still tough. A pool table rested at one end, while places for card games took up the rest of the interior. Suspicious stains covered the wooden floorboards. The booze came in buckets, taken straight from barrels transported by smugglers from the Cut out back. Several buckets rested on the counter, froth spilling over their tops. The Snake Eyes Social Club had no customers, and no apparent occupants besides the bartender.

Silver settled into a stool by the bar. "How's business?"

"I keep a loaded gun under the counter, ever since the strike," the bartender muttered. "And now this crazy Jew's declared himself emperor supreme. How the hell do you think business is?" He pointed to Clay and Harvey. "They look Hebrew. They some of that mad rabbi's spies?"

Sophie shook her head. "No, sir. They're a pair of heroic detectives, battling against the Dagger Men." Harvey blushed at the mention. "But we need a little bit of help to do so."

"That means meeting the doctor," Silver said.

"He's in his room." The bartender jabbed a thumb to the door behind the bar. "I don't know why I let him stay here. He's nothing but trouble. Still, in times like these, there are certain men who are handy to have around."

They filed behind the counter and approached the door. Silver threw it open and stepped inside and Clay and the others followed while the bartender stayed out. The back room housed a strange assortment of occult ingredients, along with a simple cot in the corner and a roll top desk. Clusters of withered herbs dangled from the ceiling, along with flesh-colored roots resembling misshapen fingers. A few shrunken heads sat on the walls, their lips and eyes sewn shut. Strange charms of bone and glass, idols of heathen gods, skulls of ravens, and odder objects joined them. A candelabrum provided flickering light—as the window had been shut to the gray sun.

A thin fellow sat at the desk, his spindly arms and spider-like fingers using a miniature blade to carefully dice some dried leaves. He turned around from his work and came to his feet, grinning when he spotted Silver. "Miss Ava Silver, it is a rare pleasure." He had dark coffee-colored skin and a pointed devil's beard on his lean, grinning face. A single gold tooth glimmered in the center of his smile. He wore a stately Edwardian suit and tie, with charms dangling from his watch chain. His top hat rested next to him on the desk, and he grabbed it to add a flourish to his bow.

"Dr. Cutte." Silver offered her hand and received a kiss on the knuckles. "A rare pleasure indeed." She indicated her companions with a polite wave of the hand. "You know my dear daughter, Sophie. And these fine gentlemen are Emmet Clay and Harvey Holtz. Mr. Clay, and young Harvey. I'd like to introduce Dr. Lazarus Cutte, a fine—"

Clay glowered at Dr. Cutte. "We've met."

"You have?" Silver seemed a little taken aback.

"We had a rather fortuitous meeting at a cabin owned by this nice young man's father," Dr. Cutte explained. "Pastoral bliss was interrupted by a local chapter of the Ku Klux Klan, and the half-made golems they summoned. We aligned our forces in order to survive." Dr. Cutte returned to his seat and folded his thin legs. "How are you, Mr. Clay? I wondered what part you played in recent circumstances which have befallen Sickle City, and what your place is in Rabbi Eisendrath's unfortunate new order." He flashed his gold tooth again.

Dr. Cutte was a witch doctor, an amateur sorcerer with a penchant for getting into trouble thanks to his various spells. He traveled from town to town, offering his magical remedies for assorted ailments, and trying to back up his big claims with bigger enchantments. It rarely succeeded, and he ended up in trouble more often than not. Clay didn't care for Dr. Cutte, or the fancy way he talked, but the man had trained under Voodoo priests in New Orleans. He might not be an expert, but he still knew his business.

Harvey politely offered his hand. "Pleased to meet you again, Dr. Cutte. Mr. Clay and I are on the run from the Dagger Men, but we're trying to gather some allies and eventually stop the Dagger Men for good and save the town. Would you please consider joining us?"

"It would be my pleasure." Dr. Cutte glanced back at his table, where he had almost finished cutting the herbs. "I knew right away that Biblical rule would be disastrous for Hogshead Street and for all of Sickle City as well. I made entreaties to certain underworld figures. The boss of Hogshead Street, a charming woman named Madam Gracie, has already agreed to send help. She should be arriving with some of her trusted lieutenants to discuss our next move. You can meet her, young Harvey, and explain what's happened to Sickle City." He paused for a moment. "It's been transformed into a golem, I take it."

"Yeah," Clay said. "Sickle City's been turned into one giant golem, under Rabbi Eisendrath's control." He paused as he stared at Dr. Cutte. "And you want to help us fight against Rabbi Eisendrath and the Dagger Men?"

Sophie looked confused. "You don't think he would?"

"He doesn't exactly seem the type." Clay didn't hide the distaste from his voice as he faced Dr. Cutte. "He's more charlatan than soldier."

"You may be right." Dr. Cutte let some of the ornamentation leave his voice. "And I'm not a particularly brave charlatan, at that. Perhaps that's why I've summoned Madam Gracie for help." He slumped in his seat. "It's simple self-preservation. The Dagger Men have sent their attack golems and reanimated Roman skeletons to capture anyone they consider a threat. They've rounded up a few people in Hogshead Street already, and I am certain they intend to come for me."

"Because you're a sorcerer," Silver suggested.

"A witch doctor," Dr. Cutte corrected. "If I wish for blood to continue to flow through my body, the Dagger Men need to be defeated. I will happily work to that end alongside you, Mr. Clay." He returned to his feet and reached for his coat. "Now, we are in agreement that the assorted sorceries come from a golem source. But how are we to stop it?"

Before Harvey could reply, the back door slammed open. The bartender emerged, his shotgun nestled in his arm. "More visitors outside," he explained. "But it ain't any guests that I'm happy to see. You'd better come out and get a look at them."

Dr. Cutte shuddered. He nodded to Clay. "Once more into the breach, eh?"

"Sure." Clay walked ahead of him and left the back room.

The others followed him. They stood in the main room of the Snake Eyes Social Club and looked out at the street. As the bartender said, trouble had arrived. A small army of golems neared the gambling joint. Dark pavement and asphalt formed their bodies, striped with strips of discarded newspapers and other detritus. They had probably emerged right out of the street, leaving man-shaped manholes in the road. Now they stood in a loose semi-circle before the Snake Eyes Social Club, like a group of shadows given substance and heft. They blocked the road completely, cutting off any escape.

Suddenly, the street golems parted. They stepped aside, chunks of asphalt dripping from their bodies and crumbling over the ground. Rabbi Geist walked to the front of the street golems, like a proud general standing before his troops. A light wind stirred his vast beard and long hair. He wrapped his fur coat around him, and glared at the entrance to the Snake Eyes Social Club.

Rabbi Geist's voice boomed throughout Hogshead Street. "Dr. Lazarus Cutte! God has whispered your name in my ear! You are needed to help with the construction of a great Temple, which will please the Lord with its beauty. Come out of this house of sin, and join us in the light of God." He held out his arms, as if he wanted to embrace Dr. Cutte. "Or we will come in and get you."

"He wants me to build a temple?" Dr. Cutte asked. "I'm remarkably ill-suited to manual labor."

"Maybe that's what the Dagger Men are doing with all their prisoners," Harvey explained. "Making them slaves to build the temple. The Torah does talk about slaves, and while it has rules for their good treatment, it says some pretty awful things too. I guess the Dagger Men are following that tradition."

"How horrid," Silver muttered.

"Will you relent, Dr. Cutte?" Rabbi Geist demanded. "Or will I have to come and get you?"

"Go get a haircut!" Sophie cried.

Silver laughed. "That's my girl." She turned to the bartender. "The boats moored outside, on the Cut—could we borrow one? We have a destination in Chinatown in mind. We'd be sure to return it to you, when this unfortunate business is over."

The bartender tossed her a set of keys.

"This is your final chance, Dr. Cutte!" Rabbi Geist called again through the door. "Will you submit?"

"I will not!" Dr. Cutte's voice boomed back. "And that is my final word on the subject." He turned to Harvey. "I do hope I do not regret this sudden burst of bravery." He shuddered suddenly, as the feet of golems pounded in a charge.

The street golems raced to the door. The first golem smashed its way against the door, shattering it in a spray of wood. It raced across the room, stomping on the floorboards as its arms reached toward Dr. Cutte. It ignored Clay and the others. It had been instructed only to grab Dr. Cutte and bring him out—Clay had no place in its command. Of course, if Clay got in the way, he would be an obstacle to be removed. Clay knew that he had to intervene.

He ran to meet the street golem, and they clashed in the center of the Snake Eyes Social Club. The street golem walloped Clay's chest, driving down its fists again and again. The golem's thick fingers wrapped around Clay's arm and started pulling. The street golem had more size and strength—but Clay was smarter, and he would have to fight smart if he intended to win. He wrenched his arms free, stumbled back, and fell into the billiards table. Green felt ripped under his body. Clay turned, reaching for something help him. He grabbed a pool cue, swung it around, and faced the street golem. It moved closer to him, as two more street golems blundered their way through the ruined door. Clay would have to take down this golem fast.

The pool cue would be weapon enough. Clay snapped it over his knee and charged the street golem, a jagged length of wood in each hand. He jumped at the street golem, reaching for its forehead. The street golem's big hands moved to stop him. A grazing blow nearly stopped Clay, but he still stabbed both pieces of the cue deep into the golem's forehead. They scratched the holy words, and the street golem tumbled back and collapsed into a heap of asphalt, burying the broken cue. Clay moved back and faced the next two golems.

Silver readied her pistol and the bartender had his shotgun. "How do we stop them, Mr. Clay?" Silver asked, cocking the pistol. "You seem to be an expert on these pieces of ambulatory geography. What's the best way to take them down?"

"Aim for the head, ma'am!" Harvey cried.

"Good advice in any endeavor." Silver's pistol cracked, sending shot after shot into the head of the nearest street golem. The fourth bullet did its job. It scraped the carvings on the street golem's forehead, and the golem fell back and came to pieces before hitting the floor. The shotgun took off the head of the next golem, scattering macadam against the walls. The shot messily destroyed the golem, and covered the card tables in pieces of street.

But even as those golems collapsed, more burst into the gambling joint. One ripped its way through the wall, while two more forced their way past the doorway. They stepped through the pieces of their fallen fellows as they approached.

The bartender pointed to a side door. "Stairs lead down to the Cut." He fired the next blast of his shotgun. "I'll tell Madam Gracie what happened. Let her know to keep her ears open, doctor, to wait for your signal before the next move—now go!"

That was all the farewell they needed. Silver led Sophie and Harvey to the side door and pushed it open, ushering them out as the street golems surged across the Snake Eyes Social Club and approached the counter. Clay ran to join them. A street golem grabbed his arm as he neared the bar, and attempted to pull him back. His side banged against the counter, upsetting buckets of booze and spilling cheap alcohol on the ground. Clay grabbed the handle of the pail and smacked it against the street golem's head—to little avail.

Harvey froze on the steps. "Mr. Clay!" He dashed back, panic in his eyes.

Dr. Cutte stepped in front of him. "Don't worry, my dear boy—I will be the one to save your guardian." He turned around, a hand leaving his coat and holding a small white bag tied with a thread. "Or rather, it will be the power of the Voodoo Gods." He raised his hand. "Turn away, Mr. Clay. Let my magic gris-gris work."

Clay twisted to the side, looking away as Dr. Cutte hurled the bag of gris-gris—a collection of powerful herbs, bone shavings, and other items—into the charging mass of street golems. The bag bounced off the golem's head, and then the string snapped and released a thick gray cloud. Clay couldn't imagine the little bag containing that much gris-gris, and yet the substance all but filled the Snake Eyes Lounge. The street golems struggled in the cloud, unable to see. They slammed into walls and furniture, smashing everything with wild swipes of their arms. Clay tried not to get any gris-gris in his face, but his vision still went foggy.

"Come along, Mr. Clay." Dr. Cutte took his arm. "Our chariot awaits."

They went to the door, where Silver and the children waited. Sophie pointed to the Cut. A few motorboats sat on the brown water in various states of rust. "We're gonna sail to safety. I prefer our personal vessel, but these will serve for now."

"Quite right, Sophie," Silver agreed. "Come along now."

She hastened down the cement steps, hopped across the dock, and landed in the motorboat at the far end of the dock. Silver started the engine, and beckoned for the others to board. Harvey and Sophie scrambled in next, and then Dr. Cutte's long legs carried him inside. Clay hopped in next. The motorboat swayed a little under his weight, but stayed afloat. Silver sent it speeding down the Cut, with large cement walls on either side.

A street golem smashed its way out of the Snake Eyes Social Club and attempted to stop them, in its own mindless manner. The golem launched itself at the cement walls surrounding the canal and plummeted downwards. It struck the water with a splash behind the motorboat. Water showered everyone in the boat, and the resulting ripple pushed their boat a few more paces along. Clay peered through the dingy water and made out the street golem at the bottom. It had damaged its forehead in the fall, and now only a pile of asphalt lay under the water.

Harvey looked down as well and then stared at Clay. "I'm glad that my uncle made you to be smarter than these golems, Mr. Clay."

"Your uncle *made* him, dear heart?" Silver asked, with a knowing grin. "Mr. Clay, are you a golem yourself?"

"I..." Clay paused. "Are you going to write a story about this?"

"Perhaps you could write that story later, Miss Silver." Dr. Cutte clutched his knees as the motorboat puttered along. "I don't think we have time for much else." He peered back at the Snake Eyes Social Club, perched above the cement walls bordering the Cut. "I do feel sorry for the old place. It took such damage. I'll have to contribute to the repairs, once this wretched business is over. Speaking of which, where is our destination?"

"Chinatown, sir," Harvey explained. "The Benevolent Merchantman's Association." He explained carefully to Dr. Cutte. "Miss Zipporah Sarfati is there, asking them for help."

"The Orientals?" Dr. Cutte asked. "Are you certain?" He brushed water off his top hat, frowning at the stains on the dark fabric. "They are a strange people, with odd rituals and customs and their own, bizarre, and frequently frightening ways of dealing with outsiders. Do you really suppose they will grant us succor in our hour of need?"

"We have to try, sir," Harvey said. "And I believe you're incorrect about the Chinese being different. They may have their own traditions, but so do we all. They're being persecuted by the Dagger Men, just like everyone else in Sickle City."

"And we need all the help we can get," Silver added.

Dr. Cutte nodded. "Sage wisdom from you, Miss Silver, as always."

Clay slumped in the back of the motorboat. He agreed with Silver. The more allies they had, the better chance they had of beating the Dagger Men. A witch doctor like Dr. Cutte would certainly come in handy. He just hoped it would be enough.

The Cut slashed down through Sickle City, leading right past Chinatown. Silver piloted the motorboat down the length of the Cut, until they found an obliging dock and ended their little voyage. They tied up the vessel, clambered up a set of cement stairs, and followed a winding alley into the heart of Chinatown. This place had been settled by Chinese immigrants for at least three generations, and it resembled something close to a foreign country, dropped in the center of Sickle City. The usual tenements rose up along the edges, but the structures inside had sloping, pagoda-style roofs. Statues of Buddhist lion dogs flanked the entrances to several buildings, and strings of paper lanterns rested overhead. Clay had taken Harvey here before, and he had watched the boy dine on chop suey served steaming from the numerous vendors. Clay had always enjoyed going there, but he didn't like what he saw now.

The neighborhood had been hit hard by the riots—even worse than Hogshead Street. Numerous structures had been burned or looted, including a Buddhist temple. The sculptures inside had been hurled onto the street. Some brave Chinaman had bundled them up and taken them to the sidewalk, where they watched everything with their sad eyes. The Chinese that risked leaving their houses tried their best to clear away the rubble. One portly woman simply stood in the center of the street, releasing endless wails. Clay looked at the neighborhood and felt a pure sadness. This was like a pogrom in Russia, but turned against a different people and carried out by American citizens.

Harvey seemed caught between disbelief and distress. He kept looking at the damaged buildings and the tearful people, and then spun around to look at Clay. "How could this happen?" His voice was small and quaked. "I know there's prejudice and I know there's hate. But someone should have done something to stop it."

"I'm sure they tried, dear heart," Silver said. "But they were overwhelmed. The hatred for those who are different is too strong in this country. The Dagger Men have lived with that hatred for a long time. It's what fuels them. They're only going to make things worse."

"We'll stop them, Harvey." Sophie patted his shoulder, trying to cheer him up. "Don't worry."

Dr. Cutte pointed to the far end of the street. "There's the Benevolent Merchantman's Association. It seems respectable enough, but I have long since learned that appearances can be deceiving."

Sophie squinted at the sky. "Is that bird following us?"

Everyone looked up. A Broxa soared over the street, its wings outstretched and its pointed beak facing the air. The bird must be scouting for the Dagger Men, scouring the city for any kind of threat. Harvey recognized it as well. "A Broxa!" he cried. "One of the Dagger Men's creatures!"

The dark bird's beak angled down, its obsidian eyes starting to scan the street. Clay didn't know if Harvey's spell would protect them from discovery when the Broxa gazed right at them. They needed to get out of its line of sight—and quickly. Clay pointed to the Benevolent Merchantman's Association. "There," he ordered. "Hurry!" He grabbed Harvey's arm and tugged the boy along, while Silver did the same to her daughter. Dr. Cutte's long-limbed gait carried him across the cobblestones, and they hastened to the large, square lump of marble and steel before them. They scrambled past the statues of lion dogs, and reached the large set of double doors.

Silver gave it a rapid knock. "Hey, open up!" she cried, to no avail. "You better let us in, or we're golem-bait!" The door remained closed. She withdrew her pistol from her purse. "What do you think, Mr. Clay? Should I try picking that bird out of the sky?"

"Better not," Clay said. "Might alert the Dagger Men."

Dr. Cutte sighed. "Why aren't the Chinamen giving us entry?"

"After what just happened, can you really blame them?" Harvey raised his voice. Above them, the Broxa began to make lazy circles. It would spot them soon, and then deliver the alarm in some rapid, far-reaching, magical manner. "Excuse m-me? I'm Harvey Holtz—Herbert Holtz's younger brother. Herbert's a friend of Bethany Hark. Do you know Bethany Hark? Maybe you could let us in, and we could contact her? I'm also Rabbi Holtz's son, and he works for Sid Sapphire, and—"

The door slammed open. Bethany Hark stood in the doorway, wearing a tattered trench coat, a flat cap pressed low on her head. A cartridge belt had been looped over her shoulder, and she carried a strange sort of crossbow, topped with wooden ridges. She moved to a kneeling position, familiar to any soldier, and aimed the crossbow at the sky. "Get in." She spoke through gritted teeth as she gazed down the sights of the weapon.

Clay held the door. The others hurried into the safety of the Benevolent Merchantman's Association, while Hark fingered the trigger of the weapon. The crossbow twanged, sending a small bolt hurtling into the sky. The bolt had been decorated with a profusion of peacock feathers, and trailed silver dust as it hurried into the sky. Its point caught the Broxa in the neck. The vampire bird tumbled to the side, its wings still pulsing. Hark fired twice more, the crossbow rapidly sending up its bolts. One caught the Broxa in the chest and the other pierced a wing. The Broxa fell to the ground, already turning to ash as it descended. Gray powder blasted against the cobblestones.

She came to her feet and turned to Clay, the crossbow still in her hand. "Enchanted bolts," she explained. "We can't let the Dagger Men know that we're here."

"What did you do in Shanghai?" Clay stared at her.

"All manner of horrid things," Hark replied. "And it seems I must do them here as well. Come inside and I'll introduce you to the others." She walked through the doorway, and Clay followed her into the Benevolent Merchantman's Association.

The lobby had the look of any respectable business establishment. Cream-colored walls surrounded ornate furniture, and appropriately oriental hangings covered the walls. The place seemed deserted. A few sculptures of dragons and lion dogs lurked in the corner, intimidating visions in polished wood and brass. Harvey touched a curling dragon's whiskered muzzle and pulled his hand away quickly, as if frightened that the sculpture would take offense. Sophie giggled in amusement. Dr. Cutte slumped into a large armchair and removed his top hat, which he assiduously began to clean of dust.

Hark walked to the head of the room and set her repeating crossbow down on the counter. She faced her guests. For a few moments, she paused—unsure of what to say. Finally, her eyes settled on Harvey. "How's Herbert? Is he safe?"

"He's back in Haven Street. He should be safe—as long as my father is." Harvey paused. The fear for his family finally got to him. "They must be targets for the Dagger Men. The golems and skeleton legionaries might already be going to Haven Street to capture them. Mrs. Cohen is protecting papa—my father, I mean—and Uncle Herbert, and Mr. Moss is as well. They'll keep them safe." He turned to Clay, eager for agreement. "Right?"

"They'll be okay, Harvey." Sophie tried to comfort the boy. "Don't worry."

Silver gave Harvey a comforting smile. "I'm sure my daughter's absolutely right, dear heart. From my reporting, I know your father is a courageous, capable, and resourceful rabbi. He'll find some way to protect his people."

"Have you heard anything from Haven Street?" Clay asked Hark.

She shook her head. "We received some very important refugees from that neighborhood, but they didn't tell us anything about Rabbi Holtz." She pointed to a small door in the corner, the same pale color as the wall. It could have been a servant's entrance. "They're downstairs. I think they need to talk with you. But no, we haven't heard anything from Haven Street." She stared at her boots, suddenly showing some fear. "I'm worried too."

"Why would the Dagger Men attempt to assault Haven Street?" Dr. Cutte asked, in genuine confusion. "They are all of the Hebraic persuasion, are they not? Why should there be dissension among the Hebrew set?"

"The Dagger Men are a very peculiar breed of Jew, doctor," Silver explained. "They're absolute nuts, and they say any Jew who doesn't subscribe to their particular brand of Judaic insanity is a heretic. They probably see Rabbi Holtz as a horrendous traitor indeed, for his, ah, extralegal activities, and the questionable nature of his rabbinic status." She glanced apologetically at Harvey. "No offense meant to your father, Harvey."

"No, I understand," Harvey said. "I'm just worried about him." He glanced at Hark. "What about Miss Sarfati? She was supposed to meet us here?"

"I've got some good news there." Hark slung the repeating crossbow over her shoulder and moved to the door in the corner. "Zipporah made it here a few minutes ago. Some Tong hatchetmen spotted her taking on a Roman patrol on the edge of Chinatown. She handled those skeletons in her usual style, then they brought her here." She gave the door a set of rapid knocks, and called in Chinese. Clay and his friends assembled behind her. "She's downstairs, and I bet she'll be eager to see that you've safely arrived."

"Hospitality from the Tongs," Dr. Cutte mused. "Seems like something out of a pulp magazine."

A Tong hatchetman opened the door and nodded to Hark. He wore a traditional Chinese robe and his fedora shaded a face covered in straight, pale scars of a bladed origin. An assortment of sharp weapons and pistols rested on his belt, ready to be used. He stepped aside, allowing entry to a few stairs winding into a basement. This had to be the underground casino that Zipporah had helped guard for Sapphire. Hark led them down the shadowed steps.

The stairs seemed to lead into another world. The Ghost Brothers Tong—the most powerful Tong in the city—knew that American gamblers wanted the mystery and romance of the Orient, and they had gone out of their way to create an appropriate setting. Potted cherry blossom trees rested in the corner, while silken screens created a maze of booths for private games. Everything seemed red and gold, from the ornaments dangling down from the ceiling to the statues of Chinese gods and warriors overlooking the games. A set of roulette wheels occupied one part of the room, a bar occupied another corner, and the rest belonged to card tables topped with red felt. The place looked very large—a cathedral of gambling—but seemed mostly empty.

A dozen Tong goons reclined around the bar, smoking and talking in quiet Chinese as they prepared knives, pistols, and rifles. But the more important guests occupied a mammoth, round card table at the center of the room. The De Brothers—the triplets who controlled the Ghost Brothers Tong—sat at one end of the table. All three portly brothers wore matching white suits and scarlet bowties. They had varying degrees of hair, and the same calm, intent look in their dark eyes. Sid Sapphire stood across from them. In his dark tuxedo, he looked like some kind of shadowy opposite of the De Brothers. Sapphire puffed smoke from his cigarette holder, and looked even more unhappy than usual.

They weren't alone. Kid Twist Deutsch leaned against a table near his boss, idly spinning the roulette wheels and listening to them whir. He had shed his suit coat, revealing twin automatics in crossed shoulder-holsters. A bandage covered his nose—perhaps an injury he had received in protecting his boss after the Dagger Men took over. But Clay's attention turned away from Kid Twist, and moved to Zipporah. She had been examining the Ghost Brothers Tong's arsenal of weapons, laid out on a long table near the back, but turned away from the various guns and blades and hurried to join Clay, Harvey, and the others.

She embraced Clay, and then did the same to Harvey. "Clay! Grand to see you." She beamed at Harvey. "You're okay, child? I had the devil of a time getting here. The Dagger Men patrols are everywhere in the city, and I had to fight my way in. Was it the same for you?"

"We had a little difficulty getting Dr. Cutte," Clay said. "But not too much."

Dr. Cutte swept off his hat in another dramatic bow. "Don't sell yourself short, Mr. Clay. You were the very picture of heroism." He beamed up at Zipporah, as if expecting her hand to extend so he could kiss it. "And how are you, my charming Miss Sarfati? Still a fiery fighter, I take it?"

"Stand up, Dr. Cutte. You look like more of an idiot than usual." She pointed to the table. "You can join our discussion. Sapphire and the De Brothers are deciding what to do." She glanced at Harvey. "We haven't heard from your pop, child. I suppose you can represent him at the meeting."

"Maybe represent Haven Street as well," Hark agreed.

"Me?" Harvey asked. "Represent my father?"

"Who could do a better job?" Sophie asked. "Come on, I'll sit next to you."

"You better join them too, Clay," Zipporah added. "You've got a rather unique perspective on golems, after all."

They walked to the large round table and sat down. Clay and Zipporah joined them. Dr. Cutte sat across from Clay's friends, and tried not to look uncomfortable at Sapphire and the De Brothers' curious stares. Silver and Hark stood a bit back, overlooking the meeting, and ready to help—but they didn't truly represent a portion of Sickle City. Clay supposed that he didn't either, but he was a golem. Sickle City was a golem city now, and his expertise would doubtlessly be needed.

Sapphire looked them over. "Mr. Clay. Miss Sarfati." He gave them polite nods. The De Brothers did the same. "I want to welcome you to the Benevolent Merchantman's Association. I've talked with the De Brothers and they agreed to offer sanctuary. We can use this place as a kind of headquarters. Put together a force." He paused. "And take back the city from these Dagger Men buffoons." He gripped his cigarette holder tightly, almost snapping the thin tube. "They're worse than goo-goo reformers. Worse than the Prohibition Agents. Worse than the goddamn temperance marchers. Their golems and legionaries have taken down all but a few of my speakeasies and trashed my liquor warehouses. They regard me as a threat, and they're acting accordingly. We've got to take this city back."

The De brothers nodded in unison. "They will come here soon," the brother on the left explained. "To try and stop us. We must stop them first."

"We've met some of their skeletons and forced them back," the De Brothers on the right added.

Dr. Cutte nodded. "I'm sure Madam Gracie and all the residents of Hogshead Street feel the same way, and I hereby dedicate my services to—"

"Clay." Sapphire's voice went low. "What's a *schwartze* doing here?"

Silence filled the table. Clay rested his hands on the red felt surface. "Mr. Sapphire, Dr. Cutte helped us escape from Hogshead Street. He is an expert on magic. We're going to need help to repel the Dagger Men." He pushed back his chair and came to his feet. "They captured me, sir, and I saw how they took over the city. They carved holy words into the Founding Stone, and turned all of Sickle City into their golem. They can summon more golems at will, and use untold power to bring about more destructive spells. All of Sickle City is endangered by the Dagger Men. All of Sickle City must rise against them. Dr. Cutte is here because we need him. It's as simple as that."

Zipporah cut in. "That means reaching out to everybody, and letting them send someone here, so we can plan some kind of attack on the Dagger Men." She tapped the table. "When I was in the Levant, during the War, the Turks had modern weapons and vehicles, vast armies, and command of all of Mesopotamia. T.E. Lawrence fought them with carefully coordinated attacks from hundreds of desert tribes, all working in concert. That's what we need to do here." She counted on her fingers. "The Italians in Campion Street. The Irish. The policemen, striking or not. Maybe even the US Military, if they wise up and send some men to help. We're gonna need them all."

The middle De brother finally spoke. "The swordswoman is right. We will need them all." He faced Sapphire. "We have traded in contraband, but now we must become something more. We must be allies, and the same to every gang in Sickle City. Do you understand?"

"I suppose I do," Sapphire muttered.

Kid Twist walked over from his place by the roulette wheels. "So we all join together. One big happy family. What then? You said it yourself, Clay—the Dagger Men control the city. How the hell are you gonna win against an outfit that has the town itself fighting on their side?"

"We can stop them," Harvey said. "We can erase the letters on the Founding Stone. That's what stops a golem, and that'll stop the golem that the Dagger Men made."

"But won't it just destroy Sickle City, then?" Sophie asked. "Won't everything just collapse?"

Silence followed her words. Harvey shuffled in his seat. "Not if we do it correctly. But I need some of the books in Haven Street to help. Also, a rabbi has to do it—and I'm not a rabbi. My father could be the one to stop the spell, though. I know he could." He smiled. "So we need to go to Haven Street and get him."

"Might be difficult," Sapphire said. "The Dagger Men have taken it over completely. Haven Street and the park are their main strongholds."

"So go at dark," the De brother in the center said. "And during the day, rest and send out more messages to our allies and gather our strength."

"I'll see if I can get word to Madam Gracie," Dr. Cutte suggested. "I know she'll do anything to protect Hogshead Street."

"Very well." The De brother came to his feet. "The meeting is over. We will go and tell our men of the plans. We wait until sunset." His brothers left the table as well, and headed to the assembled Tong hatchetmen by the bar.

Silver stood next to Harvey and her daughter. "A good plan?"

"The best one we got," Zipporah explained. "Do you have any places we could stay, Miss Hark?"

Hark pointed to some doors in the back. "Guest quarters for friends of the Ghost Brothers. I'll show you to the rooms." She led Harvey and the others to the back rooms, while Clay stayed at the table. He didn't need to rest, but he was glad that his friends got a break from the action. Dr. Cutte remained at the table as well.

Dr. Cutte stood and approached Clay. He offered his hand. "You spoke up for me in the meeting. I appreciate it." He had abandoned his refined way of speaking. "I know what you are, Mr. Clay. I'm not an expert in matters of golems, like your young friend, Harvey—but I recognized you easily enough. It's heartening, in a way, that a lump of earth could learn to overcome some prejudice. If you can, maybe there's hope for the rest of us as well."

Clay took his hand. "Maybe." He thought of the anti-Semitic mob which had attacked Haven Street, and the racially-motivated riots on Hogshead Street and Chinatown. The Dagger Men were the same way—they let their hatred of *Goyim* fuel them, and it had given them total control over Sickle City. "I hope so."

"I'll see you later, Mr. Clay." Dr. Cutte stood up and set his top hat on his head. "We'll lick the Dagger Men. Don't you fret about that."

He ambled away, walking past the Ghost Brothers' gambling equipment as he followed the others. Clay stayed behind, watching Sapphire and Kid

Twist talk quietly about what underworld allies they needed to summon. Clay didn't care much for Sid 'the Shark' Sapphire, and Kid Twist terrified him. But they could help against the Dagger Men. That was all that mattered, and there was something Clay liked about that grim finality. The battle had left the shadows and gone into the open. It was the perfect sort of fight for a golem like Clay.

As the sun set red over Sickle City, Clay and Harvey stood on the roof of the Benevolent Merchantman's Association and looked over their town. All day, messages had been going out from the Benevolent Merchantman's Association to various criminal groups throughout the city. The phones occasionally worked, but mostly just blared strange Hebrew prayers from the speakers, so Sapphire and the De Brothers used runners and notes to summon their friends. They had gotten word to some of the striking cops, including Detective Flynn. The Italians of Campion Street had been summoned as well, and several Mafia capos and representatives of various Black Hand gangs showed up with agreements to help. From Haven Street, there was still no word. The Tong runners couldn't get close. Harvey fretted, growing more worried as the hours ticked past, and he still hadn't heard from his father.

Now, they stood together on the roof and stared into the distance. The Benevolent Merchantman's Association had a decent size, and let them look across the Cut and to a section of Arcadia Park—though two skyscrapers cut off some of their view. Even from a distance, Clay could see the work going on in the park. Trees had been cut down. Statues and gazebos had been smashed. A fire pit added a warm orange glow. The Dagger Men's slaves slept on the grass, when they weren't working endlessly on some vast structure. Golem guards and full legions of skeletal Romans stood watch.

Harvey used a pair of Zipporah's binoculars to look at the park. "They're building something, Mr. Clay." He lowered the binoculars. "It's the Temple—they're going to try and rebuild it here. I think it's only supposed to be in Jerusalem, but they made Sickle City a Second Jerusalem, so I guess they figure that's okay." He shuddered. "They want Judaism to change to the way it used to be, back when Judea was powerful. I guess they want to have a priesthood, or something."

"With Rabbi Eisendrath at its head." Clay balled his hands into fists. "We'll stop them. I know we will." A dark shape fluttered overhead. Clay thought it was a Broxa at first—and then saw the gray feathers. The carrier pigeon swooped down, moved in a spiral around him, and then landed straight on his shoulder.

"Why'd he land on you, sir?" Harvey stared at Clay in amusement.

"He's a friend." Gently, Clay picked up the pigeon, and examined the speckled feathers, and the single, remaining eye. "I know this bird. His name is Hermes, after the messenger god." He reached to the pigeon's foot, where a small metal canister waited. Clay removed it, opened the case, and unfurled a small line of writing. "This is my commanding officer's prized pigeon. He must have recognized me." He showed the message to Harvey, and they read it together.

"Colonel Menelaus Montgomery Rook," Clay said. "He's coming here." The message had not been meant for him—but for anybody who happened to pick it up. It urged them to keep fighting, as the United States was not going to let Sickle City fall to the Dagger Men. Clay held Hermes in his palm. He could write back, and tell Colonel Rook their plans. It would be good to see his former commander again—though Colonel Rook always scared him a little.

"The military's going to help? Under your commanding officer?" Harvey asked. "That's swell." He smiled—for the first time since the Dagger Men had taken the city. "We've got a chance, Mr. Clay. We've really got a chance."

"Yeah," Clay agreed. He hoped they did. "Come on. We've only got another hour, and then we're going to Haven Street." They walked downstairs, ready to return home.

Chapter 8
DEALS WITH DEVILS

As soon as night fell over the troubled city, Clay, Zipporah, and Harvey made their way to Haven Street. Their forces had been growing in Chinatown for most of the day, with messages running throughout Sickle City in every clandestine manner, and men and women streaming back with the combined goal of resisting the Dagger Men. The Italians came from Campion Street, Black Hand thugs with their drooping moustaches and sharp black suits and thin knives, along with younger mobsters

representing the homegrown Mafia Families. Madam Gracie and her
Negro gangsters arrived from Hogshead Street, ready for action. Some of
the striking police officers, including Detective Flynn, managed to make
it to Chinatown as well. Without any negotiation, they seemed to have put
aside their desire to strike. Their city had fallen into the hands of madmen,
and they had more pressing matters to deal with. The De Brothers and
Sapphire welcomed them all. They gobbled down Chinese food, gambled
in the casino, loaded their weapons, and waited. Clay knew that they
would make their move soon—but first, he had to ensure the safety of
Rabbi Holtz.

The cover of night helped Clay and his friends as they snuck across
Sickle City. They took a small smuggler's coracle down the Cut, the oily
green waters turning silver in the moonlight, and then left the canal and
went in on foot. They passed through empty streets, the occasional burned-
out, gutted, or looted building, and ruined cars and wagons resting in the
center of the road like broken toys. Clay moved first, doing his best to
keep his large form silent. Harvey followed, shivering and shaking with
nervousness. Clay didn't want to bring him along, but he knew they might
need the boy's knowledge. Zipporah brought up the rear, a scimitar in her
hand. Together, they made their way to the back of Haven Street.

An old, recently-abandoned tenement provided entrance. It overlooked
Neptune Row, the poorest section of Haven Street, and it offered a fire
escape leading to the upper floors. They made their way up the spidery
steps, which creaked and shifted in the wind. Harvey needed a little help
scrambling up the ladders, and Harvey and Zipporah gave him assistance.
They reached the third floor and entered an apartment.

Harvey stared at everything as they walked through the empty set
of rooms—a kitchen, a pair of bedrooms no bigger than closets, and a
small living room transformed into another place for beds. Pictures of the
occupants hung from the wall, while a mezuzah rested in the doorframe.
"It's so small," Harvey said, almost to himself. "How does a whole family
live here?" He turned to Clay, who opened the door and led them into the
hallway. "How does everyone fit?"

"They manage it, child," Zipporah said. "They have little choice."

They stepped into the hallway. The scuffed wooden floor overlooked
a set of encircling stairs leading to the first floor, and Haven Street. But a
set of windows occupied the end of the hall, overlooking the street. Clay
wanted to get a better look. He needed to know what Haven Street had
become.

"The window." He crossed the hall, motioning for his friends to join him, and they peered down through the casement. "Let's have a look." Below them, the tenement street lay as empty as it had during the height of the riots—but the Dagger Men had changed everything considerably. They had remade Haven Street in their own image, transforming it into the biblical paradise of their imagination.

The detritus and rubble had mostly been cleared away, pushed aside into the alley or gutters. The paving stones had been torn up, wrenched away to reveal gray earth underneath. Sickle City itself might have removed the paving stones, like a snake shedding dead skin. The stones lay on the sidewalk, arranged in gray pyramids. The dirt had been cut into furrows, plowed and ready for planting. Draft and cart horses had done the plowing, and they stood on the sidewalk, tied up to streetlights which now gained their gleam by candles instead of electric lights. The horses weren't alone. Large bulls, with powerful horns and blunt, rectangular snouts, had been tied to some of the lamp posts. They snorted and thrashed the air with their horns, seemingly eager for a fight. Skeletal legionaries stood at the corner, silently holding their lances and staring into the darkness.

Clay looked over what had once been home; almost unable to believe how it had changed. He finally settled on a simple question. "What are those bulls?"

"I think they're aurochs, sir," Harvey explained. "These extinct cow creatures that used to live in Europe and Mesopotamia during Roman times. The Dagger Men brought them back somehow." He pushed up his spectacles. "I guess anything's possible with magic." Fear returned to his voice. "But where are all the people? And where's my father and Uncle Herbert? Do y-you think the Dagger Men—"

"You said it yourself, Harvey," Zipporah said. "Your father wouldn't let them." She pointed down to the street. "Let's head to Haven Street and see if we can find out anything more about what those Dagger Men bums have done to our home."

That sounded reasonable. They left the tenement building, heading down the stairwell and slipping through the front doors. They left Neptune Row and approached Haven Street, sticking to the alley to avoid the staring, empty sockets of the Roman sentries. A few more steps brought them to the main length of Haven Street, where the Dagger Men had also been at work. If they wanted Neptune Row to be their farming fields, then they had decreed that this place would be their Biblical village. The city had created a mass of cottages from paving stones and cement, built to arcane rules from the Torah, and they sprawled out in the center of the street. Torches flickered in the awnings of the cabins, where the residents of Haven Street now lived. Banners bearing Jewish stars hung limply from the walls of the larger buildings, and nobody but stone golems and skeletons walked the street. Without lights, the stars seemed to shine brighter. The moon glowed as well, matching the flickering torches. Clay and his friends watched everything, hidden in the shadows.

Harvey looked over the village from his place in the alley. "They just keep everyone here?" he asked. "And make them work in the farms?" He sighed. "They won't grow anything—not in this climate. But I guess the Dagger Men don't care. They just want everything to be like it was in Ancient Judea, and so everyone's got to live in ancient stone houses and farm."

"Bunch of nuts," Zipporah muttered. "You were right, Harvey—these kooks don't deserve power."

"They've got it, though." Clay stared down the empty street. "Let's check on the King Solomon Temple. Maybe we can find out what happened to the rabbi." He patted Harvey's shoulder. "Would you like to stay here, maybe?" If they found out the worst had happened, he didn't want Harvey along.

"No, sir." The boy remained adamant. "He's my papa—my f-father, I mean. I owe it to him to be brave." He stepped out of the alley, pressed himself to the wall, and began creeping to the sidewalk. "Come on. Atlas Avenue is this way. We can stop by my house as well."

Clay and Zipporah followed Harvey. They left Haven Street, crossed through another empty side street, and reached Atlas Avenue. They passed the Holtz house first, dark and empty, and Harvey had them wait outside while he dashed in to fetch his books. The home hadn't been looted or destroyed by the Dagger Men. Evidently, the citizens of Haven Street remained loyal to Rabbi Holtz. They hadn't ratted out where he lived. Clay and Zipporah stood in the doorway, ready to move if they were discovered, until Harvey returned, straining under the weight of his satchel. Zipporah offered him a comforting grin, and then they moved further down Atlas Avenue and reached the King Solomon Synagogue.

The Dagger Men had left their mark here and it saddened Clay to see the results. The large trees which once provided welcome shade over the sidewalk and the grassy lawn had been hacked down. They lay on the street, their branches jabbing out in broken angles. The large windows had been shattered, and the sign for the synagogue had been broken by a golem's punch. Smashed bones and several lumps of brick, stone, and dirt that had once been golems lay sprawled on the lawn. A line of barbed wire crossed the lawn, preventing anyone from reaching the entrance. Clay stared inside the shadowed synagogue, wondering if there was anyone inside. He started to the door, followed by Harvey and Zipporah.

They crossed the lawn, moving carefully around the rusted armor and broken bones of Roman legionaries, and stepped over the barbed wire. Clay walked closer to the doorway, and paused. A thin cord, translucent and almost invisible in the shadows, stretched across the door. Harvey heedlessly approached. Clay grabbed the boy and tugged him back. Harvey gasped, and Clay motioned for him to be silent. They knelt down and looked at the cord. One end had been tied to a nail driven into the doorway. The other went to a stick of dynamite, resting in the dirt. Clay knelt down to take care of the trap, when he heard a gun racking in the shadows.

"I thought the rabbi told you not to come here." Monk Moss stepped closer to the doorway, carrying his trench gun. He wore vest and shirtsleeves, one bandage brown with dried blood wrapped his arm and another knotted over his leg. A trench club and knife swung from his belt. "You get back to the main group, quickly, before they find you here."

"Mr. Moss?" Harvey asked.

Cohen hurried to the doorway next, carrying her rifle. She beamed when she saw Harvey. "Oh, thank God." She ran to Monk's side. "The niño—he's all right!" She knelt next to the dynamite and quickly withdrew it. "Monk, put that trench gun of yours away and welcome our friends to what's left of the King Solomon Synagogue."

"Little Harvey." Monk slung his trench gun over his shoulder. "It's good to see you." He held out his hand to Clay and Zipporah. "Good to see you as well." They stepped into the doorway after Cohen removed the dynamite, and stood together in the shadows. Cohen and Monk looked older in the low light, the lines of their faces deeper.

"How have you been faring?" Clay asked.

"I've been better." Monk shrugged. "Mrs. Cohen found some Passover grub in a pantry. We've been living off Matzo and horseradish for the past day, but it's been better than the slop they used to serve in the Great War. Synagogue provides more cover as well, and the rabbi kept a good stash of guns and ammunition for his businesses." He looked at Harvey. "I don't know if I should've mentioned that."

"It's okay, sir. I sort of knew about it already," Harvey replied.

"And what happened here?" Zipporah asked. "Did the Dagger Men just take over?"

"Exactly," Monk agreed. "They muscled their way in, first thing after Rabbi Eisendrath made his kooky sermon to the whole city." He pointed down the street. "You should've seen it, Miss Sarfati. An army of dead Romans came, along with countless golems. The whole city shook, and spat bricks at any automobile trying to drive away. Most of the folks were still in the synagogue, and then Rabbi Eisendrath came over with his army and ordered them out. Nobody wanted to go, but Rabbi Holtz made them— he knew what would happen otherwise." Monk smiled. "Your pop's a good man, Harvey. He surrendered himself to buy time for his younger brother and me to escape."

"So he's a prisoner?" Harvey asked. "Did the Dagger Men hurt him? And did my uncle make it away? And what about all the people camping in the street, and where is my father, and—" The questions poured out of him, fueled by fear.

Cohen raised a finger. "One question at a time, Harvey." Her eyes went sad. "We tried to get your brother to safety, but the Dagger Men stopped us. Monk and I made it back here, but they got Herbert and dragged him away. He's with your father now." She paused. "As far as I know, they are both still alive."

"Well, that's good, then," Harvey said. "We can rescue them, right?"

"We'll see, child," Zipporah said. "Monk, Mrs. Cohen—what about you?"

"We escaped and made it back here." Monk pointed out the door. "As you can see, we've done okay for ourselves. The Dagger Men tried to get in. We didn't let them. Now, they're not even keeping an eye on us. They know we're not going anywhere—not as long as they got our boss—and they're trying to starve us out." He licked his lips. "If Mrs. Cohen didn't discover that pantry, they might have succeeded. We ain't got enough ammunition to hold out for long either. The machine gun ran dry during the afternoon. We figure they'll come again in the morning, and then we'll be finished."

"No." Clay didn't like the idea of Cohen and Monk trapped here— not when they were needed elsewhere. "We're gathering our strength in Chinatown, preparing to take back the city. A witch doctor joined us, a Negro named Dr. Cutte. He's set up some kind of magical boundary around the Benevolent Merchantman's Association. Keeps the golems out."

"I know the place," Monk said. "A Tong front. Them Chinamen got a swell casino there."

"So we're to go there and wait for you? Abandon the rabbi?" Cohen spat on the ground. "I abandoned Villa. He made me leave his service, just as the Revolution ended. Now he is dead, murdered by coward assassins who gunned him down in his own car." She clasped the handle of her machete. "My husband is dead, killed by Federales in the dust of a nameless canyon. My general is gone too. I will not let it happen again."

"You're in no shape to help rescue the rabbi," Clay said. "You need to get some rest, heal up, and then help us take back the city, with Rabbi Holtz at your side." He pointed to the rear of the synagogue. "Use the secret entrance in the basement that connects to the Garden of Eden Speakeasy and get back to Chinatown. We'll return soon, with Rabbi Holtz, and then we'll fight the Dagger Men." He gripped her arm. "You won't fail your leader. You have my word."

"Go, Mrs. Cohen," Zipporah urged. "We'll join you soon."

"It's what my father would want," Harvey said. "Please." His voice cracked as he pleaded.

Cohen opened her mouth to protest and then sighed deeply. She leaned against the doorway, suddenly looking very tired. "Very well," she muttered. "But you will not turn me away from the final battle."

"I wouldn't dream of it." Zipporah turned to Monk. "Where'd they take the rabbi and his brother?"

Monk shivered. "That'd be Palisade Park—though it's not called that anymore." He leaned closer. "They call it Sheol. That's the land of the dead for you Jewish people, right? And it's lived up to that name. The place is guarded with a squad of Roman skeletons, and beyond that, they got a bunch of golems lurking around and watching things. They said that all the pagan gods get to go there, living in exile and shame. They did the same to your father, Harvey, and your uncle, and poor Professor West. I think they're gonna turn Palisade Park into some kind of prison. They'll just throw whatever they don't like into the park, and bring people by to gawk at them."

"Oh." Harvey stared at his Buster Browns. "Why is Professor West there?" he asked suddenly. "I guess they think my father is a hypocrite, and Herbert's obviously against them, but why the professor? He always seemed like such a nice man."

Clay knew, and so did Zipporah. "Professor West is a certain sort of man who has... predilections that the Bible disagrees with," Clay said. "That's why he's there."

"He won't be there much longer," Harvey announced. "We're gonna rescue them all."

"My general is gone too. I will not let it happen again."

Zipporah couldn't help smiling. "You think we can sneak past those Roman guards? Palisade Park has only one real entrance, you know."

"So we'll make a distraction." A plan appeared in Clay's hard head. "Mrs. Cohen, Monk—about ten minutes after we leave, you start firing at some of the legionary sentries posted at the borders of Neptune Row. Keep the firing light. A couple rifle rounds should do the job, and then double back here. Put up a few traps like the one we nearly triggered, and they should be kept busy for a long time." He hated the idea of using the synagogue as a trap that would be the end of Roman skeletons and golems, but there was no way around it. "The legionaries guarding the entrance will start chasing after you, and then we'll go in. Harvey has a spell that will keep the golems—and the city—from seeing us. We'll rescue Rabbi Holtz and Herbert and depart."

"And we better skedaddle quickly," Zipporah said. "I don't know how long Harvey's spell will hold."

"It should keep us safe, unless we're directly spotted," Harvey said. "Or at least, I hope it will."

"You're sure about this?" Cohen sounded skeptical.

"It's the only way." Clay held out his hand. "I'll see you in Chinatown, and then we'll put a stop to this Dagger Men nonsense for good."

"Well, hallelujah." Monk shook Clay's hand. Cohen did the same.

Then, they split up. Clay, Zipporah, and Harvey doubled back and returned to Haven Street. They hastened into the nearest alley, took a side street a few blocks further, and approached the darkened mass of Palisade Park. It towered above the docks. Usually, the park blossomed with colorful strings of neon light as soon as the sun set, making it look like some strange fairyland eager to receive visitors. That had changed now. Shadows covered the amusement park, and the struts of the roller coaster looked pale in the starlight so that they resembled pillars of bone. Enchanted green flames flickered in a few places in the park, making the air look sickly and strange. The Elephantine Hotel had no lights at all, and resembled a great elephantine shadow. The archway above the entrance had not been destroyed, though the colorful letters had been smashed and broken so that only jagged edges remained. A plank dangled below on a pair of chains, with 'Sheol' burned into the wood.

The park was guarded too. Below the archway, two columns of Roman infantry and centurions waited to attack any potential invaders. A pair of ballistae sat further back on the dock, like modern machine gun posts. Clay could make out mobile, dark shapes inside Sheol itself. Those had to be the golem guardians of the Dagger Men's prisoners.

Harvey started to leave the alley, but Zipporah took hold of his arm. "We need to wait."

"But my father—" Harvey started.

"Just wait. Just a little more." Zipporah glanced at her wristwatch. "Monk and Mrs. Cohen won't take long."

A flash of sudden light proved her words true. The flare whistled into the air from the direction of the synagogue and snaked into the sky, rocketing up on a thin tendril of smoke, and then arcing downwards with a deep rush. It bathed the street ahead of them in brilliant light, illuminating the empty tenements, the destroyed streets, and the snorting aurochs. Gunfire followed—the crack of rifle rounds echoing through Haven Street. Clay couldn't see much, but he heard the rustle of skeletal feet as the Romans raced to attack Cohen and Monk. He turned back across the street.

The legionaries guarding Sheol formed up. More seconds ticked past, and the rifle shots increased. Would the legionaries abandon their posts? Clay didn't know how much intelligence or discipline these skeletons had. They had been some of the greatest fighters in the world, but that was when they had meat on their bones. Now, they were empty shells—carrying out their orders without a care. He balled his hands into fists and waited. A second more, and the legionaries moved. Their column marched into the street and hurried away, leaving the entrance to the docks open. Clay held Harvey's shoulder and waited until they turned the corner, and they made their move.

They dashed from the alley, ran across the street, and hurried under the swaying sign welcoming them to Sheol. The two skeletons manning the ballistae remained. They swiveled the oversized crossbows at Clay and Zipporah—but didn't get a chance to fire. Zipporah hurled her scimitar at one skeleton, and the blade plunged between his ribs and stabbed out through his back. Clay reached the other before he could fire, grabbed the ballista, and ripped it from the ground. He smashed it against the skeleton. Bone and wood shattered, and Clay dropped what was left of the ballista onto the dock. Harvey hurried to join them.

He paused on the planks and stared ahead. "Okay." He breathed in cold night air and nodded in the direction of the park. "Let's rescue my father." Then he started down the pier, flanked by Clay and Zipporah. They walked inside, passed the empty Elephantine Hotel, and entered Sheol. Clay stayed close to Harvey, ready to protect him.

The Dagger Men had transformed the place into a physical cautionary tale—a temple to all the ferocious pagan gods that they hated and feared.

The oversized wooden statues of those gods, hastily cobbled together with torn up planks and old park decorations, loomed up over the visitors by the booths on the midway and the food stands. The gods looked like nightmares, oversized animals in seated positions, painted in garish red, black, and gold. Torches rested in their hands, shining over the amusement park. The Dagger Men had built effigies of modern gods as well. An oversized dollar sign leaned against the fairy floss stand, the green paint poorly applied and the nails visible. Emerald light from the torches kept shadows dancing. It made Clay think of some odd pagan temple, a place which didn't belong in the modern world. He hated to see Palisade Park like this.

"That's Moloch." Harvey pointed to a large brass bull. "And that's Dagon, over there—the fishy fellow." He turned to his friends. "The Dagger Men must want to take their worshippers through this place, and point to all the abandoned gods. I guess they'll keep idolaters here too, to show them off to visitors." He stepped carefully over a knobby plank in the docks. "But we'll put things back to normal once we get rid of the Dagger Men, right?

"Keep your voice down, child," Zipporah hissed. "We are not alone."

They neared the first set of golems—which had been made from pieces of Palisade Pier. Brightly colored wood and the planks from the dock had been smashed and assembled into the shapes of men. Nails connected some of the wooden planks and decorations, but oftentimes their pieces adhered thanks to magic alone. One golem had the wooden face of a laughing seal, while another bore the painted face of a clown. They stood still, their arms swaying idly in the wind. Clay pointed to some booths, and they crept behind those to avoid the golems. Harvey's spell might protect them, but there was no need to reveal themselves and test it.

After working their way around the golems, a few more steps brought them to the next section of the pier—where Professor West had kept his trained animals. A set of wheeled cages rested on the worn planks, with animals kept inside. Clay looked at the cages, where the animals sat sadly behind iron bars, and then his eyes fell on the cage containing monkeys and apes. He tapped Zipporah's shoulder and pointed. She nodded too, and they hurried across the pier to the monkey cage.

Harvey ran after them. "What's going on?" he asked. "Did you guys see something or—" Then he realized who was in the cage and broke into a run. "Papa! Uncle Herbert!" He covered his mouth, preventing an outcry, but still ran to the cage. Clay and Zipporah joined him. They reached the cage, where the Dagger Men kept their prisoners.

Rabbi Holtz, Herbert Holtz, and Professor West sat in the corner of the cage, sharing it with a half-dozen monkeys of various breeds, a slumbering sloth, and a single, tired orangutan. They had been keeping away from the animals, trying to put as much space between them and the simians as possible, but when Harvey appeared, they hurried straight to the front of the cage. Rabbi Holtz reached his hands through the bars. He grasped Harvey's arms and shoulders. Harvey returned the gesture, and they hugged through the iron bars. Herbert hurried over, and clutched Harvey's hand. For a while, none of them said anything.

The rabbi spoke first. His voice shook. "I'm so sorry, Harvey. My son, my *boychick*, my wonderful little boy—you should never have to see your father like this." He had a dark bruise on his cheek, and one of the lenses of his spectacles had been shattered. His tie had come undone, and stubble crusted his cheeks. "You should never have to face such danger."

"You're okay, though?" That was the first thing Harvey wanted to know. His voice cracked and tears grew in his eyes. "You're not hurt?"

"Only our pride, my boy." Professor West waved at the monkeys in the corner. "You see our current status, I suppose, and our new companions." He had lost his coat, bowtie, and top hat, and his eyes seemed sad and tired, one bordered with puckered black flesh. "The Dagger Men hauled us in here immediately and have not provided any food. The smell alone is dreadful. I think I will need to shower for a year once I get out."

"Agreed." Herbert kept his hand on Harvey's thin shoulder. "What about you, Harvey? How are you doing?" He noticed Clay and Zipporah for the first time. "Do you really think it was wise to bring him here, when there's so much danger?"

"We needed him," Zipporah said. "And we've always kept him safe."

"I trust them, Herbert." Rabbi Holtz faced Clay. "I trust you, Clay. What's been happening to our city? What about Sapphire and Detective Flynn? And has the outside world done anything, or are we on our own?"

"We're massing in Chinatown," Clay explained. "We'll move against the Dagger Men. The US Army wants in as well, and maybe we can coordinate an assault."

"Chinatown?" Herbert asked. "Is Bethany—"

"Miss Hark protected us, Uncle Herbert," Harvey said. "She's fine."

Clay walked around the cage, until he came to the back, where a lock fixed the swinging door to the bars. "Don't worry, sir. We'll stop this. We might need your help, though." He gave the lock a punch. Iron snapped and the lock fell away. Clay wrenched the door open. "Come on out."

Rabbi Holtz helped Professor West out first. The owner of Palisade Park moved with a limp. "My help?" Rabbi Holtz asked. "Why, exactly?"

"It's the Dagger Men, papa," Harvey said. "They've turned the city into a golem, by inscribing holy words on the Founding Stone. I think we can remove one letter and destroy the golem—but it might end up destroying the whole city as well. I don't know if I could do it myself, either. I'm not a rabbi. But you are, sir. You're a great rabbi. You probably know how to do all kinds of things, and you can transform Sickle City from a golem to a normal town again."

"Harvey..." Rabbi Holtz stepped gingerly from the cage to the planks of the pier. "I should tell you." He closed his eyes. Harvey walked in front of him. "I'm not a rabbi. I never attended a day of rabbinical school. I learned some Hebrew from Chaim, who attended Yeshiva, but that's all. I received a license through bribery, once Prohibition began, so I could brew alcohol for speakeasies. I can't stop a golem any more than I could give you lessons on the Talmud."

Harvey stared quietly at his father. "But I've heard your sermons, sir. You're so wise."

"I look in holy books for inspiration," Rabbi Holtz explained. "I make the rest of it up. Occasionally on the spot." He rested a hand on the bars of his former cage. "That's why the Dagger Men locked me up here. They see me as a fraud—because I am." He glanced back at Herbert. "You knew that already, of course. You've used that knowledge to poison your insults."

"I was a fool." Herbert walked to the door. He stared at Harvey. "It doesn't matter if your father didn't go to some fancy rabbinic school, or if he became a rabbi for the wrong reasons. He gave you a safe childhood. He puts me through college. He's protected Haven Street, time and time again, and he gave himself up to the Dagger Men so that innocents would be protected. He's the best rabbi that Haven Street's ever had."

Rabbi Holtz looked at them through his cracked spectacles. "You think so?"

"Absolutely, sir," Zipporah agreed.

"Without a doubt!" Professor West added.

"Yes," Clay said.

Harvey smiled at his father. "Herbert's right. You're the best rabbi Haven Street's ever had."

"Now, let's get back to Chinatown and—" Hebert moved out of the cage, but his boot landed on a monkey's tail. The monkey bounced in the air, releasing a keening shriek. Herbert tripped and fell from the cage, into his brother's arms. Other monkeys took up the cries of their compatriot. The orangutan started to hoot as well, adding another layer of sound. The cries of the apes echoed across the pier, the brightly painted buildings, and the wooden gods. The other animals in their cages, including a roaring tiger, bellowed out and increased the volume. The two wooden golems spun around and stared straight at the animal cages. Harvey's spell didn't matter now. They had been spotted.

Clay thought quickly. "Stick together. We've got to get out."

"Get to the back of the Pachyderm," Professor West said. "There's a ladder leading to a smaller dock, by the water. I keep a motorboat there, in case I need to make a rapid escape. This seems like a suitable time to use it." He closed the cage door. "But we need to hurry."

The wooden golems sauntered toward them. Behind the golems, a column of Roman skeletons charged down the docks. Clay and Zipporah hurried up to meet them and buy time for their friends. Clay ran ahead first and smashed into the skeletons. He moved at a charge, using his momentum to push the skeletons aside while his arms wheeled and delivered powerful punches to their ribs and skulls. Shattered bone flew as he battled them. Zipporah joined him, slashing at the skeletons with both blades. A wooden golem, the one with the painted clown's face, advanced on her, smashing aside Romans as it approached. Zipporah leapt over a smashed skeleton and aimed a stab at the golem's forehead. She slashed the letters above the clown face. The golem crumbled into a tide of splintered wood, and Zipporah danced out of the way.

Rabbi Holtz and the others weaved around the group of skeletons, ducking behind the booths in the midway for cover. Clay watched them hurrying along—and then a squad of Romans split off and gave chase. They hurried between the booths, their short blades shining at their sides. They would catch up to Harvey, his father, and uncle, and Professor West, and destroy them. Clay struggled to disentangle himself from the battle. He elbowed aside skeletons, rammed his way past a pair of Romans, and then broke into a run. Zipporah joined him and they raced after their friends.

They darted between the midway booths, right behind the attacking skeletons. Rabbi Holtz noticed his skeletal pursuers. "Come on, *boychick*." He grabbed Harvey's hand. "Over here." He hauled the boy up. Herbert helped him. They scrambled into the nearest booth—a baseball game. Professor West leapt in as well, his gangly limbs flailing.

The Holtz brothers popped up behind the counter. Herbert had a bundle of baseballs under his arm. "You remember baseball in the alley, Herman?" He chucked a ball at the nearest skeleton. The ball bounced against rusted steel and cracked bone. The skeleton stumbled back. "I always imagined I'd impress you by striking out the neighborhood champion. I wanted you to be proud of me." Herbert's next baseball rammed into the open mouth of a skeletal legionary, snapping open the Roman's jaws. Herbert hurled more baseballs, and they held the legionaries back—but not for long.

Rabbi Holtz grabbed the baseball bat and raised it as the legionaries reached him. "I remember, Herbert. And I was always proud of you. I still am." He brought the bat down on the first legionary in an overhead strike. Rusted metal rang out as the bat struck it. Rabbi Holtz swung the bat again, and it crashed into the skull with enough force to rip it from the skeletal Roman's neck. The skull flew through the air, struck the pier, and rolled out of sight. Rabbi Holtz met the next skeletons with similar powerful blows, while Herbert hurled more baseballs. They kept the skeletons away, protecting Harvey while Professor West unlocked the back door of the booth. Then a well-timed strike with a gladius hit the bat. Ancient steel sheared through modern wood, and the bat hit the ground in pieces. The legionaries moved to attack again.

Clay and Zipporah reached the crowd of skeletons first. Clay rammed his fist into the back of a skeleton, smashing apart a number of ribs, and wrenched the pilum from the Roman's hand. He wielded the pilum as a blunt weapon, crashing it against skeletons until the slim spear shattered. Zipporah used both her scimitars to remove the remaining skeletons. They finished off the rabbi's attackers in a few quick strikes.

Professor West kicked the back door of the booth open. "This way!" He guided Harvey out through the back, and hurried down the pier. Rabbi Holtz and Herbert darted out of the booth, and Clay and Zipporah ran around to join them. They hurried past the remaining midway booths, under the pillars supporting the roller coaster, and neared the dark shape of the Elephantine Hotel. Professor West's secret escape lay dead ahead.

Then the remaining wooden golem reared out from behind the Ferris wheel. It reached down with splintery hands, grasping madly. Its fingers caught Clay's arms and dragged him back. Clay struggled to free himself, raining blows onto the wooden golem's chest. Splinters flew, but the golem wouldn't release its hold. The big seal face loomed closer, its smile strange compared to the strength in its limbs. The wooden golem prepared a powerful punch, aiming it at Clay's forehead.

"Mr. Clay!" Harvey pulled away from Professor West, and ran back to help.

Zipporah reached the wooden golem first. She sheathed one sword, grabbed the lower rung of the Ferris wheel to pull herself up, and then leapt into the air. Her remaining scimitar shone in the moonlight. She brought it down on the wooden golem's head—a single strike that crossed out the holy letters carved into its forehead. The golem collapsed, nearly burying Clay in wooden planks. He pushed them aside with a few kicks.

"Come on," Zipporah ordered. "Almost there."

They raced to the Elephantine Hotel, and then moved along the back to the edge of the pier. Clay shimmied along with the others, until they reached a ladder leading down into darkness. Water splashed below them as the ocean rolled in. Harvey took the ladder first, and then Rabbi Holtz and Herbert worked their way down. Zipporah and Professor West followed. Clay went last. He gripped the rungs and descended, staring up at the giant wooden elephant that had been his home. A creaking ran through his body, as the shadows around the Elephantine Hotel moved. The elephant's trunk had started to sway. The painted eyes moved as well, following Clay's progress.

Clay froze. Had the Elephantine Hotel become a golem as well? No, that wasn't it—the whole city was a golem, and the Elephantine Hotel was merely a part of the city. But why wasn't it attacking? The Dagger Men controlled Sickle City, and yet the Elephantine Hotel watched placidly as Clay stood still on the ladder. He couldn't figure it out.

"Come on, Clay!" Zipporah cried. "We ain't got all night!"

The mystery would have to wait. Clay lowered himself down to a small quay, built into the pillars of the larger dock. A little motorboat waited, already overcrowded. Clay made it into the back of the boat, and then Professor West started the engine. They sped out from under the docks and shot into the ocean ahead. Clay looked back at Palisade Park, and then at Haven Street as they zoomed by. Torchlight bloomed brightly as Roman skeletons and lumbering golems darted about like bees in a disturbed hive, all mindless energy without any sort of command. A few bonfires blazed, adding to the light. The Dagger Men wouldn't be happy at their escape. For the moment, Clay didn't care.

ᴘᴀ ᴘᴀ ᴘᴀ

The motorboat brought them to the Cut, and that took them back to Chinatown and the Benevolent Merchantman's Association. Some Shadow

Brothers Tong hatchetmen spotted them in the alley and led them through the back entrance of a recently abandoned laundry, which had a tunnel leading to the Benevolent Merchantman's Association. The place had been turned into a fortress. Armed guards stood in each window, aiming their rifles at the street below. Dr. Cutte had worked his charms on the street outside, tying bags of gris-gris to the branches of some flowering trees and statues, which would prevent the Dagger Men from getting close enough to attack. The door had been boarded up, and the windows removed in case Sickle City's new defenders needed a gunfight.

They made it back a little before dawn. Rabbi Holtz had Harvey and Herbert headed straight to the guest quarters to get some sleep. Harvey protested a little, but Herbert insisted and helped his nephew along. They could get some much needed rest before the sun rose. Zipporah went to the casino below, where she could pass out on a velvet couch, and Professor West insisted on a bath. Clay was the only one who needed neither sleep nor cleaning. He went up to the roof, to look at the city again through his binoculars.

He checked Arcadia Park, examining the temple, the centerpiece of the Dagger Men's Second Jerusalem, and found that they had added more to the frame. Slave labor must be going round the clock to create that temple, and it would be finished very soon. Clay lowered the binoculars when he heard the flap of wings. Hermes the pigeon settled onto the railing, cocked his head, and emitted a gentle coo. Clay picked up the pigeon and examined the note on his leg.

He could almost imagine hearing the gruff voice of Colonel Menelaus Montgomery Rook, his former commanding officer, when he read the tiny printed words on the scrap of paper: *grand to hear from you, Clay. Happy to know that a real soldier is in that mess. Still trying to arrange everything for an aerial incursion. Expect zeppelins to play a large part. Will consider landing in Arcadia Park, to time with the attack of you and your allies. Should be a wondrous battle—perhaps the Marathon I have longed for. I will speak to you soon.* That was all the message said.

So Colonel Rook—and the United States government—was going to help. Clay didn't know how many men the colonel had with him, but he could always count on his former commanding officer to battle like a bulldog until the fight was won. Clay pulled a pencil from his coat and scratched out a return message on the back, hoping for more words and explaining that the attack on Arcadia Park would come soon. He would tell Sapphire and the others about the message, and see if the attacks could be coordinated. That would be the only way they could win, and there was still the business about erasing the holy words from the Founding Stone without destroying Sickle City.

Hermes rose on his wings and fluttered away, cooing softly as he soared into the pale dawn. "Some early correspondence?" Rabbi Holtz's weary voice came from the roof entrance. Clay turned to see the rabbi walking over and joining him at the railing. "How are you, Mr. Clay? I didn't get a chance to thank you, you know, for looking after Harvey."

"It was no trouble," Clay said.

"I'm glad he stuck with you," Rabbi Holtz explained. "Otherwise, he would have been at the synagogue when the Dagger Men arrived, and I couldn't have protected him." He stared down at Chinatown, the sunlight adding a cherry glow to the paper lanterns. "They were right about me," he mused. "I'm no rabbi. Nothing but a *goniff* with a crooked license." He gazed up at Clay. "But it doesn't matter. I'll bear that burden. I'll let them call me a liar and a crook. I'll do whatever it takes to protect my family and my people."

Clay offered his hand. "I know you will, sir."

As they shook hands, a spray of Chinese fireworks rocketed into the air in the warren of streets leading to the courtyard before the Benevolent Merchantman's Association. The fireworks exploded in the sky, adding bright purples and pale blues to the rising sun's red. Clay hurried to the railing facing the courtyard. The fireworks were a signal that the Dagger Men had entered Chinatown. The defenders of Sickle City hurried to get ready and aim their guns out of the windows. Harvey and Zipporah appeared on the roof as well, followed by Herbert, the Silvers, Hark, and the others. They gazed down at the courtyard together as a Dagger Man procession arrived.

A squad of legionaries came first, their shields raised and interlocked to form a rusted wall of moving cover. Behind them came a half-dozen ice golems. The contents of numerous iceboxes must have been emptied to build those creatures, which had the shape of men cast in stiff, blocky ice speckled with brown mud and dust. Icicle claws projected from their hands. Between them came Rabbi Giest and Rabbi Eisendrath. They dragged Orton Sinclair behind them. Rabbi Geist held the chain affixed to Sinclair's collar, and they hauled him along like he was a dog. Sinclair had been beaten badly, and his eyes remained fixed on the cobblestones. He hadn't had an easy time of his captivity.

Rabbi Eisendrath raised his voice. "We come in peace—bearing a message for the *apikoros* and *goyim* who seek to destroy our city!" He bellowed out the words, and the adjoining walls echoed his words. His image reappeared, cast on the bricks and cement of adjacent buildings, so it seemed like dozens of large, hateful rabbis were speaking to the Benevolent Merchantman's Association at once. "It is a message of unity and faith!"

The main doors of the Benevolent Merchantman's Association opened a crack, revealing the middle De Brother. The muzzles of two Thompsons, one held by Kid Twist Deutsch and the other by Detective Flynn, aimed outwards. Don of the Italian Families, Sid Sapphire, and Madam Gracie watched from their own windows. They stared down at Rabbi Eisendrath, clearly not buying his message of unity and faith.

Sapphire flicked ash from the tip of his cigarette holder. It fell down in a gray rain and sparked on the cobblestones at Rabbi Eisendrath's feet. "What do you want, Rabbi? Say your piece and get out. We're not in the mood for another sermon." Evidently, the other Sickle City kingpins had decided to let Sapphire handle the Dagger Men.

Rabbi Eisendrath didn't flinch. "I know what happened last night. I know of the invasion of Haven Street, by some of your supporters." His eyes moved to the roof, and his tattooed face broke into a scowl. "The golem was there. The abomination ruined the peace of my Second Jerusalem." His voice rose. "I am trying to build a golden city here, in this garbage heap of vice and depravity. It will be a godly city, a sanctuary, from the ashes of this cruel modern Rome."

The middle De Brother pointed at Rabbi Eisendrath. "We do not want it."

"You are fiends and fools, and I will—" He drew closer, walking straight to the door. As he approached, a thin line of smoke appeared, emanating from the bags of gris-gris, all stiff and shining. It coiled like a rope, and Rabbi Eisendrath could not continue. He stopped and tripped. Rabbi Geist ran to him and helped him, pulling him away from the smoke. Rabbi Eisendrath stared back at the Benevolent Merchantman's Association. "What sorcery is this?" he demanded. "What foul magic, born of demons, have you brought against me?"

Dr. Cutte waved from the roof. "That'd be a little of my Voodoo, Rabbi. I would not try to cross it. The same warning is again delivered to your creations there." He pointed to the golems. "I believe they will melt if they try gaining entry to our current abode. Could be most disastrous for your glad rags, such as they are."

Rabbi Geist leaned closer to Rabbi Eisendrath. "We should leave, master."

"Quiet, boy." Rabbi Eisendrath hissed the warning. He faced the building for a few more moments. "We can come to some arrangement. You can't prevail against me. You can't end my control over Sickle City. Perhaps I could find a place for you. There must be some form of crime in even my Second Jerusalem. Why should I not control that as well? You could still earn well. You could still have some measure of power."

"But all under you," the De Brother at the door replied.

"No dice," Madam Gracie replied. The Italian Don merely shook his head.

"So that's the way of it, then?" Rabbi Eisendrath asked. "Resistance." He had been struggling to hold his temper in, and now he lost it. He grabbed the chain from Rabbi Geist's hand and yanked Sinclair closer to him. Sinclair didn't struggle. He shuffled along and let Rabbi Eisendrath grab his hair and haul his head back, presenting his pale throat. "I will show you what happens to resistance." Rabbi Eisendrath withdrew the electrum blade, the same short sword that he had used to cow Asmodeus into submission in return for the Shamir. He raised the sword to Sinclair's throat. Clay realized suddenly what was going to happen.

Harvey did not. "What's he doing?" The boy stood on his tiptoes, trying to peer down at the courtyard below. Rabbi Holtz and Herbert grabbed him and tugged him back. The rabbi covered his ears while Herbert hid his eyes, so that he couldn't see. Ava Silver did the same to Sophie, turning her away from the courtyard. Clay was grateful.

"Please!" Clay heard himself speaking. "You don't have to hurt him. There's no need—"

"Lower your blade," the De Brother in the doorway ordered. "Spare his life."

Even Rabbi Geist seemed upset. He ran to Rabbi Eisendrath, his beard and long hair flying in the light wind. "Master, this is unnecessary. You do not need to spill such blood. We can find another way without slaying like the Romans before the walls of Masada and—"

Sinclair just stared at the sky. "Do it." He whispered the word. "It should have happened already. Far away. Over there." He closed his eyes. "Go on and—"

A simple slash with the knife cut his throat. Sinclair released a low, mournful groan as blood spilled over his shirt and vest. Rabbi Eisendrath released him and let him drop. He lay on the ground, convulsing as the puddle of blood grew. He died in seconds. Rabbi Eisendrath moved back, the blade red in his hand. He glared up at the Benevolent Merchantman's

Association. "That is what your resistance shall come to!" he cried. "I am armed by faith! I am armored by the Lord! Adonai, our God, shall bring me your throat, and I will bear the knife that cuts it!" He waved his blade, spraying droplets of blood at the Association building. "Eyes will be taken for eyes, teeth for teeth, and every slight against me will be revenged!" He turned to Rabbi Geist. "Come. Back to the temple."

"Master, I—"

"Follow me to the temple, my poor student." He turned around, his coat billowing, and walked away. The ice golems followed, their frozen feet crunching on the cobblestones. Rabbi Geist took a last look at Sinclair's body, and then turned away as well—clearly not liking what he had seen.

Clay stared at his friend. He thought back to all the memories they had shared—of war in the frozen wastes of Russia with the Polar Bear Expedition. He had saved Sinclair's life, and Sinclair had done the same to him, and now his friend lay dead and bleeding on the cobblestones. He had remained on the roof, unable to do anything about it. He gripped the railing and lowered his eyes as deep, powerful creaks came from his body.

Zipporah hurried to him. "Come inside, Clay. Get to one of the guest rooms. Miss Hark and I will handle Sinclair. We're soldiers too. We'll see that he's cleaned up and kept in a cool place in one of the tunnels, and he can be buried in the manner he deserves."

"Buried," Clay murmured.

Harvey took Clay's hand, reaching blindly as Herbert still held his eyes closed. "Come on, Mr. Clay. We'll go back to my room. It'll be okay."

"Come with us, sir," Sophie suggested. "Off the roof."

There was nothing for it. Clay cooperated. He let the children lead him off the roof and down to the guest quarters where all the defenders of Sickle City stayed. Sophie opened the door to one room, and Clay wandered in and sat on the cot in the corner.

They left him there for a few moments. Outside, and throughout the building, preparations continued for the attack on the Dagger Men—an attack that could end in the destruction of Sickle City if they couldn't remove the enchanted Hebrew letters from the Founding Stone without wiping out the entire town—but Clay let it progress without him. He could hear the sound of feet moving on the worn floors of the Benevolent Merchantman's Association, and the clicks of bullets being loaded into firearms. All he could think about was the cold of Russia, the wailing of the wind through the abandoned castle where they had set up their headquarters, and the death of Orton Sinclair. Death had been his constant companion then, and perhaps it would be again. He didn't know what to do.

Time passed, though Clay didn't know how much. The sun reached its midpoint, and cold gray sunlight filtered through the window. The preparations continued, and the door creaked open and Harvey stepped inside. He moved gingerly, as if he was afraid he would break the floor. "Mr. C-Clay?" he stammered as he approached. "Are you well, sir?"

"Well enough." Clay stared at the boy. "What do you want?"

"It's not me, sir." Harvey turned around. "One of your friends is here. Miss Shadowborn."

Clay looked up. Lilith floated through the open door and entered the small chamber. Her facial features had grown faint, so she seemed little more than a dark cloud hazily occupying the center of the room. She moved closer to Clay. "Harvey told me what happened." She had her voice low. "You know it will happen again, Mr. Clay, and not only from the blades of our enemies. Golems like you and me—unlike the simple creations of Eisendrath—have memory and feeling, and we cannot die unless the etchings on our foreheads are changed. But that is not the same for our friends."

"They'll die, then." Clay stared at Harvey. The boy looked away.

"They will," Lilith agreed. "Not through violence, God willing. But they will grow old, and we will not. Perhaps that is why I spend my time with ghosts and fallen angels, preferring their company to those mortals who I will someday lose. But there is a vitality amongst mortals, and that is why I love them." She reached out with a smoky hand. It brushed across Clay's arm. "I struggle to help them and I know you do the same. Now, you must do so again."

He knew why she had come. "You have a plan to defeat the Dagger Men?" Clay asked. "To remove the letters from the Founding Stone without destroying Sickle City?"

"Not I," Lilith said. "But I know someone we can ask."

The door creaked open again. Dr. Cutte emerged, a valise swinging under his arm. "I procured the needed ingredients, young Harvey, and I stand ready to—" He paused, staring at Lilith. "A golem crafted from the aether of smoke itself." He doffed his top hat. "I am Lazarus Cutte, my good woman, and it is a rare pleasure to make your acquaintance. I believe you were the one who requested that I bring all of these occult supplies, the candles, chalk, and bones and so forth. I do not know the purpose for this collection, but I have everything needed."

"We're going to build a door," Lilith explained. "A door to Gehenna, the realm of demons. And we're going to ask Asmodeus, the Demon King, for help." Everyone stared at her. "The Dagger Men captured his earthly form, but his spiritual form remains in Gehenna. We can find him. I believe we can make a common cause with him, and he will give us the aid we need." She extended a wispy hand to Clay. "Will you go with me, into Gehenna?"

For a few seconds, Clay didn't answer. He thought of Lilith's words, and the nature of forming a friendship with a mortal—even one as flawed as Orton Sinclair. Then he looked at Harvey. She was right. Golems like the company of mortals and needed to help them. Clay came to his feet. "All right. Let's go to Gehenna."

Harvey grinned. "I hope you tell me all about it, sir. I'm very interested."

"We'll see," Clay suggested. He walked out of the room, Lilith floating next to him, and they entered the hallway. Soon enough, he would be in the land of demons.

꙰꙰꙰

Dr. Cutte and Harvey worked together to build the portal. They laid out chalk, lit a few candles, and arranged bones in strange angles along the edges of a symmetrical circle broken with a swirling cross. Clay and Lilith waited patiently for them to finish. Sophie came in to help, eager to observe a portal to Hell, and she switched off the lights when Harvey asked her to. When the lights clicked back on, the darkness remained on the floor, trapped in the circle. Red smoke billowed up from the various candles, and the bones shook on the floor. Clay stared at what had once been floorboards, but now appeared to be a circle of deep, endless shadow—like a pool of tar. He glanced at Lilith. Her floating head nodded back.

"You're really going to Hell?" Sophie asked.

"Gehenna, my dear," Dr. Cutte explained. "They're hardly the same place."

"We'll be back soon," Clay said. He and Lilith clasped hands. "Wait for us, Harvey, and be ready to close the portal in case we have any unwelcome followers from the land of demons."

They jumped in, Lilith increasing her weight to drop into the hole while Clay split the surface like a stone striking a pond. The room above him vanished, and darkness covered his eyes. He tried lashing out with his arms, to swim through thickening shadows, but it didn't work. He and

Lilith simply fell until the shadows slipped back and he found himself lying on something solid.

Clay came to his feet, groaning a little as he shook dust from his trench coat. Lilith floated next to him. Before them stretched a lake of dark fire. Shadowy flames roared and flickered, breaking into the air in dark plumes. A black sky stretched into the distance, broken by the reddish crags of distant mountains and impossibly tall towers in a sheer, Arabian style that looked like they came from one of Harvey's pulp novels. Clay took it all in, and then looked back at the lake. A bridge stretched over it, thin and spindly and made from human bones. The demons—or Shedim, to use the Hebrew word—must have brought those bones down here. Clay walked to the shore, nearing the entrance of the bridge. Smoke roiled around the bridge. He couldn't tell where it went.

Lilith swirled around him and formed next to him. "Asmodeus' palace lies ahead. We'd better get moving." She started over the bridge, then stopped and turned to look at him. "Armies of demons cross this bridge. It'll hold your weight, Clay."

He walked to the bridge and started to cross. "I hope so." The railings had been made of leg and arm bones, while ribcages formed the base and skulls topped the posts holding it up. Clay started to cross. Sure enough, the bridge held his weight. He moved over the bridge, the fire flickering and dancing below him. Lilith flew next to him, never too far away. Carefully, they crossed the burning river of flame. Clay stared ahead. "So it's true?" he asked. "Golems will never die?"

"Not unless we are killed," Lilith said. "We live forever, otherwise." The bridge reached its end up ahead, on a rocky, obsidian shore. "If we don't wish to go mad, we have to find something to occupy that ever-increasing amount of time." Clay neared the end of the bridge and stepped carefully onto the shore. Lilith moved in front of him, staring at him with her shadowy eyes. "Perhaps that is why I envy you, Mr. Clay." She kept her tone light, but Clay could hear the sadness in her voice.

"You envy me?" Clay asked.

"Indeed. For you have a purpose. You were created with a purpose—the defense of your people. I was created on a whim by a few alchemists and abandoned soon after." Lilith floated to her side. "And I have been alone ever since."

A field of snow appeared before them, the white contrasting sharply with the black obsidian. In the center of the field, Asmodeus' palace stretched into the red heavens. It looked like the palace of a sultan in one of the moving pictures that Clay took Harvey to see—with bulbous turrets and minarets surrounding impossibly high spires. It had all been constructed of black marble and silver, and cherry red torches glowed from braziers by the entrance. Clay stared in quiet amazement at the palace, and started across the snow. Lilith hovered next to him. The frost crunched under Clay's boots as he hurried across. Up above, trailing comets of flame dripped down from the red sky. They smashed into the snow, causing bursts of steam to well up.

Creatures stirred in the snow. They smashed their way out, casting aside melting ice as they roared to life. These were the Shedim—the demon descendants of the original Lilith. They had the appearance of malformed, humanoid goats, with blunt snouts, curling horns, and black furred bodies. Long iron claws sprouted from their hands, and they grunted and roared as they charged toward Clay and Lilith. Some Shedim sprouted leathery bat wings, and others dragged whips alight with demon fire as they charged.

"Quickly!" Clay cried. "To the palace!" He and Lilith broke into a mad run, pounding across the snow as the Shedim closed in around them. A flying demon swooped down onto Clay's back, dragging its claws across his back. Lilith formed a fist of smoke and slugged it, her blow hitting the goat's muzzle and knocking it aside. A flaming whip coiled around Clay's leg. He let it wrap around his ankle, then kicked back and tugged the demon closer. A rapid punch to the gut sent the demon flying, and a few more swings of his arms pushed other Shedim away.

He and Lilith kept moving, racing across the snow until they reached the iron gates of Asmodeus' palace. Clay didn't wait for the gates to open. He smashed his way through, ripping aside the bars and running across bare obsidian until he reached the doors. Lilith flew behind him. The doors opened on their own, swinging wide and revealing a long, empty throne room. Lilith and Clay hurried inside and the great doors slammed shut.

Silence filled the throne room. It was big enough to be the interior of a cathedral, with a wide open gallery set below spiky arches. Clay and Lilith walked down the aisle, and approached a vast obsidian throne at the far end. Asmodeus sat there, keeping his human appearance—though he had gained a pair of pointed jackal's ears. He sat alone in the room, with no companions and no court. A cigarette smoked in his hands, and he let it rest in his mouth as Clay and Lilith stood before him, like silent subjects approaching their king.

"Hello." Asmodeus gave them a friendly wave.

"King of the Demons," Clay said. He looked around the empty throne. "It's a lonely kingdom."

"True enough." Asmodeus came to his feet and walked down the jagged obsidian steps to the floor of his throne room. He approached Clay and looked him over. "You look a little worse for wear, my friend. Been running all around your city, tangling with Dagger Men and skeletons and stupid, simple golems. Must be troublesome." He swiveled about to face Lilith. "And you, my lovely lady, named after the matriarch of my people, are—as always—delightful. What can I for you?"

Lilith kept herself composed. "You know."

"You need a way to defeat the Dagger Men. To make Sickle City back to what it was." He put his arm around Clay's massive shoulder. "But was Sickle City so great? A place of corruption, of sin, and prejudice. Is it really worth saving?"

"It is worth saving," Clay said. "It's not perfection, but it's my home."

"And it's better than the Dagger Men's alternative." Asmodeus reached into his coat. "You are very lucky, Mr. Clay. Very few of us get the luxury of choosing our own fates. That is extremely rare for golems, you know." He withdrew a short silver rod—a pointer used for indicating holy words when reading the Torah known as a Yad. But this Yad had the appearance of a snake, a coiled serpent with the fanged head as the tip. "The Serpent Yad." Asmodeus handed the Yad to Clay. "It should let anyone rewrite almost anything, or at least allow two golems to have a kind of correspondence." He waited for Clay. "Take it, you dumb lump of earth."

Clay took the Serpent Yad and tucked it into the pocket of his trench coat. "This will—"

"Save the city. Yes, it will." Asmodeus sighed. "Because Issachar Eisendrath dislikes me as much as he dislikes you. I know why, but I'll leave you to find that out for yourself." He waved his hand. "Now, farewell and goodbye. I may see you again, Mr. Clay, if you have more dealings with demons. I find myself looking forward to it."

Before Clay could reply, shadow seethed around him and Asmodeus' palace vanished. The high obsidian walls and thrones, the red braziers with burning coals, and the leering Demon King himself all slipped away. Clay fell through shadows again, though this time he was thrust upwards, as if he had been catapulted into the night sky. He reached out madly, and a small hand caught his and pulled. Clay left the shadows as Harvey yanked him out of the circle in the center of the small guest room. Zipporah and Dr. Cutte helped and soon Clay lay in a heap on the ground. Lilith floated after him. Clay rolled over and stared at the ceiling. If he could breathe, he would be breathing heavily.

Sophie's head appeared as she looked down at him. "What was Hell like, Mr. Clay?"

"Not Hell." Clay sat up. "Gehenna." He withdrew the Serpent Yad from his pocket. Emerald eyes glittered in the skull of the serpent, shining as they watched everything. "We met Asmodeus. He gave us this tool—the Serpent Yad."

"And what'll that do?" Zipporah asked.

"He said it will let magic be rewritten," Lilith suggested. "That it will let golems talk."

"It will let us fight back." Clay stood. He returned the Yad to his coat. "And it will let us win."

Chapter Nine
THE SNAKE

In the basement of the Benevolent Merchantman's Association, the gangsters and crooked cops of Sickle City—the last bastion of the city's defense—held a council of war. They sat around the great round table topped with red felt, arguing with each other and their lieutenants and men in their own myriad languages. The Italians from Campion Street sat next to the De Brothers of the Shadow Brothers Tong. Across from them, Madam Gracie and her Negro gangsters in dark suits and bowler hats shared a side with Detective Flynn and SCPD men, uniformed and plainclothes alike. Sapphire sat next to Rabbi Holtz, occasionally interjecting. Kid Twist Deutsch stood next to him like a bald gargoyle in a sharp suit. Ava Silver and Sophie sat by the bar with Hark and Herbert. Sophie slurped up a soft drink. Arguments grew and grew as Clay, Zipporah, and Harvey walked into the basement casino, followed by Dr. Cutte. They stood quietly next to the table, waiting.

Finally, Sapphire had enough. He rammed his fist on the table, again and again—pounding out a rapid beat. The pounds came rapidly, ending the conversation. Sapphire glowered at them as his fist worked like a piston. Clay stared into his hateful face and he could see why this man became one of the most powerful hoods in Sickle City. "Quiet!" Sapphire cried. "Enough!" They fell silent. Sapphire came to his feet and motioned for Clay to join them. "You. You're an expert on golems and magic and all this nonsense. You said you could stop it. Your *schwartze* quack, he said he was going to help the rabbi's boy find a way. Have you?"

Clay looked them over. He creaked uneasily. Harvey shivered at his side. "Yes." He pulled the Serpent Yad from his pocket. The emerald eyes in the snake gleamed in the low gaslights of the basement gambling den. "This will change the enchantment on the stone. It will return Sickle City to normal, without causing the town's destruction." He handed the Serpent Yad to Harvey.

"S-sir?" Harvey asked.

"You can fix it, child," Zipporah said. "You know how this sort of thing works. It must be you."

Rabbi Holtz patted the boy's shoulder. "She's right, *boychick*."

Madam Gracie fanned herself. She wore a pale striped suit and women's trousers and her face had the consistency of tanned leather. "So our fate rests in the hands of a child scarcely out of short pants? You will pardon my skepticism." She folded the fan and let it rest on the tabletop. "You Jews have caused us trouble enough and now I suppose you'll need our help in getting the boy to the Founding Stone. It's in Arcadia Park, you know. Next to that bizarre temple your yid brethren are building with the labor of their prisoners."

Dr. Cutte smiled sheepishly. "Young Harvey's got power, Madam Gracie. He truly does."

"That doesn't concern me," Madam Gracie explained. "Here's my question—how are we to get the Holtz boy and that strange serpentine stick of his to the Temple and the Founding Stone? Skeletons surround the place, along with golems."

"I can get a police cruiser," Detective Flynn suggested. "Those autos are made tough. I'll drive the lad in."

"You still won't make it." Don Brunetti, the boss of the Crime Families on Campion Street, raised his cane, which bore a silver wolf's head topper. "The enemy is too numerous." He had a thick Italian accent, and paused to let smoke from his Cuban cigar leak out of the corner of his mouth, over his silken pinstripes. "The way must be cleared first, before the child can go to the Stone. This is difficult, but we are men and women who have lived difficult lives. It can be done."

"Exactly." Rabbi Holtz motioned for Harvey to stand next to him. "He's not putting a foot in that park unless it's safe." He pushed up his spectacles. "Here's what'll happen—me and my friends will go in first. Sneak in through the woods and clear a path. I'll take Clay, Zipporah, Monk, and Cohen."

"And Kid Twist," Sapphire insisted.

"And Kid Twist," Rabbi Holtz agreed. "We'll move in through the ornamental forest. The trees will cover us. We'll go right to the meadow, attack the temple, and clear out everything around it. That's when Harvey comes in. Detective Flynn can drive him in a paddy wagon—a Black Maria, perhaps. Something strong. He'll speed right up the temple, get Harvey out, and then he can put that Yad to use and end the spell." He shuddered as he said it, but then pointed around the table. "Then you send your men in—all of them, from different sides of the park. The Negroes can get the north, the Italians from the west, the Tong from the east, and the cops from the south. We'll surround the Dagger Men and destroy them."

"We've got another edge." Clay withdrew the small roll of paper taken from a pigeon's leg. He set it on the table and unrolled it. "The US government wants Sickle City back, just as we do. They're sending in the army." The paper curled up by itself. Clay held it in place with too thick fingers. "Colonel Menelaus Montgomery Rook leads them. A good man. Brave, almost to the point of madness. He intends to land an airship in Arcadia Park and battle the Dagger Men with his doughboys."

"Airships won't work," Sapphire said. "We all heard about Eames and the *Heavenly Chariot*."

"The Dagger Men will be busy," Zippporah explained. "We'll be keeping them busy. They won't have time to watch the sky."

The middle De Brother let out a slight cough. His two brothers, along with everyone else at the table, stared at him. "We have spent too long talking." He ran a hand over his hairless scalp. "While we talk, the day passes. The hours grow long. The Dagger Men grow stronger as they see their temple built. We forget what it is to rule this city." He pointed to Rabbi Holtz. "Take your friends. Go to the meadow. Make the way safe for your son."

Rabbi Holtz nodded. "I'll be on my way, then." He pushed back from the table and motioned for Clay and the others. "Come on. Monk brought my Packard from Haven Street. It's in the alley. We'll use that."

He paused and faced Harvey. Herbert walked over as well. The two Holtz men and the one Holtz boy clasped hands. They stayed close for a few minutes, and then Rabbi Holtz pulled away and went to the stairs. Cohen followed, rifle on her shoulder and grenades clinking on her belt. Monk tucked shells into his trench gun, Kid Twist spat out his tooth pick, and Zipporah patted her blades. Harvey stayed close to the table. Clay had never seen him look so forlorn and so small. Sophie Silver hurried to his side and patted his back. Harvey hardly seemed to notice. His eyes followed his father and Clay as they went up the stairs. Conversation increased as they left—the various gangs making their plans to assemble their strength. Clay didn't know if he could trust them, but knew he didn't have a choice.

They left the Benevolent Merchantman's Association and assembled in the alley. Rabbi Holtz's second car, a compact gray Packard, lay in the alley, glistening as a light autumn rain came down in a drizzle. Rabbi Holtz got behind the wheel and slid on motorist's goggles, while Cohen opened the trunk. Rifles and cartridge belts waited. Cohen and Monk must have grabbed what they could from the armory in the King Solomon Synagogue before departing for Chinatown. The guns would come in handy now.

She handed Zipporah an Enfield. "You're used to this, aren't you? Used it in the Great War? A fine weapon. You Brits were lucky to have it." She had a Springfield for Clay, with a cruel bayonet affixed to the end. "And this is something that you are familiar with, Mr. Clay, from your time in Russia." She tossed it to Clay. He caught it and opened the breech, then slid in the first set of bullets. "There you are, Mr. Clay. You never forget."

Zipporah slung the rifle over her shoulder. "True enough." She tapped Clay's shoulder. "Clay. You got a visitor."

He turned to the mouth of the alley. Lilith Shadowborn floated there, faint in the drizzle. Her dark form seemed like liquid, as if she had dripped down from the gray heavens. Clay gripped his rifle and walked over to her. "Lilith." He wasn't sure what to say. After they had returned from Gehenna and Asmodeus' empty palace, she had vanished into the cracks between the floorboards. "Will you go with us? Will you help us?" They could certainly use the assistance.

Lilith shook her head. She had grown fainter, and Clay could barely make out the glow of her eyes. "I'm afraid you are alone in this endeavor, Mr. Clay. You must do this on your own. This is work for the world of men, and that is not a world I belong to." She leaned closer. "I was always more comfortable amongst the ghosts."

"Not among golems?" Clay asked.

"Among brutish and simple golems least of all," Lilith explained. "Apart from you." Her hand rested on the side of his face, her fingers cool and faint—like a gentle breeze that never faded. "I will wish you luck, Mr. Clay, and watch from afar." Lilith drifted back, moving into the falling rain. "Farewell."

"Thank you." Clay called after her. Lilith drifted into the distance and vanished for good.

The Packard's horn honked—a brassy, excited noise. "Come on, Clay!" Clay hurried to join them. He hopped over the runners and settled into the back, resting the rifle on his legs. Rabbi Holtz made the engine start and drove from the alley. Monk sat next to him, his trench gun loaded and ready to fire. Cohen readied her rifle and patted the handle of her machete. Kid Twist had the automatics in crossed shoulder-holsters, along with a Thompson submachine gun. The champions of Haven Street stood ready for war. Clay sunk into his seat, clutching the rifle tightly. Cohen was right. You never forgot how to handle a weapon.

"Something wrong, Clay?" Zipporah asked.

"Is this what I am meant to do?" Clay asked the question carefully as he traced his fingers along the rifle, all the way to the thin bayonet and its sharp point. "Fight and fight. Wage war without end? Is that my purpose?"

"It's something that must be done," Zipporah said. "Nothing more."

That didn't make Clay feel much better as the Packard rumbled out of Chinatown and began the journey to Arcadia Park and the battle that would decide the fate of the city.

They ditched the Packard a block away from Arcadia Park and moved in on foot. The rain had increased to a steady downpour. It slicked the streets and brought mist rolling in from the sea—a welcome cover that hid their approach as they crossed the empty street. Rabbi Holtz, clutching his double-barreled shotgun, led them around ruined and overturned automobiles and to the soggy grass of the park. They stepped over the lawn, passed a shattered statue of some Civil War general, now fallen from his horse and jabbing his sword in the mud, and entered the safety of the ornamental forest. Clay moved carefully through the trees, pushing aside low-hanging branches as they neared the forest path. Clay and Zipporah had been here before, defeating the Tree Men right before they were sent to investigate the Dagger Men's first robbery of Sapphire's shipments. The park had changed so much since then.

Beyond the forest, the rebuilt temple sprouted toward the heavens. The Dagger Men had tried their best to rebuild it in the same square style as the Ancient Israelites. In many ways, they had succeeded. The temple looked like a great white square, with slender pillars built into the wall before a rectangular entryway. Stone steps led inside, and the beginnings of more pillars and walls flanked the larger building. Chunks of steel, brick, and stone formed the temple. Unpainted and smashed together, they made the temple look like a puzzle that had been put together wrong. Burning braziers in vast round bowls and torches stabbed into the ground surrounded the temple, covering everything in flickering light. Their smoke drifted into the sky.

Clay turned his eyes away from the temple and focused on moving quietly. Cohen and Monk guided Rabbi Holtz, keeping his feet from dry branches. Clay and Zipporah followed, their rifles at the ready. Clay had done this before, in Russian forests with snow on the ground. Discovery meant death by the Bolsheviks, so the men of the Polar Bear Expedition had learned to move quietly. Clay did that now. He could be back in Russia, with the same rifle and the same cold numbness in his chest. He hated the feeling. They crossed the gravel pathway, and now could get a better look at the temple, through the thickets of trees.

The Dagger Men had fortified it well. Skeletal legionaries formed in long columns before the temple, guarded by their ballistae. Golems moved around in patrol, their thick arms swaying. These golems had been made from brick, cement, earth, sharp, jagged glass, and dozens of other substances. Their prisoners lay on the other side of the temple, their hands bound. They must not have started work just yet. Clay couldn't see Rabbi Geist or Rabbi Eisendrath, but he was certain the Dagger Men were out there, protecting the Third Temple.

Monk dropped to a crouch. He turned to the rabbi. "What do you think, boss? If I was back in France, I'd say we send a pigeon or a runner back to the artillery boys and have them pound the stuffing out all those skeletons and golems. Can't do that now, though."

"Nope," Rabbi Holtz agreed. "But we got Mrs. Cohen. She can use her grenades to—"

The barking of hounds drowned out his words. Clay stared down the gravel path. Past the gazebo, a number of skeletal Roman dogs raced through the trees. Their handlers, skeleton legionaries with cracking whips, short swords, and shields lashed to their backs, followed. The fleshless hounds had no lips and no lungs, but they still released loud, terrible barks. These dogs could take down a small horse, and their teeth remained sharp in their dusty skulls. Somehow, these long dead dogs had sniffed them out.

"Back!" Zipporah cried. "Up the trail!"

That seemed their only option. They hurried from the dogs and ran up the winding gravel trail, past the soggy trees. Clay's boots squelched on mud, but he still kept running. The dogs followed, breaking into barking runs. Cohen fired her rifle, picking off a pair of hounds as they approached. They collapsed into piles of bones, clicking and breaking as they struck the dirt. More dogs raced through the trees, baying as if Clay and his friends were rabbits to be run down. Clay certainly felt that way. The forest trail curved, and brought them to a familiar clearing. The decorative Grecian ruins rested in the grass, next to a picturesque gazebo. Rabbi Geist stood there, waiting for them. Two massive golems of living stone, rain dripping on their gray features, flanked him.

Rabbi Geist held up his hand. The barking of the dogs ceased. The skeletal canines sat on their haunches, their hollow eyes watching Clay and his friends. The legionaries moved closer, their swords, spears, and bows prepared. The rock golems stood stiffly, each like a boulder with stubby arms and legs jammed on their sides. Rabbi Geist's beard and hair clung to him wetly. He smiled. "Rabbi Holtz—though you do not deserve that title. You came to see the temple?"

"We came to destroy you," Rabbi Holtz replied.

"And you have failed. You sought to creep into our camp." Rabbi Geist waved his two fingers. "You're a fool. The eyes of every statue in Sickle City belong to the Dagger Men. There is nothing about this city—and about Arcadia Park—that we do not know."

Clay stared into the underbrush behind him. Something moved amongst the pines—a different shade of green than the pine needles, brushing past the branches. It could have been wind stirring the trees, but Clay knew it was something else entirely. He remembered the scuffle he and Zipporah had with the residents of this wood, and the peace treaty they had established. Would that treaty hold now, and give them some much needed help? Clay had to hope it would.

He faced Rabbi Geist. "Not everything."

Dark green shapes burst from the trees surrounding the clearing. The Men of the Fields—the Adnei Hasadeh as Harvey had called them— came to the aid of Zipporah and Clay, who had arranged to protect them. The Tree Men had grown in number since Clay had seen them. Now a score of the botanical creatures raced from the forest to attack. Thorny knuckles, wooden hands, and twisting vines lashed down as they struck the legionaries and skeletal dogs. The Tree Man with the mossy beard led them, swinging around a long, thorny vine that smashed into several dogs

"There is nothing…about Arcadia Park we do not know."

and their skeletal handlers. The vines wrapped around bones and broke them, scattering pieces of the Romans into the underbrush. More Tree Men fell upon the legionaries, driving club-like wooden limbs or fists spiked with thorns into their chests. Chunks of bone flew. The skeletons tried to fight back with slashes of their swords, but the Tree Men finished them quickly.

Monk and Cohen brought up their guns as the two stone golems closed in. The trench gun and rifle thundered together, both aiming straight for the head. Chunks of rock rained down. The golems collapsed, falling on their backs and rolling as their limbs struck the dirt. Dust rose, then sank down in the rain. Rabbi Geist hadn't moved. He had been master of the clearing one moment, and now his entire force had been wiped out. He tried to run, but the leader of the Tree Men waved a branch hand in the air and two of his men sent out their vines. One tendril coiled around Rabbi Geist's leg and another reached his chest. He struggled and cursed, but couldn't move. He was trapped.

Silence filled the clearing, apart from the rustling speech of the Tree Men. The bearded Tree Man approached Clay. Once again, he held out a wooden hand. Clay took it. "Thank you." The Tree Men had made Arcadia Park their home and they must not like the Dagger Men's incursion. "We may have need of you again. Help us take the temple, and we'll get rid of the Dagger Men forever. The woods will be yours again." He waited for the Tree Man to nod, and approached Rabbi Geist. Rabbi Holtz and Zipporah joined him.

Zipporah jabbed the muzzle of her rifle under his chin, the barrel poking past his beard. "Want to say a quick prayer, Rabbi?"

"Kill him." Kid Twist clutched his Thompson. "I got an ice pick. I'll keep it quiet."

"He's more useful alive." Rabbi Holtz pointed to the pillar of the gazebo. "Put him there." The Tree Men assented. They hauled Rabbi Geist to the side of the pillar and their vines snapped around his body and held him in place. Rabbi Geist didn't bother struggling. Rabbi Holtz kept his shotgun casually trained on Rabbi Geist's chest. "Where's the Founding Stone?"

"Right before the temple, *apikoros*." Rabbi Geist hissed out the final word. "You won't take it. My master stands guard before the Third Temple. God himself protects my master, and he will—"

"You didn't seem too keen on your boss back in Chinatown, pal," Zipporah said. "Back when he opened up that poor Sinclair fellow's throat. Killed him in cold blood. You didn't like that, Rabbi." She gripped his beard and gave it a tug. "You've seen cruelty before and your master's reminding you more and more of the nasty *goyim* who you seek to fight. Ain't that right?"

"I am l-loyal to Rabbi Eisendrath," Rabbi Geist murmured.

"What is he, exactly?" Clay asked. "He's taken blows that should kill men. He's lived for years—or so he claimed. What is he?"

"I am loyal to Rabbi Eisendrath," Rabbi Geist repeated.

"Let me kill him." Kid Twist sounded almost bored. He withdrew a handkerchief and tightened it into a makeshift garrote. "I can strangle him, if you're worried about the noise."

Rabbi Holtz yanked the handkerchief from Kid Twist's hand. He stuffed into Rabbi Geist's mouth. Rabbi Geist made muffled protests. "Men of the Field." Rabbi Holtz faced the leader of the Tree Men. "Keep two of your people here to look after him. Maybe the rest of you could come with us." He pointed past the line of trees bordering the clearing, out into the meadow. "We've wasted enough time in the woods. It's time to take the temple."

"Bully!" Monk said, racking his trench gun. "Off we go."

They left Rabbi Geist tied to the pillar of the gazebo with vines, shaking and growling around the handkerchief in his mouth. A few more paces and they reached the edge of the forest. Clay and his friends crouched under the cover of the branches and stared at the meadow, and the temple at its center. The Tree Men joined them, led by their moss-bearded king. The Roman legionaries in the meadow marched about, while the golems swayed in place.

There was still no sign of Rabbi Eisendrath. He had certainly left enough of his strength here to guard the temple. Even with the Tree Men, would they be able to take down that many skeletons and golems? They would have to have a plan. Clay thought quickly. "We should split up," he suggested. "Rabbi, take Monk and Cohen and the Men of the Field and see to the prisoners. Zipporah and I will go with Kid Twist. We'll get their attention, take cover in the temple, and finish them as they try to get us out. Get the prisoners out of here and then come back and help. Between us, they'll be finished."

"You want me?" Kid Twist gave Clay a humorless smile.

"I want your firepower." Clay rested his finger on the trigger. "Now let's go."

He and Zipporah broke from cover, charging for the temple. Their rifles cracked together, shooting the Roman skeletons. They fired and reloaded with rapid speed, their shots tearing through rusted armor and ancient bones. Skeletons dropped. A tall steel golem hurried in their direction and Clay took time in his aiming. His shot took the golem in the forehead and it smashed down in a heap of metal, burying and destroying several skeletons. Kid Twist followed them, and gave the Roman Legionaries a rattling salvo with the Thompson. The heavy bullets of the sub-gun ripped skeletons apart, tossing bones into the air. They moved quickly, firing as they ran, and scrambled to the steps leading into the temple. The Founding Stone lay in the dirt, next to the steps—but only Harvey and the Serpent Yad could change those Hebrew letters etched by the Shamir.

While the golems and skeletons massed around the temple, Rabbi Holtz, his enforcers, and the Tree Men moved in to rescue the prisoners. The Tree Men slammed straight into the flank of the skeletons, and battle raged in the meadow, above slick grass and mud. Branches and vines slammed and smashed against Roman armor. Short swords and pila stabbed into green bodies, spilling pulp and cutting through wood. Rabbi Holtz, Monk, and Cohen raced through the battle, adding blasts from their guns as they hurried to the line of prisoners. Cohen used her machete to cut their bonds while Monk and Rabbi Holtz unloaded their shotguns on the golems coming their way.

Clay tore his eyes away from the meadow and focused on his own part of the battle. He ran up the stone steps of the temple, followed by Zipporah. Kid Twist walked backwards, giving bursts from his Thompson to pursuing skeletons. An arrow sliced his elbow and a spear grazed his shoulder, but he didn't stop. They made it up the stairs and ducked into the doorway, using the gray stone for cover. Behind them, the temple extended in a square hall. Evidently, the Dagger Men hadn't gotten around to putting in the decorations.

"What should be the holiest site in Judaism." Zipporah worked the bolt on her rifle and fired at the Romans trying to make it up the stairs. "Hell of a place for a gunfight." Next to her, Kid Twist spent the last rounds from his Thompson. He cut down the skeletons trying to take the steps, shell casings clinking across the stone floor until the Tommy gun went silent.

"You heard Harvey." Clay's rifle cracked, dropping a centurion trying to lead his legionaries in a charge. His bullet took the centurion through the forehead, passing through steel and skull. The helmet came free, the plumes ruffling as it bounced down the steps. "Judaism's changed since Jerusalem fell to the Romans. It will never go back to the way it was. This isn't the holiest site in Judaism." The bolt clicked as he made the familiar motion. He fired again. "It's just another battlefield." He cut down another legionary before the skeleton could hurl a pilum.

Kid Twist pulled another drum magazine from his overcoat. "A lesson I learned a long time ago—nothing's truly sacred." He reloaded and fired again.

All around them, battle raged. The Tree Men had made a good first strike against the Romans, but now the skeletal legions' numbers began to take effect. Chopping gladius blades and striking spears forced the Tree Men back, cutting into plant bodies. The legion forced the Tree Men closer to the woods. Golems waded into battle with the Tree Men as well, smashing their wooden bodies with rapid swings of their heavy fists. Across from the temple, Cohen had finished freeing the prisoners. They scrambled away, running for the safety of the streets. Cohen tossed grenades into the skeletons, while Monk and Rabbi Holtz held them off with their shotguns. Bone, stone, and steel broke under the onslaughts, but the Dagger Men had endless numbers of troops to call on. They pushed Rabbi Holtz and the others back to the side of the temple, even as grenades tossed up gouts of earth and flame. The rain poured down, growing into a rapid downpour.

Zipporah pointed down the steps. "Looks like they don't like us being so close to the Holy of Holies." A group of earth golems charged up the steps, smashing aside Roman legionaries in their haste to reach the interior. These golems had been formed from compact earth, and bits of dirt crumbled from their bodies and struck the steps. The rain made streams of mud run down their chests, but they didn't look any less intimidating. They had Clay's general shape as well, though they stood a bit taller. The Dagger Men must be using all their strength to try to force out the attackers.

Kid Twist leaned out and fired at the first golem, his Thompson spitting lead. He raked the golem's chest. Mud and dirt burst from the wounds— but Kid Twist didn't get a chance to destroy the golem's head. A mud hand slapped him, knocking him across the smooth stone floor. His Tommy gun dangled on its strap, rattling against stone. Clay charged the golem next. He fired, but his bullet missed the golem's head by inches. Then the golem grabbed him, wrapping one hand around the side of his face and holding his belly with the other. Mud dripped in Clay's eyes. The golem was going to rip off his head. He thought quickly, judged the best angle, and stabbed up with his rifle.

The bayonet impaled the golem's face, driving into dirt and mud—but not the fatal letters. Clay twisted the bayonet and jammed it deeper into the mud. Dirt ran over his suit and trench coat and his legs kicked madly.

The spike dragged deeper and then the golem crumbled. Clay hit the ground. The earth golem fell to the side, the mud sticking to the stones. It covered Clay as well—just like the mud had in the battlefields of Russia.

More earth golems came up the stairs. "Look to your front!" Zipporah cried.

She ran to Clay, her rifle ready. Clay fired his rifle as well and Kid Twist joined in with the Thompson. The earth golems dropped. They dripped down the steps, turning to mud in the pounding rain. Clay and Zipporah fired until their rifles clicked empty. They reloaded while Kid Twist used the Thompson. The earth golem attack ended—but it had nearly succeeded. The Dagger Men could always summon more. Clay began to wonder how long they would last.

They ducked back behind the temple walls, letting Kid Twist keep the steps clear with his gun. "This was the plan, remember?" Zipporah asked. "Get their attention. Draw them closer and give Harvey a chance to get here and the others an opportunity to assemble."

"I'm starting to think it was a bad plan," Clay said.

"It was the only one we had." Zipporah peered out from behind the wall. A giant arrow from a ballista smashed into the wall, scattering chunks of rock. Zipporah fired at the ballista, picking off the skeletons manning it, and then pointed into the distance. "Oh nuts. Detective Flynn—that goddamn mick idiot."

"What is it?" Clay asked.

"He's coming early, damn him. He and Harvey have arrived."

Clay ran next to Zipporah and looked out over the meadow. She was right. A bulky Black Maria roared down from the street, bounced over the sidewalk and then tore across the open grass. Rain drummed on the windshield and the square back of the car, and mud sprayed from the wheels. Detective Flynn drove, his blue suit visible over the meadow. Harvey sat next to him, his newsboy hat just visible over the dashboard. Clay felt fear stiffen his limbs. The meadows in front of the Black Maria undulated and danced—difficult to see in the rain, but clear on the green grass.

"The ground's moving." Fear filled Clay's voice. The Dagger Men wouldn't make the city dance so close to this precious temple—but Detective Flynn and Harvey rode across the meadow far away from the building site. Hills bulged, the grass splitting and flying into the air. The Black Maria bucked and danced, its wheels sliding in the mud. Detective Flynn still tried to keep driving forward, but the ground roiled and swirled under his car. He wasn't going to make it.

Zipporah saw as well. "Oh no—Harvey—"

A final jab came from below the earth, the ground spiking and stabbing the bottom of the Black Maria. Metal tore. Rubber from the wheels split. The Black Maria careened along, two wheels lifting up from the earth as it slid from the side. It crashed finally, glass from the windows spilling and the door flapping. It slid on for a few moments, dragging a line in the mud, and then came to a rest. Nothing stirred inside the car. Legionaries charged it in an organized mass. Their pila hurtled through the air above them, the points driving into the dirt or bouncing and breaking off the armored sides of the automobile. They would reach the crashed Black Maria soon.

"No." Clay's vision fixed on the car. He should never have left the side of his creator's nephew. He should never have let innocents become endangered. Perhaps that was all golems were good for—protecting those that needed protecting, and Clay had failed. Or maybe his only purpose was the destruction of his enemies, and he had been lying to himself all this time.

"Clay?" Zipporah gripped his arm. "Think, man—Detective Flynn's with him. He'll get Harvey out and bring him over here. We need to clear this area, get rid of the skeletons and—" She turned as Clay dropped his rifle and faced Kid Twist. "What are you doing, Clay?"

"Give me the chopper," Clay ordered.

Kid Twist stared at his Thompson and then shrugged. "I got more than one gat." He handed Clay the Thompson and then withdrew a third drum magazine from his coat. He tucked it into the outside pocket of Clay's trench coat. "What are you gonna do, big man?"

"Protect my creator's nephew." Clay was strong enough to hold the Thompson in one hand. He hoisted the gun, aiming it upwards as he flexed his arm and prepared. "Stay here, Zipporah. Stay with Kid Twist and the rabbi and his men. Use the temple for cover. Don't let the Dagger Men move the Founding Stone. I'll be back shortly."

"Clay, you don't need to fight a war by yourself," Zipporah said.

"Why not?" Clay asked. "It's what I was built for." He leapt from cover and ran down the steps, momentum adding to his speed. Even the skeletons seemed surprised. Clay ignored them. He had fought armies before and won. It was time to do that again.

᙮᙮᙮

Time seemed to run faster, moving into a blur as the combat truly began. Clay raced down the steps, his size and speed giving him strength, and smashed through the first rank of skeletons like a wrecking ball. He swept his free hand out, driving it into the bodies of legionaries as he plowed past. Bones and rusted armored shattered on his arm. He smashed a skeleton into the air, tossing it into a pile of its fellows, and stomped on the skull with his boot as he ran past. A gladius drove into his gut. Another stabbed into his back. Clay ignored them. He reached the Tree Men and fought alongside them for a few moments, punching and kicking and driving the Romans back. Pila and arrows whistled down and stabbed into his body. They slowed him down. Clay finally decided to use the Thompson. He aimed the gun with one hand and fired. The recoil banged its way into his limb, but he held it steady. He wiped out a row of archers and cleared a path—then ran for the downed police van.

He hurried away from the building site. The rustling of bones moved around him, as a squad of Roman cavalry charged him from the side. Their swords glittered in the rain and water ran down the curves of their horses' ribs. Clay thought quickly. He grabbed the nearest brazier of fire and coals, rammed his shoulder against it, and pushed. The brazier went up, and the burning logs inside spilled out—straight into the front ranks of the cavalry. Flame clung to the bones. Dead horses leapt and danced as their armor burned. Clay gave them a burst from the Tommy gun, cutting down horses and riders, and then turned to run.

The Black Maria still seemed too far away. Clay fixed his eyes on the crashed van as he ran. The ground seemed to hunger for his boots. Mud clung to his feet, and tried to drag him down. A hill bulged out in front of him, trying to stop his approach. Clay ran over the hill, crested it, and jumped. He landed on the other side and kept running.

The door of the van swung open. Detective Flynn emerged, dazed from the crash. He raised a Browning Automatic Rifle, a portable machine gun from the tail-end of the Great War, which seemed as big as he was. Detective Flynn tugged himself out of the car, raised the gun, and began shooting at the surrounding Romans. The BAR roared and chattered, recoil ruining his aim—but there were so many skeletons that he could almost not miss. Their first line collapsed under the roar of the BAR, but Clay knew that those big guns didn't have many rounds in their square magazines. He doubled his pace, running over the ground and racing toward the Romans.

The Dagger Men's golems chased him. Golems of steel and earth followed at a run, the ground smoothing around them to make them run just a little faster. Clay turned and fired at them with the Thompson. He brought down two, ripping their heads apart with the Thompson's big bullets. A steel golem charged a little faster and reached him. It smashed a forearm built from a steel girder into Clay's shoulder, knocking him down, and then kneed him hard and kept him on the ground. Mud boiled around Clay, trying to drown him. Clay forced the Tommy gun into the golem's face and fired. Bullet holes appeared in the metal, crossing out the Hebrew word. The golem collapsed. Clay pushed it aside and came to his feet. He ejected the empty magazine, tossed it to the ground, and withdrew the second drum. A quick reload and then he kept running, racing to the back of the Roman column.

"Clay!" Detective Flynn spotted him. "Take them in the center! I'll work the flanks!"

The Tommy gun and the BAR roared together. Clay used the entire clip and Detective Flynn did as well. Their shots tore into the legionaries from both sides smashing apart skeletons and ancient armor. Romans collapsed, their rectangular shields and short swords plopping into the muck. They managed to send a few javelins and arrows whistling at their attackers as they fell—and one arrow slid into Detective Flynn's leg, piercing flesh right below the knee. He dropped, but propped the BAR on the mud and kept firing. Clay didn't let up either, until the legionaries had been cleared away. Then Clay ran to the fallen car.

He reached the Black Maria, smoke leaking from the muzzle of the Thompson. Clay dropped it and stared at Detective Flynn, who gripped the bloodied arrow jabbing into his leg. "Merely a scratch." Detective Flynn pointed to the car. "See to the lad. The poor boy's banged around some, but still all right. Get him out of there, Mr. Clay."

Quickly, Clay reached the front of the overturned van. He peered inside and offered his hand. Harvey took it. Clay pulled him out and set him down. Harvey had received a cruel bruise to his cheek and one lens of his spectacles had broken. He winced a little as he stretched his legs and gingerly stood on the now sloping meadow. "I'll be okay, Mr. Clay." He looked at Detective Flynn, his eyes widening. He gripped the Serpent Yad, holding the precious pointer between both hands as if he was afraid it would slither away. "Oh, sir. Are you all right?"

"Fine and dandy." Detective Flynn fumbled to reload the BAR. "I'll battle more of the ghouls. Try to keep them away from you. You get Harvey to the Founding Stone, Mr. Clay. Put an end to this quickly." He winced.

"Ah Hell. It seems the foul Dagger Men aren't going to let that boy reach the temple." He pointed down the meadow.

More Romans approached—an army of the skeletal legionaries. Golems joined them, hulking titans of bricks, steel and dirt, who tottered as they ambled along. Smaller, lean golems made of wood and stone moved under them, their limbs sharpened into deadly points. From the sky, a dark cloud of Broxa fluttered down from the rain. The vampire birds spread their wings, rain dripping from the points of their beaks and the tips of their talons. They flapped toward Clay, Detective Flynn, and Harvey, emitting no cries as their silent wings pulsed. The ground had sloped under Clay's feet, forming a valley around Clay and his friends. The Black Maria groaned as the earth formed a crater below it. They were trapped before all the servants of the Dagger Men.

Clay had used the last round of his Thompson, and he doubted that even his strength could keep Harvey safe from all those golems. His stony body creaked, unsure what to do. Had they fought so hard, only to be overwhelmed here?

Harvey then cupped a hand to his ear. "Wait a minute. Listen, Mr. Clay." He smiled. "Do you hear? Below the rain—it's engines! And footsteps!"

Sure enough, the hum of distant engines rumbled somewhere past the rain. Pounding footsteps joined in—and then a roar of gunfire came from every end of the park. Clay had to see for sure. He scrambled to the side of the valley and clambered up, digging his fingers into the earth to haul himself out of the pit. Harvey hurried to join him, wincing as he struggled to climb. Clay grabbed the back of the boy's collar and simply carried him, pulling him out of the shallow pit. They stood together in the broken grass, the rain rippling down, and looked at the northern, southern, eastern, and western sections of Arcadia Park. The various criminals of Sickle City had finally arrived. It had taken them a while to get organized, but now they had shown up, eager for battle.

Sapphire's Jewish Mob attacked in an array of sleek roadsters, goons poised on runners of their automobiles with Thompsons roaring. They roared over the open meadow, firing at the golems and Romans and cutting them down. More of his gunmen approached on foot, using pistols and rifles to pick off whatever the submachine guns missed. Sid Sapphire walked behind them all; an overcoat draped over his shoulders like a cape and his cigarette holder a smoldering point of cherry red light in the gray rain. Across from them, Don Brunetti and the Italians of Campion Street came in thick clusters of dark overcoats, their sawed-off shotguns roaring at close range and shattering the skeletal bodies of the Romans. Their riflemen followed, Sicilian marksmen with rain dripping on the brims of their flat caps as they put their long range weapons to use.

From the other end of the park, the Madam Gracie's gang and the Shadow Brothers Tong attacked alongside the remnants of the Sickle City Police Department. Madam Gracie led her mob from the front. They used shotguns and rifles, then crossed the Roman swords with iron bars, bats, and trench clubs. Bolo knives pierced ancient armor, and they forced their way through the first lines of Romans. The Shadow Brothers fought with their own weapons. Bethany Hark led them, her rapid-firing crossbow shooting a barrage of arrows into the Roman ranks. Tong hatchetmen cleared a path ahead of her, staffs, broadswords, and axes smashed apart the skeletons. The SCPD officers used their guns and then their nightsticks to defeat their enemies.

Clay could hardly believe it. Normally, all the gangs of Sickle City would be at each others' throats, fighting madly for the rackets of a city block, bootlegger routes, or the profits of a couple speakeasies. They would scarcely sit together without drawing weapons and picking a fight. But the Dagger Men had united them. They had tried to take a diverse city and make it uniform. They had not succeeded—but they had indeed forged the city, or at least its underworld, into something close to a unified force.

Harvey watched as well. "They've all come to help. All of them."

"This is their city too," Detective Flynn explained. "And they don't want it to be the Second Jerusalem." He gripped the edge of the Black Maria and helped himself up, gripping the ridges by the door by a support and then leaning against the vehicle. He balanced the BAR on the overturned hood. "Now, Mr. Clay. Take the lad and get to the temple. Put that serpent pen of his to good use and undo this magic which has conquered our city."

"He's right, Mr. Clay," Harvey agreed. "Let's go." He paused. "I am a bit tired, and I've never been very good at running. Perhaps we can—"

Quickly, Clay picked up Harvey and rested the boy on his shoulder. He carried Harvey like the boy was a sack of beets held by a farmer in the Old Country, and dashed across the meadow. Mud flew under his boot as they ran through the rain. Some intelligence in the Roman skeletons, or maybe the city itself, tried to stop them. Arrows flew through the air. Clay swept Harvey down and turned, letting his arm take the shafts. They burrowed into his skin, ripping his sleeve, and stabbing deep into his body. Clay ignored it, hoisted Harvey up and kept running. A Roman war dog charged toward him and he dispatched it with a kick. The temple drew closer, and Clay kept running. Harvey held on, squeaking in panic as the ground moved and bounced under Clay's feet.

"Mr. Clay!" Harvey pointed to the sky. "The Broxa—they're coming down!" The Dagger Men must have known about the Serpent Yad and the power held in that small length of gold with the emerald eyes. Rabbi Eisendrath would use everything at his disposal to stop them. Clay kept running as the Broxa descended.

The vampire crows raced around him, their claws lashing down. Beaks drilled into his back and arms, as the Broxa aimed for his head and the vital letters written there. They attacked Harvey as well. A Broxa rammed into his chest, poking him with its beak as its claws scratched. Another Broxa went for the Serpent Yad, managing to wrap a few spindly claws around the golden stick. Harvey tugged it back, wincing as talons scratched for his face. Clay pulled him to the side and slugged the Broxa. His knuckles brushed against scratchy feathers. The Broxa wheeled down and struck the ground. Clay stomped on it. Small bones cracked. Clay ran ahead before more Broxa could descend. They still flapped after him, squawking madly.

The Third Temple drew closer. It seemed strange in the gray rain, black smoke, and dancing red flame from the braziers. Broxa wheeled and fluttered around it as Roman skeletons still tried to get inside. Kid Twist and Zipporah stood in the doorway. The twin scimitars hummed in Zipporah's hands as she parried the blades of skeletons and hacked at the heads of golems. Kid Twist took a position behind her, his twin automatics blazing in his hands. He probably wouldn't be happy that Clay had ditched his Thompson. Clay didn't care. The Tree Men still battled the Romans, though they had been driven further back to the forest. The gangsters of Sickle City would reach them and help them wreck the legionaries with firepower, but Clay didn't know if they would make it in time. Perhaps the Men of the Field were just another group he couldn't help.

The Broxa still buzzed around them, their talons shredding Clay's coat. He kept his head low, staring at the shifting, muddy meadow. Harvey said something, clutching the Serpent Yad tightly as talons jabbed into his arms and drew blood. They could rip the boy apart, tearing him to pieces and carrying him away. Clay spun, putting his back to the Broxa. Beaks and talons drew lines in his back, but couldn't do as much damage. They needed to get rid of those birds.

"Clay!" Cohen roared over the sounds of the battle. "Down!"

"And keep my son safe!" Rabbi Holtz added.

Something small and olive green bounced into the mud. Clay tossed

Harvey ahead and then jumped himself—right out of the swarm of Broxa. Harvey hit the mud, bounced, and rolled—the Serpent Yad a line of gold in his hands. Clay hit the mud as well. Cohen's grenade exploded behind them, engulfing the Broxa in a burst of red flame. Black feathers rained down. More Broxa still wheeled overhead, but the grenade had bought Clay some time.

He stumbled to his feet and ran to Harvey. The boy had lost his spectacles. He reached in the mud, fumbling through grass until he found them, and set them gingerly on his nose. "Mr. Clay?" he asked, as he weakly came to his feet. "Is this what it's like? Being a golem, I mean? Getting smashed and thrown around and beaten without having a chance to catch your breath?"

"I can't breathe, Harvey," Clay said.

"Oh." Harvey straightened his tie. He wiped blood from his nose on his sleeve. "Well, I think we're almost there." He pointed ahead to the Third Temple. "There's the Founding Stone. All I have to do is make a few marks, and then this will be all over." He stood tall, sucked in air, and squared his shoulders as he faced the temple. "I c-can be brave, Mr. Clay. I can be a soldier, just like you. Maybe I can even be a golem."

"No," Clay said. "You never could."

He offered his hand and Harvey took it. They ran together across the meadow, racing for the Third Temple. Roman legionaries moved to block them. Harvey gasped and stumbled—but his father, Cohen, and Monk were looking after them. Rabbi Holtz ran to attack the Romans, using his empty shotgun as a club. He smashed the butt into a Roman's head, splintering bone and rusted metal and bringing the legionary down. Cohen wielded her machete, the blade shining as it hacked off the skulls from legionaries. Monk had his trench gun, firing it with one hand as he swatted skeletons with his trench club. They cleared aside the Romans, giving Clay and Harvey a path.

The golem and the boy raced across the meadow and reached the front of the temple. A ballista rested right before the Founding Stone, skeletal Romans already aiming the oversized arrow at Clay. They reached for the lever that would fire the arrow—when Zipporah leapt down from the steps of the Third Temple and met them with swinging swords. She cut her way through the crew, cutting apart the remaining skeletons, and then gave the ballista a push. It swung to the side, its arrow aiming at an oversized earth golem trundling their way. Zipporah pulled the lever, driving a heavy arrow straight into the earth golem's skull. Dust trickled down as the earth golem collapsed into the mud. Zipporah lowered her blades and smiled.

Harvey ran to her. "Miss Sarfati." He tripped on a destroyed skeleton, stumbling in the sloping dirt, and then reached her. Clay followed. Zipporah patted Harvey's head. "You're okay. You're safe. And what you did with the ballista? That was—that was swell, ma'am."

"Just some quick thinking," Zipporah said. "But Harvey—you look terrible."

"Well, I was in a car that crashed, and then attacked by skeletons, and then vampire birds." Harvey shrugged. "There'll be time for resting when this is done." He readied the Serpent Yad. "I'll go save the city now, I suppose."

He walked to the Founding Stone, followed by Clay and Zipporah. Battle raged all around them, but the front of the Third Temple seemed calm. The attacking gangsters kept the attention of the legionaries and even fired at the Broxa. Rabbi Holtz and his enforcers held off the skeletons, and Kid Twist kept his pistols thundering from the doorway of the temple. The Founding Stone looked much like it had in the lobby of City Hall, and in the sewers—a great boulder, inscribed with ancient words. The Hebrew letters had been etched along the top by the acid of the Shamir, and they glowed a faint green. Moss had grown along the base, giving the entire stone an emerald cast. Harvey walked straight up to the stone and raised the Serpent Yad. It shook in his hands and he planted the point, the serpent's snarling mouth, right in the middle of the Hebrew letters. He would just have to turn the word 'truth' to 'death' and all of this would end.

Something spiky and cold stabbed into Clay's back. He stumbled and fell, then turned with his fists raised. "Mr. Clay?" Harvey looked up from his work. "What's going on?" Another icicle whistled down, big as a spear. Zipporah raised her swords and tried to deflect it, but the icy point still slashed against her arm and drew blood. Clay stepped in front of Harvey and caught another icicle in his chest. He stared ahead at the meadow. "Mr. Clay?" Harvey asked.

"Keep writing!" Clay called. "End this!"

"Use that Serpent Yad, child!" Zipporah added. "We'll keep you safe!" But she and Clay both stared across the meadow and wondered how that would be possible. They had cleared away the legionaries and the simple golems of the Dagger Men. Now, the Dagger Men sent their elite.

Rabbi Eisendrath himself had finally chosen to arrive. He walked down the meadow, his tattered frock coat dragging behind him. His hands rested in the pockets of his vest, and rain pelted his bald, tattooed head, the water looking dark as it covered the occult script on his face. Behind him, six hulking ice golems walked together through the rain. The city must have made them with the contents of ice boxes and Rabbi Eisendrath had done the rest. The ice golems had slim frames, but they stood head and shoulders taller than Clay. Jagged icicles sprouted from their shoulders and wrists, and they shook their arms to send icicles flying through the air. The frozen projectiles smashed into the mud, stabbing deeply into the dirt, or shattered on the stone pillars and walls of the Third Temple. Roman soldiers and smaller earth golems joined Rabbi Eisendrath. He had massed a powerful force around him, and intended to take the temple back.

Harvey stared at them, looking over his shoulder. "No. There's too many of them. Mr. Clay, you'll never—"

"Finish removing the enchantment," Clay ordered. He stared at Rabbi Eisendrath, looking into the dark eyes of the Dagger Man. Rabbi Eisendrath had survived pummeling with a golem's fists, which should have pulped his organs and broken his ribs. He had lived for centuries. Clay began to have some idea about the exact nature of this high priest of Dagger Men. He stepped closer to the ice golems, his fists swinging at his sides. "Rabbi Eisendrath!" he called, trying to show some of Zipporah's bravado. "What kept you?"

"Marshaling my forces to defend my city," Rabbi Eisendrath called back. "From abominations like you, golem!"

Clay didn't flinch at the comment. "It ain't your city anymore!" Zipporah called.

"I will make it more than a city!" Rabbi Eisendrath replied. "I will make it a Garden of Eden, a paradise on earth! There will be no persecution, no harm to innocents. Jews will be powerful here, as they were in ages past, and we will praise God with our very breaths!" His snarled as he talked, his lips curling back to reveal perfect, square teeth. He looked more like a sculpture than a man. "But you seek to ruin my perfection. You have put a snake into my garden, a serpent! I will cast it out with a fiery sword. I will protect my Eden!"

"Come on, then," Clay said. "Come and try."

The ice golems charged, racing from Rabbi Eisendrath and running to meet Clay and Zipporah. Their spiky limbs swung down as they attacked. Two ice golems reached Clay, and drove their icicles into his chest. Spiked ice punched into his body, nearly impaling him. He twisted to the side, breaking the ice, and punched at icy faces. Ice shattered under his fist. Chunks rained down, spilling onto the grass. Clay rammed the outstretched leg of an ice golem, breaking its knee. It fell back. Clay drove his elbow into the golem's head, breaking the ice and finally destroying it. Ice floated in the rivulets of water caused by the rain. Clay turned to the next, only for fingers tipped with icicles to stab into his chest and lift him up. He kicked the ice golem in the chest. It didn't work. The ice golem hurled him back. Clay flew past Harvey and smashed into one of the stone pillars of the Third Temple. Stone broke under his back. He tumbled down to the mud and lay there.

Zipporah fought the ice golems as well—with limited success. She cut apart icy fingers as they reached for her, slicing through frost and sending the frozen claws spinning away. They still forced her back, closer to the Founding Stone. Clay stumbled to his feet and ran to join her.

They stood together, protecting Harvey as the ice golems closed. "M-Mr. Clay? Miss Sarfati?" Harvey's voice came from behind, very faint. "I think there's some kind of problem. With the Serpent Yad, I mean. It doesn't appear to be—"

"Not now, Harvey!" Zipporah cried. An ice golem reached for her, trying to entangle her in frost fingers. She drove her sword through its wrist, stabbing it through ice, and then hacked to the side. The ice golem's hand fell free and hit the ground, where its fingers moved and carried it along like an ice blue spider. Zipporah looked back at the temple steps. "Twist—a rifle!" She sheathed a sword and held out her hand. Kid Twist dutifully tossed her a rifle, Clay's Springfield, from the door of the temple. Zipporah caught the gun, twisted it around, and impaled the crawling hand with the bayonet. She hoisted it up, the icy hand still stuck on the end, and fired at the ice golem before it could attack again. The bullet caught the ice golem in the head, and it fell back as slush and snow.

Despite their efforts, they couldn't hold out against the ice golems. Clay knew it as two ice golems attacked him at once. Their ice fingers slashed at him and held him in place while Rabbi Eisendrath watched. The leader of the Dagger Men had started to wave his hands, forming his fingers into occult symbols. Clay grabbed a lump of mud and tossed it at him. Dirt splashed onto Rabbi Eisendrath's tattooed face. He sputtered and stumbled, his spell ruined—but mud wouldn't hold him for long. An icy arm grabbed Clay's leg and pulled. His leg went out from under him and he fell to the mud. Battle raged above him, as he stared into the gray sky.

The ice golem raised its thin hands again, preparing another strike.

Something red and glowing roared down from the sky before a plume of smoke. It shot down like a comet and smashed into the back of the ice golem. Ice broke and melted. The ice golem fell in half, the pieces tumbling down onto Clay and falling into the muck. Clay rolled over and pulled himself to his feet. His legs ached. Bits of his limbs had chipped off and they fell through his ripped sleeves and struck the ground. Clay still managed to stand and look at the sky.

A zeppelin hung there, a gray sausage growing larger as it came down through the rain. Water ran down the gasbag and splashed onto the undercarriage. Steel plates protected the doughboys inside, and they aimed cannons and machine guns down at the field below. The guns of the zeppelin roared as it drew closer, sending rockets, machine gun rounds, and artillery into the clusters of legionaries. The name of the airship, *Terrible Swift Sword*, had been emblazoned in gold lettering on the side. The doughboys inside wore goggles under their tin bowlers, and readied rifles and submachine guns as the airship touched down. Gangplanks fell into the muddy earth and the soldiers hurried to attack the enemies. They had been fighting rebels in Haiti, Nicaragua, and Honduras. Compared to those jungle guerillas, the antique Roman soldiers and mindless golems must be duck soup.

Cheers came from the assembled gangsters, which echoed over the park. Clay felt better as well. He stood next to Zipporah as rifle fire tore into the ice golems and remaining legionaries, while cannon shots and rockets rained down from the deck of the *Terrible Swift Sword*. Fire split the rain and skeletons dropped under the blasts. Some charged the doughboys, backed up by golems. Rifle fire, submachine guns, and then bayonets met them. The doughboys held their firing line, and golems and skeletons melted under the blast.

Colonel Menelaus Montgomery Rook stepped before the firing line. He hadn't aged a day since Clay had seen him after the War in Russia—still a man who was never happier than in the middle of a battle. His uniform was spotless and he waved his sword as he urged his men onward. A trim, down-swept moustache covered his face, and Hermes, his prized carrier pigeon, sat on his shoulder. Colonel Rook fired at the attacking Romans with his pearl-handled revolver, and then moved in and finished them with sweeps of his saber. He had fought in the Spanish-American War, the Philippines, Mexico, the Great War, Russia, and countless smaller conflicts. And now, he fought in Sickle City as well.

He parried a gladius with his saber and blasted apart the Roman's skull, before turning to face Clay. Colonel Rook snapped off a salute. "Clay! My word, son—this is a grand battle you've arranged. I always wanted to test myself against the might of Rome and the Caesars!" He grinned as he shot an attacking earth golem, fanning off his revolver to make sure that his bullets drilled a hole in its head. "We fought creatures like this in Russia, time to time. I enjoyed slaughtering the supernatural even more than I did the Bolsheviks, and it's a fine thing to repeat that here!" He called to his men. "Fan out! Engage these Romans and defeat them! Leave nothing standing, boys, until the city is ours!"

The battle was all but won—even though the earth still shifted and danced under the feet of the Third Temple's attacker. Then Clay remembered Rabbi Eisendrath. He could summon monsters with his spells, and that may turn the tide. Clay scanned the battlefield and found the familiar scrap of black. Rabbi Eisendrath watched the battle in horror. His hands rose, preparing another spell. A barrage of cannon fire enveloped him first. Clay turned away from the blast. Fire blanketed the grass, along with bursts of smoke. That should have obliterated a normal man, but when the smoke cleared, Rabbi Eisendrath remained. His coat had been tattered and the tattoos blasted away from his skin. He looked more like a lump of clay than a man. He started walking to the Founding Stone, hate in his flinty eyes.

Zipporah stared at him. "He's not human."

"No." Clay ran to Harvey, Zipporah close behind. They stared at the Founding Stone as Rabbi Eisendrath approached. "The spell—you said there was trouble?"

Harvey looked up from the Founding Stone. He gripped the Serpent Yad with both hands and tried to drag it across the stone. "It's not working. It's like the stone is resisting me." Mud covered his boots, trying to drag him down. "Maybe it's Sickle City, sir. The city doesn't want to go back to how it was." He turned to Clay. "I don't know what to do. Could you— could you talk to it?"

"Me?" Clay stared at the Founding Stone.

"You're both golems. You and the city," Zipporah suggested. "Talk to it."

"But it's a golem," Clay said. "It has to follow the orders of the Dagger Men. It's mindless." Then he remembered the Elephantine Hotel, watching them with sad painted eyes as they escaped from Palisade Park. It could have stopped them, and it didn't. "Mindless," he repeated.

"No, sir," Harvey said. "It's not. No more than you are." He kept the

Serpent Yad aimed at the stone. "Please. Just try and talk to it."

Clay rested his palm on the stone. He knelt down and put his head close to the carved letters. He could hear something behind the stone—perhaps the beating of a heart. He whispered to it. "You must have seen a lot of pain in your time. A lot of cruelty. I have as well. But we don't need to let that pain control us. We don't need to let ancient prejudices from the past rule our lives. We can choose our path. It doesn't matter why we were created, or what orders we were given. We can find a better way." He tapped his fingers on the stone. "You know this isn't right. You know what the boy has to do. Maybe part of you can stick around, but there's no Second Jerusalem. There's no paradise. There's just a city and the people who live in it. They have to learn to live with each other."

A second ticked past. The gentle pounding in Clay's ears grew. Then the earth below him shifted. It flattened, the mud falling away from his boots. Hills and valleys straightened, the dirt filling itself in. All the golems stopped running. They collapsed, falling to the grass in piles of steel, wood, glass, brick, ice, and dirt. Their pieces scattered in neat piles. Rabbi Eisendrath wordlessly shouted and Clay turned to look at him. A hole had opened in the earth below him, trapping him for good. The pit surrounded him, and though he clawed and struggled, he could not get out. The legionaries fought on, but gunfire quickly finished them. The battle had been won.

"What h-happened?" Harvey asked.

"The city chose a side," Zipporah said. "It decided to defend its people."

Shouts of victory came from the defenders of Sickle City. Fedoras, newsboy caps, and bowler hats sailed through the air. Rabbi Holtz ran past the piles of dead golems and hurried to his son. They embraced. Colonel Rook hurried to the Founding Stone, along with everyone else. They gathered around Harvey, who held the Serpent Yad over the Hebrew character that would return Sickle City to normal. There was no hurry. He could strike it at any time now, without danger. The city was on their side.

For a while, Harvey stared at the stone as the cheers echoed. "I almost feel bad about it," he said. "Sickle City was alive, and now it's free. Do I really have the right to kill it?" He looked at the Serpent Yad and then at the stone. "But if the city's truly alive, it could cause trouble for people—

making streets break or buildings fall over. That sort of thing." He tapped his finger on the stone. "Maybe there's some kind of solution."

"Do what you think is right, *boychick*," Rabbi Holtz said. "We trust you."

"Okay," Harvey agreed. "I think I'll—"

Dirt and mud flew behind him. Hark shouted a warning as she raised her crossbow. Clay spun. Rabbi Eisendrath had clambered out of the pit. His body had changed—his fingers fusing together and elongating into powerful, jagged blades. His tattoos remained, blurred and smudged on skin like melted wax. He raced through the crowd, leaping into the air and lunging for Harvey with his bladed hands. Clay stepped in front of him. He caught Rabbi Eisendrath and they struck the ground together. Clay grappled with him, but Rabbi Eisendrath broke and reformed.

"Golem!" Clay called out the name. "That's what you are."

"Yes." Rabbi Eisendrath leaned down, his tattooed face melting. "Rabbi Eisendrath died a century ago—stabbed a hundred times by the blades of Cossacks. He built me with his blood and his bones and the dirt from the road, and I have continued serving him ever since." He lunged for Clay's head. Clay grabbed his arm and twisted. "I will always serve him. That is a golem's job. I will pay back the world for all the injustice I have seen." His other hand lashed for Clay's head, the bladed edge cutting through the air. It struck Clay's cheek and kept cutting. From far away, Clay heard Harvey shouting in panic.

Zipporah ran to help. Her scimitars hummed down, aiming for Rabbi Eisendrath's head. They sliced the letters—but it was too late. The bladed hand had done its job, cutting through Clay's head. Momentum carried it along, even as Rabbi Eisendrath collapsed into rot and dust. Clay's head was cut in half. Darkness consumed him and he saw nothing at all.

Chapter Ten
ALL OF CREATION

Something close to life flashed back to Clay after an instant of darkness that could have lasted an eternity. Candle light, faint and quivering, appeared in his eyes. He stared at the candles, the tall sort used for Shabbat, with a deep, smooth whiteness below a dancing flame. He stared at the candle flame for a while and then rolled over, staring at an arched ceiling.

Garish carnival posters looked back at him from the walls, along with dusty bits of furniture. Rain drummed on the windows, overlooking the gray sea and the roller coaster. A carriage moved along the wooden rails, the grinding mixing with the crashing waves and the calliope music of Palisade Park. Clay was in the attic of the Elephantine Hotel, lying on a table and surrounded by candles. He sat up.

A tall man with a face like a vulture stood in front of him. He wore a shaggy robe, with a circular, completely round fur cap, a *shtreimel*, on his lean head. He kept his beard, almost completely gray now, in a neat triangle that matched his thick sideburns and moustache. Thin, round spectacles perched on his nose. Clay recognized him instantly.

"Rabbi Chaim Holtz." He nodded, almost politely, to his creator.

"Golem." Chaim stepped aside. Clay's clothes, his shirt, and a new brown suit, matching vest, and a trench coat, hung on an old coat rack. "Get dressed." Chaim folded his arms and watched as Clay hopped off the table. His feet slid on the floor. Clay grabbed the table to support himself. Chaim watched. "Your body is strong. It will take a few moments to remember that strength." Clay slipped to his knees, then grabbed the table and pulled himself back up. He stumbled to the coat rack and started to dress. He buttoned his shirt and slid his tie under the collar, not looking at the rabbi who had built him.

Shlomo Ben Shlomo, their dybbuk informer, remained in his fishbowl. His grating voice filled the attic. "What's going on? Has the golem awoken yet? Has the *schnorrer*—" A dusty tablecloth covered the fishbowl, which sat in the corner.

"Shut up." Clay didn't bother facing Shlomo Ben Shlomo. "Or we'll toss you out the window." That made Shlomo shut up. Clay kept his eyes on Chaim. "How long has it been?" His hand went to his face, his fingers tracing across his features. He couldn't feel any scar left by Rabbi Eisendrath's claws. No mark remained and his face was as smooth as ever. He had new eyes at least—another pair of round stones, jabbed into his face.

"A few weeks," Chaim explained. "My younger brother sent a letter to me, begging for my help, and so I arrived. I have left Russia, and Poland as well. The war, and chaos—it is not safe for my people, if it ever was." He rested his hands in his pockets, refusing to look at Clay's face. "I live in Germany now. There is still fighting, still battles, but at least is it safe."

"For how long will it be safe?" Clay asked.

"That, golem, is not your concern." Chaim took the fedora from the top of the coat rack. He set it on top of Clay's head. "My brothers asked for my help. They wanted you rebuilt and so I arrived and now you are rebuilt. That will be the end of it."

"Thank you."

Chaim stroked his beard, his fingers moving through the stiff, spiky hairs. "I didn't do it for you, golem. I have little love left for my brothers—one was always a criminal and the other has grown up to hate his people and his faith—but there is still enough of a bond between us that I was willing to rebuild my creation."

"Am I still an abomination?"

"In my eyes, you will always be an abomination," Chaim replied. "When I see you, I see the blood on your knuckles and the swords driven into your skin. I hear the cries of men and horses as you destroyed them." He leaned closer and tapped Clay's stone eyes. "But there are other eyes that have seen you. They don't see you as an abomination at all."

The hatch on the floor of the attic fell open with a clatter. Zipporah Sarfati and Harvey Holtz, wearing a dark formal suit and a matching bowtie, walked into the room. For a moment, they stared at Clay in surprise, and then they ran to him. Clay opened his arms. He embraced both of them, his thick fingers strong against their backs. They held each other for a few moments. Their bruises and wounds had faded and healed. Harvey pushed up his spectacles and wiped tears on his sleeve. Zipporah simply smiled. They were glad to have him whole.

Zipporah clasped his hand. "You're back. Right as rain, eh, Clay?"

"You're okay?" Harvey asked. "No parts of you will fall off or anything?"

"I don't think so," Clay agreed.

Harvey faced his uncle. He bowed politely to Chaim. "Thank you, Uncle Chaim. I would like to extend an invitation for you to stay with us, for as long as you like. You can join us for dinner or spend the night and the weekend. We have guest rooms, and I would be very happy to talk to you about your mysticism, and particularly those books that you dropped off." His voice shook. "Please?"

"No, my child. I cannot." Chaim's eyes remained on the round window and the dancing waves outside. "I must find passage on a ship and return to Europe. I cannot stay in this country, so crude and cruel. I belong back in my home." He patted Harvey's shoulders. "The books I gave you are precious. I brought them here because they are not safe in Europe. Tell your father, and watch them yourself. Read them if you'd like—but make sure they are protected and do not fall into the wrong hands. Do you understand, Harvey?"

"Yes, sir," Harvey agreed.

"Good." Chaim folded his fingers. "Then I have nothing more to say. I have burdened my brother enough." He reached for his valise, his thin fingers curling around the handles, and then went to the stairs in the floor. He left the attic without looking back, humming some prayer to himself as he strolled into the shadows. Harvey made to follow him, but then paused and thought better of it. Chaim Holtz had walked out of Clay's life again.

Clay adjusted his tie and buttoned his vest. "Don't mind him, Harvey. That's the way he is."

"I suppose so," Harvey said. "But I would like to see a little more of him. He is my uncle, after all. Whatever else he is."

"He's a bum," Zipporah replied. She grinned at Clay. "We got dinner at the rabbi's house—the real rabbi, as far as I'm concerned. You're invited, Clay, even if you can't eat. He's sent out quite a few invitations and it should be a real dandy soiree. You in?"

"A dinner party?" Clay asked.

Harvey nodded, full of boyish excitement. "It's Shabbat, sir. Do you want to go?""

He was right. It was a Friday, several weeks or so after the battle in Arcadia Park. Clay could think of nothing he would rather do than see his friends. "Of course," he agreed. He pulled his trench coat around him and walked down the stairs. Harvey and Zipporah trailed after him. They left the attic and walked down the length of the Elephantine Hotel, passing the two floors and emerging from the front onto the porch. The park had its usual Friday crowd, and the roller coasters, midway, and freak show all did a brisk business. Clay looked it over and scanned the rest of Haven Street, past the end of the pier.

The damage from the Dagger Men's occupation remained, but a great deal of the repairs had already been completed. The flagstones had been replaced, covering up the gray dirt. The stone cabins had been removed as well, and all the Judaic detritus had been cleared away, replaced by the usual collection of vendors, horse-drawn wagons, and automobiles fighting with pedestrians for space. Newspaper boys advertised their wares even as the sky darkened, and the families had returned to their crowded tenement homes. Their lives, hard and unmerciful as they were, had returned.

Zipporah followed his gaze. "Things ain't quite getting back to normal," she said. "But we're getting there." She pointed to the end of the dock. "Come on. We got your Studebaker ready. We're giving Professor West a lift as well."

They walked down the pier, passing the line of visitors eager for a Friday night at the Palisade Park, and then reached Clay's old Studebaker, looking somewhat battered but still ready to drive. Professor West leaned against the side of the car, reading a new copy of the Sickle City *Halcyon*. The professor had returned to his sartorial splendor, with his usual crimson suit and upturned moustache. He looked up from the pages and stepped aside from the Studebaker.

"Mr. Clay. Miss Sarfati. Young Master Harvey." He doffed his top hat. "I was merely perusing the latest periodical, and seeing what the authorities made of our recent troubles. Apparently, there was no attack from the Dagger Men at all. An earthquake and severe storm struck the city, along with a simultaneous attack from an anarchist group which released hallucinogenic gasses into populated areas. That explains all of the recent strangeness, according to our civic leaders."

"The government doesn't want to tell anyone the truth?" Harvey asked.

"Apparently not." Clay held out his hand. "Can I drive?"

"You can." Zipporah dropped the keys in Clay's fingers. "Come along, Professor West. We're going to the rabbi's house."

They piled into the Studebaker and Clay started the engine and peeled out from the pier entrance. The sun had started to set in the distance, and then the Sabbath would truly begin. Clay didn't mind. He knew that he would reach Rabbi Holtz's house in time. He gunned the engine and drove into the usual crowd of traffic, ready for Shabbat.

אא אא אא

That evening, they munched on brisket and wine around the large table in Rabbi Holtz's dining room. The long table usually just seated Rabbi Holtz, Harvey, and a few guests—but today it was packed with visitors. Clay sat at one corner, next to Harvey and Zipporah. Rabbi Holtz helped the maid and the cook dish out the food. Herbert and Hark, still not quite welcomed in Rabbi Holtz's home, sat together at the other end of the table. Detective Flynn joined them, wearing his dress uniform with polished brass buttons. Ava and Sophie Silver had been invited as well. Lucky the panda cub raced around below their feet, eager for any kind of scraps. Sophie waved to Harvey as Rabbi Holtz finished with the prayers and the boy blushed. Monk Moss and Carmen Cohen had a place at the table too, and they had arrived without any sort of weaponry—or at least they hadn't brought their guns to the Shabbat. They talked and ate together, while Professor West poured wine and Clay watched without a plate in front of him. He enjoyed sitting quietly and letting the conversation fill the dining room.

Detective Flynn sawed at his brisket as he talked about what Clay had missed. "The Wigwam Club and the policemen's union agreed to make peace—or something close to it. My poor brothers in blue won't be getting all the benefits they desired, but their pay has increased and the department agreed to clear out the rats and roaches from the SCPD bunkhouses. Sounds like a windfall." He munched on the brisket. "But they did put the fear of God into Grand Sagamore Edwin Eames."

"His career's not through?" Clay asked.

Ava Silver snorted. "Hardly. The wretch is a master at manipulating events. He's made it seem that he stayed steadfastly at his post as the city crumbled around him—a rock of order in an ocean of chaos, as he called it. His popularity's increased and now his candidates are guaranteed to win."

"The Shark's back on top as well," Monk added.

"His bootlegging and smuggling routes are back in business. Making up for all the lost time." Cohen ripped her bread into smaller chunks and tossed them in her mouth. "The same with all the other gangsters and hoodlums in town."

"Corruption has returned," Detective Flynn said. "God bless it."

"True enough." Silver spooned sauce onto her plate. "I'll get him, though, given time. I've been doing my best to cover the truth in the *Weekly Sophisticate*, but my editor doesn't much care for tales of magic and mayhem. I'll convince him, though. Don't worry, Mr. Clay." She flashed him a grin. "I'll keep your name out of it."

"Thank you," Clay replied.

"Oh, it's no trouble, dear heart." Silver wiggled a finger at Sophie. "And mind the panda, darling. Don't let him onto the table. And don't feed the blasted bear anymore. He's chubby enough as it is."

"Yes, ma'am." Sophie set Lucky back onto the floor. The cub whined piteously, but accepted it. "Harvey, did your uncle want to stick around?"

"I don't t-think so, Miss Silver," Harvey said. "He seemed very keen on going back home."

"His loss," Herbert said. "There's nothing left in the Old Country, from what I hear. The future is in America."

"He obviously didn't feel that way," Hark said. She had been hesitant about speaking, and watched Rabbi Holtz. He kept his mouth shut. "Some men take comfort in tradition. They need the familiar to survive, and

Sickle City is anything but familiar. Chaim is your brother, Herbert, and you should forgive him for not wanting to dip his toes in the same churning waters that you bathe in so regularly."

"True enough," Herbert agreed. "Didn't he leave some books, Harvey?"

"He did." Harvey leaned closer, his food forgotten in his excitement. "There's some very rare manuals of Kabala, a treatise on Merkabah mysticism—that's chariot mysticism—and, most impressively, a set of travel journals from this Radhanite merchant and adventurer named Malachi the Mamzer."

"Malachi the what?" Zipporah asked.

"Mamzer," Rabbi Holtz explained. "It means bastard."

"Well, I think was a bastard." Harvey lowered his voice, his cheeks reddening as Sophie stared at him. "Literally, I mean. But he became a very well-traveled merchant, and always wrote about magic in his various travels. His journal is tremendously rare and tremendously valuable. He writes about lost worlds, ancient civilizations, mysterious ruins, and valuable artifacts in all the big cities in Europe, in Egypt, and even in Asia as well."

Silver nodded knowingly. "Sounds like the makings of a treasure hunt. Could be a delightful excursion, particularly after this mess with the Dagger Men."

"As long as it doesn't lead you into danger, *boychick*," Rabbi Holtz said.

"Of course, papa," Harvey agreed.

They returned to their dinner, talking about gangland politics and all the ways that Sickle City had struggled to return to normalcy. The meal seemed tasty enough, and the cook and the maid returned with seconds for those who wanted them, and then a puffy cake drenched in frosting and a pile of freshly-baked rugelach for desert. Clay watched them eat, glad that his friends could get a break from the chaos that had conquered their city. It didn't matter if the corruption had returned. They had each other and that would be enough.

After the meal, Rabbi Holtz and his guests retired to the drawing room. They played cards and watched Monk juggle apples—a trick he had learned during his youth on the streets of the slum known as the Rookery. Herbert fiddled with the radio and found some strumming, easy jazz. Clay stayed with them for a few minutes, watching everything, and then left the parlor. He walked past the bookshelves and headed out to the porch, where he could look at the stars.

Electricity had returned to Sickle City, and the flashes of lights drowned out the stars, as they always did. The sky seemed dark and far away. Clay sat on the steps of the porch, looking at the faint glimmer of stars through the extended branches of the great tree in Rabbi Holtz's yard. It seemed that Sickle City had been rebuilt without lasting damage—just like him.

The door opened behind him. Harvey and Zipporah stepped out, both shivering a little in the night's chill. They went to join Clay on the steps, and looked up at the night sky together. Nobody said much for a while.

"What happened with the Founding Stone?" Clay asked. "And the letters?"

Harvey stared at his polished dress shoes. "I did end up turning the word for 'truth' to the word for 'death,'" he admitted. "It wasn't easy, and I didn't like doing it—but a living city was too dangerous. I did something else too, though. On the back of the stone, I used the Serpent Yad to write the word for 'freedom.' I had read about that in some of my books, but I'm not sure it worked. It keeps the spirit of the golem around, freeing it from the physical confines of the body, and letting it filter into the air and fill another frame. In this case, the frame is still around." He smiled sadly. "So in many ways, Sickle City is still alive."

"Maybe it always was," Zipporah said. "All the magic that went on here, thanks to Bathsheba Barebone and her witches in the old days, and all the occultism that's taken place since—maybe they did give the city some kind of consciousness and Harvey just set it free."

"It could be," Clay agreed.

Zipporah put a hand on his shoulder. "He's wrong, you know."

"Who?"

"Your creator. Chaim Holtz." Zipporah settled onto the steps, almost reclining—a rare position for her. "He's wrong in the same way that the Dagger Men are wrong. He's set in his ways and he can't accept the truth about you." She stared back up at the faint stars. "But you need to accept that truth, Clay. You truly do."

"I don't know if it is true," Clay muttered. "Maybe Eisendrath's right. Maybe all a golem can do is hate, and live for decades off that hate. Maybe my creator is right as well and I am nothing more than an abomination."

"No, Mr. Clay, that's not—" Harvey started.

"But Zipporah? Harvey?" Clay faced them. If he could smile, he would. "I am eager to prove them wrong."

Rabbi Holtz's voice came from the doorway. "You want some tea? And Harvey, that radio show you like is on. We're all gonna give it a listen. Come on, *boychick*. Don't stay out there and catch cold."

"He's wrong, you know."

"Okay, papa." Harvey turned back to the door. "Mr. Clay? Do you want to accompany me?"

"Give me a few more moments," Clay said. He turned back to the sky.

"Come on, child." Zipporah steered Harvey to the door. She looked back at Clay. "Don't take too long, Clay. Don't be as slow as the mud that made you." She and Harvey returned to the house and walked to the parlor. Light and laughter came from the drawing room. Harvey and Zipporah shared in the conversation.

Clay remained sitting on the steps for a little more, as an evening breeze fluttered his trench coat. Then he walked down to the street and knelt down. He rested his palm on the notched pavement. He could feel the city under his skin. It was free now, and so was he. He wondered if he could feel the pulse through his fingers. Clay kept his hand on the street for a few moments, and then stood. He returned to the rabbi's house to rejoin his friends.

THE END

MODERN GOLEMS
A Bonus Tale of the Clay Shamus

Haven Street had changed. The tenement buildings had been transformed into high-priced condos, suburban streets, and spacious apartments. The old speakeasies and kosher butcher shops and bakeries had all but vanished, with only a core surrounding Haven Street's Jewish enclave, and trendy coffee shops, upscale toy stores, and boutiques inhabited their empty shells. Bicycles replaced the pushcarts, and they buzzed around streets that had become greener, with trees and flower beds shading the assembled chairs of outdoor eateries. Banners advertising some new exhibition in the city's art gallery dangled from the streetlights, while one-sheet posters for some new album, or movie, or whatever, had been plastered on barren walls. Emmet Clay, a golem turned detective who had lived in Haven Street since the Twenties, didn't quite know what to make of the changes. Everything had changed, but him—or at least, not in any way that mattered.

He parked his car—a beautifully restored classic Studebaker—outside one of the new high-end coffee shops on trendy Atlas Avenue. Clay had spent a fortune on the Studebaker, with its white-rimmed tires, boxy form, and jutting runners, and he considered it money well-spent. Because he was a golem, he didn't really need many other amenities. He didn't like the look of modern automobiles either. He walked onto the sidewalk, aware of the occasional odd gaze sent his way. Clay still wore a trench coat and brown suit like he had in the old days, though they were both of a modern cut. He sported the fedora as well. He looked like someone pretending to be a detective from a black-and-white movie, but he didn't care. In Haven Street, people wore plenty of outlandish costumes and he could still fit right in. At least he projected an illusion to hide his stony skin and round rock eyes, though he couldn't hide his bulk. He strolled across the sidewalk, paused to let a bicycle and a couple walking their oversized dogs pass, and headed into the coffee shop.

It bore the name JOVA—purposefully misspelled—and featured a mix of overpriced coffee, assorted pastries, and concoctions that reminded Clay of milkshakes and had some Italian name. Clay entered JOVA, ignored the occasional glance and scanned the interior of the coffee shop. A small boy in a booth in the corner turned and spotted him. He waved wildly and

Clay headed over. He emitted a happy creaking as he slid into the booth.

"Hello, Henry," Clay said.

The youngster—a boy no older than twelve—beamed at Clay from behind a cream-topped milkshake. He seemed slight for his age, with very dark hair over a pleasant, round face mixed with freckles. Square spectacles perched on his nose. He still wore his school uniform, his collared shirt with the school's crest marked on the pocket, under a light camo jacket. "Mr. Clay." He turned to the young woman at his side. "This is Emmet Clay. He's a friend of my family." Henry Mackintosh-Holtz turned back to Clay. "He's been a big help to us, many times."

One of Henry's ancestors—a great, grand-uncle and rabbi by the name of Chaim Holtz—had created Clay, bringing him to life in the chaos of the Russian Revolution and then casting him out. Clay had then traveled to America, and found sanctuary thanks to Henry's grandfather. Clay had been helping with Henry's family ever since. However, the young woman sitting next to Henry didn't need to know all those details. She probably wouldn't believe that Clay was a golem anyway.

"Henry's been talking a lot about you." She held out her hand and Clay shook it. "I'm Talia Goldstein. Henry's mom hired me to look after him. I picked him up from school and I'm taking care of him until she gets home from work in the evening." Talia had auburn hair in a neat braid and an easy smile. She wore a light coat over a dark sweater, with a silver Star of David shining just past the collar. "You know, babysitting—well, kidsitting." She corrected herself quickly. "I live in the apartment next to Henry, actually. We're good friends. I stop by to play his video games, sometimes."

"Talia was in the Israeli Army, Mr. Clay," Henry explained. "She's an excellent soldier."

Clay couldn't help smiling at the boy's enthusiasm. "Really." He settled into the booth.

Talia shrugged. "Not exactly. I joined up after a sponsored trip, did a few tours. Just camping in the Negev, mostly. Weapons training and combat simulations. The IDF's not dumb enough to let a bunch of American kids see any action." She had a sip of her coffee. "Now, Henry was saying that you're, like, a detective? Like a private investigator. Is that true?"

"That's right," Clay agreed. "I'm a one-man agency. Clay Investigations." He handed her his card.

"Is that why you're dressed like Humphrey Bogart?" Talia asked.

"I'm used to the get-up," Clay replied.

"That's pretty awesome." Talia seemed impressed and Henry beamed. He obviously cared for his babysitter's approval. "So, what sort of cases do you do? Do you like spy on people cheating on their wives or husbands or anything like that?"

"No. I mostly leave that to other detectives," Clay explained. "I tend to handle strange cases."

"The occult, Talia," Henry explained.

"Like ghosts?" Talia asked. "Werewolves? Dracula?" She grinned into her coffee.

"You'd be surprised," Clay said.

Before Talia could reply, a commotion came from the door, followed by a series of screams. The line scrambled away from the counter as the glass door smashed open. A pair of strange, spindly figures, each standing head and shoulders taller than any man, rammed their way through the door and sprang into JOVA. They had the general shape of humans, with chests, arms, legs, and lumpy heads—but every piece of them had been assembled from garbage. Broken machinery formed their limbs, with crushed aluminum cans and bottles as their fingers. Wrappers from fast food burgers covered their bodies, mixed with torn pages from magazines and aluminum foil. Rotten fruit and vegetables protruded from their chests, making them stink as they rushed into JOVA.

Tattered hand-written pages had been stapled to their foreheads, which dangled down over their bodies. Clay spotted some of the lettering on those pages. He had similar letters, carved onto his own forehead—the Hebrew word for truth. That meant these were golems, just like him. He sprang to his feet, squaring his shoulders as the garbage golems hurried across the coffee shop. Diners darted out of the way as the strange forms loped closer. One smashed aside a shelf of easy-listening CDs and crockery. Metal jugs and cups bounced their way across the tiled floor. It couldn't be a coincidence. These garbage golems were here for him.

Clay faced the foremost golem. "Protect Henry!"

He charged for the garbage golem, his hands swinging at his side. The garbage golem grabbed a nearby stool and hurled it in Clay's direction. The stool smashed against Clay's shoulder, the curved wood shattering against his skin. Clay took the blow, letting the stool break, and slugged the garbage golem with both fists. He punched through the golem's chest, ripping into garbage and sending litter flying through JOVA. The garbage golem fell on the ground, becoming a heap of trash.

The next garbage golem leapt on Clay from the side. It crawled on top of him. Clay felt like he had been buried in a junkyard avalanche. He stumbled back, his boots sliding on the tiled floor, and banged into the counter. Clay struck out wildly. He drove his fist straight through the golem's chest. Trash sprayed out from the wound and clattered on the floor. Clay grabbed the golem's head next and rammed it into the counter. But the golem didn't collapse. Powerful bonds held the garbage together. It coiled around Clay like a serpent, one of its hands elongating and reaching up. The hand reached Clay's face, welled up like it had suddenly ripened, and unleashed a spray of liquid sewage into Clay's face. It blinded him. He crashed back against the counter.

"Mr. Clay!" Talia hurried out of the seat. "Hold on. I'll think of something."

She kicked the garbage golem, driving a rapid series of blows with her boot into what passed for the monstrosity's head. The garbage golem fell to the side, rolling off Clay and striking the ground. It lunged for Talia and she held her arms out, caught the blow, and deflected it. Her arms reached out, found hand-holds in the garbage golem's head, and drove it into her knee. Her elbow rammed into the back of its head, and it struck the ground.

Talia looked at the counter. She reached past the terrified employee in his dark apron and grabbed a heavy steel cylindrical keg of coffee. Steam boiled up from the spout. "I'm sorry. You can bill me later. If you want." Talia tossed the keg down onto the garbage golem. It broke. Steaming coffee spilled over the garbage golem, drenching it in dark liquid. Steam roiled up from the golem, which quivered and shuddered, but did not move.

Henry stared at them from the booth. "That was amazing!"

"Just a little Krav Maga," Talia explained. "We'd practice a lot, during my army training." She glanced at the garbage golem. "Weren't there two of these weirdos? Where'd the other—" Garbage rustled across the floor near the booth. Clay and Talia turned. "Henry!" Talia cried. "Hurry! Get over here before—"

The garbage golem lunged up from the ground and reached Henry. The boy let out a single, terrified squeak as the garbage golem wrapped him in an embrace, and then tucked him under one of its elongated arms. It raced to the door, dragging Henry with it. Talia and Clay raced after the garbage golem, pounding through JOVA and pushing aside bits of furniture. The drenched garbage golem on the ground rolled over, and sprang up as well. It broke into a run and raced past Clay and Talia. The two garbage golems reached the door together. Clay groaned in panic. He had been wrong.

The garbage golems hadn't come for him at all—instead, they had come for Henry.

"Don't worry, Henry!" Talia cried. "We'll get you back! We'll rescue you."

"Talia! Mr. Clay!" Henry cried their names as the garbage golems leapt through the damaged doors and onto the sidewalk. Clay and Talia hurried after them, the two golems leapt into the street, landed on separate cars, and launched themselves into the air. Tattered paper and straightened aluminum slid out from their sides, fringed with pigeon feathers. They flapped rapidly, and the garbage golems soared up into the sky. Their legs whirred like propellers to speed them along. Clay and Talia stood on the sidewalk, watching in stunned silence as the garbage golems escaped— taking Henry with them to some unknown destination.

"Oh no." Talia let out a slight moan. "That poor little guy." She turned to Clay. "We gotta help him. We need to find out where those garbage men things took him and rescue him." She thought for a few moments, thinking calmly. "I'd normally suggest telling what happened to the police, but I don't think they can help with this."

"True," Clay said. "But I know someone who can."

Talia stared at him. "You said you were an occult detective, right? So where those garbage dudes come from is some sort of occult thing? Like some magic spell summoned them, joined them together, and animated them?"

"They're golems," Clay explained.

"Golems." Talia shrugged. "Okay. Sure. Well, Mr. Clay, who do we go to for help?"

Clay led her to his Studebaker. He opened the door and motioned for her to join him. "She's in North Haven Street. I'll drive."

"You drive an old-fashioned car too. Great." Talia slid into the passenger seat as Clay started the engine. "You know, in the IDF training, we got a lot of lectures from some of the old timers—veterans of the wars in Lebanon, as well as ex-Shin Bet agents and soldiers who had gone into Gaza or the West Bank. They had one piece of advice that stuck with me: be prepared for the bizarre. You never know how surreal and strange modern warfare can be, and nothing prepares you for it." She glanced Clay. "I guess this is something similar, right?"

"Could be." Clay started the engine and they roared off down the street as sirens wailed in the distance.

They headed to North Haven Street, and a psychic and fortune teller's store, nestled between a community garden and a feminist bookstore. North Haven Street had always been a little Bohemian. Time hadn't changed that—it had only made North Haven Street more expensive. Clay parked the car, and he and Talia headed into the fortune teller's store, a square, cozy structure called Mama Lilith's. Clay had switched trench coats in the car, which helped with the smell. He would have to take a careful shower when this case was closed and Henry was safe.

The bell on the door tinkled as Clay and Talia stepped into the lobby. The place looked like it belonged in Tibet. Strands of prayer flags dangled down from the ceiling. Various statues of Buddha from all across Asia sat in the corner. There were no chairs, only thick cushions. The beaded curtains in the back rattled and a portly woman in her fifties entered. She had long hair, dark and streaked with gray, and a friendly, knowing smile that said she knew plenty and didn't mind sharing. She sported a shimmering crimson sari, with a large necklace and a silver Chai symbol dangling over her chest.

"Ah—Emmet Clay. Namaste." She pointed to the beaded curtain. "Come on in, and introduce me to your friend."

She slipped back through the curtain. Clay and Talia followed her into the back room. They stepped carefully through the beaded curtain and entered a room resembling a cross between an office and a meditation chamber. Thick cushions lay on the carpet, Hebrew calendars and colorful pictures of Sanskrit writing covered the walls, and more Buddha statues squatted or sat on almost every fat surface. Their hostess torched an incense candle, and then moved to the mini-fridge in the corner and set a large jug and a pair of glasses on the table.

"This is Cornelia Deutsch," Clay explained. "She's a psychic, mystic, and Jewish Buddhist." He pointed to Talia. "And this is Talia Goldstein."

"A Jewish Buddhist?" Talia asked. "Is that a real thing? I heard of it, I guess, but I never met one."

"I'm a regular Jewbu, honey," Deutsch explained. She filled two tall, colorful glass cups with some thick, green liquid that resembled toxic waste from a cartoon. She offered Talia a cup. "Herbal juice. I make it myself. That's the only way to handle it." She faced Clay. "I'm glad you stopped by, Emmet. Lots of trouble going on in Haven Street. Lots of bad vibes." She slumped into a large cushion, resting her hands behind her head. "And I think I found the source."

"What would that be?" Clay asked.

Deutsch sighed. "Well, it's the Kosher Kave getting bought out." She turned to Talia. "You grew up around here, right? You know about the Kosher Kave?"

"Sure. I used to have my birthdays there, when I was a little girl." Talia sighed. "It's a neighborhood institution. They sell kosher burgers and hot dogs. An old Orthodox family has owned the place since the Sixties. Every kid in the neighborhood goes there for burgers and homemade lemonade after Hebrew School. But I guess that won't happen anymore. It's been bought out, and the new owners are going to close it down and demolish it."

"It's a tragedy," Deutsch said. "I'm a Pescetarian, but I loved their tofu burgers." She faced Clay. "And now you're here. That usually means some other kind of big time danger is gonna strike Haven Street. What is it this time?"

"Other golems," Clay explained. "Made of garbage. They attacked us when we were in some coffee shop on Atlas Street." He paused. "They kidnapped Henry."

"That nice little boy?" Deutsch frowned. "Terrible." She stood up, grabbed her juice and drained it in a few gulps. "I'll meditate on it. Send out some psychic feelers and see if there's any major outpourings of mystic energy in the city. Hopefully, I can figure out what created the golems." She set down the cup and moved to a large cushion in the corner, flanked by two statues of a handsome Indian Buddha. "Don't interrupt me." Deutsch sat down, crossed her legs, and began to meditate. Her eyes rolled back and she released a slight moan—then said nothing at all.

Talia stared at her. "How long does this normally take?"

"Not too long." Clay sat down on another large cushion. It flattened under his weight.

"Okay. Well, I've got a few questions for you, Mr. Clay." Talia pointed at Clay. "First off, how do you know Henry's family? He seemed very excited about meeting you, and he said that you've helped his mom and dad in the past?"

"I'm just an old friend of the family."

"I don't buy it. You're clearly immortal." Talia lowered her voice. "Are you... a vampire?"

Clay let out a slight laughing creak. "Nope." He decided she could be trusted. Harvey certainly trusted her. "I'm a golem."

"You're kidding." Talia walked closer to Clay. "You've got normal skin, it looks like." Clay let his illusion drop. "Oh." Talia moved back. "Well, maybe not. But a golem? Maybe you're just a guy with a skin condition. With weird eyes." She folded her arms. "Look, I know about golems. I've heard the story about the rabbi in Prague making one. They're supposed to be mindless, right? Unstoppable engines of destruction. Maybe those garbage guys were golems, but you've definitely got a mind and a heart too. You really care for Henry and you want him to be safe."

"Maybe I'm just a different sort of golem," Clay explained.

Then Deutsch let out a sudden cough. Her eyes winked open. "Crap." She came to her feet. "I made a mistake. I found the source of the psychic energy, but it found me as well." She straightened her sari as she paced around the room. "It caught me peeking and didn't like getting spied on. I think it sent something my way—to come after me." She spun and pointed to the wall behind Clay and Talia. "Oh God. There it is."

The outlet in the center of the wall suddenly released a crackling blast of electric energy. The energy tore out of the outlet, falling to the floor in a stream of flashing lightning. It boiled and bounced around the floor, coiling together and growing into a vaguely humanoid shape. Soon, an entire human form of glowing electricity stood before the wall. Sparks flew down from its limbs as it walked toward Deutsch, its glowing arms outstretched like a zombie. Brilliant energy composed the creature, which danced and shifted and made Clay's eyes ache. Still, he looked at the forehead. He could make out the Hebrew characters, cast in dancing lightning letters. This creation of energy was a golem.

Talia realized it too. "Another golem."

"Yeah." Clay stepped in front of the golem. It lashed out, its fingers slapping against him like whips of lightning. The energy coiled around Clay, burning his skin and knocking him back. He stumbled, tripped on a cushion, and fell to the floor. Clay kicked the energy golem, ramming a boot into his chest. The force surprised the energy golem, buying them some more time—but the strange creation slid past Clay and continued to advance on Deutsch. Clay reached behind him, trying to grab onto the energy. His fingers passed through, lightning burning his fingers.

Quickly, Talia ran to the table. She grabbed the jug of herbal juice. "Hold on!" Talia hopped onto the table, stood above the golem, and then upended the jug. Green sludge spilled down and covered the golem. The liquid splashed over the energy golem. Steam rose from the contact, as the juice started to melt. But the energy golem still sunk down to its knees. Talia kept shaking the jug, spilling every last drop of herbal juice onto the energy golem.

The juice clung to its limbs and midsection. It thrashed about, its lightning limbs kicking back pillows and cushions as it began to fade. Then the energy crackled a final time and vanished. The last drops of herbal juice hit the ground. Nothing remained of the energy golem but a thick puddle. Talia sighed and dropped the jug. She slumped onto a cushion. Clay came to his feet and Deutsch picked up the empty jug and set it on the table.

"Quick thinking with the juice, honey," Deutsch said. "Though it will take me a while to get the stains out..."

Clay brushed himself off and kicked a pillow aside. "What did you learn? Did the creator of this energy golem also make the garbage golem?"

"I don't know. But the mystic forces are coming from an Uptown penthouse, in the Harwood Apartments. That's strictly millionaire country. I don't know why some silver spoon is summoning golems, but that's the source. It might be where Henry is, but I can't be sure." Deutsch sighed. "You're gonna have to go in on foot and see for yourselves."

"Thank you," Talia said. "We really appreciate your help. And I'm sorry about, ah, the energy golem."

"Don't sweat it," Deutsch replied. "This kind of thing happens all the time when Clay's around."

"Let's go to the Harwood Arms." Clay adjusted his trench coat and headed for the door. Talia waved goodbye to Deutsch as they stepped outside. She was adjusting very well to all this supernatural insanity and the various golem attacks. Henry's mom had picked the right babysitter. Clay led her back to his Studebaker and they got inside. Henry needed their help, and they were ready to rescue him from any sort of danger.

By the early evening, they reached the Harwood Arms. It stretched up to join the other skyscrapers, towering above the green expanse of Arcadia Park—one of the most expensive chunks of real estate in the city. That was as true now as it was in the Twenties. Clay found a lucky parking space near the park for his Studebaker and filled up the meter with quarters. Then he and Talia headed inside. Even for someone who had spent several decades in the city, the Harwood Arms was still impressive. Clay stared up at the rows of windows, and then the glassy palace at the very top. They entered the lobby, bribed the doorman, and went to an elevator in the corner that resembled a small garage. Clay punched in the buttons for the penthouse. They waited as the elevator rushed its way up with a whispered hum. Soon, the doors noiseless slid open.

Talia and Clay walked into a small hallway, outside a steel door. Clay walked over and gave it a knock. A security camera above the door swiveled around, making tinny, electronic noises as it zoomed in and stared at the visitors. Then the door opened. A broad-shouldered black man in a somber suit and tie stepped into the hall. He had Clay's size, if not his bulk, and a thin scar crossed his face from his cheek to his ear. He had no hair to speak of.

He looked over Clay and Talia. "Do you have an appointment with Mr. Amir?"

"No," Talia explained. "But we really need to see him—whoever he is. It's very important."

The guard stared at Clay. "You don't even know who Mr. Amir is? You must be lost. Or maybe you're the press playing dumb. Either way, he doesn't want to see you. Go back in the elevator and leave. Be glad you're getting off with a warning."

He moved back, when a shrill voice came from the penthouse. "Hold up, Saladin. I never said I was busy—because I ain't. And that girl is fine!" He dragged out the last word, making it last several seconds. "You send that girl in, yo! Let me get better acquainted." Evidently, Mr. Amir wanted to see them. The guard held open the door, let out a weary sigh, and motioned for them to enter. Clay and Talia headed inside.

The penthouse had been furnished in a cross between a hip-hop mogul's pad and a terrorist training camp. Everything, from the angular furniture to the ground, seemed to have been composed of thin, spiking metal. Television screens turned to various channels flickered in the corners, and posters of terrorists and dictators gleamed down from the wall. A massive TV took up one wall, where Amir sat, hard at work at some explosive video game. Large windows covered the other walls, looking down at Arcadia Park and the city.

Amir paused his video game and bounded up from the couch. He waved Clay and Talia to join him. "What's up, yo? I'm Alex Amir." He looked about Talia's age, with smooth dark hair and coffee-colored skin, his thin frame under an olive green track suit. He wore numerous gold and silver rings, a set of swinging golden chains that seemed to weigh him down, and sported an Arabic verse in inscribed on diamonds in a grill on his mouth. "Come on. Let me check you out." Talia walked over, rolling her eyes. "Damn. Damn. Damn. I thought you was fine—but you're *hella* fine!" He waved past the couch. "Come on. Let me show you something. Your swole homeboy there can come too."

"Is he always like this?" Clay asked Saladin.

The bodyguard shrugged. "His dad's one of them oil magnates from the Middle East. Pays me a mint to babysit and watch his boy waste fortunes on dumbass business ventures and mangle ebonics." Saladin, Clay, and Talia followed Amir to the rear of the apartment. "Beats the Marines, that's for sure."

Past the couch, a small armory of gold and silver weapons had been mounted on the wall. Amir pulled down a golden assault rifle. He posed with it, grinning as the light shone on the rifle. Silver machine pistols and jeweled handguns also gleamed down. "Check it. I keep my weapons iced—just in case I gotta ice some dude. Got that Jihad swag, know what I mean?" He set down the assault rifle and grinned at Talia and Clay. "Say, what are your names? And why exactly have you chosen to swing by my crib?"

"I'm Emmet Clay," Clay explained. "Private detective."

"And I'm Talia Goldstein." She glanced at the weapons behind Amir. "I see you got the full size Uzi and the Mini. I fired both of them when I trained with the IDF." She turned past Amir, to a large map of the city set up on a frame. "What's this?" Talia walked closer and Clay joined her. They looked at the poster, which showed Haven Street. A large property had been circled, and surrounded with posted blueprints. "This is the Kosher Kave. You're the guy who bought it up?"

"Uh, yeah," Amir agreed. "I had a hard time getting the owners to agree, but that place was losing money and they took my deal eventually." He pointed to the map, and then to a large set of posters on the far wall. "I'm gonna tear that old burger joint down and bring in the new hotness. Check it—my banging club, Gangsta Gaddafi." The pictures, artist's sketches, showed crowded dance floors, with glowing, neon camo assault rifle decorations flashing on the walls and a DJ in bandoliers and a turban working the turntables. "I already got one Gangsta Gaddafi at an Uptown location, and now I'm branching out into Haven Street. It'll be the trendiest place in the city. Get some of that franchise swag going." He clapped his hands and grinned at Clay. "Gonna be collecting mad cheddar, bro."

"You're tearing down the Kosher Kave to put up some goddamn Jihad-themed club?" Talia asked. "That's not cool. Haven Street has been the center of a large Jewish population since before the turn of the century. You can't demolish a Jewish institution and—"

"Times are a-changing, baby girl," Amir explained. "Haven Street gotta change too." He waved his hand at the map and the blueprints. "Gangsta Gaddafi will do just that. Now there may be some resistance from the, ah, local population. And it's not like the Zionist types have the right to complain. They been forcing people out of their homes since 1948, for real. I even had some trouble coming my way from them, and already got it handled." He tapped his foot on the marble floor. "Gangsta Gaddafi all day, son!"

Talia glared at Amir. She drew closer, her face flashing with rage. "You're talking trash about Israel now? We fought and died to create our homeland—and the Jewish people need a home. You don't need another stupid, tasteless night club."

"It's called terrorist chic, bro," Amir explained. "That's far from tasteless."

Clay had a feeling Talia wanted to use some Krav Maga on Amir. He stepped between them before she could strike. "What sort of trouble?" he asked. "What kind of trouble did you face from the Kosher Kave?"

Amir stared at Clay. "Not enough to make me shook, if that's what you're asking."

"Did it involve golems?"

The question made Amir's eyes widen. He stumbled back, his chains swaying. "All right. I've had about enough of you fools questioning my stee-lo. You better bounce, now." He turned to Saladin. "Yo, Saladin. Throw them out of my apartment."

Saladin stood by a computer bank in the corner. "Actually, Mr. Amir, it looks like you got another visitor."

Everyone clustered around the bank of computers. It showed a view from the security camera in the hall, fixed on the elevator door. Henry Mackintosh-Holtz stood there, staring at the door and fidgeting. His collared shirt and jacket looked a little rumpled, and he had a slight bruise on his cheek, but seemed otherwise unharmed. He knocked on the door. "Mr. Amir?" His voice piped in through the computer speakers. "Excuse me, is there a Mr. Amir in there? I've got to warn him about something." He moved nervously from foot to foot and pushed his glasses up.

"Henry." Talia smiled. "He's all right. Thank God."

"You know that kid?" Amir asked.

"I'm a friend of the family. Talia was babysitting him when he was kidnapped by garbage golems." Clay motioned to the door. "We thought you stole him. That's why we're here. Evidently, that isn't the case. You better let Henry in, so we can see what he has to say."

"Yeah, no problem." Amir punched a spacebar on the computer screen and the door slid open.

Henry stepped hesitantly into the penthouse. He stared at the furnishings in quiet awe. "Mr. Amir?" he asked. Then he spotted Clay and Talia. "Mr. Clay! Talia!" Henry hurried to join them.

Talia patted his head. "Thank God you're all right, Henry. I was freaking out. One of Mr. Clay's friends pointed us here, and we thought we might find you—but I guess the garbage golems took you somewhere else." She motioned to a nearby chair and Henry sat down. "Why don't you tell us what happened, and why are you trying to warn Mr. Amir?" She pointed to Amir. "He's right there, and that's his bodyguard, Saladin."

"My real name's Jonathan," Saladin added.

"Thank you." Henry settled into the chair. Amir popped open his fridge, withdrew a soda, and handed it to Henry. "Oh—thanks." Henry smiled as he popped the seal on the soda. "My mom only lets me have one of these per month, so they're sort of a treat." He sipped the soda. "Okay, so those garbage guys picked me up and then they flew away and they took me to the Kosher Kave." He pushed up his spectacles. "I know—it's so weird. I've had all my birthdays at the Kosher Kave and their buffalo burgers are really good. I was wondering why the garbage golems took me there, and then they brought me to the back, and I met this guy named Shmuel Horowitz. He's the son of the owner, and he's the one who created the garbage golems." He nodded to Amir. "He was really angry about you buying out the Kosher Kave and wanted to fight back, so he made golems. And he had said that you made golems to fight his golems."

"Is that true?" Talia asked. "You made that energy golem, I bet."

Amir shrugged. "Hey, if someone steps to me with a gat, I go for a gat. Someone steps to me with a golem, and I look up how to make golems from some weird-ass website and build my own." He stared at Clay. "What? You got a problem with that?"

"Too many golems—and all mindless creations, made by amateurs," Clay explained. "It's bound to cause trouble. They'll get their orders mixed up, mindlessly pursue their goals, and not care if anyone gets hurt in the crossfire. They'll tear Haven Street apart until they're destroyed." He faced Henry. "So what happened after that? And why exactly did Horowitz want to capture you?"

Henry had another sip of the soda. "He said it was because my ancestors were great golem-makers. My great-grand uncle made you, after all." He shrugged. "He wanted me to help. But I remembered what you said about creating golems, Mr. Clay—I refused. I wouldn't make golems and send them on a mission of destruction." He smiled hopefully and Clay nodded proudly at the boy. "Well, then Shmuel got worried. He seemed like a nice guy, but he said that he really wanted me to help get his golems under control. They're all going after you, Mr. Amir. They're going to come here and attack you. Shmuel said you deserved it—but that's not true. Nobody deserves to be attacked by golems. So I escaped through the window, and took a cab over here to warn you."

"Why would you risk your life like that, Henry?" Talia glared at Amir. "For someone like him?"

"He's just a person, Talia," Henry said. "It's the right thing to do."

"Well, thanks, little man." Amir scratched his head. "I'd never think anyone like you would risk your life for someone like me. But you can bet it's appreciated." He turned to Saladin. "So, the garbage golems are coming here. I say we lock the doors, load up the burners, and start blasting soon as they show. You down to roll, bro?"

"Jesus Christ." Saladin sighed. "We can't hold them off here—not in this goddamn penthouse surrounded by windows and massive heights. We need to go somewhere more defensible." He moved past Amir and stared at the wall of gold and silver guns. He reached for a silver assault rifle and the extra magazines. "We need to start heading to the lobby now and leave."

"How about we slide to the Uptown location of Gangsta Gaddafi?" Amir asked. "It's closed now and that seems pretty defensible."

"Fine." Saladin turned to Clay and Talia. "Mr. Clay, can you handle a firearm? And what about you, Talia? You said you had IDF training with the Uzis?"

Talia stared at the wall of guns. "Well, it was just training." She picked up a golden assault rifle with an attached grenade launcher. "And I practiced a little more with this." She slung the gun over her shoulder, holding it like a pro. Clay selected a combat shotgun and a belt of shells. "But I don't know if I'm ready, exactly." She glanced at Henry. "How long until the garbage golems show up, Henry? Did Shmuel Horowitz happen to tell you?"

"I d-don't think so," Henry admitted. He set down the soda.

"Then we'll leave now." Saladin started toward the elevator. "Amir, you stay back with the kid. Keep him safe, okay? Stay behind us a bit when we go through the lobby. Your ride's on the curb. We get inside and then we'll start driving to the club."

Amir grinned at Henry. "You stick with me, little man. Everything's gonna be fine."

They headed to the elevator. Clay rested his shotgun on his shoulder. Talia switched off the safety on her assault rifle as Saladin opened the door. Clay hoped Amir was right. With two groups of feuding golems, everything working out seemed nearly impossible. Golems made with this sort of hate had a propensity to get their orders mixed up and cause all kinds of terror and destruction. Clay hoped that things wouldn't get too bad. Haven Street had seen enough trouble in the past.

The elevator descended swiftly, the floors ticking down. Clay and his friends stood inside, nobody saying much as the elevator moved down at a whispered hum. The doors slid open, revealing the wide, marble expanse of the lobby. Clay, Talia, and Saladin emerged first, carrying their weapons. The concierge stared at them and their guns in surprise, and then let out a yelp of panic as the glass doors shattered. Clay turned down the lobby. Henry had warned them just in time. The garbage golems had already arrived.

Four of the garbage creations raced across the street, bounding from the roofs of the cars, and then lunging through the air at the hotel. They smashed their way through, shattering the glass like they were projectiles fired from some gun. The garbage golems pierced the glass door, rolled on the ground, and sprang up to attack. Bits of litter dripped behind them, and each golem left a trail of refuse as they closed in. They bounded toward Clay and the others like wolves on the attack, rustling as they moved in. They pushed aside a stanchion and rippled around a geometric modern art sculpture in the center of the room as they advanced.

Saladin raised his assault rifle. "Contact!" He moved ahead of the others, leveling his assault rifle with practiced precision. "Give them some long bursts. Put some suppressing fire on them!"

"Look down the sights." Talia whispered to herself as she moved to join him. "Squeeze, don't pull." She was repeating her training. She raised her rifle and joined in with Saladin. Clay didn't need any training. He had been built to be a killer. He joined them and racked the pump on his shotgun. They formed a firing line, aimed at the garbage golems, and then started shooting.

Gunfire roared and echoed through the lobby. The blasts struck the first two garbage golems, the bullets shredding their cobbled-together forms and spraying litter into the air. Tattered magazines, chunks of rotten organic matter, and ruined car parts bounced off the ground, staining the pristine floors of the lobby. They concentrated their fire on the first garbage golem, shredding the creation as it drew closer. Saladin fired his clip into the golem's chest, the bullets cleaving their way through. The golem continued its charge, sliding along the floor and advancing even as the shots dismantled it. Talia fired at its outstretched limb, ripping it from its body and letting it fall on the ground in a heap. Then Clay moved close to the garbage golem. He rammed the butt of his shotgun into its chest, knocking it onto the ground. The garbage golem tried to rise and Clay's shotgun fired through its forehead, stopping the mindless monstrosity for good.

"Go!" Saladin cried. "Stay close and watch your angles!"

They hurried across the lobby, firing to keep the golems away. Amir and Henry hurried over next, racing through the lobby after Clay, Talia, and Saladin. A garbage golem reared up above Saladin. He fired the last shots from his assault rifle, swung the gun behind him, and pulled his automatic. Every shot from the pistol blasted into the golem, knocking it against the wall and buying them more time. He hurried ahead and reached the door, then motioned for the others to join him.

Amir and Henry hurried over next, followed by Clay and Talia. The garbage golems sprang at Talia and Clay fired the remaining shots from his combat shotgun into their mass. Garbage splattered across the walls and Talia winced as she stepped onto the sidewalk. Clay hopped out after her, and they reached the curb.

Their car waited for them—a hulking pearl white Hummer limo with oversized golden rims. Saladin slammed open the front door and got behind the wheel. The Hummer limo's engine came to life with a lion's roar. "Get in!" Saladin ordered. "And let's get out of here!"

But before they could, a garbage golem spread its malformed wings and leapt over the heads of Clay and Talia. It landed next to Henry, and reached out with a jointed hand ending in a pair of clicking, pointed pincers made from discarded pens and knives. As Clay predicted, the golems must have gotten their missions mixed up. Kidnap Henry and kill Amir fused together, and the garbage golems didn't know what to do—so they simply tried to destroy everything. The golem lunged for Henry. He tried to scramble away, but the pincer closed on his coat and tugged him back. The golem raised another hand, a fist made from dead fish and rebar, to strike.

"No!" Amir dove in front of the boy. "You want me, man—don't you? Don't hurt the kid, bro. I'm the guy who's destroying Kosher Kave. I'm the one you're after." The garbage golem faced him, and then turned from Henry and attacked. It swung its fist out and Amir closed his eyes to wait for the strike.

Luckily, Talia reached the golem first. She lunged out, caught the blow, and deflected it with some Krav Maga—then fired her assault rifle at close range, into the golem's chest. Garbage flew from the wound and the golem collapsed. Amir sprang to his feet, grabbed Henry's hand, and helped him into the open door. Talia hopped in next, followed by Clay. He slammed the massive door shut as the golems recoiled and prepared to attack again.

The heavy door closed with a metallic crack. The garbage golem smashed against the tinted window, delivering a blow with a paperweight fist. Cracks appeared in the tinted glass, but the window didn't break. Saladin slammed on the gas. The Hummer limo zoomed away, honking madly and clearing the street as it sped along. The garbage golem hung on for a few more movements, still smashing the glass—and then got side-swiped by a passing panel truck. Litter flew over the street as the Hummer limo rolled down the street and escaped. Saladin turned the corner, and they began the drive to Gangsta Gaddafi.

Amir leaned back in his seat. "Damn. That was tight!" He pointed to Saladin. "You was like being all military." He turned to Clay. "And you was rocking that shotty!" He grinned at Talia. "And you were like some kind of Israeli Amazon warrior."

"Well, thanks." Talia smiled, then grew serious. "And thank you very much for protecting Henry. That took a sort of courage that—well, that I didn't think you had."

"Thank you, Mr. Amir," Henry added.

"Nah, bro, it was nothing." Amir reached into a mini-fridge in the corner of the Hummer limo, situated between the pale, elongated benches. He popped the door, grabbed another can of soda, and tossed it to Henry. "I'd never let some kid be hurt by a garbage golem trying to attack me." He reclined in his seat. "And Henry was brave enough to warn me. That took major guts, and I don't ever want to see an innocent person like him get hurt. Besides, it gave me a chance for a little heroism." He paused. "I've always kind of wanted to have that and this was an opportunity. YOLO all day, you know what I'm saying?"

"Well, your energy golems might end up harming innocent people," Talia explained. "They attacked us earlier, when we were visiting a psychic friend of Mr. Clay's."

"Seriously?" Amir asked. "Damn. Believe me, Talia, I would never want that to happen."

"But that's the price of making so many golems," Clay explained. "It will always cause trouble."

"I hear that." Amir adjusted his various chains. "First chance I get, I'm shutting all those energy golems down. I'll think of some other way to defeat this Shmuel Horowitz dude and make Gangsta Gaddafi 2.0 a reality."

"Do you have to, Mr. Amir?" Henry asked. "Shmuel reminded me a lot of you—he tried to be angry, but I could tell he was a nice guy who was just trying to protect his family's restaurant. And Kosher Kave is really good! I don't even really keep kosher, and I still like going there. Maybe you can, I don't know, partner up with them instead? Make some kind of cool kosher nightclub, or something." He had another sip of soda. "This is really good, by the way."

Talia took it from Henry's hand and tossed it in the garbage can in the corner. "One soda's enough, Henry. We don't want you to have trouble sleeping—beyond the nightmares you'll probably get from being pursued by living chunks of garbage."

"It's okay, Talia." Henry stared forlornly at his soda in the garbage can. "I've seen way more terrifying things than garbage monster people before. Mr. Clay's always there to protect my family and me, and to make sure we're safe."

"I guess I'm learning something new." Talia smiled at Clay.

"I guess so," Clay agreed.

The Hummer limo slowed as it turned the corner. The partition between the front and back rolled down. "Okay, we're coming up on Gangsta Gaddafi's," Saladin explained. The Hummer limo rolled to a stop on the curb, in front of a rectangular cement building resembling a concrete bunker draped in neon. Amir pushed open the door, and Clay and the others emerged. Saladin stepped out as well, and walked to the bolted, iron doors. He unlocked them and swung them open, then switched on the lights. Clay glanced up the street, but there were no signs of the garbage golems. Hopefully, they had left those pathetic creatures behind. They stepped inside and Saladin carefully closed the doors and locked them behind him.

Amir walked ahead, clapping his hands, and then darting to switches on the walls to turn on lights. "Check it." He switched on a bank of lights above the main dance floor, which bordered a small bar, and then a row of tables. Neon camo glowed on the dance floor. Sculptures of camels and turbaned, gun-toting mannequins, all painted camo, rested in the corner. "This is what the new location of Gangsta Gaddafi will be like—only, I'd say with a good fifty percent more swag." He walked to the DJ's booth, at the far end of the dance floor. Crossed assault rifles, hopefully props, stood above the booth. Amir's hands flew over the controls, and he grabbed a pair of records from the racks above the turntables. "Let me give you a demonstration of the fresh beats I'll be blasting every night at Gangsta Gaddafi." He started a pounding hip-hop beat, interlaced with sounds of machine gun fire. The music filled the club. Saladin sighed and settled in a chair at the bar. Amir grinned at them. "Well? What's the verdict?"

Henry tapped his feet. "It's pretty catchy, actually."

"What about you, Mr. Clay?" Amir asked. "You like my turn on the wheels of steel?"

"I prefer jazz," Clay said.

"Like from the Jazz Age?" Talia asked, with a grin.

"Hey, I can feel that." Amir spun around, looking at his records. "Electro Swing—or maybe Swing House? Say, that'd actually be pretty sweet. You could make some kind of speakeasy club, with Electro Swing and Swing House beats blasting while people drink fancy cocktails. Some old timey swag." He clapped his hands. "Or maybe we could use some of that music that you Jews have—what's it called again? Klezmo or something?"

"Klezmer," Talia suggested.

"Yeah. Now that would be cool." He turned to his bodyguard. "What do you think, Saladin?"

"It's your money, Mr. Amir," Saladin said. "Waste it however you want." He paused suddenly, and stood up from the table. "Hold on. Can you turn that music down for a second?" He reached into his coat, going for his pistol.

"You're gonna make me stop the jams?" Amir asked.

Then Clay heard it too—a moaning buzz echoing just above the music. "Switch it off," he ordered. Amir dutifully shut off the music. The high-pitched buzzing continued, echoing out of the large banks of speakers facing the dance floor. Clay moved toward the largest speaker. The hum grew in volume. Clay reached out and tapped the speaker. The hum instantly ended.

A second later, all the lights on the dance floor flashed on, and music erupted from the speakers—a pounding hip-hop beat loud enough to make Henry jump in panic. Colored lights flashed below their feet on the dance floor. The glass on the floor shattered, colored lights blooming out as sparks crackled through the air. Clay and the others hurried back, moving closer to the bar. The speakers erupted as well, blasting fabric and emitting powerful whines of static as they fell back. Electric limbs burst through the ground and pushed out of the speakers. Glowing torsos and lumpy, flashing heads composed of woven strands of lightning emerged next. Dozens of the electric golems seeped their way out of the speakers and the dance floor. They stood in shimmering ranks, electricity coursing between them. Then they advanced on Clay and the others.

"What's happening, bro?" Amir asked. "These energy golems are supposed to ride for me!"

"Too many commands for too many poorly-made, amateur golems," Clay explained. He fired his shotgun into the mass of golems. The blast ripped through several of the electric shapes. Sparks flew from their wounds, but they still advanced. "They're assembling here because you attracted them, and they're filling with rage and bloodlust for their final assignment."

"They're going to attack the Kosher Kave," Talia said.

"What?" Amir asked. "Hell naw! I never asked them to attack the Kosher Kave. I just wanted them to beat up those garbage golem scrubs causing me problems." He stared at his hands. "I guess they misinterpreted my commands."

Henry gasped. "Oh no. There will be tons of people there. We have to warn them, and make sure they evacuate."

Saladin nodded. "Sounds like a plan. We get back to the limo and ride down to Haven Street." He turned to Clay. "In the mean time, you got any way to put an end to these golems?" His pistol flashed after his words, shooting an energy golem as it crept closer.

"Aim for the head," Clay explained. "Now let's go."

They ran for the far doors, charging rapidly away from the dance floor. Pulsing hip-hop music still blasted from the speakers placed throughout the club, and colored lights moved and shifted. The mannequins and camel statues lit up, flashing with light and going dark a second later. Clay pushed aside a fake camel as they hurried to the door. The music, colored lights, and sculptures made him feel like he was running through a funhouse. He grabbed Henry's hand and hauled the boy along. They neared the door. Amir unlocked it, revealing the cool night air.

The energy golems raced after them, many lifting off the ground and floating in to attack. They left crackling trails of sparks as they hurtled their way through the air. One reached Talia. It grabbed her arm and she winced and sank down. Clay hurried to help her, but Talia turned her assault rifle in the energy golem's direction and sent a burst of bullets into its head. That undid the Hebrew writing etched in its forehead, and the golem winked out of existence. Clay helped her up and they scrambled to the door. Saladin fired the last shots of his pistol. Clay spun around and did the same with his shotgun. He fired and worked the pump until the silver shotgun clicked empty, and then he tossed the gun down and swung his fists against the energy golems. They broke against his knuckles, searing his stony hide but not stopping him. He dispatched an energy golem with an upper cut, then elbowed another. Saladin grabbed his shoulder and hauled him back.

They hurried to the Hummer limo. Saladin got behind the wheel while Amir held the door. Once again, everyone piled inside. The engine roared and the Hummer limo flew down the street. It zoomed along, burning rubber. Clay turned and looked out the back window. The electric golems followed, floating through the air like chunks of suspended lightning. They were headed to the Kosher Kave. Hopefully, the Hummer limo could get there first.

The limo zoomed down the road, cutting through side streets to avoid traffic and make it to Haven Street as quickly as possible. Talia set the assault rifle on her lap. She was the only one who had conserved her ammo, and still had bullets for the gun. Henry sat next to her, his face pale and frightened. Talia gave him a quick pat on the shoulder and a comforting smile. "Don't worry, Henry. We'll figure it out. We'll protect the Kosher Kave."

"I'm sorry." Amir said the words suddenly. "You gotta believe me—I never knew this would happen. I just wanted to stop some garbage golems."

"Well, this is what happens," Clay said. "You've got two sides playing with supernatural forces that they don't understand and they can't control—it's obviously going to lead to unintended consequences." He stared at his thick hands. "Maybe I'm one of those unintended consequences. But no matter what happens, it's always innocents who pay the price."

"Speaking of those consequences." Saladin rolled down the partition between the driver's seat and the rest of the Hummer limo. "You said that aiming for the head was the best bet with these things. Is that so, Mr. Clay?"

Henry nodded. "Well, they're golems, Mr. Saladin—and that's how you stop a golem. You see, they all have the word 'Truth' etched somewhere on their foreheads. I guess it's written in electricity somehow, in the case of the energy golems. But if that name is obliterated, the golem is destroyed.

It will just fall apart." His face reddened as everyone stared at him. He reminded Clay a great deal of his grandfather, with his shy knowledge. "So, yes. Aim for the head."

"You know a lot about golems, little man," Amir said.

"It runs in the family," Talia explained, giving Clay a sly grin.

They sped down the dark streets, hurrying back to Haven Street. Night had fallen on the city. Clay could only hope that it wouldn't be too late for the Kosher Kave.

꙳꙳꙳꙳

They arrived at the Kosher Kave after a few minutes of frenzied driving. As Clay feared, the place was packed. It lay on the corner, a bright banana-yellow structure with an oversized plaster burger on the roof. The Hummer limo careened onto the curb and came to a halt. Clay and the others hurried outside. They scrambled across the pavement, Talia tucking her assault rifle into her coat so she didn't frighten anyone. Clay reached the door first, followed by Henry. They stepped inside. Almost every round table in the Kosher Kave was occupied. Teenagers sat together and texted over baskets of fries. Large Orthodox families minded their children while they dined. Tourists snapped pictures of the menu and their meals while workers sporting yarmulkes assembled burgers behind the counter. One of those workers spotted Henry and hurried out from behind the counter.

He ran over to them, slipping off his apron. "Henry. Look, I can understand why you ran away—and I'm so sorry. I had no idea that those garbage golems would kidnap you." He was about the same age as Talia, though still had the awkwardness of youth. Like all Orthodox Jews, he wore sidelocks which drooped down beside his cheeks.

"You must be Shmuel Horowitz," Amir said. "The punk-ass sending garbage golems everywhere."

"And you're Alex Amir—the son of a wealthy oil baron who is going to ruin Haven Street by making some tasteless memorial to thugs and gangsters." Shmuel glared at him, and then turned to Henry. "Has he kidnapped you? Are you in some kind of danger, Henry? I can maybe summon another golem, who will—"

"Shut up." Talia glared at Amir and Horowitz. "Both of you." She pointed to Amir. "He's right about Gangsta Gaddafi being tasteless." She turned on Horowitz. "But your idea of sending garbage golems everywhere is even worse. You can't control them, and it made Amir build his own golems out of electricity—which he can't control—and now all of Haven Street is gonna pay the price because of your stupid supernatural arms race." She caught her breath. "Now, here's what needs to happen. Shmuel, you gotta get all the customers to the back of the restaurant. Henry, Mr. Amir—you can help. Mr. Clay, and Saladin, and I will head outside and see if we can take out all the golems who will be soon be showing up here."

Horowitz stared at her. "Golems are coming here?"

"They're getting their orders mixed up," Clay explained. "It's what happens when amateurs try to create such complex supernatural creatures." He pointed to Talia. "You better listen to her. We don't have much time."

"Okay." Horowitz turned around. He raised his voice. "Um, excuse me? We've got a bit of a problem. There's been a—um—a gas leak, outside. So if everyone can just take their food and move to the back?" He grinned at the customers. "We'll throw in a free basket of kosher hot wings for your trouble." He hurried over to help them, followed by Amir and Henry. Then the lights in the Kosher Kave flickered. Clay nodded to the door. The golems had arrived.

Clay stepped outside, joined by Saladin and Talia. They stood together on the Kosher Kave's porch, looking at the street. Both varieties of golem emerged from the street and the alleys. The garbage golems showed up first, slipping out of an alley and congregating together in a festering horde. The electric golems came down the street, floating along like kites carried by the wind. They floated down and landed on the street, next to the garbage golems. The two types of golems stood together, the glowing from the electricity casting strange, dancing shadows over the misshapen forms of the garbage creations. They stared ahead at the Kosher Kave, as if waiting for some signal.

"Why aren't they fighting?" Saladin asked.

"They both have orders that align," Clay explained. "The energy golems want to take out the Kosher Kave. The garbage golems want to take out Alex Amir, who's in the Kosher Kave. That puts them on the same side." He sighed. "It's what happens with these poorly made golems." He pointed at the crowd. "And it looks like the situation is getting worse."

The garbage golems merged together, the litter combining and melding to form the same mass. Some of the golems became the arms, while others formed arms and legs. They didn't hold hands, but simply merged and reformed, their rotting exteriors clicking into shape like the joints of some strange machine. The odd creation fused together, and slowly stood. It moved to its knees first, and towered above the Kosher Kave—forming a great giant of seething garbage, big enough to tackle a small building. The fake burger of the Kosher Kave's roof came only to its waist. The giant garbage golem stared down at them with a face made from tattered papers, all covered in occult Hebrew lettering. It took a single step and made the street shake.

Then the electric golems joined in. They formed together as well, losing their humanoid appearances and becoming a twisting, crackling band of electricity. The energy snaked around the legs of the garbage golem, crisscrossed its chest, and fused together. Electricity filled the garbage golem, bright enough to light up the whole street. The whole creation stared down at Clay, Talia, and Saladin. It seemed to realize that they were a threat.

"Oh no," Saladin muttered. "It's like some kind of golem Godzilla. How are we gonna take it down without calling in an airstrike?"

The giant golem raised a hand. Its misshapen fingers, each as big as a person, radiated with electricity. "Get back!" Clay cried. He grabbed the shoulders of his friends and hauled them back, but it was too late. The electricity slammed down and blasted into the ground behind them—a lightning strike that sent shockwaves of heat and pressure through the air. Saladin flew back and crashed into a dumpster. Clay hit the ground and rolled. His heavy limbs clattered across the street, cracking before coming to a rest. Talia had managed to avoid the blast. She stood back and stared at the golem.

The door of the Kosher Kave opened. Henry peeked out. "Talia!" he cried. "Remember—the golem's head!"

"Okay." Talia raised her assault rifle. "Aim for the head."

She used the attached grenade launcher. It shot into the air, trailing a line of smoke, and then struck the giant golem straight in the forehead. Fire consumed the golem's head. The explosion ripped it apart, shredding the papers and sending pieces of electricity flying away. Fire consumed the giant golem's head. It took another step, and collapsed. The energy vanished. The garbage descended, falling onto the street. Talia lowered her gun with a slight sigh. Clay sat up. The garbage golem had been defeated.

Shmuel and Amir joined Henry in the doorway. Amir looked at the golem and then at the grenade launcher. "Everyone okay?" he asked. "Looks like you iced all those golems, Talia. Pretty cool, I must say." He adjusted his gold chains. "And you know, checking out the Kosher Kave—and being pursued by killer golems—has given me a new perspective. I was thinking that I wouldn't demolish the Kosher Kave. Instead, I'll partner up with it, and build an addition." He beamed. "An add-on nightclub. Get some Klezmer hip-hop fusion going on, mixed with some Jazz Age swag." He turned to Saladin. "What do you think, Saladin?"

"I'm sure it will good, Mr. Amir." Saladin stood up and winced. "Well, I don't know about you guys, but I'm pretty hungry. How are the burgers here?"

"They're very good. And all on the house." Shmuel motioned for them to come inside.

"Come on, Talia!" Henry called, as he stepped inside. "We better call my mom too. I bet she'll be worried. But she'll be very happy to know how you protected me and saved all of Haven Street." He glanced at Clay. "With some help from Mr. Clay."

"Sure," Talia agreed. She lowered the golden assault rifle and walked over to Clay. "Well." She stared at the remains of the garbage golem. "That was something. I had no idea that kidsitting the good-natured, nerdy little boy from next door would get so intense." She offered Clay her hand and he came to his feet. "How'd I do?"

"Wonderfully," Clay said. "Henry and his family will always have one protector. I'm glad to know they've got another." He turned to the Kosher Kave and Talia followed him. They walked inside as a night wind blew the remains of the other golems along the street.

THE END

ABOUT OUR CREATORS

AUTHOR -

MICHAEL PANUSH – Only twenty-six years old, Michael Panush has distinguished himself as one of Sacramento's most promising young writers. Michael has published numerous short stories in a variety of e-zines including: *AuroraWolf, Demon Minds, Fantastic Horror, Dark Fire Fiction, Aphelion, Horrorbound, Fantasy Gazetteer, Demonic Tome, Tiny Globule,* and *Defenestration.* A graduate of UC Santa Cruz's Creative Writing program, he currently lives in Sacramento, where h teaches at Encina Preparatory School.

He has written several books with Curiosity Quills all of which are available digitally and in paperback. He has also written a webcomic entitled, illustrated by Masmi Kiyono, which is available on the Curiosity Quills website at http://curiosityquills.com/looters-taking-tomes/

ARTIST -

ZACHARY BRUNNER – graduated from the School of Arts with a degree in filmmaking. Upon graduation, he realized that he would rather pursue a career in illustration, needing a more creative job than the high-stress environment of film production. He began working with comic writer Jim Krueger on two graphic novels, "The High Cost of Happily Ever After," and "Runner." "High Cost" is currently available at Amazon, "Runner," is expected out this year.

While studying at SVA, Zachary worked as a concept artist on an animated film called "Brother," directed by Sari Rodrig. The short film went on to win countless awards all over the world, having been shown at festivals such as Cannes and the Student Emmys. Zach currently is working on Sari's second short animated film, "Essence."

For the past year, he has also worked as a storyboard artist for Torque Creative, the in-house advertising agency for Mercedes-Benz. He is also currently working on several storyboards for short independent films.

Other print projects included "Christopher Rising," "Penny Dreadful" and "The Poisonberry Fortune" and "Foot Soldiers,Volume 1." He plans on furthering a career in concept art and in the comic book industry.

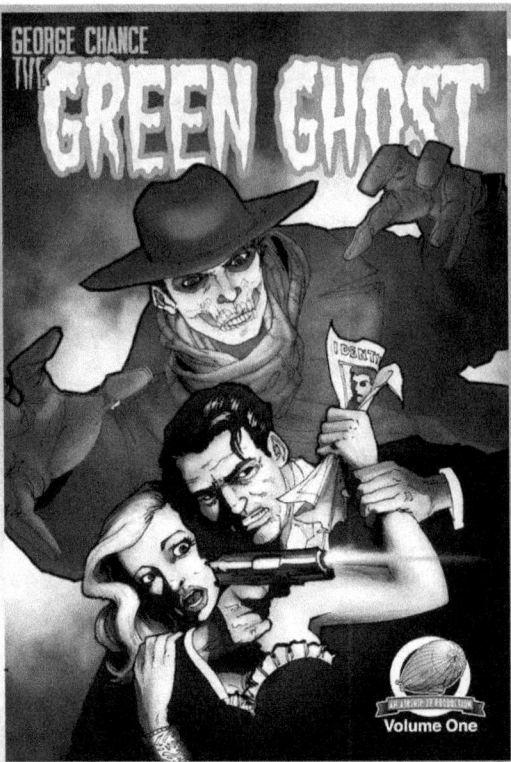